PRAISE FOR
MIKE DELLOSSO

"Every time I read a Mike Dellosso inspirational thriller, I find a new favorite—until another hits bookstores that tops the last. Definitely the best yet, *Centralia* is not just a nonstop thrill ride with Dellosso's signature spine-chilling suspense edged with the supernatural. It is a deeply moving story of one man's desperate search for all that has been ripped from him—family, identity, honor—and ultimately his greatest loss and heart longing—a restored relationship with the heavenly Father all logical evidence would indicate has abandoned him. *Centralia* is a story I will not soon forget."

JEANETTE WINDLE, award-winning author of *Veiled Freedom, Freedom's Stand,* and *Congo Dawn*

"With mind-bending twists and tangled truths, *Centralia* is one killer story! Mike Dellosso has outdone himself with this heart-pounding story of one man's fight to find the truth—but is it the real truth? This one will keep you guessing right to the end. If you're a Bourne addict like me, you can't afford to miss this novel!"

RONIE KENDIG, bestselling author of *Raptor 6* and *Hawk*

"Mike Dellosso's *Fearless* packs an emotional punch. His engaging characters and riveting plot pull the reader right into the story. He's a true craftsman!"

TOM PAWLIK, Christy Award–winning author of *Vanish*, *Valley of the Shadow*, and *Beckon*

"Mike spins a tale that combines suspense and compassion, intrigue and hope. Born of fire but created in love, [*Fearless*] is a ride that will keep you wondering until you turn the final page."

ACE COLLINS, bestselling author of *The Yellow Packard* and *Darkness before Dawn*

"With hints of Frank Peretti and Stephen King, *The Hunted* is a chilling debut."

CRESTON MAPES, author of *Nobody*

"A vicious enemy, a family secret, a thirst for revenge, and a need for reconciliation all drive *The Hunted* from intriguing beginning to thrilling conclusion."

KATHRYN MACKEL, author of *Vanished*

"Read this someplace safe as you experience the incredibly descriptive world of *The Hunted*. And sleep with the lights on."

AUSTIN BOYD, author of the Mars Hill Classified trilogy

THINGS ARE NOT WHAT THEY SEEM

MIKE

CENTRALIA

DELL

 TYNDALE HOUSE PUBLISHERS, INC., CAROL STREAM, ILLINOIS

OSSO

Visit Tyndale online at www.tyndale.com.

Visit Mike Dellosso's website at www.mikedellossobooks.com.

TYNDALE and Tyndale's quill logo are registered trademarks of Tyndale House Publishers, Inc.

Centralia

Designed by Dean H. Renninger

Edited by Caleb Sjogren

Published in association with the literary agency of Les Stobbe, 300 Doubleday Road, Tryon, NC 28782.

Scripture taken from the New King James Version,® copyright © 1982 by Thomas Nelson, Inc. Used by permission. All rights reserved.

Library of Congress Cataloging-in-Publication Data

Dellosso, Mike.
  Centralia / Mike Dellosso.
    pages ; cm
  ISBN 978-1-4143-9041-3 (softcover)
  1. Psychological fiction.   I. Title.
  PS3604.E446C46 2015
  813'.6—dc23   2015000555

Printed in the United States of America

21	20	19	18	17	16	15
7	6	5	4	3	2	1

For Jen

I remember when you told me,

"Live like it's already happened."

PROLOGUE

. . .

Peter Ryan tossed his head back, rested it against the leather wing-back chair, and stared at the ceiling. A symmetrical swirl pattern in the plaster covered the entire surface. He wondered how long it had taken the plasterer to complete it. Must have required a ton of patience. These old buildings had such unique touches, such character and craftsmanship. The longer he stared at it, the more the pattern appeared to move and shift and change. The swirls curved in alternating directions, some clockwise, some counterclockwise, like an intricate network of cogs and gears skillfully crafted by a master clockmaker.

"Something you want to talk about?"

The gears on the ceiling halted their motion. Peter tilted his chin down and eyed Dr. Audrey Lewis. She was a plump woman, full-figured with a large frame that fit nicely into her pantsuit. With her glasses on the end of her nose and her legs casually crossed, she smiled at Peter and waited for his response. Walter Chaplin, the departmental dean at the university, had insisted he see her, said it would do him good to talk to someone, to get things off his chest and out of his mind.

Peter wasn't so sure. He'd seen Lewis three times already, and she'd been no help. All she did was listen and ask questions, smile, and take notes. He could get that from any child in any first-grade classroom. And what did she do with all the notes she took, anyway? No doubt she used them as fodder for her social-media alter ego.

But there was no use resisting. If Chaplin wanted him to use Lewis as a psychological dumping ground, he would do it. It certainly didn't harm him any or cost him anything but a couple hours a week. "I've been having the dream again."

Lewis's eyes went to her notepad. "The house."

"Yes."

She looked up, eyeing him like an interesting specimen to be poked and jabbed, dissected and studied, and finally pinned to a foam board. "And the rooms—are they the same?"

"Yes."

"Same layout?"

"Yes."

"Same number of rooms?"

Peter closed his eyes and filled his memory with the inside of the house that he'd been visiting in his dreams. "Same everything." It had two stories, mostly unfurnished, and every room seemed to contain pieces to a giant puzzle; only the pieces never fit neatly together. The first-floor living area consisted of four spacious rooms. There was also a kitchen he'd never entered, only caught a glimpse of the tiled floor and white cabinetry. The second story had a hallway lined with four rooms along the right side. The walls were gray, the wood worn. It was an old house, well used, stately yet sad. Many memories hid in the walls and paint and floorboards.

Lewis was quiet for a long moment, and Peter didn't know if she was thinking about a response or waiting for him to continue.

Finally, "Go on."

He sighed and recalled his latest dream, which had been exactly like all the other ones. "I'm in this house, the same house."

"And does it look familiar yet?"

"Nope. Never seen it before except in my dreams." At least not that he remembered.

"Go on." Those were two of Lewis's favorite words, and combined, they made up the majority of her contribution to shrink sessions.

The office was a room in Lewis's home. She lived down a county road, five miles outside of town. With the windows open, the curtains moved gently on a midafternoon breeze, but the outside world was quiet save for the occasional bird singing or squirrel chattering.

"I seem to have access to every room, just like always, except that one."

"Does the door look the same?"

"Everything's the same. The staircase, the hallway, the doors. They're all the same. Nothing ever changes."

"And did you go in any of the rooms?"

"Sure. I made my way down the hallway, just like I always do, checking each room. I have a feeling like I'm looking for something. An urgent feeling."

Lewis cleared her throat and apologized. "The same feeling you've had before."

Peter nodded. "Same as always."

"And what did you find in the rooms?"

"Same stuff I always find. Mementos, different objects from my life, from childhood up to just a few weeks ago. My old baseball mitt. A stack of comic books. Spider-Man. Daredevil. Archie. The tuxedo I wore when Karen and I got married. Lilly's favorite teddy bear. A pile of unpaid bills. Just the stuff of life. My life."

"And do you find what you're looking for?"

"Nope. The feeling never goes away."

"Is Karen in one of the rooms?"

"Yes. The same room. Third one. She sits in a chair, one of those overstuffed ones you find in a furniture store. We had one just like it when we were newly married. Checkered blue and white with some flecks of red. We bought it with a Christmas bonus I got that year."

"And did she talk this time?"

"She never talks." Peter closed his eyes again and saw Karen in the chair, her legs crossed, skirt just above the knees, hair pulled back from her face. "But she looks like she wants to. She has that look on her face, you know, when someone has something to say but either doesn't quite know how to say it or wants to but something's holding them back. Do you know that look?"

"I do. And then what?"

"And then nothing. I say hi to her, tell her I love her, ask her what's wrong, but there's never any answer. I plead with her, tell her it doesn't matter what it is—just tell me; I can handle it. But no answer."

Again Lewis remained quiet as the clock on her desk ticked softly. A shadow flitted across the ceiling, a flutter of activity, and then it was gone. Probably a bird outside caught between the house and the sun's midafternoon rays. Peter kept his eyes on the ceiling as those gears began to move again, setting in motion some major mechanism, maybe the machinery of his mind.

"And after finding Karen, do you still have the feeling that you're looking for something?"

"Or someone. Yes."

"So the someone you're looking for isn't Karen."

Peter thought about that for a moment. He'd always assumed that he was looking for Karen. Or Lilly. But the feeling was persistent and wasn't quenched with the discovery of Karen in the room. "I guess not."

"What about the last room? It's the same as always too?"

Peter massaged his hands and glanced around the office. It was nicely furnished, mostly with antiques. A floor lamp in the corner always attracted his attention. Its carefully sculpted brass stand was polished to a high sheen, and from the top dangled a bell-shaped glass shade with a hand-painted stylized C on it. Peter often wondered what the C represented but had never asked Lewis about it. "Yes, the last room. It's the same thing. I try to open the door, but it's locked. I dig through my pockets—all of them, frantically—but I have no key. I have no way of opening the door. I think whatever or whoever I'm looking for is in that room."

"That's new."

Peter lifted his head and looked at Dr. Lewis. "Is it?"

"I don't remember you ever mentioning that before—that you know the room contains what you're looking for."

Peter thought back to his other dreams. They were so vivid, so real, he could still remember each one in detail. "Or who. And I suppose it is new. Does that mean something?" Peter didn't really expect Lewis to answer his question directly.

"What do you think it means?"

"I thought you were supposed to have the answers."

"I don't have all the answers. In fact, I have few answers. More times than not, the answers are in you."

"Well, give this one your best shot."

Lewis removed her glasses and placed her notepad and pen on the little round colonial table with a tripod pedestal beside her chair. "I think it means your subconscious mind is keeping something from you."

"Keeping secrets?"

"In a sense. Protecting you from some memory you may not be ready to recall, some event in your life you may not be ready to deal with."

Peter drummed his fingers on the arm of the chair. "So what do I have to do?"

Lewis laced her fingers and rested her hands on her lap. She looked directly at Peter as if she were about to reveal to him not only the secrets of his past but the mysteries of the universe. "Find the key."

ONE

. . .

Peter Ryan rolled to his side and peeled open his eyes. Hazy, early-morning light filtered through the blinds and cast the bedroom in a strange, dull, watery hue. For a moment, his mind fogged by the remnants of a dream filled with mystery and anxiety, he thought he was still in the same unfamiliar house, exploring room after room until he came to that one room, the room with the locked door that would allow him no entrance. He closed his eyes.

Peter pawed at the door, smacked it with an open hand. He had to open it; behind it was something... something... A shadow moved along the gap between the door and the worn wood flooring. Peter took a step away from the door and held his breath. The shadow was there again. Back and forth it paced, slowly, to the beat of some unheard funeral dirge. Somebody was in that room.

Peter groped and grasped at the doorknob once again, tried to turn it, twist it, but it felt as if it were one with the wood of the door, as if the entire contraption had been carved from a single slab of oak.

Peter gasped and flipped open his eyes, expecting morning sunlight to rush in and blind him, but it was earlier than he thought. Dusty autumn light only filled the room enough to cast shadows, odd things with awkward angles and distorted proportions that hid in the corners and lurked where walls met floor.

He couldn't remember last night. What had he done? What time had he gone to bed? He'd slept so soundly, so deeply, as if he were dead and only now life had been reinfused into him. Sleep pulled at him, clung to his eyes and mind like a spiderweb. It was all he could do to keep his eyes open. But even then, his mind kept wanting to return to some hazy fog, some place of gray void that would usher him back to the house, back to the second story, back to the door and that pacing shadow and the secrets it protected.

He shifted his weight and moved to his back. Hands behind his head, he forced his eyes to stay open and ran them around the room. It was a habit of his, checking every room he entered, corner to corner. What he was checking for he didn't know. Gremlins? Gnomes? The bogeyman? Or maybe just anything that appeared out of...

There, in the far corner, between the dresser and the wall, a misplaced shadow. No straight sides, no angles. It was the form of a person, a woman. Karen. His wife.

Peter lifted his head and squinted through light as murky as lake water. Why was...?

"Karen?"

But she didn't move.

"Karen, is that you? What are you doing, babe?"

2

Still no movement, not even a shift in weight or subtle pulsing of breath. For a moment, he didn't know if he was awake or asleep or caught in some middle hinterland of half slumber where rules of reason were broken routinely, where men walked on the ceiling and cats talked and loved ones roamed the earth as shadowy specters.

Peter reached for the lamp to his right and clicked it on. Light illuminated the room and dispelled the shadows. If he wasn't awake before, he certainly was now. The corner was empty, the image of Karen gone.

Propped on one elbow, Peter sighed, rubbed his eyes, and shook his head. He kicked off the blanket and swung his legs over the edge of the bed, sat there with his head in his hands, fingers woven through his hair. The remaining fog was dispersing; the cloudy water receded. His head felt heavy and thick as if someone had poured concrete into his cranium and sealed it shut again. The smell of toast and frying bacon reached him then, triggering his appetite. His mouth began to water. His stomach rumbled like an approaching storm.

And that's when it hit him, as suddenly and forcefully as if an unseen intruder had emerged from the fog, balled its bony hand, and punched him in the chest.

He needed to see Karen, needed to tell her something.

It was not some mere inclination either, like remembering to tell her he needed deodorant when she went to the supermarket. No, this was an urgent yearning, a need like he'd never experienced before. As if not only their happiness or comfort depended on it but her very existence. He had information she needed, information without which she would be empty and incomplete, yet he had no idea what that information was. His mind was a whiteboard that had been wiped clean.

Had he forgotten to tell her something? He filed through the events of the past few days, trying to remember if a doctor's office had called or the school. The dentist, another parent. But nothing was there. He'd gone to work at the university lab, spent the day there, and come home.

But there was that void, wasn't there? Last night was still a blank. He'd come home after work—he remembered that much—but after that things got cloudy. Karen and Lilly must have been home; he must have kissed them, asked them about their day. He must have eaten dinner with them. It was his routine. Evenings were family time, just the three of them. The way it always was. He must have had a normal evening. But sometimes, what must have happened and what actually happened could be two completely different animals, and this fact niggled in the back of Peter's mind.

Despite his failure to remember the events of the previous evening, the feeling was still there: he needed to find Karen. Maybe seeing her, talking to her, would be the trigger that would awaken his mind and bring whatever message he had for her bobbing to the surface.

Downstairs, plates clattered softly and silverware clinked. The clock said it was 6:18.

Karen was fixing breakfast for Lilly, probably packing her lunch, too, the two of them talking and laughing. They were both morning doves, up before sunrise, all sparkles and smiles and more talkative and lively than any Munchkin from Oz. Some mornings he'd lie in bed and listen to them gab and giggle with each other. He couldn't make out what they were saying, but just the sound of their voices, the happiness in them, brightened his morning.

Peter stood and stretched, then slipped into a pair of jeans

4

before exiting the room. He stopped in the hallway and listened, but now the house was quiet, as silent and still as a mouseless church. The smell of bacon still hung in the air, drew him toward the kitchen, but the familiar morning sounds had ceased. The sudden silence was strange—eerily so—and the niggling returned.

"Karen?" His voice echoed, bounced around the walls of the second floor, and found its way into the two-story foyer. But there was no answer.

"Lilly?" He padded down the hall to his daughter's bedroom, knocked on the door. Nothing.

Slowly he turned the knob and opened the door.

"Lil, you in here?" But she wasn't. The room was empty. Her bed had been made, bedspread pulled to the pillow and folded neatly at the top. Her lamp was off, the night-light too. And the shades were open, allowing that eerie bluish light to fill the room. On her dresser, next to the lamp, was the Mickey Mouse watch they had gotten her for Christmas last year. Lilly loved that watch, never went anywhere without it.

Peter checked the bathroom, the guest room, even the linen closet. But there was no one, not even a trace of them.

Down the stairs he went, that urgency growing ever stronger and feeding the need to find Karen and put some life-rattling information center stage with high-intensity spotlights fixed on it. And with the urgency came a developing sense of panic.

On the first floor he tried again. "Karen? Lilly?" He said their names loud enough that his voice carried from the foyer through the living room and family room to the kitchen. The only response was more stubborn silence.

Maybe they'd gone outside. In the kitchen he checked the clock on the stove. 6:25. It wasn't nearly time yet to leave for school, but they might have left early to run an errand before Karen dropped Lilly off. But why leave so early?

He checked the garage and found both the Volkswagen and the Ford still there. The panic spread its wings and flapped them vigorously, threatening to take flight. Quickly he crossed the kitchen and stood before the sliding glass door leading out to the patio.

Strange—he hadn't noticed before, but the scents of breakfast were gone. Not a trace of bacon or toast hung in the still air. He'd forgotten about it until now, so intent was he on finding Karen and Lilly. It was as if he'd imagined the whole thing, as if his brain had somehow conjured the memory of the aroma. There was no frying pan on the stove, and the toaster sat unplugged in the corner of the counter. Prickles climbed up the back of his neck. He slid open the glass door. The morning air was cool and damp. Dew glistened on the grass like droplets of liquid silver. But both the patio and backyard were empty. No Karen, no Lilly.

Peter slid the door closed and turned to face the vacant house. "Karen!"

Still no answer came, and the house was obviously in no mood to divulge their whereabouts. His chest tightened, that familiar feeling of panic and anxiety, of struggling to open a door locked fast.

The basement. Maybe they'd gone down there to throw a load of laundry into the washing machine. At the door, facing the empty staircase and darkened underbelly of the house, he called again for his wife and daughter, but the outcome was no different.

Had they gone for a walk before school?

At the kitchen counter, he picked up his mobile phone and dialed Karen. If she had her phone on her, she'd answer. But after four rings it went to her voice mail. He didn't bother leaving a message.

Peter ran his fingers through his hair, leaned against the counter, and tried to focus, tried to remember. Had she gone out with someone? Maybe Sue or April had picked them up. Maybe they'd planned to drop off the kids at school and go shopping together. They'd done that before. Karen must have told him last night, and he was either too tired or preoccupied with something that her words went acknowledged but unheard.

He picked up the phone again and punched the Greers' contact. Sue answered on the second ring.

"Sue, it's Peter."

"Oh, hi, Peter." She sounded surprised to hear his voice. If she was with Karen, she wouldn't be surprised.

"Do you know where Karen and Lilly are? Are they with you?"

There was a long pause on the other end. In the background he could hear music and little Ava giggling and calling for Allison, her big sister. The sounds stood in stark contrast to the silence that presently engulfed him.

"Sue? You still there?"

"Um, yeah." Her voice had weakened and quivered like an icy shiver had run through it. "I'm going to let you talk to Rick."

That sense of panic flapped its wings in one great and powerful burst and took flight. Peter's palms went wet, and a cold sweat beaded on his brow. "What? What is it?"

"Here's Rick."

Another pause, then Rick Greer's voice. He'd be leaving for work in a few minutes. "Hey, man, what's going on?"

"Hey, Rick, I'm not sure. Do you know where Karen and Lilly are? Are they okay?"

The pause was there again. Awkward and forced. Seconds ticked by, stretching into eons. In another part of the house, Ava continued to holler for Allison. Peter wanted to scream into the phone.

"I'm... I'm not sure I understand, Peter."

Irritation flared in Peter's chest. What was there to not understand? "I'm looking for my wife and daughter. Where are they?"

"Man, they're not here. They're... gone."

"Gone? What do you mean, gone? What happened?" The room began to turn in a slow circle and the floor seemed to undulate like waves in the open sea. Peter pulled out a stool and sat at the counter. The clock on the wall ticked like a hammer striking a nail.

Rick sighed on the other end. "Are you serious with this?"

"With what?"

"What are you doing?"

Peter gripped the phone so hard he thought he'd break it. He tried to swallow, but there was no saliva in his mouth. "What's happened to them?"

"Pete, they're dead. They've been gone almost two months now. Don't you remember?"

TWO

• • •

Catching memories can sometimes be as difficult as catching raindrops. A memory was there for just an instant, but as quickly as it came, it slipped through his fingers. A funeral outside, the sky overcast and ridged with thick clouds as though the world had been turned upside down so a field freshly plowed now formed the canopy above and the ground on which they stood was made of unstable clouds.

As numb as if his blood had suddenly turned to ice water, Peter forced his brain to engage and fumbled for words. "I… uh, I…"

"Pete." It was Rick again. He sounded confused and concerned. "You okay, man? You need help? You need me to come over?"

"No." He rubbed his eyes, scanned the room for any sign of Karen or Lilly, any evidence that they'd been there this morning.

Any proof of their existence. Crumbs on the counter, trash in the wastebasket, a dirty dish in the sink. Anything. But there was nothing. It was like they'd never set foot in the house, never walked from room to room, never made a mess, never used anything. Never lived. "No, I'm fine, Rick."

"You sure? You don't sound fine."

The last thing Peter needed right now was Rick Greer coming over and talking holes in his head. Rick was a financial counselor. He spent his days staring at numbers and helping people balance their checkbooks. So when he got out from under his calculator, he didn't know when to give his mouth a rest. He was a nice enough guy, but the relationship was between Karen and Sue, not Peter and Rick.

"Yeah, uh, I'm okay. Just had a bad dream and… forgot for a moment."

"Hey, it happens, you know? You're grieving; you're still trying to come to terms with your loss, make sense of it. You know?"

So he was using his counseling wisdom on Peter. "Yeah. You're right. Hey, listen, sorry to bother you. I hope I didn't scare Sue. Man, this is embarrassing."

"No, no. Don't worry about that. No harm done here. Totally understandable." There was a pause again. The background was noiseless now. "Pete, if you ever want to, you know, talk about this, I'm here, okay? I think I can offer you some advice to help you through it, but I don't want to push. Just say the word and I'm there."

Peter knew Rick meant well, but he was in no mood to be questioned and counseled like one of Rick's financially challenged clients who'd gotten themselves buried in too much debt. "Thanks, Rick. Hey, sorry again. I'm okay. Really. I'll see you sometime."

He clicked off the phone and let it slip from his hand and fall to the counter. Again a memory was there, dropped out of nowhere. They'd been killed in a car accident. It was a Friday morning. Overcast and dreary. A light rain had fallen since darkness crept in the previous night. The report said Karen had somehow lost control and the car had run off the road, hit a tree, and rolled into a ditch. A fuel line ruptured, ignited. The car became an inferno.

Peter had just gotten to the lab at the university when Dean Chaplin stopped by and told him there had been an accident. Chaplin's watery eyes couldn't hide the truth, and immediately Peter knew it was Karen and Lilly, that fate had reached a bony finger from the dark side of reality and poked them.

And then the memory evaporated and was gone as quickly as it had arrived.

Peter dropped his head into his hands and tried to remember more, to recall the funeral. It had to have been at the church. Reverend Morsey had to have been the one who presided over it. Friends would have been there, colleagues from the university too. There would have been a viewing and memorial, then a graveside service and burial. Peter would have dropped a handful of cold soil on the caskets.

But this hazy image of inverted earth and sky seemed more like a dream. He had no distinct memory of it. As if it had never happened or had happened and Peter had somehow slept through it.

Was this part of grieving, blocking out the memories of the funeral like a disfigured man might hide from his own reflection? Had his mind shut out whole chapters of images and text, refusing to acknowledge their existence, refusing to deal with reality?

Maybe he should call Morsey, get his take on this. Peter's throat tightened and he balled his hands into fists. No. Morsey would want to come over and counsel him or pray for him, and Peter wanted no part of that. Morsey would go on about how merciful and caring God was. How these things just happened and there was no use getting angry at God because of it. Morsey was a good man with good intentions, but Peter was in no mood to be preached at and prayed for.

And yet some spark of familiarity ignited in his soul just then. Though he couldn't remember the last time he'd been inside a church, Peter had the slightest feeling, like the itch of a loose thread, that God knew him deeply and, what's more, that he himself had once known God the same way. There had been a relationship between him and the Almighty, but somewhere along the line, Peter had forgotten. Strangely, he had the sense that it had been taken from him, that he had been ripped from God's presence. Or at least been blinded to it. Was that even possible? But like everything else this morning, the idea was all faded and vague, images behind frosted glass.

But even as these muddled thoughts roiled in his brain, the morning's horrific, tangible question came rushing back to him: Karen and Lilly. How could they be dead? Even if he didn't see evidence of them having been there this morning, he felt them in this house. Felt their presence, their life. That wasn't something that could be conjured out of thin air. Or could it?

No. They were alive. He didn't care what anyone said. Didn't care if Rick wanted to counsel him, didn't care if Morsey wanted to pray with him. He didn't care what any police report said. Karen and Lilly were not dead. Not even his own damaged mind could convince him of that.

Peter grabbed his phone and stood. As he did, another sequence of images landed and pecked at his memory. Two caskets suspended

12

above their graves by wooden supports covered with green indoor-outdoor carpet. An arrangement of flowers topped each box, and under the tent, dressed in black and varying shades of gray, sat a group of sniffling people, their faces shielded and hidden by handkerchiefs.

Peter rubbed his eyes again. They were memories, for sure, but they didn't feel like *his* memories. He felt no personal connection to them, as if they were memories of a movie he'd watched or snippets he'd imagined after hearing of someone else's terrible misfortune. No, his beloved Karen and Lilly weren't dead. Everything in his rational mind scoffed at anything metaphysical or spiritual, and yet his heart—his soul—were loud witnesses. As strange as it seemed, he was certain of it. He felt them there, felt them with him. They were alive. Somewhere.

He just had to find some proof of it.

Starting in the kitchen, Peter opened every drawer, every cabinet, rummaging, emptying, searching for any sign of Karen's recent presence.

Next he moved to the family room, then the living room and downstairs bathroom. In the foyer he found Lilly's jacket, and though it still held the aroma of her shampoo on the collar, it meant nothing. He needed concrete evidence that they were still alive, that they had recently been in the house, that he had interacted with them, talked to them, laughed with them, loved them. He had no idea what he was looking for but would know it when he saw it; he was sure of that much.

Upstairs he started with the guest room but came out empty-handed. In Lilly's bedroom, he stopped and sat on her bed, almost panting, his heart beating out a steady staccato rhythm. He needed to calm himself. Getting frantic meant getting sloppy, and sloppy was something he could not afford. He might miss something he was meant to find, something that would solve this strange mystery and lead him to his wife and daughter.

Lilly's room had remained untouched. Everything was exactly how it had always been. Except one thing. The Mickey Mouse watch. If she had truly been lost in a tragic accident, she would have been wearing the watch, and it would not be here. It would have been destroyed.

But maybe he'd brought it home from the morgue. He tried to remember if he'd received a bag with personal belongings retrieved from the car or bodies. But he had no memory of any of it. It was as if a wall had been erected, blocking access to an entire bank of memories.

Peter stood and took the watch from the dresser. It showed no signs of being in a fire and worked fine. The second hand ticked steadily, evenly, reminding him of the gears on the ceiling of Dr. Lewis's office, churning, grinding, turning, tick, tick, ticking. Suddenly he was struck with the sentiment that there was something else at work here, something larger than Karen and Lilly and his own fleeting memories. Like the tiny second hand on the watch, time kept pressing onward, but it was merely a facade. Behind it there was a much more intricate mechanism at work, controlling each movement... each memory.

Holding the watch, he scanned the room again for any sign of misplaced objects. Another memory came to him, floating out of the fog that had clouded his mind. That morning, the last time he had seen them, Lilly had kissed him good-bye and told him she loved him, that he was the best daddy in the world, and that she'd pray for Jesus to keep him safe. She must have noticed he was worried about something, because when he knelt to hug her, she cupped his face in her soft hands and assured him that they would be okay, that Jesus would protect their whole family. She was only eight but so intelligent. She had an incredible ability to read people, to intuit what they were thinking.

If they were dead, Peter would know it; he would feel the deep sense of loss, the emptiness of a life without purpose, without a reason to continue. Even if he was going nuts and simply denying reality, somewhere deep in his psyche he would know the truth and feel it. And he didn't. All he felt was a powerful sentiment, a *knowing*, that they were alive.

But still he needed to prove it to himself.

After searching Lilly's bedroom, he moved to his and Karen's room. This was it; he had to find something here. And he would; he knew he would. He emptied every drawer, tore the sheets off the mattress, yanked the boxes from under the bed, went through every corner of the closet. And when he had finished, he had nothing.

Tears now pressing against his eyes, Peter stumbled into the bathroom like a man suffering extreme dehydration and its resultant dementia and collapsed onto the floor. Maybe he was wrong. Maybe he *was* going nuts, refusing to accept the reality of his loss. Jesus hadn't kept them safe, had he? Maybe Karen and Lilly were gone.

Another memory scratched at his mind. Reverend Morsey, concern and sorrow clouding his eyes, telling Peter that he'd see Karen and Lilly again, that they might be absent for now but that there was still hope of being reunited with them in heaven. The words were kind and sincere but meant nothing. For the first time, this memory was accompanied by emotion. Such loss, such grief. Peter felt as though his heart had been torn from his chest, cast onto the floor, and trampled. He wanted to die, wanted to crawl into a hole somewhere and just wither away.

On the floor of the bathroom, knees pulled to his chest, bile surged up his throat. He barely made it to the toilet in time. Violent heaves racked his body; sweat soaked his T-shirt; tears poured from his eyes.

When he finished, he wiped his mouth and flushed the toilet. He sat on the floor, head in his hands, for a long time, searching the corners of his mind, the shadowy places he rarely visited, trying to remember anything else, any detail, any lasting image. But nothing came to him. Perhaps he was wrong. Perhaps they were dead.

He noticed then that the toilet was still running. Peter stood and lifted the lid of the tank. Sometimes the stopper didn't fall right and he had to jiggle the...

In the bottom of the tank was a small black object, one of those old 35mm film containers. He reached into the water, retrieved it, popped the cap. Inside was a stack of quarters that had kept the canister from floating. As he poured them into his palm, Peter saw they were rolled in a piece of paper. Heart pounding like the beating of massive wings, he unfurled the paper.

It was Lilly's handwriting, scribbled as if she was in a hurry. With tears blurring his eyes, Peter read the words: *Daddy, we went to Centralia.*

THREE

. . .

Peter held the note with numb, trembling hands, his heart in his throat. He glanced at the toilet tank. It didn't stick with every flush, sometimes not for days, even weeks. Lilly had known he'd be sure to find it eventually. But whom had she been hiding it from? Karen? Someone else?

His mouth suddenly gone as dry as sawdust, he stared at the note. Those words glared defiantly back at him.

Daddy, we went to Centralia.

He knew of no Centralia. Had never even heard the word before. Was it a company? A town? A park?

Centralia.

It seemed he'd known what it was at one time. But why couldn't he remember? Why had whole chunks of his memory been surgically removed while other areas remained unscathed?

The toilet was still running, so Peter reached into the tank and repositioned the stopper.

He walked to the bed on weak legs and sat on the edge, still holding the note in front of him as if it were some magic incantation that if recited long enough would summon the memory he sought.

"Centralia." He said it out loud, hoping the auditory stimulation would trigger something, anything. But it didn't. It was just a word, nothing more than a string of letters, a compilation of sounds.

Again tears came to his eyes, and he brushed them away. Regardless of whether he knew what the note meant, this was the proof he'd been looking for. Lilly was alive. And her note said they'd both gone together. If Lilly was alive, he had every reason to believe Karen was too.

He had to find them. He had to figure out what Centralia was and what he was supposed to remember.

"Oh, God, help me."

Peter shuddered. The ease with which those words had passed over his lips surprised him, and again the sense was there, the feeling of frayed fragments just out of reach of both memory and soul. As far as he knew, the words meant nothing to him. But their weight tugged on him until a noise outside startled him from his reverie.

A car door closed, then another and another. They were close. In the driveway.

With prickles of anticipation swarming his arms, shoulders, and neck, Peter stood, crossed the room, and slid the blinds far enough to the side that he could peer out and get a view of the driveway below. A dark-gray SUV was there, one of those jumbo jobs the size of a small apartment. There were no corporate or government markings on it that he could see. And from where he stood, he couldn't get a look at the license plates.

Then, from downstairs, came the sound of someone tampering with the front door. The knob rattled softly, turned, and the door opened.

Peter froze, still holding the blinds with one hand and the note with the other. His pulse thumped in his neck.

After releasing the blinds and shoving the note into his pocket, he crossed the room again, back to his dresser, and slid open the top drawer. From there he retrieved a handgun. It was a Glock 19 he'd bought last year after a rash of home invasions in the neighborhood. At the time he wasn't sure he'd have the resolve to fire at another person. Now the reality that he might have to face that uncertainty put a ball of dread in his stomach. He rooted through the drawer for the magazine, but it wasn't there. Not beneath his underwear, not tucked into the mess of random socks. Had someone taken it? He was sure he'd put it in the same drawer as the pistol. Crossing the room quickly and quietly, he slid open the drawers of his bedside table, but the magazine wasn't there either. Peter tossed the useless gun onto the bed and returned to the doorway.

His mind reeled in a hundred different directions, spinning like an off-balance top. He drew in a deep breath in an attempt to steady his nerves, but it did little. He had no idea how many intruders there were. Three closed car doors would suggest three men, but there might be others.

Footsteps sounded downstairs, soft and careful. This was not a breaking and entering done by amateur thieves in search of electronics or jewelry they could hock to a local small-time dealer. These intruders knew he was home, and they were taking extra precautions. They knew—or at least thought—he was armed.

Peter returned to the bed and snatched up the gun. The intruders didn't know it was useless, and that could be his only advantage. He stepped easily to the bedroom doorway and peeked around the corner. From there he had a view of the stairs and a partial view of the foyer. He saw no one but could hear movements in the kitchen now.

As silently as a cat creeps across an open room full of sleeping dogs, Peter slipped into the hallway and made a dash for the top of the stairs. There he pressed his back against the wall and tried to settle his breathing. Light footsteps moved across the first floor from kitchen to hallway. Peter peeked around the corner. From where he stood, he could now see the entire foyer area and some of the living room. A man dressed in dark jeans and a khaki jacket exited the kitchen and appeared in the foyer. His hair was trimmed close, showing a lot of scalp, and he carried a silver handgun equipped with a silencer. As the intruder turned toward the stair-case, Peter ducked behind the wall and held his breath.

These were definitely not concerned neighbors stopping by to deliver a casserole.

Footsteps ascended the stairs at a cautious but even pace.

Peter thought about rounding the corner and rushing the man while he was on the steps. He had the high ground and the element of surprise on his side. Any attack from above would throw the intruder off-balance and send him tumbling down the stairs. But such an aggressive confrontation would produce a lot of noise and would call the others to the scene. Abandoning the idea of such a frontal assault, and without so much as creaking a floorboard, he took three steps to his left and ducked into Lilly's room, leaving the door open.

The footsteps stopped at the top of the staircase, and a few seconds' worth of silence hung in the air. Peter held his breath, afraid the intruder would hear his increased respiration and get a bead on his location. With a handgun but no ammunition, he'd have to find another way to take the man out. He needed to keep the element of surprise as long as he could. Right now, surprise was his only advantage—that and the fact that this was his home, his turf, and he knew every angle, every vantage point.

When the footsteps started again, they headed in the direction of Lilly's room.

Peter's pounding pulse moved from his neck to his ears. He strained to listen, to determine where exactly the gunman was. The soft footfalls grew so close that he could now hear the man's steady but deep breathing just on the other side of the wall.

Peter slipped his Glock into the waistline of his pants at the small of his back and braced himself behind the open door. An empty gun would do him no good in a situation like this.

On the other side of the door, a handgun came into view. Two thick-knuckled hands grasped it. As the man moved forward, more of his arms became visible: the wrists, then the elbows.

Peter knew he had only one chance, and he had to act now before the intruder pushed the door all the way open and found his prey crouched and vulnerable behind it.

In one smooth motion, surprising even himself with the agility and force with which he moved, Peter grabbed the man's gun with his left hand, pulled forward, and jammed his right elbow into the gunman's face. One, two, three times. Nasal bones cracked and the gun discharged with a muffled pop. The man stumbled backward, his nose broken and pouring bright-red blood down over his lips and chin. But Peter and the intruder still each had a grasp on the gun. Quickly Peter clutched the weapon with his right hand and swung around to drive the back of his left elbow into the side of the man's head. It connected solidly with the force of a hammer.

The man grunted and finally lost his grip on the gun. But Peter lost his hold on it too, and it clattered to the floor.

Getting his feet under him, the trespasser righted himself and squared off against Peter. The two men stared at each other like gladiators battling to the death, panting, sweating. The intruder ground his teeth and narrowed his eyes. He wiped at his face with the back of his hand, smearing blood from his nostril to his cheekbone. He opened and closed his fists as if squeezing strength from his muscles. The gun lay on the floor between them. Peter instinctively knew he had to act fast. The others downstairs had no doubt heard the commotion and were on their way.

The gunman shifted his attention to the pistol on the floor, and seeing his opportunity, Peter reacted. He jabbed his hand forward and found the big man's throat with his knuckles. The guy's head snapped back, his face paralyzed in agony. He pawed at his throat and gagged. Taking advantage of the opening, Peter lunged forward and drove a fist into the man's face, catching him square in the nose and pushing him back against the doorjamb. The intruder's eyes rolled back in his head, and he gasped for air.

Peter followed with another right to the jaw, then a quick left to the temple area. His adversary teetered on rubbery legs, tried to sniff, tried to lift a hand. Peter raised his leg and landed a foot in the man's abdomen. The gunman doubled over, then slumped into the hallway and crumpled to the floor.

Immediately the sound of heavy but quick footsteps advanced. They were up the steps in no time.

FOUR

. . .

Now on his knees, Peter reached for the handgun, leaned out the doorway just far enough to get a look at the hall, and squeezed the trigger as another of the intruders rounded the corner. The slug hit the man solidly in the chest and pushed him back and down the steps.

Ducking into the room again, Peter pressed his back against the wall and waited. There was at least one more trespasser to deal with, possibly two.

Sweat stung his eyes; his hands trembled. His breathing was quick and heavy, like the chugging of a steam engine pushing at full throttle. Adrenaline surged through his veins, sharpening every sense.

The man on the floor in the hallway was still out cold.

"Ryan!" a man shouted from the staircase. "That's enough, Ryan." Fear strained and tightened the voice.

"Who are you?"

"Let's finish this the easy way. Put the gun down. There's more of us. There's no way out of this."

"What is *this*?"

"Ryan, you need to come with us."

"You didn't answer my question. What's *this*? Why are you here?"

"To take you in. It doesn't have to happen like this."

"Take me where?"

"You know where."

"I don't know where."

None of this made any sense. He had to finish it soon. If there were more than one intruder left, the longer this went on, the more advantage the others had. Even now they might be repositioning, blocking exits, cordoning off whole sections of the house. If he knew for sure there was only one left, he'd try to take him alive, question him, beat answers out of him if he had to. The man might know where Karen and Lilly were. But he couldn't take that chance.

Peter grabbed a stuffed hippo from Lilly's floor and aligned himself in the doorway so he could see flush with the wall the whole way to the corner of the staircase. He then tossed the hippo down the hall, away from the staircase. The hippo hit the wall and fell to the floor with a muffled *thunk*. The man popped out from around the corner for a quick scan of the area, but before he could duck back behind the wall, Peter aimed and pulled the trigger.

The man howled and cursed.

While the intruder struggled, Peter hurried toward the staircase, slid his gun around the corner, and squeezed off three rounds in rapid succession.

There was a weak grunt, the sound of a mild exertion, followed by the loose thumps and soft knocking of a body toppling down the stairs.

The entire incident with this third intruder had taken less than ten seconds.

All was quiet again, but Peter didn't feel safe. He needed to know if there were any more intruders. Still in a crazy fog of adrenaline, he pushed himself across the hallway until his back found the wall, then leaned to his left to get a view of the staircase. One man lay on the steps, head down, the front of his shirt soaked with blood. Another man lay sprawled on the floor at the base of the stairs, bullet wounds to the chest and abdomen. He appeared to be dead as well.

The sound of fabric against fabric snapped Peter's attention back to the intruder in the hallway. The man groaned and pushed himself to his hands and knees, looked around and found Peter with glassy eyes. Clumsily, he slid up his left pant leg, revealing a small revolver holstered to his shin.

"Don't," Peter said, pointing the pistol at him.

But the man didn't heed his warning. Grimacing, fury and hatred now cascading over his face, he eased the gun from its holster.

"Stop," Peter warned again.

Defiantly, as if he knew this would be his final volitional action in this life and was resolved to make it count, the man pulled back his lips in a painful sneer and raised the revolver. But he never got a chance to bring it high enough to aim. Peter squeezed off one shot, hitting his mark just below the collarbone. The man dropped his gun and fell back, chuffing like a sick dog and groping at the fresh wound. Peter acted quickly and retrieved the revolver, shoving it in the back pocket of his jeans.

The man tried to roll, tried to sit, but the gaping wound in his chest oozed blood and kept him down. His eyes as wide and blood-shot as tomatoes, breathing shallow and rapid, and still coughing sporadically, he looked at his bloody hand and cursed Peter.

There wasn't time for niceties and formal introductions. Peter knelt on the man's abdomen. "Where are my wife and daughter?"

More cursing. The intruder tried to take a feeble swing at Peter but barely had the strength to lift his arm. He was losing blood rapidly.

"Where are they?" Peter asked. He had to make this interrogation quick and efficient in case there were more unwanted visitors.

A crooked smile stretched across the man's face. His teeth were stained red and blood pooled in the corner of his mouth. "You have no idea what you're dealing with." He drew in a deep, gurgling breath.

Peter put the end of the handgun's barrel over the wound and pressed. "Where are my wife and daughter?"

The big man gnashed his teeth and moaned pitifully. Again the lips parted and the man smiled. "You're in deep, Ryan." His eyes lolled back in his head, his jaw went slack, and he lost consciousness.

After checking the rest of the house and carefully scanning the yard through each of the windows, Peter determined that there indeed had been only three intruders. But who they were and why they had broken into his home was still a mystery.

He started with the man on the floor at the bottom of the steps, searched his pockets, but found nothing. The intruder at the top of the stairs yielded no information either. But on the big man in the hallway, the brute who wouldn't heed Peter's warning, he found what he was looking for: a small wallet in his right hip pocket.

Opening the wallet, Peter stumbled back until he found the wall, then slid down to sit on the floor. He fumbled with the guy's identification card, yanked it from the wallet, and held it an arm's length away. The photo was definitely him. Peter's heart banged and his breathing quickened. Tears pooled in his eyes.

The intruder's name was James McNally.

The guy was a cop.

FIVE

. . .

When questions come like lightning strikes, answers rarely follow.
Holding the dead cop's ID between his thumbs and forefingers,
tears now streaming down his cheeks, Peter suffered a barrage of
those lightning bolts. Why had a cop broken into his home? Why
the silencer? What did he mean by "You're in deep, Ryan"? Deep
into what? Why were these three men after him? And *were* they
even after him? Maybe they were after something...

He remembered the note in his pocket. *Daddy, we went to*
Centralia.

Maybe the gunmen were after the note. What was so important about Centralia? And why had Karen and Lilly gone there?

He began to tremble then as more questions rained from the
sky, pummeling him with a full-scale attack. Where had he learned

to fight and shoot like that? He had no memory of ever taking any kind of self-defense course. And he had no memory of visiting a firing range or even once firing a gun. The salesman at the gun store had shown him and Karen how to use the Glock, but when they brought it home, Peter had stuck it in the drawer and that's where it had stayed. And the speed with which he had acted and reacted, the quickness and precision of his movements, the accuracy of his shooting—Peter had moved as if he'd been trained to fight. There was apparently more to him than he could remember. And the answers to most, if not all, of his questions were wrapped up in one word: *Centralia.*

Peter looked at the man on the floor in front of him. The hole in his chest had stopped spouting blood. He was dead. His eyes were open, staring at the ceiling as if he were expecting something miraculous to happen at any moment.

"What have I done?" A sorrowful wave of guilt rushed upon him, but though the sorrow remained, the guilt was just as quickly washed away in a sense of relief. These men had been prepared to use lethal force. And their presence proved that something was amiss.

A memory came then, just bits and pieces of images and sounds, like the scattered wreckage of a downed plane surfacing in the middle of a churning ocean.

A man's thick, deep voice hollers at him. It's muffled but clear enough that Peter can make out what he's saying. "Ryan, get up. Get up!"

Then there is water and something pressing down on him, holding him in place. He's underwater and can't breathe. His lungs burn like they've been set on fire; his mind clouds. He tries to free himself, but something holds him in place, and the more he struggles, the firmer the pressure grows.

Then the water is gone and there is gasping, air filling his lungs, a rush of pain to his head. Someone squeezing his brain like a soaked dishrag. He's sure his skull will explode.

The image changes to a room and a bright light above, brighter than the sun, scorching him, sapping every ounce of energy from him, sucking him dry, so dry, as dry as sand. He needs water, craves it, thinks of nothing else.

The memories faded, and Peter was left sitting on the hallway floor, still holding the handgun.

"God, what's happening to me?" The words breathed out like a reflex. Once more, that niggling was there. A lost relationship. Feeling stranded. A notion that he no longer needed someone on his side. Convinced he could go it alone. But before and after were a jumble in his mind, and he couldn't figure out where any of these feelings had originated.

He was going nuts, he was sure of it. He'd wind up in the psych ward of a state prison being pumped full of all kinds of medication and poked and prodded like some lab animal, condemned to spend the rest of his days standing in a corner mumbling about the little men who came and took his brain away. Or he'd wind up on death row with a simpler fate, strapped to a gurney waiting for a cocktail of poisons to flood his bloodstream. Maybe he could plead insanity and at least get a stay of execution. He was, after all, surely insane.

Again he studied the note in Lilly's handwriting. *Daddy, we went to Centralia.*

Was he supposed to recognize the name? Somehow it seemed to fit those images of water and drowning and dying of thirst. Was that where Lilly and Karen had gone?

He ran his fingertips over the letters. It made no sense.

Another memory came in short bursts.

31

Karen is with him, as is Lilly, seated at a table, a man in a suit across from them. The man sits erect, posture that would make any chiropractor beam with pride, shoulders back, chin up. His hair is perfectly groomed, combed to the side and carefully sprayed in place.

"It's a remarkable school, I assure you," he says. There's an air of confidence about him that is reassuring. This is a man who knows what he's talking about.

He smiles and dips his chin. "Children like Lilly—gifted children— need someplace special to hone their skills. She deserves that, don't you think?"

The setting changes to their bedroom at home. They're lying in bed, he in his boxers, Karen in nothing but a long nightshirt. She looks worried, concerned. Her brow is tense, and she's doing that biting on her lower lip she does when she has something to say about being worried and concerned.

"Are we doing the right thing?" she asks. She looks at him, and in her eyes he sees the shadows of uncertainty that whisper doubt in her ears. "Can we trust them?"

The memories vanished just as quickly as they had surfaced, and Peter once again ran his fingers over the words on the piece of paper, tracing each slanted line, each curl and curve. As far as he knew and remembered, Lilly went to Middleton Elementary School. Other than this fragmented glimpse, he didn't remember anything about a school for gifted children. But apparently such a conversation had taken place. His thoughts were disconnected, unfamiliar, like some stranger had taken residence in his mind and was now inserting pages haphazardly torn from unrelated books.

One thing Peter did know was that he couldn't stay in this house. Whoever was after him or the note would soon realize their hit men were missing, and reinforcements would no doubt be sent to finish the job.

He thought about going to the police—that would be the logical thing to do—but if this guy on the floor was a cop, that could not end well for Peter. Cop killers, no matter the reason, were not treated kindly.

His mind began to spin like an auger, digging up questions without answers. If the cops were involved, then who else was? Maybe this was a case of mistaken identity, of confusing him with some drug kingpin or mob godfather. But what if it wasn't? What if he had unknowingly become some national security threat? Or what if, buried somewhere deep in his past—a past he no longer remembered—he had done something worthy of drawing the attention of law enforcement? Something so heinous they felt it needful to break into his home with silencers in place and murder him without an arrest or trial?

Unlikely.

He couldn't risk going to the police right now. First he had to locate Karen and Lilly. And to do that, he had to find out what Centralia was and then determine what he needed to know about it.

He'd leave the house exactly as it was. If someone did come looking for their pet thugs, he wanted to send a message to them that he would not be an easy target. Plus, he had no time to dispose of the bodies of three grown men even if he did know what to do with them.

In the bedroom, he retrieved his duffel bag from under the bed and threw some clothes and toiletries into it.

Downstairs in the kitchen, he filled a cooler with bottled water, a few apples, an orange, and a handful of cheese sticks. He went into the study and opened the safe hidden in the closet and retrieved the thousand dollars—his and Karen's emergency fund, cash on hand if they ever needed it in a pinch.

Before leaving the house, he dialed a number he had thought he'd never dial again. But it was necessary. And she was the only one besides Karen and Lilly who might not think he had officially swan dived into the deep end of life's pool and surfaced clinically bonkers.

She picked up on the second ring. "Peter?"

"Amy. I need your help."

There was a brief pause, then: "My help? The last time we talked, you said I'd never hear your voice again."

"Forget all that. Now I need your help."

"How can I forget? You were—"

"Amy, please."

Amy huffed. "What's going on, Peter?"

"Can I stop by your place?"

"Are you in trouble?"

This time he hesitated. He didn't want to lie to her. Lying would do no good. "Maybe. I don't know. Probably. It seems that way."

"Have you gone crazy?"

"What?"

"You sound like you've gone crazy. 'Maybe. I don't know. Probably.' It's like telling someone you think maybe, probably they have cancer. It's not real reassuring, you know."

"I just need to crash somewhere for a few hours. Figure this out. Can I come?"

She sighed. "You're not much of a sales guy, are you? Figure what out?"

"I'll explain when I get there."

"Does this have to do with Karen and Lilly?"

Peter checked his watch. The three dead men in his house weren't rogue hit men out for a stroll in the neighborhood when they randomly chose his home to terrorize. They worked for someone, and that someone would be checking in soon to see if they had completed their mission. And when that person received no answer... He needed to get on the move. "Amy, I really don't want to talk about this over the phone."

"Just answer that one question. Does it have to do with Karen and Lilly?"

"Yes. Everything has to do with them."

"Okay. Come. But why do I feel like I'm going to regret this?"

"Because you probably will."

SIX

· · ·

Lawrence Habit had his orders. The trio of stooges had failed—it was that simple. He wasn't given any details, didn't even know their names; he knew only that they'd not succeeded at their mission. Like most, they had underestimated the target, who had knocked them off one by one.

Peter Ryan, a research assistant. How some poindexter had gotten the best of his attackers was beyond him, but Lawrence wasn't going to be taken by surprise. He made it a habit to stay a step ahead. No pun intended.

Lawrence had gotten the call just a few minutes ago. It had taken him mere seconds to respond. This was his specialty now, cleaning up messes. He was a glorified janitor of sorts, only he *made* a bit of a mess in the process.

As with every job, they liked to keep him in the dark, and he was just fine with that. He had a name and a location. The less he knew, the less involved he had to get. And he was a man who didn't like getting involved. Distance was good.

When the call came, he didn't recognize the voice of the speaker. It was a woman this time, and she told him only that he was needed. Lawrence didn't probe for details. He asked a single question of the woman. "Where's he headed?"

The voice gave him an address and one instruction: Bring Ryan alive if at all possible. The woman with him was expendable. Lawrence sighed silently. He hated collateral damage, but it sometimes came with the territory.

In his brand-new Lincoln MKZ, he adjusted his mirrors and seat, tuned the radio to the oldies station, and backed out of the parking space. He could have afforded something a little more image-enhancing, like a Mercedes or BMW, but Lawrence wasn't the pretentious type. He liked to think of himself as simple, useful, functional. Besides, the Lincoln gave a nice ride, offered plenty of room for his largish frame, and was chock-full of bells and whistles he would never have use for.

The destination was a good thirty miles away, so he had to make time. But first he needed gas.

Two blocks over, Lawrence steered the Lincoln into the parking lot of an A-Plus Mini Mart, pulled up to a gas pump, and killed the engine. On the other side of the pump island, some punk kid filled his customized Honda Civic, equipped with ground effects, window guards, aftermarket headlamps, and alloy wheels. The kid's pants were down around his thighs, his smiley face boxers in full view. He wore a bulky black hooded sweatshirt and a red Miami Heat cap pulled low, hiding his eyes. Loud rap music thumped from the car's speakers and vibrated Lawrence's chest. The kid nodded to the beat.

Before exiting the car, Lawrence glanced at himself in the rearview mirror. The smooth, silvery scar that stretched from his right temple to the corner of his mouth had turned an odd shade of blue. It did that sometimes. From pink to blue to bright red. The injury had partially paralyzed the right side of Lawrence's face, affecting the way he spoke. For that reason, Lawrence spoke only when he had to.

While pumping his own gas, Lawrence avoided the kid, who was posturing like he had some turf to protect here at the mini-mart. He was the type who put on like he was king of the world, a tough guy, but really he was just as scared as the rest of them. Just as defenseless and vulnerable as a cornered rat staring down a shotgun.

When he finished, the kid returned the nozzle to the pump and glared at Lawrence.

This time Lawrence didn't avert his eyes.

The kid squared up and stuck out his chest. "What you lookin' at, man? You got a problem?"

Lawrence said nothing but smiled at the kid. He could have jumped across the island and snapped the punk's neck like a twig. This kid had it coming, for sure, but Lawrence made a point of only getting his hands dirty on the job. Besides, there were cameras monitoring the area. He needed to remain just another joe at the pump, minding his own business.

The kid stared at him for another long second, eyeing up the freak with the scar. He thought he had the upper hand, that he was intimidating Lawrence, but if he only knew what Lawrence was capable of, what pain he could inflict upon the kid while keeping him alive and aware, he would get in his beater and leave.

But he didn't. He no doubt saw Lawrence's unwillingness to look away as a challenge.

The punk stepped up onto the concrete island and thumped his chest with an open hand. "What's yo problem, old man? Huh? You got that crazy scarface and you think yo sumpthin'? You want to go?"

Lawrence finished pumping and held the nozzle at his waist in one hand, aimed at the kid. With his other hand he discreetly reached into his jacket pocket and retrieved a lighter. He eyed the punk carefully, no longer smiling. "Beat it, kid. You don't want this."

The kid stepped back off the island and smirked. "You crazy, man, you know that? That freaky scarface don't intimidate me. Yo, this ain't over. You hear? It ain't over."

But it was over. Lawrence got into his car and drove away. If the kid bothered to follow him, he'd be happy to pull off along some scarcely traveled stretch of road and give the piece of filth what he deserved. But that wouldn't happen. Punks like that were all bark and growl but had no guts when it came to backing it up.

Back on the road, Lawrence donned his shades and cranked the radio. Little Richard sang "Good Golly, Miss Molly." Lawrence enjoyed his job. He didn't enjoy the killing; he wasn't sure anyone really *enjoyed* killing. Well, certainly there were some who did, those crazies who saw themselves as some kind of hero for cutting people up or some whacked-out thing like that. But that wasn't Lawrence; he was a professional. He didn't kill for pleasure; the killing was simply part of his job. A man had to make a living doing something. It was never personal, and he tried to keep it that way. He tried to keep emotions out of it because emotions only complicated things, and in his line of work simplicity was best. Get in, get out. No regrets, no apologies, no second-guessing.

As he drove, he stuck mostly to county roads and remote areas. Less traffic, less people, less congestion. And besides, Lawrence enjoyed the scenery and wide-open spaces. The farmland reminded him of his childhood home, where fond memories resided. For most of his childhood he had been raised by foster parents who loved him and gave him every privilege and right a real son would enjoy. Except one. They refused to legally adopt him. They had a biological son who was ten years older than Lawrence and upon their death wanted their entire estate and substantial wealth to be bequeathed to him. Though they showed young Lawrence every kindness and outward display of love, their true son was always their favorite. And upon their most untimely and unfortunate deaths when Lawrence was just fourteen, his older brother had rejected him and cast him back into the foster system. Lawrence had spent the next three and a half years moving from one horrid home to the next, suffering neglect, anger, jealousy, and a myriad of abuses he'd never even thought possible. The day he turned eighteen, he packed his sole bag with everything he owned and walked out of a nightmarish situation to do the one thing he'd dreamed of doing since he was fourteen and abandoned. He joined the Army.

And like it or not, the Army had made him what he was today. Turned him into a killing machine, then cut him loose. Naturally he'd brought his training into the private sector. What other skills did he have to work with?

Lawrence glanced at the clock on the dash. This time of day he'd cover ground quickly. Nothing personal, Peter Ryan. Just business.

SEVEN

$\bullet\ \bullet\ \bullet$

Footsteps sounded outside the door. The familiar steps that came every day at the same time. Three men. Always three men. But never the same group of three. Always, though, they were large, broad-shouldered, thick-chested, and stern. Rarely did they speak more than two or three words, usually just commands.

The woman clutched her daughter and put her face in the girl's hair. She drew in a long breath. "Be strong. Be strong."

The girl hugged her mother. "Mommy, I can feel your heart beating."

Of course she could. Each time the men came, the woman thought her heart would bound right out of her chest. "I know, baby. It means I love you so much."

The girl lifted her face and kissed her mother on the cheek.

The touch was so gentle, so tender, so sweet and innocent and everything a little girl's touch should be. When she spoke, her voice was hushed but not hurried. Never hurried. "Don't worry, Mommy. God's with me. I know that. Do you know that?"

"Yes. Yes, baby, he is. I know it. Always remember that. Hold it close to your heart."

The men were just outside the door now, talking in quiet but harsh tones.

"I'll be here when you get back. Like always. Okay?"

"Okay, Mommy. Don't worry about me. God will protect me."

The woman wiped tears from her eyes, smearing them across her cheeks. She sniffed and forced a smile to hide the fear that gripped her heart like an iron claw. "I'll pray for you. The whole time."

The lock disengaged and the door swung open. Light from the hallway slanted across the concrete floor. Two of the men entered, both wearing khakis and black long-sleeved polo shirts. One was taller than the other and bulkier. The smaller one wore glasses and had his head nearly shaved. High and tight, military style. The woman's father had been in the Army, a career soldier; she was raised a military brat. Her husband had been in the Army too. She knew the type when she saw it.

The men said nothing because they didn't need to. The woman and her daughter knew the routine. Her daughter pulled away from her and approached the men like a willing sacrifice resolved to place herself on the altar. They looked at her as if she were some lab freak and handled her indifferently, clinically: no emotion, no tenderness, one hand on the upper back, keeping an arm's distance between them.

If they only knew how sweet she is, how innocent. How brave. They wouldn't treat her so coldly. They couldn't.

Before she left the room, the girl turned, made eye contact with her mother, and smiled. It was a smile that said everything would be okay, a smile that told her mother not to worry, to trust God because he would protect his child. Then the door closed, and the woman was once again alone with her tears. And guilt.

Every day they took her daughter, and every evening different men returned her. The girl said they did things to her—she called them "experiments"—but she never went into detail. The woman prodded her, even pleaded with her to tell her what they did, but she would never say. She'd only ever say that God was with her, that he gave her strength and protected her. At least she referred to experiments and not abuse, and there were never any marks on her. But did an eight-year-old even know what abuse was?

Regardless, the girl was immovable in her faith. It was incredible. Almost inhuman. As far as the woman knew, her daughter had performed no miracles, but still she should be sainted for her faith.

The woman went to the bed and sat there, her hands in her lap, tears falling from her eyes. She thought of her husband as she did every day. They told her he was dead, that he'd died a hero's death and that she should be proud. She was proud, but she was also angry. Not at him—goodness, no. They had both agreed that he needed to do what he'd done. It wasn't his fault. She was just angry. Maybe at herself, maybe at God—it was hard to tell. But besides anger, there was the guilt—such terrible guilt. It was her job to protect her daughter, to make the right decisions, to keep her sweet, precious girl from harm, but instead she'd led them right into the devil's lair.

They'd been in this place so long she'd lost track of the time. It could be weeks but was probably months by now. Time seemed to move in a circular fashion here rather than linearly as it did in the outside world. Days ran together, and if she didn't know better, she wouldn't be surprised if they repeated themselves. If days became more days before turning into weeks. Maybe weeks didn't even exist here in this secluded world, months or years either. It could just be days and days and more days. Just an endless string of hours ticking by with no beginning and no end.

She didn't know who it was who held them, but their captors provided decent care. Three meals a day, a shower a day, and the room. It was nothing special, certainly no five-star accommodations, but it had a double bed, a dresser, a table and chairs, some area rugs, and a lamp. Everything she and her daughter needed to at least not be uncomfortable. There was no television, but they supplied her with books to pass the time, mostly classics like Austen and Brontë and Steinbeck and Twain. She'd never been much of a reader before, but now she devoured books—sometimes two a day. After all, there was little else to do. After a while, passing the time in one's own mind could lead to all sorts of thoughts. The mind had a tendency to wander, to meander to strange places and alternate realities. Rooms in the mind opened to more rooms, which opened to yet more rooms, and in each one resided endless possibilities for the imagination. The woman felt it was best to stay out of those rooms as much as possible, and the books allowed her some different rooms to explore.

There were no windows in their cell, leading the woman to believe they were either in an interior room of some thick-walled building or possibly in a subterranean bunker of some sort. Maybe a military installation.

On the rare occasions when she wasn't reading and she did let her mind drift in and out of those dangerous rooms, she thought about the days before any of this happened, before the cursed room, before the men who came every morning to take away her daughter, before she'd lost everything and become nothing more than a caged animal, the mother of a lab rat.

And when she wasn't reading or remembering, she kept her mind busy and focused by praying. Sometimes, admittedly, she had to force herself to pray. Her faith was not as strong as her daughter's. It faltered; it failed. She questioned and sometimes cursed. But when she saw her daughter, her faith was renewed. The girl had that effect on her and used to on everyone she came in contact with. It was a gift, no doubt about it. She was special. So special.

And that's the reason they were here.

EIGHT

• • •

Peter pulled his Jetta into the driveway and shut off the engine. He'd tucked the intruders' gray SUV into his own garage after backing out the Jetta. He didn't need snooping neighbors prematurely stirring up trouble when they noticed the SUV hadn't moved in a while. Anything out of place or out of the ordinary made them nosy. And nosy neighbors eventually surrendered to their curiosity and knocked on doors and peered into windows. And if there was no answer or if the home looked like it had been disturbed, nosy neighbors would sometimes take it upon themselves to locate the hidden key to the back door and let themselves in. All out of neighborly concern, of course. And when nosy neighbors found three dead bodies lying on the stairs and in the upstairs hallway, they called the police.

So because Peter didn't want to add to any nosy neighbors' curiosity, he left the house as naturally as he could. Just another day of heading off to a boring day at the lab. Nothing to look at here, folks.

Amy Cantori, assistant professor of psychology, lived alone in a two-story brick Victorian on the edge of Candleburg's historic district. At twenty-five hundred square feet, the house was way more than she needed, but she managed to keep up with it.

A large maple with sprawling limbs that forked into more sprawling limbs shaded the front of the house. Meticulously clipped knee-high boxwoods lined the sidewalk, and twisted wisteria shoots, like the many entangled tentacles of a graceless octopus, framed the wide front porch. The lawn was freshly cut and edged with razor precision. She'd had the porch painted since the last time Peter saw it. The framing was now a light cucumber green.

Peter exited his car and stepped up onto the porch. It was nicely furnished with wicker chairs and a love seat, potted cannas and ferns. Stained natural-wood flooring had replaced the old worn boards. It looked to be a nice place to sit on a summer evening and enjoy a gentle breeze and iced tea.

The front door opened, and Amy folded her arms across her chest. "So this isn't a friendly visit to make amends."

Peter stopped. "I know we need to deal with that, and we can. Later. Can I come in?"

She stepped to the side. "Only if you tell me what this is really about."

Walking past her and into the house, Peter said, "There's not much I can tell."

She closed the door. "Still as elusive as ever, I see. You said it was about Karen and Lilly. I'm sorry, Peter; really I am. And I'm sorry I didn't come to the funeral. It just didn't feel right after—"

"I'm not here to talk about the funeral." Peter scanned the foyer area. Not much had changed since the last time he'd been there. Amy had a distinct style of interior decorating, kind of a mash-up of early-nineteenth-century Victorian with its intricate woodwork and colorful fabrics and twenty-first-century modern with its smooth surfaces, sharp angles, and brushed steel. Normally the two would go together like bow ties and tattoos, but she had a way of pulling it off. "Place still looks the same," he said.

"I like it. It works for me."

"Me too. I always did." He glanced at her. "Can I use your computer?"

"My computer? Is yours broken?"

"No. Can I use yours?"

He took a step toward the living room, but she stopped him with a hand on his chest. "Hey, are you okay? What does my computer have to do with Karen and Lilly?"

"Karen and Lilly are alive."

Her hand dropped to her side. Confusion contorted her face. "Come again? I saw the obituary. It was the talk of everyone at the school. A lot of them were at the funeral. They told me about it. Peter, are you all right? I mean, you've gone through an awful lot. If you're having a hard time dealing with all of this, you can always talk—"

"Don't analyze me, Amy," he said. He pushed past her and entered the living room, a softly lit area furnished with a claw-foot sofa, a floor-to-ceiling bookshelf, and two ornately carved end tables each topped with a brass lamp. Amy kept her laptop on an antique secretary's desk in the corner. "I already have a shrink and do enough talking. I need a computer. Is your laptop still in here?"

How was he able to recall details of Amy Cantori's house when he couldn't even remember what happened yesterday?

Leaving her in the foyer, he found the computer on the desk, opened it, and sat in the chair.

But Amy was right there, shutting the laptop before he could get his hands on the keyboard. "Not till you tell me what's going on."

Peter sighed and sat back. "Okay, I don't think Karen and Lilly died in a car accident."

•   •   •

Lawrence Habit pulled his Lincoln into the driveway behind Peter Ryan's Volkswagen, blocking any getaway. He cut the engine, removed his sunglasses, and examined his face in the rearview mirror. He hadn't been particularly attractive even before the scar; he could admit that. He traced his finger along the length of the scar. It was smooth and numb and at various points sent electric zingers to remote locations on his face. It ached at the moment. It always did right before a kill.

Lawrence smiled at himself, checked his teeth, then tossed the glasses on the passenger seat and exited the vehicle. He made no attempt at being covert. For one thing, he was too big to be sneaking around, with his broad shoulders, deep chest, and thick arms. And second, that just wasn't the way he operated. He wasn't arrogant about it; on the contrary, he never boasted about his success rate. His foster dad had taught him that a humble man was a respected man. And an arrogant man would eventually wind up a prematurely dead man. Lawrence considered that the fear of death caused some in his profession to sneak and slink around, hiding in shadows and using the element of surprise. But to him, death was a nonnegotiable part of life, something everyone had to deal with regardless of location or situation or occupation, so he dealt with it. He dealt with the fear head-on, not out of arrogance but out of practicality.

At the front door he didn't bother to knock. He looked side to side and across the street, checking to make sure no neighbors were nosing around outside. The last thing he needed was for some little old lady out for a walk with her dog to witness him forcibly entering the home. She'd call the cops for sure, and those local schmucks were idiots. Fortunately the large maple and other assorted shrubs on the property provided seclusion and privacy the woman must have enjoyed. No wonder she had the front porch so comfortably furnished. It was a place where she no doubt spent much of her time.

Drawing his silencer-equipped Smith & Wesson from his shoulder holster, Lawrence took one step forward, lifted his right foot, and planted it solidly just to the left of the door handle. The door shot open, splintering the wood along the jamb, and Lawrence rushed in.

NINE

. . .

The front door crashed open with the suddenness and intensity of
a gunshot and nearly pushed Peter out of his chair. He instantly,
instinctively, grabbed Amy by the arm and ducked into the
kitchen, drawing the pistol he'd stashed in his waistband at the
small of his back.

His reaction time was amazingly quick, and a feeling of déjà vu
came over him, as if he'd done this exact thing at some other time
in some other place. If indeed he had been the target of assassins
and hit men before, and if indeed he had been shot at before—and
enough times to have developed an almost-involuntary reaction
to it—at least he'd been lucky. His body had no scars from gunshot
wounds.

Amy eyed the weapon, then Peter. Fear widened her eyes,

and her mouth formed an almost-perfect O. From the look on her face, Peter assumed she was just as surprised at his newfound skills as he was. He put an index finger to his lips and shook his head.

Heavy footsteps sounded in the foyer, then the dining room. Quickly Peter pulled Amy by the arm and shuffled across the kitchen to the back door. They would have to make an escape that way. He didn't know how many uninvited visitors there were and didn't want to get into a shootout and put Amy in the line of fire.

After lifting a key ring from a peg by the counter, he opened the door and the two of them slid onto the back porch. Peter said, "Is the garage unlocked?"

"You have the keys," Amy said.

Down the porch steps they ran and to the garage, where Peter handed the keys to Amy, who opened the door to the garage.

In the garage sat a late-model Ford F-150, red and shiny, with knobby tires and tinted windows.

"Really?" Peter said.

Amy tossed him the keys. "You drive."

Peter got in and cranked the engine to life as Amy hit the button to open the overhead door. The electric motor hummed, the chain engaged, and the door lifted with a low rumble. When it was four feet off the ground, Peter saw two legs from the knees down—khaki dress pants, military-style boots—standing in the middle of the driveway.

Amy saw too. She pushed back against the seat and braced herself. "Go!"

Not waiting for the door to reach its full height and give the invader a clean shot at the windshield, Peter shifted into gear and stomped on the gas. The engine roared triumphantly as if it were a beast that had been caged for far too long and had finally found its freedom. Tires screeched on the concrete flooring as the truck lurched forward and the grille crashed into the lower edge of the door. The door tore loose from its track, dragging the rubber-coated edge along the truck's hood and up the windshield.

When the truck cleared the garage and the door, the man came into view, feet wide, handgun pointed at the cab. His eyes drilled Peter with intensity but not hatred, not like the big man who had invaded his home and tried to kill him. Peter thought he saw a flash of surprise, too, just long enough to prevent the man from aiming and squeezing off a shot. The truck was upon him in a fraction of a second and he dove to the side.

Peter lifted his foot off the gas pedal for an instant. His Jetta and a black Lincoln blocked any exit from the driveway.

Amy looked out her side window, whimpered, and banged the dash as if she could push the truck forward simply by willing it to do so. "Ram 'em," she hollered.

Once again Peter hit the gas and the truck's engine growled and pushed forward. But instead of striking the Jetta and shoving both it and the Lincoln into the street, he yanked the wheel to the right and steered the truck into the yard beside the driveway, toppling three shrubs and a portion of a neatly trimmed hedge.

Bouncing back onto the driveway, the truck's side front bumper clipped the back of the Lincoln, causing an awful screech as metal bent and twisted and the paint was stripped off the Lincoln's rear quarter panel. Peter stole a quick glance in the side mirror. The gunman was back on his feet, lumbering after the truck.

Peter pressed harder on the gas as a bullet struck the cab's framing.

• • •

Furious and spitting curses, Lawrence threw open the Lincoln's door and jumped in. He brought the engine to life, jammed the gear stick into reverse, and laid down rubber getting out of the driveway.

Jed Patrick. The job might have identified someone named Peter Ryan, but Lawrence knew the man he'd seen in the cab of that truck. After training together, after facing countless life-and-death situations, how could he not know the man on sight? Jed Patrick was the only reason Lawrence was alive today. And Lawrence had allowed that personal connection to get the better of him. He was not only angry with himself for not taking the shot when he had it, but he was infuriated by Patrick's audacity. He would have run Lawrence over had he not dived out of the truck's path.

Tearing down the road after the truck, Lawrence slammed his palm against the steering wheel and once again released a string of the most extreme curses he could devise. His blood bubbled in his veins and his foot pressed heavy on the accelerator. Up ahead, the F-150 slowed and turned right. Seconds later, Lawrence did the same. The tires of the Lincoln stuttered around the turn, and he had to fight the steering wheel to keep from ending up in a ditch that bordered the shoulder.

• • •

"What was that? Who was that man?" Amy said, bracing herself against the dash with one hand while gripping the seat belt with the other.

Peter checked the mirrors. The black Lincoln hung on their tail but was still a good ways off. The truck had a nice engine under its hood, lots of horses for getaways just like this one. "I don't know."

"You don't know? You're gonna have to do better than that. He had a gun, Peter." In his peripheral vision, Peter saw her glance at his pistol, which now lay in the center console. "And so do you."

The brief glimpse he'd had of the gunman's face before he dove out of the path of the truck had triggered a shotgun memory: *A series of rifle blasts—pop, pop, pop, pop—concealed behind a wall, a closed door. The door opens and a man steps out, crouched, hollering. He wears a black ski mask and swings the gun around in a wide arc. He reaches up with a gloved hand and yanks off the mask.*

It was him, the gunman. Same short-cropped dusty hair, same heavy eyelids, full lips, thick nose. Same deadness in his gray eyes. But without the scar that marked the face of the man in the Lincoln behind them.

Peter had seen the man before, even had the feeling that he knew the man, but had no idea how or why. It was like a memory transplanted from another time. Maybe another life altogether. Some lone image floating in a sea of lost memories.

"Are you gonna start talking now?" Amy said.

Peter leaned on the brake and steered the truck off the main avenue and onto a secondary road where there were fewer homes and longer stretches of asphalt. "I'm kind of busy right now."

They were beyond the town limits now, pushing sixty-five down a narrow road that cut straight through the surrounding farmland. On either side of the truck stood acres and acres of browning cornstalks as tall as a man, their tassels waving gently in the morning breeze.

Behind them, the Lincoln gained ground. Amy turned and

looked out the rear window. "He's getting closer. We need to do something to lose him."

"Got any suggestions?"

Amy checked the rear window again. "Drive faster?"

"Hang on." Peter hit the brake and pulled the wheel to the right. The truck bounced and bumped over the shallow ditch that ran parallel to the road, climbed the short incline to the field, and plowed into the corn, laying down a path of stalks four rows wide.

Amy leaned forward in the seat and put both hands on the dash. "Oh, my truck." Cornstalks slapped at the grille like broom handles, broke, and released drying ears of corn, which slid up the hood and bounced over the windshield. "Keep going," she said. "Make some turns, then head that way." She pointed to the left. "We can come out on the other side of the field, and he'll never know where we went."

• • •

Lawrence pushed himself back in his seat and stomped on the brake. The car's tires slid on some loose gravel; it fishtailed a bit, then came to a stop. There was no way the Lincoln could navigate the terrain through the field and follow the truck. He got out and removed his sunglasses, scanned the area carefully, and chewed on his lower lip as if it were a piece of beef jerky. The field was slightly elevated, and with the height of the corn, he couldn't tell which way the truck had headed. He hit the trunk with his hand and cursed again.

He'd have to call and let the agency know he'd lost them. He hated the thought of it. Failure was not tolerated. If he was lucky, they'd keep him on the assignment, give him another chance to redeem himself and right this wrong. If he was unlucky, which he had yet to be, they would take him off the case, and he knew exactly what that meant.

If it came to that, he'd go rogue; he'd drop everything and take himself off the grid. They wouldn't take him. He wouldn't let that happen.

TEN

. . .

Five minutes and thousands of broken and crushed cornstalks later, the truck emerged from the field and the tires found pavement again. For Peter, it had been a ride more bumpy and jolting than any amusement park's wooden roller coaster. But there was nothing amusing about these twisted turns of events that kept finding him. As the truck hit the road, shedding the remains of the field, Peter's white-knuckled hands gripped the steering wheel and his heart hammered in time with the pistons of the heaving monster under the hood.

Amy glanced behind them, then relaxed a little in her seat. Her face was as pale as chalk, her lips colorless. "Peter, you mind telling me what's going on here?"

"Do you have your phone on you?" Peter said, ignoring her question.

"My what?"

"Your phone. Do you have it?"

"Yes. Why?"

"Get it out."

She pulled the phone from the back pocket of her jeans. "You want to call for help now?"

"Take the battery out."

"But—"

"Amy, do it. Take it out. It's a trackable device. They can use its signals to pinpoint our location." It was crazy and some of the strangest timing he'd ever experienced, but the thought had struck him while they rumbled through the cornfield, getting battered by drying cobs.

Moving quickly, Amy popped the back off the phone and removed the battery. Peter then fished his phone from the front pocket of his pants and handed it to her. "Mine too."

She repeated the process with his phone, then stuck them both in the glove box.

Peter massaged the steering wheel as if he could milk hope from it. He stole a glance at Amy. "I'm sorry, Amy. Really."

"You know, for someone who vowed to never talk to me again, you sure have a weird way of keeping your promises."

"I never meant for this to happen. I needed help, and you were the only one I could think of." He turned left at the next stop sign and drove past a large white farmhouse. The house was old, at least a hundred years or so, and appeared in need of updating and repairs. Clothes hung on a wash line outside, and a girl—no more than seven or eight, Lilly's age—wearing jeans and a purple sweatshirt played with a kitten.

Amy craned her neck to look at the family. "That's the Bruces' home, and that's Jenny. Theirs is the field we just destroyed."

"Do you know them?"

"Yes. Sort of. His wife works part-time at the Food Lion. We talk. She's a very kind and soft-spoken woman."

Peter sighed. "Give them my apologies?"

"Apologies won't bring their corn back. That's their livelihood."

"We had to."

"I know. I'll pay him back for his loss."

"I'll pay. I drove."

"It's my truck covered with his corn. We'll split it."

They drove in silence for a minute or so, Peter pushing the truck just beyond the road's posted speed limit.

Finally Amy said, "Where are we going, anyway?"

Peter shrugged, checked the mirrors. "I don't know. I just want to get away and think. I need to think." There was so much to process, so much to sort out. His mind reeled with questions and possible answers and scenarios that made absolutely no sense and others that made partial sense but only under extraordinary circumstances. But he had yet to come upon an explanation that made perfect sense. It was there; he was certain of it. But he needed time and quiet to sort through all the weeds and find it.

"Peter, that man had a gun. He was there to kill one of us or both of us. Who was he? How did he know you'd be there?"

"I don't know."

"That was two questions."

"I don't know on both accounts." He forked his fingers through his hair. "I need to think."

"You said you needed help. What kind of help? And why me?"

Peter checked the mirrors again, glanced out the side window, scanned the dash's instrument panel. She had so many questions.

It was time to start giving her some answers. "Karen and Lilly are alive."

"Yeah, you said that already. What does that mean?"

"Exactly what it sounds like: they're still alive."

"But the accident. The funeral."

He shook his head, rubbed his temples with one hand. "It must have been staged. Faked. I don't know. All I know is that the funeral wasn't real and they're alive." More memories of the funeral materialized and peppered his mind with splintered images and fragments of running video. There were so many people there, people he didn't even know. Friends of Karen, parents of Lilly's schoolmates. The preacher went on and on. He was a good man, Pastor Morsey, but he didn't know when to quit talking. Not that Peter wanted to hurry the service up; he didn't. He just wanted to be left alone to grieve. He wanted some time without well-wishers and condolences and all the tears. Eventually the clouds released their rain and Morsey was forced to wrap things up. When everyone had gone, Peter asked the caretaker if he could have a few minutes at the graves before they put the caskets in the ground. The man, an older gent with a weathered face and tired eyes, nodded and backed away. And that's when Peter let the tears come. Rain ran off his head and mixed with the tears. He was angry, hurt, lonely. How could God abandon him like this? Take what was most precious to him? How cruel was that?

But this morning changed all that. How he'd forgotten, he didn't know. It was as if someone had gained access to his mind as he slept, hacked into his internal hard drive, and erased file after file. His mind, scrambling to repair the damage, had then reverted back to the last configuration that made sense, that it knew to be true: Karen and Lilly were indeed alive. Again he wondered how much he could believe what his mind was telling him. But he wasn't imagining the gunmen. Or the note in Lilly's handwriting. None of the pieces seemed to form the right picture.

Amy held her head with both hands. "Staged the funeral? Okay, so let's say they are alive somewhere. Who would want to do such a thing? And how do you know? Didn't you see the bodies after the accident?"

They'd told Peter the car had been so engulfed in flames that there were no remains to identify. "No. They told me there was nothing left. And I have no idea who's behind this."

Amy's hand went to her mouth. "I'm sorry. And I'm sorry I didn't come to the funeral. Didn't call or write or anything. I thought…"

"I understand, Amy. Really. When I think about it, I can't really blame you." Peter reached into his pocket and retrieved the note he'd found in the toilet tank. "Look, I'm not going nuts, okay? I thought I was at first, but I'm not." He paused to consider all that he had told her so far and put himself in her shoes, on the receiving end of such outlandish and improbable theories. "Okay, maybe I'm a little nuts."

"What are you talking about?"

He handed her the piece of paper.

She unfolded it and stared at it. "Centralia. What's that?"

"That's why I needed your computer."

"But why couldn't you use your own computer?"

Peter checked the mirrors. No black Lincoln followed. He slowed the truck and turned right onto Long Acre Lane. The road was lined with mature sycamores, their branches sprawling overhead, forming a canopy thirty, forty feet above the ground. Beyond the trees were acres of field that had lain fallow. Grass, shin-high and brown, swayed slowly, pushed about by the air's gentle currents. He didn't want to tell Amy about the gunmen. He'd trusted her at one time, trusted her with his career until she'd betrayed him and nearly cost him his job and reputation. But when he needed someone he trusted, hers had still been the first name—really the only one—he could think of. Regardless of what had happened between them, he knew where he stood with her. "Can I trust you?"

If the question startled Amy or took her by surprise, she didn't show it. "After what just happened? I think I should be asking you that."

He said it again. "Can I trust you, Amy?"

She studied the note for a long moment, then turned her head toward the window and watched the trees whiz by. "Yes. Yes, Peter, you can trust me."

"Do you think I'm nuts?"

Her hesitation didn't bother him. Anyone sane would deduce that he was playing on the edge of lucidity, walking that very fine line that separated sanity from utter madness. After checking the note again, she said, "No. I think you're confused, I think you still haven't made sense of any of this yet, I think you're a total jerk for pulling me into this, but I don't think you're crazy." She paused, glanced at him, and smiled. "Well, maybe a little nuts."

He couldn't argue with any of that. "Fine. I think I was being tracked or bugged or monitored or something."

"Big Brother?"

"Worse."

"What do you mean, worse? And why?"

He paused, swallowed. A light sweat had broken out on his brow and upper lip. If he wanted her help, he'd have to tell her.

She was the only one who would listen to him and take him seriously without writing him off as a mourning husband and father
who'd misplaced his last piece of sanity somewhere in the land of
paranoid psychosis. "Big Brother with guns and an intent to kill."

"Is that who that was back there? Big Brother?"

"I really don't know. I think he was sent to clean up Big Brother's
mess. Three men broke into my home shortly after I found that
note. They had guns. Silencers. They weren't there to play nice."

"They were professionals?"

"Apparently."

"And they knew the moment you found this note?"

Unbidden, tears came again, pressing behind his eyes and ooz-
ing out the corners. He dashed them away. "It looks that way, yes.
I was being monitored."

"What happened? How did you get away?"

He glanced at her but didn't answer.

"We need to call the police," she said.

Peter shook his head. "No way. I have to stick with people I can
trust. People I know."

"And you can't trust the cops?"

"Not anymore."

"Why ever not?"

Outside the truck, the line of sycamores ended and the fields
gave way to a more populated stretch. Small homes, mostly ranches
and mobiles, lined the road now. Each sat on a nice-size lot with a
paved driveway and trees for shade. In them lived families who
shared memories and played games together, maybe watched
movies at night, ate popcorn. Families that hadn't been destroyed
by lies and hunted like criminals. A mile or so down the road,
they'd enter the town of Five Forks. Peter massaged the wheel

again. "Because one of the intruders—one of the men who would have shot me in cold blood—was a cop."

Amy didn't say anything to that. She stared out the side window for a long time before asking again, "How did you get away?" She seemed surprised that a lab researcher, a man who spent most of his academic life in a white coat, a man who would rank at least in the upper tenth percentile when it came to nerdiness, could escape the clutches of three trained killers.

Peter glanced at his hands. He had once again clenched his hands until his knuckles lost their color. "That's enough for now, okay?"

ELEVEN

• • •

They rode in silence for the next thirty minutes, across oceans of open farmland striped with rows of corn and blanketed with fields of golden wheat, and through the towns of Five Forks and Crossroads. Peter kept glancing in his mirrors but never saw the black Lincoln or any other vehicle following them. Though satisfied that he'd temporarily shaken his murderous shadow, he didn't believe for one moment that he'd lost his pursuers but had merely stalled them. They seemed to have resources beyond his ability to truly hide. He only needed to lie low long enough to collect his thoughts, formulate a plan, and figure out what to do with Amy. He certainly didn't want to endanger her any more than he already had but knew that she was part of it now—she was involved—and whoever was after him wouldn't stop until they had both of them.

When they arrived in Bentleysville, Peter said, "We need gas, and I need to get some answers."

Amy said, "I need answers too."

"You'll get them. As much as I know." She deserved to know what he knew, which wasn't much. During the drive following their cornfield escape, his mind had sprouted a whole new crop of questions. All without answers. He'd spare Amy the finer nuances of his tortuous soliloquizing and share only the facts he'd learned or deduced.

After filling the truck at a small local station on the fringe of town, he found a coffee shop on one of the secondary streets and parked behind it in the employee parking area.

"Why not go to the library?" Amy asked.

"Cameras," Peter said. "Libraries have security cameras, even in small towns."

"Yeah, these little towns are real hotbeds for book thieves. You wouldn't imagine what the street value is for the latest Dan Brown novel."

"We need to stay off the grid, out of view. No cameras, no credit cards, no phone calls."

Amy sighed, ran her hand through her hair. "You think they can tap into some country library's closed-circuit system?"

"I'm not sure what they're capable of right now. They tracked me to your house. How did they do that? My car? My phone? It could be anything. It's like they know my next move before I do. They're resourceful, and until I figure out how they operate, we need to be as invisible as possible."

"And who exactly are they?"

Peter pulled the key from the ignition and opened the truck's door. "That's what I'm trying to figure out."

• • •

It took Lawrence Habit a full twenty minutes to make his way around the cornfield and find the road that Patrick and the woman had taken. It was obvious civil engineers had tractors, not assassins, in mind when designing the grid for rural roads. Oversize, tread-heavy tires could go where luxury sedans could not. Lawrence primarily made his living maneuvering through city streets with stop signs and traffic lights and the occasional pedestrian to deal with. This land of corn and wheat and shoulderless roads was as foreign to him as a grass-covered savanna was to a mountain goat. He glanced at his watch. He was now thirty minutes behind them. He'd have to be liberal on the gas pedal.

Shortly after Lawrence had lost Patrick and reported his miscalculation, his employer had phoned back and given him the route and direction Patrick and the woman were headed. The call came from a different number this time, and it was a different voice on the other end, masculine but with an effeminate quality to it—so mechanical and lifeless Lawrence at first thought it was a recording. To make sure it wasn't an automated caller, he asked the voice what its favorite rock group of the 1970s was. An odd question, but personal enough that a computer-generated identity using artificial intelligence would not be programmed to answer it. The voice hesitated, then mumbled that it didn't listen to seventies rock. Eighties was its music of choice. Red Hot Chili Peppers.

Satisfied that he was indeed speaking to a real person, Lawrence told the voice to phone him again when Patrick reached his destination, wherever that might be. The voice agreed but said yet another individual from yet another phone number would call Lawrence the next time.

Lawrence was not surprised.

Ten minutes later he received another call. A man this time, no mistaking it, with a hint of a New England accent. Bostonian. Patrick's location was given with specific orders to take him alive. This made Lawrence's job a lot trickier. Still, it was better than the alternative. He did not want to kill Patrick; after all, he owed the guy his life.

Lawrence thanked the caller for the information and was about to disconnect the call when the man said, "One more thing you should take note of."

Lawrence pressed the phone harder against his ear. "I'm taking notes."

"If you fail this time, you will be discontinued."

That was it. Spoken coldly as if he'd read it from a script and didn't realize what he'd said, the weight of his words, the finality of his simple sentence, until after the words had crossed his lips.

"Thanks for the warning," Lawrence said.

The man disconnected.

Discontinued. Lawrence ran his finger around the steering wheel. It certainly didn't mean fired. The agency didn't fire people. Either you were in or you were out. And if you were out, it meant you were dead. Discontinued.

He wouldn't fail, though. He never had and never would. Persistence was a trait of his that had gotten him through too many tours in desert wastelands and landed him countless scores for the agency. He was their most successful tool. A pit bull when it came to completing a mission. That wasn't about to change now.

• • •

Upon entering the coffee shop, another memory assaulted Peter.

He's at a booth, sipping coffee. He's wearing a uniform, dark blue, short sleeves. Beneath the shirt is a thick vest, tight against his chest and around to his back. Another man is with him, another officer, presumably his partner. On the wall behind the booth is a large clock with a round white face and bold black numbers, its hands showing 7:45. The other cop—what was his name?—smirks and says, "You hear what happened with Rodriguez?"

Peter shakes his head. "Which one?"

"The old man."

The waitress behind the counter hands them each a steaming coffee. She smiles at Peter's partner, but it isn't the friendly type of smile that would normally pass between a waitress and her customers. No, this is a knowing smile, a more-than-friendly smile that makes Peter suspicious of their relationship.

When she glances at Peter, he merely nods at her, then says to his partner, "What? Did someone get to him?"

His partner drags his eyes from the waitress's slender figure long enough to take a slow sip of coffee. "He's gettin' out."

"What do you mean he's getting out? He was put away for thirty."

"Struck some kind of deal with the DA and they got him out early."

"What kind of deal?"

His partner shrugs. "Confidential, they say."

Peter was still standing in the doorway, one hand lingering on the door's handle, when Amy touched his shoulder. "Hey, you okay?"

"Uh, yeah. Yes." The memory had come out of nowhere like a fleet of kamikaze planes. This place, this café, was familiar to him, but he'd never been here; he was certain of it. And he'd never been a cop—of that he was certain too. His mind was misfiring, splicing together images and memories from his past—maybe movies he'd watched or stories he'd read—and creating some alternate reality.

"You sure?" Amy said. "You look like you just saw a ghost."

"And what does that look like?"

"The look or the ghost?"

Peter shook his head. "I'm fine. Just thinking."

"Planning, I hope."

Inside the coffee shop were five patrons. An elderly couple at a corner table, both with coffees. The man read a brochure about a cruise to Iceland; his coffee was black and hot. His wife held her mug with both hands and watched the lazy morning traffic out the window. A young woman, no more than thirty, sipped an iced coffee while paging through a magazine. She wore a beret and scarf, no jacket but a heavy wool sweater. Then there were two men at the counter, both middle-aged, rugged and unshaven, jeans-and-sweatshirt types, both taking their time with their black coffees. One read a newspaper while the other made small talk with the woman behind the counter. She seemed uncomfortable with his attention but remained polite.

After ordering a coffee and a latte, Peter and Amy seated themselves at a table for two toward the back of the shop. Peter faced the front door but was aware of the customer restroom behind him and the entrance to the kitchen to his right. Beyond the kitchen would be the rear exit. He turned his chair a little to the right so he could clearly see both the front door and the kitchen come-and-go area.

Sipping his coffee, he said to Amy. "Sorry about your landscaping back there."

"Peter, we need to go back."

Peter shook his head. "Can't. They'll be waiting for that."

"Who will be waiting?"

"I don't know."

"I'm not a fugitive. I can't just abandon my home, my career, and go on the run."

Peter bit his cheek and nodded slowly. "Maybe you should go now."

"Go where?"

"To the cops. There must be a police station in this town."

"You said the cops weren't safe."

"Not for me. But there's no reason to put both of us in the line of fire. Besides, they'll believe you."

Amy turned in her seat but hesitated.

"What's the matter?" Peter said. "Go. I can handle it on my own from here."

Amy faced Peter again. "Whoever is after you, if they've gone this far, surely they wouldn't just forget about me."

"Go, Amy."

"I can't. If you have a price on your head, then so do I by now. Besides, whatever happened in the past, you're still… very important to me."

Peter sighed. "Amy, I never meant—"

"I'm not trying to make this awkward. But I'm staying. I'd rather know where the danger is coming from for a while than live the rest of my life looking over my shoulder, wondering whether they're coming for me."

Peter glanced around the shop. For the moment, nothing seemed out of place. "All right. Thank you, I guess. And I'm sorry. We need to stay off the grid. We use only cash from here on out."

"And how long do we have to do that? How long before we can go home again?"

Peter shrugged. How long before either of them could go home again? "When all this is over."

Amy sipped her latte again and stared at the table. "Who are they, Peter? Seriously."

"I honestly don't know. The government, I think."

"Why are they after you?"

"I don't know."

"Okay." She set her latte down and folded her hands on the table. "Let's start here. What do you know?"

Peter paused, swirled the coffee in the cup. The black liquid reflected the lights of the café in alternating black-and-white concentric circles. In the dark swirls Peter found Amy's face, distorted, etched with pain—no, agony and fear. A chill passed through him as easily as frigid air penetrates loose-knit fabric. Quickly he took another sip of the coffee to erase the image. Her question was valid, though. What did he know? The problem was that he wasn't sure what he knew—really knew—and what he'd only imagined or dreamed or concocted in a distant corner of his mind. Wherever the line was between the actual events of his past and his memory of it, Peter had no idea. His mind was feeding him lies, and he didn't know what to hold on to: the reality he experienced or the reality other people were telling him about. Regardless, he had a lot to explain to Amy and would do his best to share only what he knew or perceived to be factual. "I know I awoke this morning and Karen and Lilly were gone."

"Because they died and were buried." She didn't say it without feeling; she wasn't cold like that. But Amy had always been matter-of-fact. It was one of the qualities that made her a great psychologist and researcher.

"Only I don't believe that. Not anymore. I'm not even sure I ever believed it." He downed the remaining coffee in the cup. "Then these three guys show up, break into my home. They had guns. Looks like they meant to kill me."

Amy leaned in. "But why?"

"I don't know."

"You must have done something, known somebody, made enemies somewhere. Something. Did you tick anybody off? Cheat somebody?"

"No. Absolutely not." At least not that he could remember. Not that he could even trust his own memory anymore. So he stuck to what he could be sure of. "You know me. Am I the type to make enemies? Those kind of enemies?"

She took the latte cup in both hands. "Of course not."

"There was one thing, though. That guy at your house."

"Baldy."

"Yeah. I recognized him from somewhere."

"Where?"

"I can't put my finger on it. I know I've seen him before, though." He didn't want to tell her about the flashback. The gunshots. The ski mask. Not until he figured out where his memories were coming from and what and who they involved.

"So where do we go from here?"

"Centralia."

"But we don't know anything about the place—not what it is or where it's located."

Peter pushed back his chair and stood. "Then we'd better find out."

TWELVE

· · ·

The contact had phoned him one last time, another unfamiliar voice from another unfamiliar number. It was a man again, deep, raspy voice with a slight Southern drawl. Maybe North Carolina, maybe Virginia. They were taking extra precautions this time, following additional steps to check on him and guide him along. Making sure he did his job. But Lawrence didn't need them to hold his hand. He was well-versed in what he was about to do. Their lack of confidence in him only served to heighten his level of irritation.

After clicking off the phone and dropping it into a cup holder in the center console, he cranked the radio louder than usual. Perry Como was in the middle of crooning "Can't Help Falling in Love."

Lawrence relaxed in the seat of the Lincoln and maintained

a steady speed. He used music to focus himself, and he needed to focus. While he had no doubt he could take Patrick, he still needed to respect his old friend. Patrick's abilities were unmatched by many; he'd always shown promise, carried so much potential. When he failed to become all that was expected of him, the disappointment around the agency was palpable. For months everyone paid the price for Patrick's failure. The director was furious and intolerable and wanted to make sure a similar breakdown never happened again.

Lawrence steered the Lincoln into the parking lot of an empty warehouse and next to a receiving dock. The place looked like it had been abandoned for years. Weeds, knee-high and thick as a finger, poked up through cracks in the asphalt. The block walls of the building were cracked and stained with rust from the metal roofing and rainspouts. The concrete foundation had crumbled at one corner, causing the building to sag in that area.

Leaving the car, Lawrence moved on foot around the corner of the warehouse, down the short alleyway, and to the street, sticking close to storefronts and staying in the shadows of overhanging roofs. Running his hand over his head and retrieving the handgun from its holster, he quickened his pace. The café was just a block away.

• • •

Peter headed over to the woman at the table across the room, the magazine reader with the beret and scarf. Late twenties, with smooth skin, dark-brown hair, and large, innocent, dark eyes. As he neared, she appeared to not notice him. She sipped at her iced coffee through a straw but kept her eyes on the magazine the entire time.

Approaching her, he said, "Excuse me, ma'am."

She looked up, not startled that a complete stranger would approach her in the coffee shop but rather surprised that she hadn't seen him coming, so engrossed was she in her magazine. "Yes?"

"Hi. I know this is a strange request, but might you look something up for us on your phone? A friend recently mentioned a place we've never heard of. Can you help us out? We're both still in the dark ages with dumb phones."

She glanced at Amy, seated across the café, and smiled. It was a nice smile, friendly, warm, welcoming. This was a woman who naturally assumed the best in people. "Sure. What's the name of it?"

"Centralia."

The woman reached for her phone and tapped the screen. "Centralia. Hm. Never heard of it either. Is it the name of a town?"

He had no idea. "I think it is."

Her fingers went to work on the screen, and within seconds her eyes were scanning back and forth. "Sure is. Looks like it's a town in Pennsylvania. It says Centralia is a near ghost town. Its population has dwindled from over one thousand residents in 1981 to its current ten as a result of a mine fire burning beneath the town since 1962." She tapped the phone several more times with her index finger. "Interesting. Over the years they've made several attempts to put the fire out but have had no success. In 1981 a twelve-year-old boy fell into a sinkhole and nearly died."

So it was a town. But was he supposed to recognize the name? What connection did Karen and possibly he have with a town in Pennsylvania? And what about this town could have brought hit men to his home? It still meant nothing to him. He now had a town in Pennsylvania, a ghost town, burning for decades, but nothing more to go on. No hook that affixed the town to either himself or Karen.

He smiled at the woman. "That is interesting. Thank you. Can I ask one more thing of you?"

"Sure." She looked at him expectantly.

"I'm sorry. I know this is all very intrusive and I'm interrupting your reading."

She shook her head and smiled. "No, no. Don't apologize. This is fascinating. I love learning new things, especially little factoids like this. Now I can wow all my friends by telling them about Centralia, the burning town."

Peter leaned forward. "Thank you so much. Can you pull up a map of the town's location in Pennsylvania? Just out of curiosity. I was born in PA and have never heard of it. I'm interested to see where it is."

"Absolutely." Her fingers went to work again, and in short time she handed him the phone. "There you go. Looks like, true to its name, it's near the center of the state."

"Sure does," Peter said. He handed the phone back to her. "Thanks. You've been a big help."

"Where were you born?" the woman asked, putting the phone in her purse.

"Near the PA–Maryland line, little town called Fairfield. I was actually born in Gettysburg Hospital."

"Interesting," she said. "I grew up in western PA. Went to Pitt, then got married and moved here. My husband is from Vermont."

"Well," Peter said, "from one Pennsylvanian to another, thank you for your help."

She smiled wide, and those big, amicable eyes twinkled in the café's lighting. "Glad I could be of help."

Peter turned away from the woman and glanced out the large plate-glass windows that made up the café's front facade. Stepping up onto the sidewalk, just as casually as if he were out shopping on a Sunday afternoon and had decided to take a break for a coffee, was the bald gunman from Amy's house. In his right hand, keeping it close to his thigh, he held his handgun. He'd found them. But how? Pulse suddenly racing, adrenaline flooding his arteries, every nerve fiber, every sense on high alert, Peter turned to the woman who had just so kindly offered her assistance and said, "Get down. Under the table."

She must have seen the intensity in his eyes because after a quick glance out the front window, she slid off the seat, squatting beneath the table.

Peter hurried across the café to Amy.

Her eyes were wide and worried, her lips parted. "What's going on? What's the matter?"

Peter took her by the arm. "Quickly. Back door."

She slid her chair away from the table and stood without hesitation.

But even as they left the main seating section and entered the area behind the counter, the gunman pushed through the front door.

Peter made eye contact with the woman taking orders and running the register; he presumed she was the owner of the small establishment. There was uncertainty in her eyes and a spark of fear. "Get down and stay down," he said.

Like the dark-haired woman in the beret at the table, she obeyed immediately and dropped to her knees.

Peter shoved Amy ahead of him into the kitchen. "Out the back, get the truck started. If he comes out first, gun it and get out of here." Silently cursing himself for leaving one of the handguns in the car, Peter drew the other from the waist of his jeans and passed it to her. "Just in case."

Amy ran through the kitchen and disappeared out the back door. Peter ducked behind a stainless steel shelving unit, not expecting it to conceal him indefinitely but looking for any advantage he might gain. Moments later the gunman entered the kitchen. Peter had to act quickly. The owner was probably already calling the police, and while they would be helpful in a situation like this, he wasn't ready yet to engage the cops in his current predicament. They would want to take him to their offices for questioning and would keep him occupied for hours. They'd want him to stay in town so he'd be easily located for further questioning. He could be detained for days, and he felt in his bones, in the core of the fabric of his soul, that staying in one spot, easy to locate, would be disastrous.

When the most opportune moment came, Peter swung out from behind the shelves and caught Baldy by surprise. He brought his elbows down on the big man's arms, knocking the handgun loose and sending it sliding across the tiled floor and under the boxy stainless steel commercial oven.

Baldy reacted quickly, shoving his elbow toward Peter's abdomen, but Peter anticipated the attack and sidestepped, simultaneously landing a forearm across his rival's face, catching him across the jaw and cheekbone. The bone-to-bone contact was solid, and Baldy staggered back but quickly regained his bearings. Setting his feet in a wide stance, he opened his powerful hands, forming them into claws, chuffed like an annoyed bear, and charged at Peter. The sheer size of the man was enough to intimidate even the most fearsome professional wrestler. He had Peter by at least forty pounds, most of that muscle. He was nimble for his size, too, and well-trained. Not clumsy and lumbering like most men carrying his bulk.

Baldy came at Peter swinging. Each jab and punch had a precision to it that spoke of years of training and use. But Peter blocked nearly every blow and managed to get a few in himself, landing them to Baldy's face, neck, and upper chest. But the big man was resilient and absorbed each impact like he was made of rock.

The fight took them across the kitchen to the prep area, where Baldy reached for and grabbed a utility knife. He squared up, slightly crouched, feet wide, and sneered at Peter. A trickle of blood ran from one nostril to his upper lip, and he had a small cut over his right eye that leaked blood as well. "I don't want to use this, Patrick."

Patrick. The name rang familiar to Peter, but he didn't know why. It was like a voice calling from a distant location, a voice he'd heard before but was now unable to tie to a face or a name.

"Do I know you?" Peter wasn't interested in having a heartfelt conversation with his opponent, and he had no expectations of the two of them leaving the café the best of friends, reunited after a long separation, but he was hoping to gain even a morsel of information, another piece to the jigsaw puzzle.

Without answering, Baldy lunged, but Peter had anticipated his move. He sidestepped the jab, grabbed the man's arm, and twisted it up and out. Spinning to his left while still grasping his assailant's wrist, Peter brought his elbow down hard across Baldy's upper arm. The blow would have broken a normal man's arm but not Baldy's; his bones must have been infused with concrete. Baldy did grunt and curse and drop the knife, but Peter didn't let go. Instead, he continued twisting the arm until it was behind Baldy, then ran the big man across the open space between the prep area and the grill.

Just before ramming the grill, Baldy lifted both feet and planted them against the grill's upper edge. He pushed hard, doing a leg press and driving Peter back.

Peter nearly lost his balance. If he went to the floor, Baldy would be on top of him like a bear on a salmon, and he wouldn't stand a chance under the bigger man's weight. Those fists would rain down like chunks of rock and pummel Peter into mash.

Peter stumbled backward and reached for the prep counter, steadying himself against its edge before he toppled over. But in doing so he lost the grip on Baldy's arm, and the big man yanked himself free and turned to face Peter.

"That's it, Patrick," Baldy said. He was panting, and sweat glistened on his head. Bright-red blood now smeared along the right side of his face. Crouched like a linebacker, the man shifted his eyes from Peter's hands to his feet and back again. "You don't remember me, do you?"

Peter said nothing. He didn't remember the man—not exactly. There was a familiarity about his face, but Peter wasn't sure if that was because of the flash memory he'd had or not. It could just be that his brain was equating Baldy with the memory of someone who appeared similar. Yet the man seemed to know Peter... and was calling him Patrick.

Baldy shifted his weight and glanced around the kitchen. "Let's call it a draw and we both walk away."

But he didn't mean it. Men like him never meant it. It was a trick to get Peter to let down his guard. "Why are you calling me Patrick? What does that mean?"

Baldy opened both hands and turned his palms up. His eyes no longer held the shadows of hatred and contempt; he no longer appeared to thirst for Peter's blood. There was respect in them now and maybe a hint of pity. "You don't remember yet. You will. Give it time."

"Time for what?"

In the distance, the low, eerie moan of a police siren sounded, and something changed in Baldy's eyes. The shadows had returned. He lunged at Peter with fists swinging. Peter deflected the blow coming from the left, but the fist attacking from the right struck him just below the ribs and nearly knocked the air out of his lung. He doubled to the side as another fist rained in from the left and caught him in the back of the head, sending spheres of light sailing through his field of vision. Baldy hit with tremendous force, his hands like battering rams.

Under the barrage, it didn't take long for Peter's knees to buckle and for the room to go dim.

Baldy's boot landed in Peter's side with all the force of a gunshot, shoving him against the counter. Hot-poker pain radiated through Peter's trunk. It seemed obvious to Peter now that Baldy was a hired gun, probably sent by the same employer who had sent the threesome to Peter's house, who wouldn't let up until Peter was dead or the cops came. Peter had to end this. He had no other choice. An image of Karen and Lilly stuttered through his mind. He couldn't abandon them; he had to find them.

Peter rolled to his side and swung his foot around, landing it along the side of his adversary's knee. Baldy stumbled and lurched but didn't go down. It was enough, though, to buy Peter the second he needed to scramble to his feet and go on the offensive.

He went at Baldy with both hands jabbing, cutting, delivering precise blows designed to induce damage that would accumulate exponentially, but the big man parried every advance. Renewed by a will to live and find his family, Peter relentlessly kept Baldy in the defensive position. He drove him back, closer to the grill, throwing punch after punch at varying angles. Finally Baldy backed up against the grill. The jolt was enough to break his concentration for a split second, enough time for Peter to slip in a jab unencumbered.

His hand connected with the big man's nose. Baldy's head snapped back and a fresh stream of blood trickled from his nostril, but he recovered quickly and came at Peter with a right roundhouse.

Peter stepped back and blocked the blow with both hands, then moved closer to use his weight to twist the arm behind Baldy's back.

The siren grew louder, a low moan that escalated into a high-pitched squeal. They couldn't be more than two blocks away.

Not giving Baldy a chance to counter his move, Peter once again drove the man toward the grill. But this time Baldy wasn't quick enough to block with his legs. He stuck out his hand to brace himself and it landed on the grill top. Skin scorched and sweat sizzled. Reflexively Baldy lifted his hand, and Peter saw his opening to catch his rival off-balance. He drove him farther forward, doubling him over the grill until his face touched the hot surface. A scream escaped Baldy's mouth, and his legs gave out beneath him. Peter followed him to the floor, grabbing the man's neck with one hand and a free wrist with the other. The left side of Baldy's face was red and raw, saliva oozed from his mouth, and hatred burned once again in his eyes.

"Who are you?" Peter hollered. "Why are you calling me Patrick? Where have we met before?"

Through his sweat and blood and vitriol, the big man smiled. "You'll have to do better than that. Remember your training, Patrick? Huh? It'll come back to you. It always does. And you'll remember who I am."

The sirens were nearly there, just outside now.

Peter retrieved the man's handgun from under the grill and pointed it at Baldy's forehead. There wasn't a shadow of fear in the man's eyes. His life meant nothing to him. But Peter couldn't do it. It was one thing to take down a clear and present danger, but he couldn't murder an unarmed man in cold blood like this. Peter didn't care who he was in another life or what he'd been trained for; it wasn't him now. And somehow he had to believe it never really had been.

Releasing Baldy, he stood, turned, and made a dash for the rear exit.

THIRTEEN

. . .

Leaving Bentleysville behind and heading north on State Road 74, Peter was back to massaging the steering wheel, attempting to squeeze some rationality out of it. His heart still pounded in his chest, and his hands, when they weren't working the wheel, shook like the last autumn leaf hanging on for all its worth. The confrontation with Baldy had left him upset, angry, and confused. The man apparently knew Peter, but by a different name. And though he had obviously been dispatched to take Peter out, he seemed for a moment to not want to go through with it; he seemed almost remorseful and relieved that there might be another option.

Suddenly Peter was acutely aware of Amy beside him in the truck. She huddled against the door, feet pulled up on the seat, knees to chest, biting at her fingernail.

"How did he find us so quickly?" she asked. "And who is he?"

Peter checked his mirrors to make sure Baldy hadn't raced for his car and followed them. He didn't know how he could with the burns he'd suffered. The left side of the man's face was sushi raw. He had to be in tremendous pain. But he was a trained killer, a hired gun, and men like him didn't stop because of pain. They were motivated by something deeper, something more visceral. There was a reason they chose to take life for money rather than hold down a respectable job in business or medicine.

Peter didn't answer her directly because he had no direct answers to give. Instead he said, "We need to get rid of this truck."

"What do you mean?" Amy said. "This is my truck."

"It's bugged. There must be a tracking device on it." It was the only explanation short of clairvoyance for how Baldy had found them so quickly in Bentleysville.

"But how? How could they have known you'd come to me?" Amy put her fist to her mouth and turned her head toward the side window.

How could they have known? Peter hadn't talked to Amy in months, not since she betrayed him and nearly ended his career, almost destroying his marriage in the process. He'd vowed to never speak to her again. How could anyone possibly have known that he would seek her help? Unless she was being watched as well. But why?

"I don't know."

Amy shook her head. "There you go with the I-don't-know routine."

"Amy, I'm just as much in the dark about this as you are." But he wasn't. Not quite. He'd recognized Baldy. He knew the man from somewhere, had had contact of some kind with him, but the answer still eluded him.

"*You don't remember me, do you? . . . Patrick.*"

Again Peter searched his memory, fishing to hook something tangible and bring it to the surface, but again, nothing came. The memory he'd had of Baldy had faded, and though he tried, he could not retrieve it. He thought that in it he might find some detail, some hidden trigger that would bring the full memory back into the light. But all his attempts at retrieval were futile. His mind was like a deep, dark tunnel in some subaquatic cavern. Memories, floating as effortlessly as dust on the currents of the air, bobbed near the surface but only close enough that general forms could be distinguished or a few indistinct features noticed before they disappeared into the lightless depths.

They drove in silence, heading north to put distance between them and Bentleysville and give them a lead on any pursuers that might be coming after them.

After several long minutes, Amy faced Peter and said, "Are you okay?"

Peter nodded. "Yeah."

"Peter, did you kill him? Back there."

"No." But he felt he should have, and he had the odd feeling that at another time he would have. But not now. He couldn't do it now. He was different. He didn't know how or why, but he sensed it; he sensed that at another time he had been another man, that his past held malefic secrets that had been repressed and buried in the darkest, remotest, most godforsaken corner of his brain. And yet, at the same time, he now felt more like the man he'd always truly been, whatever that meant.

Just like that, as quick and sudden and jolting as the clangor of a cymbal in the still of the night, another memory slammed through Peter's mind. It was the memory he had been waiting for, searching for.

"Take the shot. You have it."

He hesitates, his finger lingering on the cold metal of the trigger.

"Patrick, take it now!"

He exhales, depresses the fat pad on the end of his finger.

He can't. The target is there, a thousand yards away, reclining on his patio by the pool. He's got a drink in one hand and phone in the other. Dark shades hide his even darker eyes.

The crosshairs center on the man's forehead. This is the finest look they've had at the target yet, and it's such a clean shot. He'd be dead before anyone around him even heard the distant concussion of gunfire.

But he can't. The target's wife is there. She's younger than the target but not by much. And across the pool is his daughter, no more than seven or eight. Cute kid. Dark hair, dark eyes, olive skin.

"Patrick! Take it now." His spotter pulls away from the telescope and turns his head. Confusion hardens his face.

It's him. Baldy.

Even after the memory faded back into the dark, cloudy waters of Peter's mind, Baldy's eyes remained. The man was a machine, his mind calculating and his will driven by orders dictated by a handler who was even more heartless.

Amy nudged Peter's arm. "Hey, you there. Will they keep coming?"

Still trying to process the memory that had hijacked his mind, Peter looked at Amy and found fear in her eyes. For an instant, the duration of a single tick on a clock, he wished he would have killed Baldy. But back in the café, there was something in the man's eyes.

It was brief and Peter would have missed it altogether had he not been paying attention, but he saw a humanness there, an emotion that belied the actions of a killer with a rock for a heart. Besides, killing Baldy wouldn't have stopped them. Whoever was after him seemed to have unlimited resources, and if Baldy was erased, another would take his place. Wanton killing would offer no solution to this problem.

"They will," he said. "They won't stop until they get what they want."

"And what's that?"

"Me, I think."

"But why?" She was crying again.

Peter said nothing. He thought of the recurring dream he had. The house, the rooms, the locked door. The shadow that paced back and forth, back and forth. The answer was behind that door; he was sure of it. There was a part of his life he couldn't remember, something from his past that was hidden in the room behind the locked door. Half of him was afraid to find out what it was, afraid to open that door and face the other self who resided there, afraid he might be something this Peter Ryan loathed, someone violent and hateful and driven by a carnal need to take life. Someone Karen would despise and Lilly would fear. Like Baldy. But the other half of him knew he needed to open it; he needed to face whatever was there, needed to look it in the eyes and find the truth. His questions would be answered, the mystery solved. His life would be exposed for what it really was once and for all, and he could deal with it and move on.

He needed to find the key. He needed those answers.

A few miles down the road, they passed through a small, one-intersection town called Marsville. It wasn't much: one blinker light, a hair salon, a small grocery store, a hardware store, and a few dozen aging homes, most in need of updates and repairs. East of Marsville, a half mile past the last home, they came upon a large packaging plant rising out of the countryside like an alien mother ship that had been buried for centuries beneath the Indiana soil and only just recently broken loose. To the left of the plant, a sprawling parking lot held at least a thousand vehicles. Captives of the alien race who enslaved them with hard labor.

Peter pulled the truck into the parking lot and headed for the back corner. There he found an empty spot and shut off the engine. "Get anything you'll need. We're leaving it here."

"Leaving what?" She looked at him questioningly.

"The truck."

"*My* truck?"

"Your truck. It's bugged, Amy. If we keep driving it, we might as well have a flashing sign on the roof."

"So find the bug and get rid of it."

Peter shifted in his seat so he faced her. "Amy, listen to me. We don't have time to search the entire truck. It could be anywhere. They know where we are—"

"Who's *they*, Peter? You keep saying *they*. *They* are after us. *They* are coming. Who are *they*? Huh? Who?"

He didn't know, and she knew he didn't. His ignorance was a glaring blemish on the face of this entire ordeal. Peter swallowed and tried again. "There's probably someone headed to this location right now. We need to move quickly. We can't keep driving the truck. It stays." He declared the last two words with the same finality that a judge would use to deliver a death sentence.

Amy pursed her lips and nodded subtly. "I just need the keys."

Peter handed her the key chain. "Do you carry tools?"

"There's a small toolbox behind the driver's seat."

It didn't take Peter long before he found an old blue Honda Accord that would do nicely. The owner would report it stolen, but how many blue Accords were on the road? And fortunately, the car was unlocked. Folks in rural Indiana, where the incidences of grand theft auto were as rare as Nessie sightings, weren't as cautious as those in the city.

After switching the Accord's license plate with that of a royal-blue Ford Fusion parked a few cars down, it didn't take him long to get the car started using a screwdriver and hammer. Surprisingly, though he had no memory of ever hot-wiring a car using a flathead screwdriver, his hands instinctively knew what to do.

Amy slid into the passenger seat and eyed Peter suspiciously. "Where's a research geek learn to do that?"

Peter shifted the Accord into reverse. "I think you know the answer to that."

"Right. You don't know. You're beginning to scare me, Peter."

"Beginning to?"

"You're right. I'm already there."

FOURTEEN

. . .

He'd failed again. Patrick had gotten away. The agency would most assuredly be after him now. They'd try to *discontinue* him. But he was resourceful too, more resourceful than they could ever imagine. And he knew more than they gave him credit for. He remembered what they thought they had caused him to forget. His mind was sharp, nimble, and much more resilient than they expected.

He knew where Patrick ultimately was headed even without their vast resources.

Lawrence crouched behind a Dumpster and lightly touched the left side of his face. Pain shot through his nerves like high-voltage electricity. His left hand ached and throbbed too. He needed to care for his wounds before they got infected.

After Patrick had escaped, Lawrence too had bolted out the

rear exit of the café, down the alley, across the street, and behind a small strip mall. He couldn't go back to his Lincoln. He was sure it had been bugged by the agency. He'd have to find a new vehicle, then get some supplies to treat his wounds. But he'd need to be careful. The folks at the café had no doubt already given the cops a complete description of the parties involved in the brawl. Hopefully they would see it as just that—a brawl. Maybe two men fighting over a woman. An ex-husband going after the new boy-friend. With any luck, it would stay local, and once the town was cleared, the cops would be glad to be rid of the nuisance and not get the state police involved.

Of course, the Lincoln would be found eventually. But Lawrence had thought ahead as he always did and registered it under an alias, Richard Barton from San Francisco. If the local cops put two and two together, they'd assume the abandoned vehicle belonged to the bald man in the brawl who had escaped on foot, and they'd begin a search down a long and endless path, looking for a man who existed only on paper and in various databases around the country and who had quite the history to muddle through.

Setting out on foot, ignoring the pain in his face and hand, he made his way across town, keeping to side streets and alleyways until he came upon a supermarket. Behind the store he slid into an unlocked aging Chevy pickup and easily hot-wired it. By the time the owner discovered his truck missing and reported it to the police, Lawrence would be far out of town, and the local cops would be on the trail of Richard Barton.

On the road, he headed east and an hour later entered the town of Stubbsville. There he found a small drugstore and grabbed antibiotic soap, two spray bottles of bacitracin, a large bottle of ibuprofen, and six rolls of gauze from the shelves.

At the counter, the clerk, a shaggy-headed kid, said, "Dude, that burn looks nasty."

Lawrence forced a smile. "Got in a fight with a grill." He didn't want to spend too long in the store. He knew they had security cameras that had already captured his image. The agency would be on his trail soon. There were cameras on the exterior of the building as well, and they'd now know what kind of truck he was driving.

The kid at the checkout scanned the items. "Looks like the grill won. You sure you shouldn't see a doctor about that?"

"I'll be fine."

The kid shrugged. "Whatever, man."

Lawrence placed two twenties on the counter, more than enough to cover the bill, and said, "The rest is for you." He grabbed his supplies and made for the exit.

The kid hollered after him. "You don't want your receipt?"

But Lawrence was already headed out the door.

In the truck he closed his eyes, took a deep breath, and cleared his mind. This was how he coped with the pressures and stresses common to his line of work. He quickly performed a mental inventory of every major muscle group in his body and concentrated on relaxing it. Tension seeped from his muscles; his circulation improved; his breathing calmed; the pain in his face and hand slowly dissipated.

An image entered his mind, unbidden yet in a strange way welcome. He sat on the edge of a bed, his handgun ready, a round chambered, the safety off. He was going to do it. He was going to pull the trigger and end the torment. With the barrel to his temple, he rested the fat pad of his index finger on the trigger. He was that close. And then the phone rang. It was Patrick.

Lawrence pushed the memory away, opened his eyes, and gripped the steering wheel. He needed to find a bathroom and a new vehicle.

• • •

Back on the road, behind the wheel of the Accord, Peter drove east, pulled there not merely by his newly acquired knowledge of where Centralia lay on the map but by some unseen and barely felt force urging him onward, leading him as if with invisible guide wires. Was it God pulling him? Leading him? The thought came out of nowhere, like a puff of wind in the dead of a still night, but Peter was immediately skeptical. When had God shown up before? He hadn't in the house; he hadn't in the café. Peter had done that alone; he'd survived on his own. Again that distantly familiar feeling of abandonment was there. Apparently God had issues with showing up when he was needed most.

The mysterious force pulled Peter eastward, toward Centralia, toward Karen and Lilly, and, he was sure, toward the key that would open that fourth room of his dream and reveal what wonderful or wicked secret it held.

After several quiet minutes of being lulled by the drone of the wheels on asphalt, Amy finally said, "Where are we going now?"

"Centralia," Peter said and liked how familiar the word now felt on his tongue. "It's a town in Pennsylvania."

"Pennsylvania?"

"Yeah, Pennsylvania. Is that okay?"

Amy shook her head. "Peter, none of this is okay. My home was broken into, my garage door busted up, my landscaping ruined; my truck is gone. We've been shot at and attacked. How is any of that okay?"

They drove in silence another few minutes. Outside the car, fields of drying corn planted in perfectly straight rows stretched to the horizon, where they met a crystalline-blue sky. Looking out the side window, Amy said in a low voice, "I've never been to Pennsylvania before."

"I haven't either." At least, not that he could remember.

"And you know how to get there?"

"Of course. I have the map in my head."

"How?"

"That woman back at the café—she had a map on her phone."

"Is that what that was all about?"

He glanced at Amy. "Getting answers. Collecting information."

"And you memorized the map?" She sounded cynical.

"Does that surprise you?"

"No. I mean, sort of. You didn't look at it for very long."

He'd studied the map for only a second or two, but that was all he'd needed. He remembered every road, every highway, every state park and Podunk town along the way to Centralia. He could see the map in his head just as clearly as if he were holding it in his hands. "Weird, huh?"

"Yeah. Weird. Tell me something," Amy said. "How did you know that woman would help you? I mean, a strange man approaching a woman in a café, asking her to look something up on her phone. How did you know she wouldn't think you were a creep and tell you to get lost?"

"Why? Do I look like a creep?"

"No. It's just, you know, nowadays you can't be too friendly or you risk coming off like a creep."

Peter thought about that. Of course he'd considered the chance he was taking. He'd considered every risk he'd taken since he hid in Lilly's room when the intruders had busted into his home. It was part of who he was now: analytical, calculating, constantly running a menu of options through his head, weighing them for the best outcome. But the fact of the matter was, there were risks to be taken. The woman in the beret could have gotten nervous and called the police.

But he'd known she wouldn't. "Did you notice anything about her?"

"She was a woman. She was alone. She was looking at a magazine."

"Right. But did you notice anything else?"

Amy shrugged. "She had brown hair, shoulder length. She wore glasses."

"She had a button on her purse that said 'Have you hugged a librarian today?' She's a knowledge junkie and is into sharing knowledge, turning others on to knowledge. She's married and has three kids, girls. She's used to interacting with people, caring for them, helping. She carries pepper spray but isn't anxious to use it. She had a canister on her key chain, but her keys were in her purse on the floor. She works out, sometimes at home, mostly at a gym. She's confident, self-assured."

Amy sat in silence while, outside, more fields passed by in green-and-brown streaks. "You noticed all that from where we were sitting?"

"Yes."

"How did you know about the kids?"

"Her wallet was on the table. It had one of those clear plastic fronts where you can put a picture. Karen had one just like it. Carried a picture of Lilly and me in it. That woman's had a photo of three small girls, looked to be ages six to two."

"And how about the working-out part? Were you checking out her calves?"

"Nope. The key chain again. She had a membership card to a gym. It was well-worn."

Amy glanced out the side window. More perfectly striped corn-fields moved by. "Wow."

Peter ran a hand over his face. "Amy, how does someone do that? How did I even know to look for those things, to take notice? How did I know, of the five people in that café, she'd be the one to help us?"

"Did you notice stuff about the others too?"

"Every detail. But I don't recognize myself anymore."

"You're Peter Ryan. Research assistant. Batman."

"Seriously, who am I?"

"I guess now it's my turn. I don't know."

FIFTEEN

. . .

The door's lock disengaged again, catching the woman off guard.
She wasn't expecting her daughter to be returned so soon. It was
only two o'clock. She usually didn't get back until closer to five,
sometimes even later than that.

A bar of light from the hallway widened as the door opened.
Three shadows darkened the light, silhouettes of two men and a
child. Her daughter entered the room, shoulders back and chin up,
the same way she always did. The woman had once thought this
posture was a sign of her daughter's defiance, an outward expres-
sion of the unbreakable will within. But she soon learned that it
had nothing to do with the girl's temerity and everything to do
with her faith. She held her shoulders back and her head up not
out of rebellion to her captors but because of her reliance on her
Lord. If he was for her, who could be against her?

But the early return was not the only thing out of place this time; her daughter's appearance bore signs that the "experiments" had gone physical. Her hair was mussed, and her upper arms were colored with a faint reddening of the skin.

The woman lunged for her daughter and pulled the girl to her chest even as the door closed and the outside light was cut off.

"Oh, baby, baby girl, what did they do to you?" Tears leaked from her eyes and the words squeezed from her constricted throat. She had to do something. What kind of a mother stood by and idly allowed her daughter to be abused?

She pulled away and held her little girl's face in her hands, scanning every inch of skin, searching for any other marks or wounds. How dare they touch her daughter! Anger rose in her like a lava flood, burning her from the inside. Leaving her daughter, she rushed to the door and pounded on it, venting the anger and hurt and pain that tore at her with hooked claws. "How dare you! How dare you harm her. You animals!"

Turning around, she found her daughter there, arms relaxed, face turned upward. She was so innocent, so gentle, such a sweet, loving child. She did not deserve to suffer pain. "Oh, baby." She hugged her. "I'm sorry. I'm so sorry. What did they do to you?"

The girl, though, appeared unfazed by the torment she must have received. If the woman had not noticed the tousled hair and reddened skin, and if she had not been privy to their current circumstances, she would have thought her daughter had returned from a common day at school or an outing with friends. "Mommy," she said, suppressing a tremor in her voice, making it just as calm and even as earlier in the day, before she had been taken, "don't cry for me. I'm okay. God was with me. He was right there, holding my hand the whole time." She lifted a hand and wiped the woman's tears from her cheeks.

The tears still came. What kind of a God would stand by and let an innocent angel be hurt by grown men? "Did they hurt you?"

The girl shrugged.

The woman took her daughter's face in her hands again. Such a sweet face. "Baby, listen to me. I'm going to ask you a question, and I need you to answer me, okay? Tell Mommy the truth. Okay?"

She nodded.

"Did they touch you in your personal places?"

"You mean my girl parts?"

"Yes, honey." The fact that she even had to ask the question brought a fresh wave of tears.

Her daughter shook her head. "No."

"Have they ever?"

"No."

She knew her daughter was telling the truth. The girl didn't lie; it wasn't in her, wasn't woven into the tapestry of her soul. She might seem distant at times, and she'd become adept at avoiding questions, but she'd never outright lied.

The woman drew her daughter close, hugged her, stroked her hair. She thought of what life would be like if circumstances had been different. If they were free; if her husband were alive; if they lived a normal life in a normal home in a normal neighborhood. If they were happy.

"Baby," the woman said, still holding her girl, "why won't you tell me what they do to you?"

"I can't."

"But why? Why can't you?"

The girl hesitated, and the woman could tell she was wrestling with whether to answer the question directly or give another vague nonanswer.

Stepping back and out of the woman's arms, the girl said, "Because they said if I tell you, they'll hurt you."

"Oh, my sweet girl." Once more, the woman took her daughter into her arms. She didn't want to let go of her. Ever. She wouldn't let them take her again.

"Mommy?"

"Yes?"

"There is something, though. Something else."

The woman lifted her head from the girl's hair and held her at arm's length, hands on her daughter's shoulders. In her sweet girl's eyes she saw indecision and hesitancy but not doubt. Never doubt. "What is it?"

Again the girl hesitated, unsure whether she could share what else she knew.

"You can tell me," the woman said. "It's okay." She knew the room was bugged and knew her daughter was taking a chance by telling her information that might land her in the lab too.

The girl closed her eyes and swallowed. When she opened her eyes, there were tears in them. It was the first time the woman had seen her daughter cry since the news that her daddy was dead.

"Baby, tell me. I'm right here."

"Mommy, there's other kids."

SIXTEEN

· · ·

Several miles from the Ohio–Pennsylvania line, Peter steered the Accord into the parking lot of a strip mall in the town of Abbey, a small village populated equally by Amish and Englischers. It was early afternoon and there were plenty of cars and a few horse-drawn buggies in the lot. They'd easily get lost in the crowd. The mall was neither new nor newly renovated and consisted of ten units with a large superstore anchoring the north end and a rather large furniture store boasting Amish-made wares on the south end.

Peter shifted the car into park and let the engine idle. Heat radiated off the hood in tendrils that rose like watery fingers until they dissipated and became one with the cooler air. The sky was cloudless, a washed-out shade of blue.

Amy looked around the parking lot. "Problem."

"I know," Peter said.

"You know what?"

"Cameras. There." He pointed at the gray security cameras mounted high on light poles scattered throughout the lot, eyes in the sky keeping watch over the entire shopping complex. "There and there. And no doubt the stores have them as well."

"So what are you gonna do now, Batman? You don't have your mask."

Peter checked his watch. The day shift at the plant back in Marsville hadn't ended yet, so the owner of the Accord wouldn't have found it missing. They wouldn't be looking for a stolen blue Honda for another hour. He surveyed the parking lot. A few cars away, a woman wrestled to maintain control of a stroller while lifting her child from a car seat. One row over, an elderly gentleman exited his car, looked around, smoothed his shirt, and headed for the front door. A woman met him there and gave him a peck on the cheek before taking his hand in hers.

"They don't know what we're driving yet," Peter said. "For all they know, we're still in your truck."

"That's to our advantage."

"Yes…"

"But…?"

"But if they're running this surveillance footage through facial recognition software, they'll find us."

"Can they do that?"

"Do what?"

"Run it in real time like that?"

"I don't want to underestimate their capabilities. We need to assume they can tap into any video feed and run it through their own systems." Peter made a quick scan of the parking lot again, measuring the distance between the drop-off zone and the front doors and looking for any sign of law enforcement or security personnel. He didn't know if the home intruders and Baldy worked for the Feds or not, so until he had firm evidence either way, he'd have to assume they did. And if they did, they would have already circulated photos of him and Amy, public enemies one and two. Every local and state cop and security guard in eight states would have received one or gotten a special bulletin in their e-mail. That notion sent a chill through his blood. If the Feds were behind this covert manhunt, their resources were all but unlimited, and he was just one man with a tagalong.

But if the Feds were involved, that led to a myriad of other questions. Questions he'd have to deal with later, though. Right now they needed a change of clothes, food, water, first aid supplies. They could get all that in the superstore, but Amy would be the best candidate to go inside.

Peter turned to her. "You ready?"

Eyes wide, she said, "For what?"

"To get supplies."

"I'm going in?"

"It'd be better if it was you. Let your hair down and hide as much of your face with it as you can. I'll drop you off at the door. As soon as you get in the store, head for the sunglasses and the hats and put them on. Tell the clerk you just saw the eye doctor and he dilated your eyes. He can scan the tags while you're wearing them."

"What do we need?"

A gray-and-blue police SUV entered the parking lot and rolled slowly past the store's entrance. They couldn't have gotten a bead on Peter and Amy that quickly. It was impossible. Whoever was after them might have resources, they might have the ability to track and scan and survey, but they weren't omnipresent. Peter waited until the vehicle meandered its way out of the lot and back onto the primary route that passed the mall.

He turned his attention back to Amy. "Food. Water. Clothes. Get me a baseball hat and sunglasses. A pair of khakis and a couple T-shirts too. Pants, thirty-two waist; T-shirts, large."

"Anything else?"

"Get yourself some clothes. Toiletries. Deodorant, soap, tooth-paste, toothbrushes. Anything we'll need for a few days on the road. And first aid supplies."

"You think this will be over in a few days?" She was questioning his optimism.

Peter scanned the parking lot again, his eyes covering the entire area in seconds. "One way or another."

"That's not reassuring," Amy said.

Peter put the car in drive and pulled to the front of the store. There were many people milling around, coming and going, entering and leaving the store, and each one seemed to have an eye on them, seemed to watch them, study them, wonder if they were the couple they'd seen on the news before leaving the house. Peter had to remind himself that they were just people, and generally speaking, people were not very observant.

Amy shifted in her seat, smoothed her pants, glanced around the parking lot.

"You okay?" Peter said.

"No, I'm not okay."

"Just relax. Be yourself."

"But this isn't me. I'm not a criminal sneaking around, trying to avoid being seen."

Peter sighed. "I know. I'm sorry." He turned in his seat to face her and handed her a stack of twenties. "You can do this, okay? When you're finished, I'll pick you up right here."

She nodded, opened the door, and exited the car.

He watched until she got inside the store, then parked at the back of the lot, out of the watchful range of the security cameras but at a location where he could see the entrance. He rolled down the windows and waited. A gentle breeze moved across the parking lot, stirring up paper litter and sending it skittering across the asphalt. To the left, a stray dog emerged from behind a Toyota minivan, sniffed the ground, then lifted its leg on the vehicle's tire. It nosed around a bit, then—spooked by something unseen—raised its head, ears perked, looked around, and ran off.

The sight of the dog unearthed another memory that had been buried somewhere in the soil of Peter's mind.

It's hot. Blistering hot. The sun is a blazing orb hovering in the sky, scalding the earth's surface. And this area looks like it's been scalded countless times, stripped of all vegetation. Nothing but dirt and sand and drab block buildings and heat. Occasionally a car will drift by, covered in dust and half falling apart.

A dog saunters into view, running its nose along the ground, looking for anything worth eating. The thing is just bones and flesh; its fur is matted and clumped and missing in areas, mostly around the hips.

The dog noses up to a bicycle that's parked outside one of the homes, sniffs it, lifts a leg, and waters it.

The sight causes Peter's mouth to burn with thirst. He unscrews the cap of his canteen, puts it to his lips, and lets the tepid water linger in his mouth before swallowing it.

To his left, a gunshot cuts the silence. A single shot. The dog's hind end whips around as the mangy beast lets out a pitiful yelp.

"Whatcha do that for, ya jerk?" someone says.

Another voice answers, "It's just a stray. What? You wanna take it home or somethin'?"

"Maybe."

The dog limps, whines, pulls itself along with its front legs. The entire back end of it is red with blood.

"Well, someone put it out of its misery."

"I'll do it."

But before another shot can be fired, the final shot, Peter stands and approaches the dog.

The police SUV returned and glided to a stop in front of the entrance. The officer in the vehicle spoke into his radio, then opened the door and stepped out. He was a big guy, thick arms and neck, made larger by the body armor he wore beneath his uniform. He turned and scanned the parking lot as if looking for someone, then slipped a phone from his utility belt and proceeded to make a call. He spent no more than a minute on the phone, searching the lot as he spoke. Finally he finished his conversation, adjusted his pants, and stepped inside.

Peter's heart thumped. Had his pursuers somehow tracked them that quickly? If so, they were more resourceful than he'd ever expected, and their response time was incredible. If this was the federal government, it had to be the work of some little-known agency, highly specialized, not found on any budget sheet or under the attentive gaze of any congressional oversight committee. He'd wait a few minutes and see how things played out. The cop might just be responding to a report of a stray dog watering cars in the parking lot.

Moments later a cruiser pulled up behind the SUV. A cop, shorter but stockier than the first one, exited the car and spoke into his shoulder radio. He waited a few seconds before entering the store.

Peter tensed. The gears of his mind engaged, running through various scenarios, weighing options, calculating responses. He needed to act quickly and get Amy out of there. He shifted the Accord into gear and hit the gas.

But just as he reached the fire lane, Amy emerged carrying three bags, a baseball cap resting low on her head and large sunglasses hiding her eyes.

Peter pulled forward and she got into the car. Her face glistened with sweat and her cheeks were flushed.

"What's going on?" he asked.

She put the bags in the backseat. "Did you see the cops?"

"I saw them." And he'd come terribly close to engaging them. He pressed the accelerator and moved the car out of the drop-off zone and through the parking lot. Amy's hands trembled. "You okay?" he asked.

"I thought they were coming for me."

"They weren't?"

"No. Some guy was caught shoplifting. A real loudmouth. He was going on about how much the government owes him and what he's entitled to."

Peter pulled the car into a parking space and stopped. He breathed deeply and relaxed his hands on the steering wheel. "I'm sorry, Amy. I didn't want to get you involved in this. You can go anytime, you know. If you want to get out right now and just go, that's okay."

"I haven't changed my mind. Whatever this craziness is, I'm stuck in it too. Where would I go now, anyway? To the cops? And tell them what?" She was nearly frantic. Tears pooled in her eyes, and her chin quivered.

She was right. Whoever was after him—and now her,

too—might or might not be working with local police. She had no car; she couldn't go home; she couldn't go to the cops. All he could say was "I'm sorry."

Amy touched his arm. "Don't worry about that now. We can't. Let's keep moving."

She was right again. "We need to get to Centralia," Peter said.

SEVENTEEN

· · ·

The Oceanview Motel was not your typical wayside overnighter. Located in the heart of Pennsylvania near the state's coal region, it wasn't anywhere near an ocean. But due to its proximity to the borough of Jersey Shore—a small town with a population just exceeding four thousand, located sixty miles from Pennsylvania's northern border and 260 miles from the real New Jersey shore— the name was oddly appropriate.

When Peter slowed and steered the Accord into the Oceanview's lot, Amy said, "You're kidding right?"

The motel was a two-story throwback built in the late sixties. It consisted of twenty rooms, ten on the ground level, ten on the second story. A concrete staircase with a landing midway was at one end, while the other end of the building was framed by a small office with a blinking Vacancy sign in the window. The bulbs behind the *A* and *C* were both burned out, so the sign read V ANCY. The teal paint on the doors and molding outside each room was in desperate need of a fresh coat. Cracks and fissures spiderwebbed the sidewalk, and the asphalt parking lot was faded and warped. The lot was empty except for a big rig parked on the far west side.

Peter imagined at one time the motel did a decent business from coal workers wanting to take their sweethearts somewhere oceanic and shore-like, somewhere away from black dust and subterranean mazes. Now, with the coal industry in decline and more families going to the real Jersey Shore, business had dried up.

Peter shut off the Accord's engine. "You're used to the Hilton?"

Amy looked around the premises. "The Holiday Inn would do just fine."

"Stay off the grid, remember?" Peter said.

"Yeah. And this is certainly off the grid. You think they have running water in the rooms?"

They entered the office, a small room sporting teal shag carpeting and paneled walls painted white and teal, a color scheme better suited for a motel along the real Jersey Shore, where ocean-thirsty vacationers came to play, rather than in a motel on the edge of coal country, where locals and passers-through came to hide. The manager met them at the desk. "Evenin', folks," he said. A thin, middle-aged man with dark hair, a pencil mustache, and a goatee, he had hooded, watery gray eyes and a plastic smile. "Like a room?"

"Yes. Please," Peter said.

The man reached under the counter and pulled out a sheet of paper. "Wonderful. Just fill this out and I'll get you a room key. You have a preference?"

"Ground level—"

"Just one that's been cleaned recently," Amy said.

The man stopped, hesitated, then blinked rapidly and forced a smile until his lips disappeared. The flesh on his face was as thin and translucent as onionskin. He had an appearance of someone more suited for life in the basements of funeral homes, interacting with the deceased, than for managing a motel so brightly garnished, interacting with the living and breathing. "All our rooms are cleaned daily, miss." He reached for a key, then paused and glanced at Peter's left hand, then at Amy's. "One room?"

The guy was no doubt used to catering to traveling businessmen and their mistresses popping by for a few hours of imagined seaside bliss. He'd learned to be observant. "Yes, please," Peter said.

The manager retrieved a key from the Peg-Board behind the counter, held it between his index finger and thumb as if it were coated with flesh-eating germs, and handed it to Peter. "Room five." Then, shifting his eyes to Amy: "It was cleaned just this morning."

Peter slid the half-completed form across the counter.

The manager scanned it. "Mr. and Mrs. Cooper. Minnesota." He looked up, that strained, disapproving smile parting his lips again. "You're a long way from home. Headed anywhere in particular?"

"The real Jersey Shore," Peter said. "Thought we'd stop here for the night—you know, a little teaser before the real thing."

The manager cleared his throat and coughed once. "Very well, I'll just need to see some photo identification."

Peter handed him more cash than was required. "That's not necessary."

There was a brief moment when electric tension arced through the space between the two parties. Finally the manager tightened his lips, pocketed the cash, and said, "Very well. Enjoy your stay.

Checkout is by ten tomorrow morning. If you need anything, just ring for me."

Peter nodded. "Thanks."

• • •

When the odd guests left for their room, Conlan Slenker headed back to his lounge area, where Sandy, his aging bulldog, and reruns of *Knight Rider* were waiting for him.

He sat in his recliner and rubbed Sandy's head. "What a couple a' weirdos, huh, girl? Think they can fool me. No one fools me. I knew from the second they walked in that they were up to no good. Sneaking away to the Oceanside for a little hanky-panky, that's what they're up to." He slipped out the wad of twenties the man had handed him. What did he care if they weren't married? If they were cheating on their spouses? He wasn't the morality police. Let 'em do what they wanted to do. Let 'em screw up their own lives. What did he care? He had a business to run and profit to turn, which was becoming more and more difficult.

"What'ya think, Sandy girl?"

Sandy lifted her head and looked at him with lazy, disinterested eyes.

"Aw, what do you know? You like the weird types. That's why you hang out with me, huh?" When Sandy gave no response, Conlan laughed and rubbed her head harder. "That's my girl."

As the show transitioned to a commercial break, Conlan reached for his beer and took a long, steady swig. He should hate this place, the motel. It was the only thing his old man had left him when he died. No money, not even a house, just this broken-down motel. At least it wasn't in debt. The entire thing was paid for and all his. He should hate it, though. It was such a ball and chain around his ankle, holding him back from having any kind of social life, holding him back from having a woman in his life, holding him back from becoming really successful at something else. But he was successful, wasn't he? He was a motel owner, a business-man, a proprietor. And when he attended the hotel/motel manager conferences, he was really somebody. Besides, there were lots of good-looking women who attended those conferences.

He held the can close to his mouth and looked around the lounge area. Besides the recliner, there was a small table, a plastic tree of some sort in the corner, a mounted marlin on the wall that his dad caught off the coast of Maryland, and an old TV with an annoying flickering screen. Some dream.

He thought again of the couple he'd just given room five to and chuckled. Conlan had read them like a lusty paperback, them and their little rendezvous. The guy's wife was probably home with the kids, wondering where her hubby was, wondering if he was pulling a double shift to earn money for the kids' college funds or maybe at a church meeting learning how to be a better husband. Instead, he was here, at the good ole Oceanview with his little woman.

On the TV a commercial pushing car insurance ended, and a special breaking news announcement came on. The talking head, that woman with the nice figure and pretty face from the local sta-tion, said something about a couple fugitives on the run, a man and woman. A picture flashed on the screen, and Conlan sat up like he'd taken a thousand volts to his backside and dropped his beer can. It landed in front of Sandy and poured its contents onto the rug.

"Holy sam hill, Sandy, that's them!"

Not impressed in the least, Sandy inched forward and slid her tongue along the carpet, lapping up the spilled alcohol.

Conlan stood and moved closer to the TV, drawn there by a sudden mesmerization of good fortune and destiny. The woman said if viewers spotted the two, they were not to call 911 but rather were to call the number on the screen immediately.

Conlan froze, his mind a blank. He stared at the screen as the special report graphic faded and another commercial, this one for hot dogs, came on. He noticed then that his heart was racing so fast it felt like it would burst out of his chest and go bounding across the room, and his palms were all clammy. This was it, his big break. He'd be the one to capture the fugitives or at least to turn them in. News crews would be here, probably FBI and all kinds of cops. Reporters, detectives, maybe a SWAT team. The Oceanview would be on every news channel. They'd probably interview him, put him on morning talk shows; maybe he'd get a movie deal out of it.

Folks from all over would want to come to the Oceanview, the place where the modern-day Bonnie and Clyde took refuge and where they were captured. His rooms would be full; he'd have money to make repairs, give himself a pay raise, and retire early. *Thank you, Dad.*

Making his feet move, he went back out to the front desk, where the phone was, rounded the counter, and peered out the big front windows. Yep, their car was still there, and the door to room five was shut. Wouldn't they be in for a surprise.

Returning to the desk, he lifted the phone with a trembling hand and dialed the number that had been on the screen.

EIGHTEEN

· · ·

Peter sat at the small round table by the front window of their room in the Oceanview. The room offered nothing more than your typical lonesome motel, inaccessible to any major thoroughfare. It had two double beds, the table and two chairs, and a TV on a dresser. The seashore motif continued in the room with more teal carpeting, a seashell design bedspread, and white oak furniture. The room was at least clean. Whether it had been cleaned this morning as the manager had claimed was doubtful. A musty, earthy odor hung in the air as if the windows hadn't been opened in days, maybe weeks. As Peter leaned on the table, he wondered if clean, salty ocean air from a distant sea would magically waft through the room if the window were open.

Amy sat on the bed, one leg tucked under the other, and stared at the wall.

"What is it?" Peter asked.

She glanced at him. "What do you mean?"

"You want to say something."

"I do?"

"Don't you?"

"How can you tell?"

He smiled. "You have that I-need-to-say-something look on your face."

"You know, I think you make half this stuff up."

He waited a moment, then said, "Well, don't you want to say something?"

"I thought I was supposed to be the psychologist here." Then, sheepishly, as if caught in a lie she'd been keeping for years and now must finally reveal, Amy shrugged and said, "Actually, I do have something to say."

Peter waited. He could tell it was something weighty, some burden she'd been carrying and needed to unload. The tension in her face and hands and the way she nervously shifted her eyes gave it away.

After a few silent beats, Amy sighed. "I'm sorry, Peter. Very, very sorry."

"For what?" He thought he knew what she was referring to but wanted to hear her say it. The air between them that had been polluted and fogged with regret and resentment and discord needed to be cleared once and for all.

They'd been working together on a professional research paper on circadian rhythms and chronobiology with a goal to submit it for publication in *Biological Psychology*. The project had required them to spend a lot of time together. Time outside the office. Time at Amy's home. Amy's behavior had changed subtly at first, so subtly he didn't even notice. But things had escalated, and one day at her house she told him she thought she was falling in love with him. He was floored and flattered at the same time. He initially downplayed her interest in him, told her—and himself—it would pass, that they just needed to keep the focus on the project. They needed to finish it and get it to the review board. But as time passed, her interest didn't. Finally Peter had to cut it off. He told her the feeling was not mutual and that she needed to put a stop to her behavior.

But instead of setting aside her personal feelings and resuming their professional collaboration, Amy put a stop to the relationship altogether, publishing the paper under her own name and intimating that Peter's research was flawed and unusable. Peter lost credibility at the university and nearly lost his job. As a result, hateful words had been spoken and the friendship had shattered.

"I'm sorry for what happened between us. I don't know what got into me. I was irrational and did and said some really stupid things."

"Well, I can't argue with you there," Peter said. "But you already apologized. I remember it well."

A month after the blowup, Amy had shown up at the Ryan house with tearful eyes and apologized to Peter. She'd said that if Peter never wanted to speak to her again, she would honor his wish. He didn't argue and said that was probably for the best.

And that was it. Though he'd pass her on campus or catch her eye in the science building, he never spoke another word to her until he called her this morning, asking for help.

Amy hesitated. "I'm not sure I fully meant it then. I was so hurt. So ashamed. So embarrassed. I did what I thought I needed to do to make it all better."

"But it never got better. Not really."

"No, it didn't. I wanted so badly to make it all right, to make it as if it had never happened."

"But it did happen."

"I know." She wiped a tear from her eye and hooked a loose strand of hair behind her ear. "How can I ever make it up to you?"

"Why do you feel like you need to?"

Amy lifted her shoulders and let them drop. "It feels like something needs to be done."

Peter shifted in his chair, pushed the curtain aside enough to see most of the parking lot. "I think you're doing it now, being here with me. Being here *for* me."

"Is it enough?"

He let the curtain fall back in place. "Right now, it's everything."

A moment of silence passed between them until Peter finally said, "You know, I've been having this recurring dream."

Amy smiled. "What's the dream?"

He told her about the house and the open doors that led to rooms full of memories. He also told her about the one room with the locked door, the room he could never gain entrance to no matter how frantically he tried. The room with the shadow, the secret. He failed to tell her, though, that he thought the room likely harbored some evil from his past, some part of his history that his mind had tried to lock away, imprison forever.

When he was finished, Amy said, "Did you tell your shrink about this?"

"Yes. I told her."

"And what did she say?"

Peter ran his finger over the table's top, making concentrically

enlarging circles. "She told me I need a key to open it. That the challenge was going to be to find the key."

"There's something important in that room," Amy said. "Something terrifying and life-changing—you know that, don't you?"

Peter thought for a moment. He did know it. He'd been wrestling with just that fact since seeing that menacing shadow darken
the light under the door. Again the thought squeezed its way into
his mind that whatever was terrifying and life-changing might
be a some*one* rather than a some*thing*. But it wasn't Karen. Maybe
Lilly. Maybe God. But if it was God, then Peter had to think that the
Almighty didn't want to be found. "I do. Is that why I can't open it?"

"Possibly. You intuit that there's some horror there and you
don't want to open it. Not really. The key will be a trigger, something that kicks your memory in the seat and tells it to remember
at least part of it. Then you'll have to make a decision on whether
you want to find out the rest or not."

"So where can I find the trigger?"

Amy tapped the bedspread. "It could be anywhere. It might be
a very common item right under your nose, but until you see it in
a certain light or under a certain set of circumstances, you won't
recognize it as such. Or it could be something totally unseen and
unknowable until you see it, and then you'll know. And it doesn't
have to be an object. It might be a word or a sound or a voice. It
might be a simple piece of knowledge."

"I think my shrink might have some competition," Peter said.

Amy grinned. "Well, the competition needs to use the bathroom and wash up."

She grabbed the bag of toiletries she'd picked up at the superstore and headed for the bathroom, closing the door behind her.

Peter parted the curtains covering the front window of the

room and surveyed the parking lot. The place was as barren as any uninhabited beach, minus the water and sand. Above the forest across the road, the sun bowed low, almost brushing the treetops, and cast long shadows that stretched nearly to the motel like dark, sinister hands inching closer, bringing with them a touch that would reveal every tenebrous mystery Peter hid. He shuddered and let the curtains fall back into place. As he did, another memory made itself known, but it was brief—like the surfacing of a whale to draw in air before plunging once again to the ocean's depths—and gone before it had any chance to form fully.

It consisted wholly of stuttered images and the residue of a seemingly familiar odor. Karen, Lilly, and he returning to a hotel room after a day at the beach. Damp towels, sunburned flesh, sandy flip-flops, and smiles all around. The feeling of the chilly air on his warm skin the moment he unlocked the room's door and stepped into the air-conditioning. The aroma of chlorine and sunscreen. The sweet music of Lilly's giggles.

He tried to hold on to the memory, tried to grasp it and massage something more out of it, some scenario that he could probe. But as quickly as the images had materialized, they vanished, and he was left with nothing more than a feeling, that same feeling of needing to tell Karen something of importance.

Peter rapped his fingers on the table, drumming an unfamiliar tune from some distant, long-forgotten world. For some reason, like the beckoning of ancient drum telegraphy, the rhythm conjured another image in his mind.

Lilly is there, her sweet face turned up, her deep-blue eyes penetrating his. She holds his hands. Hers are so soft and tiny, so fragile, as if to squeeze too hard would break them into a million shards of china glass. "Jesus will take care of us, Daddy. Don't worry, okay?"

"Jesus will take care of us." She had such faith; he remembered that. It was unshakable. Faith that could be possessed only by a child who had yet to experience the horror and pain the world had to offer and the doubt that accompanied both. Peter only vaguely remembered having faith like that as a child. But his memories of childhood were spotty at best, and he had no recollection at all of his parents. He knew he was raised in Indiana. North Manchester. But that was it; that was where his knowledge ended and disappeared into a fog of forgetfulness as dense as swamp water. And yet some kind of lighthouse was penetrating the fog, drawing him closer, still faint but seeming just a little brighter all the time. Something he'd once known—or thought he'd known. Something deeply rooted in himself, if only he could access it.

From behind the closed bathroom door, Amy said, "Oh, great." She opened the door and poked her head out. "Toilet doesn't flush."

Peter pulled himself from his jaunt into the past. "Did you jiggle the handle?"

"Of course I did. I live alone. I know how a toilet works. The chain in the tank is broken."

Peter pushed back the chair and stood. "I'll go tell the manager. He may have a spare one or he can take one from another room."

"Be careful; that guy gives me the creeps. I wouldn't be surprised if his name was Norman. Make sure he doesn't have a kitchen knife behind that counter."

Peter laughed. "I'll be sure to ask him how his mother is doing."

NINETEEN

. . .

Outside the Oceanview, the air was cool and dry, the sky a gradient of blue to black as the sun slid lower on its downward arc, now nearly touching the treetops. Soon the light of day would be a thing of the past and the sky would become a speckled mantle. Darkness would move in, and shadows would rule the night. Peter would have to keep watch while Amy slept. Lately, shadows had a way of turning into something much more malevolent, and Peter didn't want any more surprise guests.

The light in the office was off, which was odd because motels usually expected late-night travelers to pop in unannounced, looking for a place to catch a few winks before heading back onto the road in the morning. The V ANCY light was off as well.

Peter took off the sunglasses as he approached the office door, only slightly cautious, and tried the knob. It was unlocked. He pushed open the door and, standing in the doorway, said, "Hello? Anyone still here?" In a remote location like this one, a motel with an oceanside theme most likely rarely saw any of those late-night travelers and no doubt was wont to close up shop early. Possibly the manager had stepped out to attend to some plumbing issues in the trucker's room, or possibly he'd turned in for the night and saw no need to lock the office door. Or he was in another room having a heated debate with the skeletal remains of his mommy.

But in the back room Peter could see the flicker of a television. He rounded the counter. "Hello?"

A muffled growl came from the room, then a louder one. Peter began to backpedal as a pudgy bulldog sporting a severe underbite emerged from the room. The dog stopped five feet from him and chuffed. It eyed him with sagging, bloodshot eyes and snorted as if it couldn't muster the strength for a real bark.

Peter knocked on the counter. "Hey. Anyone here?"

The overhead light flicked on and the manager stepped out from the shadows. He stood in the passageway between the front office and the darkened room, the dog at his feet. He had no kitchen knife in either of his hands. "Help you?"

"Hey, yeah, sorry to bother you. The lights were out and I wasn't sure if anyone was here or not."

The man scratched his head and shifted his focus over Peter's shoulder to the front of the building. "Uh, I turn them out at ten. I'm the only one here and I need some sleep sometime, you know?"

Peter checked his watch. "But it's only eight o'clock."

The guy forced a little laugh and nervous smile. "Well, I mean, it's not like we got a line or anything. On slow days I usually close up early."

"Sure, sure. Well, look, the chain in our toilet tank is busted, and it won't flush. You mind getting us another one?"

The guy glanced over Peter's shoulder as if he was waiting for someone else to arrive and join their late-night get-together. He shoved his hands in his pockets, then removed one and ran his fingers through his hair. Furrowing his brow, he said, "The chain?"

"Yeah, you know, the chain that connects the plunger to the handle."

"Oh, the chain. Okay. Um, yeah, okay. I need to find one. If you, uh—" he started for the counter, then backed up—"you know, if you just reach in and lift the plunger, it'll flush. You don't really need a chain."

"You want us to manually flush the toilet every time we use it?"

The guy glanced at his watch. "Well, you know, you're only here for the night. I mean—"

"We paid for a toilet that works the way it should. Now, do you mind?"

"Uh…" He ran a hand through his hair again. "Do I mind?"

"Getting a new chain."

"Oh, uh, yeah. Sure. Of course. If you just want to head back to the room, I'll find one and be right there."

The guy was acting odd. Too odd. "Sure. Room five, then," Peter said. "Soon as you get that chain."

The bulldog growled and chuffed again, then ran a pink tongue up and over its nose. "Yeah," the manager said. "Be right there."

Peter left the office and hurried back to room five and Amy. He opened the door and quickly shut it behind him, then moved to the front window. To Amy, he said, "Pack the stuff up. We need to get out of here."

He parted the curtains with his finger just enough to get a good look at the parking lot. Nothing had changed. The truck was still in its place at the far end; the Oceanview Motel sign was still lit. The road was empty. The sun was almost hidden by the trees and the sky was darkening.

"What's wrong?" Amy said, stepping out of the bathroom.

Peter kept his eyes on the parking lot. "The manager. He knows something. Was acting very strange. Nervous."

"He's a strange guy. I thought we'd already settled that."

"No. There's something else going on. He knows something about us."

"You think we were on the news?"

"Possibly. Regardless, we need to get out of here."

As Amy packed their belongings back into the bags, the sun continued to dip until it was completely behind the trees and the heavens turned a deep blue. A few stars dotted the sky and the sodium lamps in the parking lot cast tents of light onto the cracked and faded asphalt.

When Amy had finished, she placed the bags on the bed and said, "Okay, so what now?"

"Time—" Peter stopped. Three pairs of headlights rounded the bend in the road and approached the eastern end of the parking lot. "Time to go."

Before he could shut the curtain, the headlights came nearer and Peter could see the vehicles more clearly. Three black Chevy Tahoes. Tinted windows. No plates. Unmarked. And turning into the Oceanside parking lot.

TWENTY

...

Peter and Amy had arrived at the Oceanview less than an hour ago. Even if the manager had called as soon they left the office, it would have given their pursuers barely forty-five minutes to assemble and travel. As he had suspected before and now realized in truth, their response time was incredible.

But what did the Feds want with him? What had made him such a wanted man?

Peter quickly surveyed the situation. Three SUVs, but he had no idea how many men per vehicle. Could be upwards of six. Eighteen total. Too many. He'd be severely outmanned and outgunned. He needed to think. The room had only one entrance, the front door. There was a small window in the bathroom but it wasn't large enough to fit an adult through. They were trapped like mice in a corner with nowhere to hide. And a clowder of tomcats was on the way.

He had to change the playing field, which at the moment was unfavorably tilted toward the tomcats.

Turning to Amy, he said, "Get a gun from my stuff and lock yourself in the bathroom. Get in the bathtub and keep your head down. If anyone comes in who isn't me, shoot."

Five rooms lay between theirs and the staircase to the second level, a distance of about sixty feet. He could cover that in a couple seconds. And that's all the time he had. The last of the SUVs had stopped as soon as it entered the parking lot, blocking any exit by vehicle. The other two were slowly approaching the motel. Peter could feel vigilant eyes behind the tinted glass of the two lead vehicles scanning the area, planning, anticipating.

Amy hadn't moved yet. "Go!" Peter said. "Now."

He pulled open the door and, as quickly as he would dash across a bed of fiery coals, ran for the staircase, keeping his head down and his eyes straight ahead. The vehicles braked, the tires stuttered on the asphalt, and the doors clicked open. By then, though, he was on the bottom step, throwing himself up the stairs two at a time.

At the top of the stairs, a breezeway partially concealed by a supporting wall made of cinder block offered some cover. A cylindrical sconce with a yellow bulb was attached to the wall. Peter hit the bulb with the handle of his gun, shattering it and welcoming partial darkness to the breezeway.

He caught a glimpse of how many men were on the ground below. Eight total, all dressed in black combat gear as if they'd been deployed to take down an international terrorist guilty of murdering thousands. Just like the Feds to overplan. The third SUV, the one that had stopped by the entrance, remained where it was, doors closed, engine idling. A sentinel keeping close watch over the events unfolding.

One of the men signaled to two others to go into the room. They knew Amy was still in there. Peter didn't have long to do what he needed to do. The men wore body armor, so his shots had to be precise.

Two more men headed for the staircase, while the remaining four crouched by one of the SUVs. Peter's only tactical advantage was his high position.

Before the two ascending the stairs reached the landing, Peter rushed down the steps. Rounding the corner at the landing, he found the two men three steps away. By the looks on their faces, it was obvious they weren't expecting him to run into their line of fire.

Quicker than their eyes could register his movements in the dimming light, and certainly quicker than they could aim and fire, Peter squeezed off two shots, hitting the lead man in the forehead and the one behind him in the neck. Even before the lead man's legs could buckle, Peter tackled him and tumbled down the steps.

At the bottom of the stairs, still clutching the dead gunman's body close to his and now in full auto mode, Peter rolled and positioned himself so he was protected by the man's body armor. Without taking time to plan or reason or even aim, he fired twice more, hitting one of the remaining four men square in the face.

From inside room five, Peter heard a gunshot, then another and another.

The shots distracted the three remaining men by the SUV long enough that Peter could squeeze off another two rounds, hitting one man with a fatal shot.

Standing, Peter lifted the dead gunman with him. He wouldn't be able to hold the guy for long; he was too bulky in his gear and too heavy. In an act of calculated desperation, Peter sidestepped closer to the room, shifting his eyes from the men taking cover behind the SUV to room five's open door.

No more gunshots came from inside the room, and he hoped it didn't mean the worst.

Before Peter reached the room, one of the gunmen emerged, eyes wild and mouth in a snarl, clutching Amy in his arm, the barrel of his handgun pressed against her temple.

But there was only one. Did that mean Amy had shot and killed the other? What had Peter gotten her into? What had he done to her? She'd be the one needing counseling if they got out of this.

Sweat poured from the man's brow and wet his face. He gritted his teeth and said, "Put it down, Ryan! Now. Or she's a goner."

Before Peter had time to weigh the potential consequences of his action, before he had time to argue with himself that Amy's safety came first, before anyone had time to react, he pointed and squeezed. A single shot struck the man directly in the nose. He collapsed as quickly as if someone had cut off his legs at the knees, and the gun rattled to the concrete. Amy screamed and jumped back into the room.

There were two left, plus those in the SUV by the entrance, idling quietly, hiding behind the vehicle's tinted windows, waiting.

From inside the room, another muffled gunshot pierced the evening air, and a bullet ricocheted off the exterior of the SUV. Amy had fired it.

The two men behind the Tahoe shifted away from the room's opening and returned fire. Amy shot again.

Seeing his opportunity, Peter dropped the dead man from his arms and rushed the SUV, advancing on the men from behind.

As he rounded the rear bumper, he met one of the gunmen head-on. They were close enough to shake hands. The man lifted his weapon to fire, but Peter was quicker, and before his opponent had a chance to squeeze the trigger and lodge a round deep in Peter's skull, he shoved the guy's arm to the side and simultaneously drove the palm of his hand into the man's face, jamming upward on the nose. The gunman's head snapped back as if a coiled spring had been released. Blood immediately oozed from his nose, and he stumbled back into his comrade. Peter lifted his own gun and squeezed off one, two shots, and that was all it took.

Not waiting to see if the third Tahoe would awaken from its slumber, Peter made a dash for the motel room and shut the door.

TWENTY-ONE

. . .

Inside the room, one of the gunmen lay on his back, his eyes blank and staring at the ceiling, jaw slack. A single hole just above his right eye oozed blood.

Peter looked at Amy, who was crouched behind the bed and shaking. She clutched the handgun with both hands at chest level. "Did you do that?" Peter asked.

She glanced at the body, then back to Peter. "He didn't shoot himself."

Peter positioned himself so he could see out the front window but remain concealed by the curtain and wall. "We have one more vehicle. I don't know how many are in it. It's just sitting there."

"What are they waiting for?"

"Us. Waiting to see what our next move is."

"What is it?"

Keeping one finger hooked on the curtain so he could maintain a visual with the lone Tahoe, Peter scanned the parking lot, the road, the carnage outside the room's door. The sky was almost black now; only a subtle glow of light remained above the treetops. More stars had appeared too, glistening in the evening sky, watching from above but totally oblivious to the violence that this parking lot had just seen. Peter's heart still pounded, adrenaline-infused blood still surged through his arteries, but his stomach had twisted itself into a tight knot. He didn't like killing. If he had at one time, it was a different Peter Ryan because this Peter Ryan, this man who was a foreigner to his own past, handled killing as well as he handled eating chicken gizzards. In the heat of battle, it seemed like some base instinct took over, and his combat skills went into full self-preservation mode. But in the aftermath, looking at the collection of casualties in the parking lot, he wondered who these men were when they weren't being used as killing machines. Did they have wives who would grow ashen at the news? Children who would never again hear their father's voice reading a bedtime story? The thought made Peter sick.

God in heaven, forgive me. Deliver me from this evil.

He immediately wondered where this impulse to pray had come from and, at the same time, marveled that he honestly felt the pressure lift. He still felt remorseful, yes, but somehow absolved as well.

He took another look out the window. The Tahoe hadn't moved, but its headlights seemed to glow brighter in the darkening night. "We need to get out of here."

Amy said, "I was hoping for something a little more specific than that."

No matter what they did now, the men in the Tahoe would see them and be ready to react. And the longer they waited, the greater the chance that more men with guns would arrive, this time coming in larger numbers and toting heavier weaponry. Only one option remained.

"We need to make a run for it," Peter said.

They'd have to take one of the other Tahoes because the Accord was boxed in. And besides, if it came to a game of bumper cars, a Tahoe would hold up much better against another SUV than the smaller, lighter Honda. He hoped the keys were still in the ignition, waiting for a fast getaway.

Amy stood and moved toward the door on rigid legs.

"I'm sorry it came to this," Peter said, nodding toward the dead gunman on the floor.

Amy closed her eyes and drew in a deep breath.

"Amy, we need to do this now."

She opened her eyes and nodded.

"Give me your gun. I'm going to go first and cover you while you make a run for the nearest SUV. Get in the passenger side and start it. I'll be right behind you."

The only time she'd be exposed was from the door to the front of the Accord. From there she would find cover from the Accord and then the Tahoe. If the men inside the distant Tahoe decided to show themselves and start throwing bullets, they wouldn't have a clean shot at her. Peter hoped they wouldn't have any shot.

He put a hand on her shoulder. "Ready?"

She swallowed hard. "Do I look like I'm ready?"

"You can do this. Just stay low, behind the car. It'll give you the cover you need. On the count of three."

Amy wrung her hands like she was trying to squeeze water out of an invisible dishrag and took another deep breath.

"One. Two."

He slid in next to the door so as soon as she opened it, he could slip out and lay down fire on the Tahoe. It was a good thirty yards away.

"Three."

Amy turned the knob and swung open the door.

Peter stepped out, aiming both handguns at the black SUV and squeezing off rounds as he ran for the Accord, Amy right on his heels. He squatted behind the hood of the car and continued shooting.

The Tahoe's doors opened, but Peter couldn't see how many men emerged. He thought it was two. Short bursts of gunfire echoed through the air, and rounds popped against the Tahoe at the rear of the Accord. Some of the rounds hit the motel's facade, busted room five's window, tore the wood molding to shreds.

Peter ducked, trying to stay as low as possible, and made his way around the Accord to the other Tahoe's driver's side door. Amy was already in, the engine running. Another burst of gunfire came, as quick and sudden as thunder on a summer's night. One round hit the top edge of the SUV's rear window, shattering the glass.

"Get down," Peter yelled.

Amy put her head between her knees and screamed.

Peter threw the Tahoe into gear and stomped on the gas. Adrenaline surged through his veins like nitromethane. His heart sledgehammered against his sternum. Yanking the steering wheel to the right and laying down rubber on the asphalt, he just missed the beams supporting the motel's second-story deck and made a tight U-turn in the parking lot. He wasn't about to head directly at the other vehicle, not with the men sending so many rounds their way. The chances were too great that one would find its way into the cabin and ricochet around until it found a soft target. Instead he headed for the far end of the parking lot, intent on running over the ten yards of lawn and overgrown gardens and getting to the road that way.

But the other Tahoe predicted his move and, with the gunmen already inside, was heading toward them, positioning to intercept Peter's path.

With no other course of action, Peter pressed the accelerator to the floor and, right before impacting the opposing SUV, spun the wheel to the right. His vehicle smashed into the rear quarter panel of the oncoming Tahoe and spun it around so the two slammed together in an odd metal-on-metal waltz, facing opposite directions, driver's side against driver's side.

Not waiting for his opponent's next move, Peter kept his foot on the gas while the Tahoe's wheels clawed at the dirt. Finally the tires found traction, and the SUV jerked forward, bounced through the garden, and landed on the solid asphalt of the road.

In the rearview mirror, no more than twenty yards behind them, the pursuing vehicle stuttered onto the road and spun its rear wheels, stirring up a cloud of smoke.

Again the concussion of rapid gunfire cut through the air; rounds banged against the back of the Tahoe like leaden popcorn. One entered the cab and destroyed the rearview mirror.

"Stay down," Peter said to Amy. "We'll get out of this."

"How?" She still had her head between her knees and now her hands covered her ears.

Peter didn't answer because he didn't know. But they would get out of it. They had to. Karen and Lilly were waiting for him, and they were all that mattered now. Getting to them. Finding them. Hugging them again.

A flash memory assaulted Peter's mind.

He's in the passenger seat of a Humvee, bouncing over a desert road, stirring up a storm of dust.

Shots pop off the vehicle's armor, enter the cab, and ricochet around. Men holler, scream, curse, return fire. Someone's been hit. Droplets of blood cover the inside of the windshield.

It's chaos. Utter chaos.

Heading north, the road was lined with oaks and maples and pines; a mantle of darkness had descended on the forest. The Tahoe's headlights cut a swath of light across the road and about twenty feet on either side. A gully ran along both shoulders, two feet deep and at least five feet wide. There was no hopping off the pavement this time like he'd done back in Indiana. Doing so would get them no farther than ten feet before the thick trunk of an ancient oak stopped them dead in their tracks.

Ahead the road turned slightly to the left. Peter took it without slowing; the Tahoe handled well for an SUV and managed the curve with only minimal drift.

Behind them the other Tahoe's headlights grew larger in the side mirror. More gunshots erupted, and Peter could see the muzzle flash from the automatic weapon on the driver's side. He instinctively ducked and swerved into the oncoming lane. The speedometer read sixty-five. He'd have to go faster, but the road was unfamiliar and the darkness now almost suffocating.

He pressed the accelerator closer to the floor, but still the headlights behind them grew closer until the vehicle tapped their bumper—a monster with blazing eyes, nudging them, sniffing its prey, calculating its next attack.

Seventy-five miles per hour. Undergrowth whizzed by in darkling blurs. Peter didn't want to go much faster. To lose control and spin into the trees would mangle not only the Tahoe but its occupants as well.

More shots cracked through the air. Peter's Tahoe found a will of its own and lurched to the right and almost ran into the gully, but Peter was quick on the wheel and corrected course. One of the rounds had struck a tire. He couldn't tell which one at first, but the vehicle kept wanting to pull. Then came the awful grinding sound of the rim on asphalt. The right rear tire had been shredded.

Peter needed to make a decision. The Tahoe couldn't last long on three tires, and it was only a matter of time before they shot out the other ones.

He hit the gas hard; the SUV's large engine whined and moaned and pulled the vehicle forward, putting some distance—at least four car lengths—between them and their pursuers.

He said to Amy, "Sit back and put on your shoulder belt. And hang on."

They were approaching a slight bend in the road to the right. Midway through the curve, Peter cut the Tahoe's headlights and took his foot off the gas. The lights behind him rounded the bend and approached rapidly. When they were merely two car lengths away, Peter mashed the brake. The antilock braking system kicked in, vibrating the pedal beneath his foot.

Peter braced himself. *This is crazy.*

Less than a second later, the oncoming vehicle met the Tahoe's bumper. The impact was sudden and violent.

TWENTY-TWO

. . .

Peter slammed against the seat as if it had broken loose from its anchor. Air squeezed from his lungs, and his head jerked violently. If he had been clubbed in the back of the head and tossed down a flight of stairs, he couldn't have felt worse.

For a second, maybe two, he forgot where he was and thought his Humvee had been struck by an improvised explosive device. He tried to speak, tried to produce sound from his vocal cords, but his lungs didn't want to cooperate and take in air. Finally, though, the awareness of reality returned, and it didn't take him long to get his bearings and regain his composure. Ignoring the throbbing in his neck and the relentless swirling sensation in his head, he checked Amy to make sure she was okay.

"I'm fine," she said, her voice shaky and weak. "Fine."

Peter unhooked his seat belt, opened the vehicle's door, and nearly fell out of the cab. The odor of gasoline and burnt rubber was everywhere. Beneath the Tahoe, something ticked, ticked, ticked. His legs trembled, not willing to support his weight, but he pressed on. He had to. He had to finish this. As he moved, his head settled and cleared. One of the pursuing Tahoe's headlamps was busted and the front end was crumpled like tissue paper, but the other headlamp was somehow still intact and emitted cloudy light around the scene of the accident.

Peter assumed that since no bullets had flown his way, the occupants of the other Tahoe must be too injured to fire, unconscious, or dead. Sticking close to his vehicle, he slipped out the handgun that he'd tucked into the waistline of his pants, and in one fluid motion swung it forward and fired a string of shots at the Tahoe's windshield.

When he reached the driver's side door, he yanked it open. The driver toppled out, his face blood-covered, his head swiveling on his neck like a ball on a string.

Peter looked across the driver's side to the passenger seat. Another gunmen was there, his body folded almost in half and wedged into the footwell. He too appeared dead.

The back driver's side door opened and a man, about six-two and built like a grizzly bear, eased out. His eyes were glassy, and he wobbled on his feet as if he were honey drunk. A large gash below his left eye oozed bright-red blood down his cheek. When he saw Peter, his eyes widened and he swiped at the blood, smearing it across his face to his ear. He looked from Tahoe to Tahoe, then to the dead driver on the road. His face twisted into an awful scowl as understanding dawned.

Before Grizzly could go on the offensive, Peter struck him in the face with a fist, connecting just below the gash. The man stumbled back, grunted, and reached for his weapon, which was seated in a shoulder holster. Peter raised his weapon to fire, but nothing happened. He'd used all his rounds. Before Grizzly could aim and fire, Peter was there, delivering a quick kick to the man's hand and dislodging the gun. It flew into the darkness and rattled across the asphalt.

Seeing an opportunity that was never really there, the big man lunged for Peter, his eyes blazing, teeth gritted. His hands were like meat hooks.

Peter sidestepped and delivered a blow to the man's abdomen, but it didn't even faze him. He turned and growled at Peter, bared his teeth and clenched his fists, and snorted like the angry bear he was.

If Peter was going to survive this night, he needed to regain control of the confrontation. He stepped forward and jabbed at the man's face. But Grizzly was surprisingly quick for his size, and his reaction time was sharpening by the second. He blocked Peter's advance and threw a punch of his own. Peter deflected it. Another punch was thrown, a large roundhouse that had lights-out written all over it. Peter deflected it as well. A third punch came at him. This time Peter not only deflected it but simultaneously stepped forward and drove his elbow into the man's face.

That one landed solidly, causing Grizzly to stagger backward, arms falling to his sides.

Peter wasted not even a fraction of a second. He immediately followed that blow with another one, a sharp jab to the throat. That was followed by a battering ram to the abdomen, which succeeded in doubling the man over. From there all that was needed was a double-fisted hammer to the upper back, and Grizzly collapsed onto the road. He didn't get back up.

Breathing like he'd just run a hundred-yard sprint through six inches of mud, Peter put his hands on his hips and scanned the darkened perimeter, looking for any other gunmen. There had been four in each of the other vehicles; why would this one carry only three? His neck still ached, but there was no time to let that slow him. They needed to get out of there, get on another road, and find a place to lie low for the night.

Amy leaned against the vehicle, tears streaming down her cheeks. She was shaking and sniffling, wringing her hands.

Peter went to her. "Are you hurt?"

She ran a fist across her cheek, then held up a quivering hand and said, "Look at me. I'm a wreck."

"It's okay," Peter said. He put a hand on her shoulder. "It's fine. We're all right. We'll be okay."

Amy shook her head. "No. It's not all right." Her eyes met his, and in hers he found sorrow so deep one could drown in it. And fear. Such fear. "Peter, I'm so sorry. I didn't know it was going to come to this. I didn't know you'd come to me. I had no idea they'd go this far." She was rambling, jumbling her words together as if she knew she needed to release them in a torrent while she had the chance—and the will.

"Whoa, slow down. What are you talking about?"

Amy drew in a long, stuttered breath and exhaled through pursed lips. She wiped at her tears again and shook her head. "Things aren't what they seem. They're not what you think. It's all been an act."

"What's not what I think, Amy? What do you mean?"

"This. You. Me. Everything. We need to find Abernathy. It's—"

Amy's head snapped back at the same time a crack pierced the air. Even as her body slumped against the car and another shot cracked like thunder, Peter was on his knees, then his stomach.

Amy's body collapsed next to him.

TWENTY-THREE

• • •

The woman had fallen asleep holding her daughter in her arms, stroking her hair, wishing with every ounce of strength and faith left in her that their circumstance would change. Someway. Somehow.

But her daughter's soft voice, like the muted babbling of a stream in a dense forest, murmuring something incoherent, had awakened her. She put her nose to the girl's hair and drew in a long breath.

Again her daughter mumbled, her voice as soft and gentle as the whisperings of wind through the slender branches of a willow. This time the woman caught the word *Daddy*. She kissed her precious girl on the head even as a lump formed in her throat.

Her daughter stirred, exhaled, lifted her head. There was

sleep in her eyes, a glassy faraway gaze that focused on nothing. "Mommy?"

"Shh. It's okay, baby. You're all right. Go back to sleep."

"Mommy, I fell asleep."

The woman ran her hand over her daughter's hair. "I know. You sleep now. Get your rest."

But instead her girl pushed herself to a sitting position and rubbed her eyes. She looked around the room as if it were her first time seeing it, and the woman couldn't tell if she was awake or still asleep.

The woman put her hand on her daughter's cheek. "Sweetie, are you awake?"

The girl's gaze shifted quickly to the woman and made perfect contact. Clarity filled her eyes now. "Yes. I'm awake. I was dreaming of Daddy."

"I know."

"Was I talking in my sleep again?"

"You were, yes."

Her daughter was quiet for a moment, thinking. She thought a lot. The woman would often notice her just sitting and staring and when asked what she was doing, she'd respond that she was thinking. But rarely did she reveal the details of what she thought about.

"Mommy," her sweet girl said, inching closer and putting her head on her mother's shoulder. "Do you think Daddy knows where we are? Do you think he's coming for us?"

Tears stung the woman's eyes, and her throat swelled. She sniffed and swallowed past the lump. "I think he's doing everything he can to be with his family again."

At first the girl had believed her father was dead when the men told them he was, that he had died a hero's death and had been given a hero's burial overseas. They said the woman and her daughter should be proud, that he had served his country valiantly and would want them to do the same. But as time passed, her daughter grew more and more resolute that her daddy was not, in fact, dead but was very much alive and searching for them. The woman never corrected her daughter, never argued the point, never dashed her hope. Hope was all they had left in this place, and to take that away from her daughter would be cruel and senseless.

The fact was, though, that the woman couldn't trust the men who fed her the information. There were two of them; they'd come in suits and neatly combed hair. Their faces showed remorse but their eyes betrayed them. They had the eyes of wolves, hungry for power, hungry for dominance. And why should she trust them anyway? These were the same men who experimented on her daughter, who did things to her she would not even speak of. They said her husband was dead, but they very well could have lied.

In fact, she told herself often that they had lied. That her husband was still alive. That even now he was on his way to find them and rescue them. But in her heart, in the silence that resided there when her daughter was gone and she was alone with torturous thoughts, she questioned her own hope and whether it was misplaced, whether it was nonsense and only wishful thinking. The deluded optimism of a grieving and frightened wife.

Primarily, the doubt came when she was alone and felt nothing. Oh, she tried. She tried to feel, to sense that he was still alive. A wife would know, wouldn't she? Shouldn't she? But she didn't. She felt nothing. Was that what it felt like when your husband was dead? Nothing?

Her daughter's body grew heavy against her shoulder. She was asleep again. She laid the girl down on the bed and stroked her hair, kissed her on the cheek. Then she sat on the bed next to her and offered a whispered prayer to heaven. "God, please let him still be alive."

"He is," her daughter whispered back.

The woman patted the girl's head. "Shh. Go back to sleep now."

• • •

With no time to think or plan or even check for Amy's pulse, Peter rolled to the edge of the road, then scurried into the woods, taking cover behind a stand of serviceberries. The shot had come from across the road. A fourth gunman must have slipped from the wreckage as unnoticed as any ghoul and taken refuge behind the veil of darkness.

Quietly Peter stood and moved from tree to tree toward the back of the Tahoe. The taillights illuminated the area in a bloody glow. He remained in the woods, hidden in darkness, and moved with the stealth of a cat.

When he was thirty feet behind the wreckage, Peter stepped out of the woods, crouched at the knees and waist, and scanned the area. He checked the woods along both sides of the road, looking for anything that didn't belong, any shadow out of place, any glint of metal. But the darkness was too oppressive. The trees seemed to swallow up any light from the starry sky, and the residual illumination from the vehicles only made it to the edges of the road, lighting the first line of trees and underbrush. Beyond that, deep darkness resided and somewhere in there, the man who had shot Amy.

Still crouched and moving silently, Peter took two, three steps toward the wreckage, then stopped and listened. Without the luxury of light, both he and the gunman would have to rely on their other senses. Hidden by the darkness, they could move about almost freely, but any sound—the scuff of shoes on the asphalt, the crackle of a leaf, the snap of a twig—would give away their location. Peter only hoped his own hearing was better than his rival's.

When he started moving again, Peter sidestepped across the road to the far shoulder. And there he waited. Minutes passed, and with each tick of the clock, Peter grew more anxious. It was another minute wasted, another minute that Amy could be cling- ing to her last strands of life. He had to do something.

In desperation, Peter decided to expose himself, to make himself the bait needed to catch that elusive last fish. Launching himself from the roadside like a man dashing through six lanes of rush-hour traffic, he sprinted across the asphalt toward the wreckage, keeping his eyes on the dark woods to his left where he presumed the gunman to be. The crack of gunfire sounded and with it a muzzle flash. Still running, Peter aimed his weapon and fired at where the muzzle flash had been, then two more shots to the right of the flash. He was taking a chance, assuming the gun- man was right-handed and, after firing once, would quickly move to his right.

He assumed correctly. A grunt came from the darkness, fol- lowed by a complicated rustle of leaves. Another flash, and a bullet whizzed by Peter's head. Slowing, he fired twice more, each shot a little to the right of where the flash had been. Another grunt, more rustling of leaves, branches snapping, then a heavy thud.

All was quiet, but Peter had to make sure. He rushed to the tree line, staying low and ready, his heart doing double time, every sense on alert. From there he moved from tree to tree until he reached the area where the last flash was seen.

There he found the gunman, not breathing, no pulse.

In a near panic, Peter returned to Amy and felt for her neck. "C'mon, Amy, be here."

He couldn't find a pulse. "C'mon. C'mon."

Still nothing. She was gone.

Peter wanted to grieve; he wanted to sit by Amy's side and not move; he wanted to stay with her until... until what? Until his pursuers showed up and apologized for having no idea things would get so out of hand and people would lose their lives? Until they suggested a truce and a round of hugs?

He had to get out of there. It was a public road, and though it was in a remote area and no doubt saw very little traffic this time of night, there was always the chance that some unsuspecting traveler on his way home from work or en route to a night of poker playing with his buddies would stumble upon the collision and find Peter there with five dead bodies.

It took him less than fifteen minutes to change the tire on the Tahoe. It was in bad shape, but hopefully the vehicle could get him far enough to find a new one—one without a tracking device. He gleaned everything he could use from the four dead gunmen and their SUV: two automatic rifles, four handguns, and a dozen magazines.

Leaving everything else exactly as it was, Peter touched Amy's shoulder, said again that he was sorry, then jumped into the Tahoe and headed off. He had to find a new vehicle and get back on track to Centralia. Tomorrow would bring a new set of challenges.

TWENTY-FOUR

· · ·

Lawrence Habit was a patient man, but he hadn't started out that way. As a young man, he was as impulsive and stupid as a monkey in a mall. He functioned primarily on instinct and reactions. He did what he wanted, when he wanted, where he wanted and simply walked over anyone who opposed him or got in his way. But the military had drilled that out of him. He'd learned discipline, honor, the importance of planning, and respect. And his time with Patrick had taught him patience.

Now that patience would be tested. He'd arrived at his destination an hour ago, concealed his vehicle under a blanket of heavy brush, and settled in for a long wait. From where he sat in the driver's seat, he could see the incoming road and any traffic on it.

It would be a sleepless night. He was fairly certain Patrick wouldn't arrive until daybreak, but he didn't want to take any chance of missing an early arrival. He knew the agency had dispatched another team to take care of Patrick. It was simply their way of dealing with problems. But he also knew that team had failed as well.

Because he knew Patrick.

He admired Patrick, respected him. The world needed more men like him. The deal to bring him in had been business and nothing more. But now that the deal was off and Lawrence had become a target himself—a target for *discontinuation*—the two shared a bond. Lawrence could use that bond to his advantage.

The agency would be coming for Lawrence, so he needed to get to them first and destroy them. But he couldn't do it without Patrick. The man possessed skills that Lawrence had never seen before. His ability to stay calm under the most stressful situations was remarkable. And his aim was dead-on. The man simply didn't miss. He was, in every aspect of the term, the perfect soldier. Tough, resilient, flexible, loyal, intelligent, he was the complete package. Even outside the war zone, outside that valley of death, he'd proven to be all those things. The memory hit Lawrence again, the one he'd kept buried for too long. Not because he didn't want to remember it, but because he thought it no longer held any relevance; he'd thought he'd never see Patrick again.

Patrick had talked him down off that ledge, convinced him to pull the handgun away from his head and lay it on the bed. The apartment was quiet, empty; the only thing to fill it was Patrick's voice over the phone. It was the voice of reason, of truth, of hope. He'd proven that day that he wasn't only a loyal soldier; he was just as much a loyal friend.

Lawrence had thought Patrick was dead, that he'd been discontinued.

Sipping a cold coffee, watching the empty road, Lawrence smiled. It'd be just like old times.

TWENTY-FIVE

• • •

He was in the house again. The same one as always. He never got a
look at the exterior but could tell from the layout and architectural
details that it was an old home. The decorative molding around the
windows and doors, the hardwood flooring, the large double-hung
windows, the archways between rooms, the ornate brass chandelier in the foyer area.

There wasn't much on the first floor. The rooms were mostly
empty with only a few stray items of furniture: an oak straight-
back chair with a caned seat in the dining room, a cherry pedestal
table in the living room, an old toaster on the granite counter in the
kitchen. But each room had a feeling about it that it was waiting
for something, waiting to be filled with objects, with furniture,
with memories. He'd been through the first floor multiple times,

165

searched each room as if it were a rare archaeological find and he a treasure hunter. And every time he'd found nothing but dust and splinters and a couple loose nails. And that persistent feeling of expectancy, of waiting, of longing.

The real intrigue, though, for Peter, was always the second floor.

Up the staircase he plodded, the aged wood of the steps creaking under his weight, a curious excitement building in his chest. The closer to the top he drew, the harder and more rapid his heartbeat.

Just like always.

And as always, he expected to find something up there, something of value or a piece of important evidence, anything that would trigger more memories, clear the fog, and clue him in to what was going on.

The sensation he experienced in this house was like none he'd ever had before. He was dreaming and yet he knew he was dreaming and was in a kind of semiconscious state. Yet he was fully asleep. It was a dream like any other dream he'd had at any other time in his life, but he could think, he could reason, he was aware of where he was and what he was doing. He was in control and not at the whim of the irrational side of his subconsciousness.

Once he reached the top of the steps, he rested his hand on the banister and surveyed the hallway. Four rooms lined one side, three with their doors open as if inviting him in. But that last door, the fourth one, remained closed, warning him away.

He needed to do a more thorough search of each of the open rooms. He hoped that in them he'd find clues, signs to point him to even more clues, and puzzle pieces. This was where he needed to focus his efforts, not on discovering the source of the longing on the first floor, not on finding the key to the locked door and exposing the source of the shadow. These rooms, the ones open to him, begging him to explore, to find, to remember, were where he'd find his answers.

The first room consisted of a dresser, a bookshelf, a desk, and a floor lamp. No bed. No closet. No mirrors. And there were boxes of all sizes. Shoe boxes, gift boxes, trunks, lockboxes... all stacked and arranged in a haphazard manner. On and around the boxes were objects from Peter's past—mementos, photos of times he didn't remember, toys he had no recollection of ever playing with yet knew were his. There was his baseball glove, worn and flimsy though he couldn't remember using it, not even once. He picked it up and slipped his hand into it. The glove was too small now, but still it felt right, like he'd worn it for hundreds of hours and caught thousands of balls with it. Why couldn't he remember ever playing baseball?

Peter walked to the dresser and pulled open the top drawer. It was stuffed with underwear and socks, nothing out of the ordinary. In the second drawer he found shirts, ties, sweaters. The third drawer held pants, mostly khakis. No jeans or shorts. In the bottom drawer were four lab coats, white, mid-thigh length. Over the left breast of each was stitched *Peter Ryan, Biology.*

Peter pulled out one of the coats, unfolded it, and tried it on. He wore one just like it when he worked in the lab. He slipped out of the coat and let it fall back into the drawer without bothering to refold it.

The bookshelf reached from floor to ceiling and consisted of seven shelves, all stuffed full of books, mostly biology texts and reference books. One shelf was reserved for journals and another for a variety of other books, ranging from classics—Jack London, Edgar Allan Poe, Dickens, Austen, and Henry James—to biographies. On the end, separated from the other books as if it were something too precious to be in the presence of other texts, was a book that caught his eye: a Bible.

Sliding the Bible off the shelf, he cracked open its faded leather cover. On the first page was the handwritten inscription: *May these words always be a lamp to your feet and a light to your path. Love, Mom and Dad.*

Mom and Dad. He thought it odd that he had no memory of his parents. No real memory, anyway. Nothing specific, nothing that made them any different from every other mom and dad out there. It was as though he'd been raised in some television life, where everything was scripted and stereotyped and nauseatingly typical but nothing was real.

Peter flipped through the thin, crisp pages and landed in the book of John. He scanned the page and finally came to rest on some familiar words, comforting words. Words he'd read before. Words that at one time had meaning to him. His eyes lingered on those words, drew them in as a mother welcomes her newborn, the child she feels she's known all her life but has only just met. He lifted a hand and ran his fingers over each word. The feeling he had when reading them was incredible. Such peace. Such hope.

And then it vanished as quickly as a mist is dispelled by the wind.

He returned the Bible and moved to the desk on the other side of the room. It was a wide, thick partners desk made of oak. The top surface was as wide and deep as a dining room table and littered with papers and photos and forms and receipts. It was an exact replica of his desk at home in his study.

On the left side of the desk was a notepad, one of those small steno pads detectives and reporters used to jot down phone numbers and important information. Peter reached for it and opened it. A phone number was on the first page, written by Peter's hand. He didn't recognize the number, but the name under it—*Nichols*—was oddly familiar. He knew it from somewhere but couldn't place where; he'd said that name before, used it in conversation, used it to address a man of some stature. But no specific memories were attached to it, only a distant familiarity. Peter closed the pad and placed it back on the desk. He needed to remember that name when he woke up.

On the right corner of the desktop, a brochure attracted his attention. A photo of a school and a smiling boy standing with his parents adorned the cover. Across the top in a scrolling font, it read *The Andrews Academy.*

Peter opened the brochure, but the interior panels were all blank, just white space. On the back was the name of the school again and a motto: *The place for gifted students to develop to their fullest potential.*

That memory returned to him then, floating out of the ether. It was the same memory he'd had before, when he'd been awake and searching for the meaning of Centralia.

He and Karen and Lilly sit around a table, and a man in a suit sits across from them. His face is chiseled, his brow heavy, his hair perfectly groomed, combed to the side and carefully sprayed in place. His eyes are a piercing green. He sits erect, chin up. Statuesque.

"It's a remarkable school, I assure you," he says. There's an air of confidence about him that is reassuring. This is a man who knows what he's talking about.

He smiles and dips his chin. "Children like Lilly—gifted children— need someplace special to hone their skills. She deserves that, don't you think?"

An address was printed on the bottom of the page. The school was located in a town called Buck's Valley in Indiana. But below the address in small, italicized print were the words *A Centralia School*.

Centralia.

At once, Peter felt a great urging tugging at his mind, his heart, his soul. He had to act now, had to move. There was someplace he needed to be, someplace that *needed* him to be there, and there was no time to waste. He glanced at his watch, but there were no hands on it. Only numbers—solitary, lonely numbers that told him nothing he didn't already know: that there were a mere twenty-four hours in a day and time stood still for no one. And his time was up.

And then he was standing in front of the closed door. The fourth door. Behind it lay the answers to his questions, he was certain. He reached for the knob and tried to turn it, but it wouldn't budge. He rattled it, pulled on it, but got nowhere. It was stuck as fast as rebar in concrete.

Below the door, in the space between the bottom edge and the wood flooring, the shadow moved, back and forth, pacing, always pacing.

"Who are you?" Peter hollered. He put both hands on the door and pressed his ear to it, hoping to hear some breath or whisper or anything. But there was only silence, not even the sound of footsteps.

He had an idea. Peter reached over his head and ran his fingers along the ledge of the molding above the doorway. Maybe the key was there, out of sight, hidden from anyone who was not supposed to enter the room. But no key was there. He ran his eyes along the floor, searching every angle, every corner, but still no key was to be found.

Again he tried the knob, but the outcome was no different from before. The door was locked fast.

• • •

Peter did not awake from his dream casually as he had done countless times before when dreams had entertained his sleeping hours. This time the transition out of the dreamworld house full of strange rooms and misplaced memories was harsh and jarring. Peter awoke suddenly and with a frantic feeling in his chest. His hands were sweaty and the muscles in his forearms ached. His hair was wet, but he couldn't tell at first whether it was because of sweat or not.

Then he realized he was outside, lying in the grass, damp from the dew that had settled overnight.

A Ford Fiesta was there, the latest in his string of grand thefts auto, its driver's side door open, the soft electronic bell still chiming, letting him know the keys were in the ignition.

He was in a clearing in the woods. Trees like sentinels rose around him, spreading their leafy arms across the light-gray sky. A gentle breeze blew and surrounded him with the earthy odor of grass and fallen leaves. If he were a child of the forest, raised by rabbits or squirrels or coyotes, he would have thought it a beautiful morning and would have stretched contentedly after a comfortable night's sleep. But the wood was foreign to him, and awaking there was as unnatural as discovering he had somehow sunk to the bottom of the ocean and could miraculously breathe water.

Peter sat up and rubbed his eyes, ran a hand through his hair. He tried to remember how he'd gotten there, how he'd come to spend the night with nature, but couldn't. He recalled the events of the previous evening. The Oceanview, the gunmen, three Tahoes, twelve men. All dead. And they'd killed Amy. It was his fault. Sorrow threatened to overwhelm and shove him into a very dark and uninhabitable place, but he pushed it aside. Remarkably, he didn't find it all that difficult. His mind was a weapon he had at one time mastered and tamed and trained, but now he couldn't remember when or how.

Amy's final words, that last conversation they'd had right before a single bullet pierced her skull and snuffed out her life, surfaced and pricked at his mind.

"Peter, I'm so sorry. . . . I had no idea they'd go this far."

What did she mean? Who were *they*? And how did she know anything about them?

"Things aren't what they seem. They're not what you think. . . .

"This. You. Me. Everything. We need to find Abernathy. It's—"

Questions stabbed at his mind. So cryptic, so mysterious. And no answers. It was nearly too much for Peter. He wanted to claw at his own flesh. What had he gotten involved in? And had Amy somehow been a part of it, even before he'd dragged her into the danger?

He'd left her there, lying on the cold road, lifeless and staring into the night sky. He'd driven the Tahoe... but to where? And where had he procured another car? He didn't know where he was. At some point he must have pulled off the road and found this clearing, then fallen asleep.

And dreamed. He'd had the dream again. It was still so vivid—the stairs, the hallway, the rooms and open doors. The room he'd explored with the dresser and bookshelf and desk and floor lamp.

The floor lamp. He remembered it now. He hadn't noticed it in his dream, but now, viewing the room through his mind's eye, he recalled it perfectly. It was the same lamp Dr. Audrey Lewis had in her office, the one with the stylized *C* painted on the shade.

And then there was the brochure on the desk with its scrolling fonts. The Andrews Academy. *A Centralia School.*

He thought of that conversation he and Karen had with the gentleman across the table. The guy with the chiseled features and brilliant-green eyes. The guy with the perfect posture and smooth voice. There had to be more to the event than just his fragmented memory. Had they gone through with it? Had they sent her? They couldn't have because Lilly was with Karen when they were...

No, they weren't killed in the accident. They were still alive. Lilly had left him the note.

But Lilly didn't go to any Andrews Academy; she went to Middleton Elementary School.

And there was also the Bible, set apart from the other books as if he was meant to find it, meant to turn to the exact page he'd turned to and read the exact words he'd read. Only now he couldn't remember what he'd read. It had meant something to him, though, something special; he knew that much. The words had stirred some inkling of hope in him.

Peter stood and stretched his legs and back and looked around. Trees, underbrush, and more trees. About thirty yards to his left was the road, but he didn't know which one. His watch said it was nearing seven o'clock. He rubbed his neck; it still ached.

He didn't know how long he'd been out on the grass and hoped the car's battery still had enough juice in it to turn over the engine. He tried the ignition and was pleased when it revved to life. Now to figure out where he was and redirect himself to Centralia.

TWENTY-SIX

. . .

Outside the town of Trout Run, just off Highway 15, Peter pulled
to the side of the road, behind a row of Dumpsters, and got out.
He'd managed to hot-wire a beater with a radiator that kept over-
heating, and this was a good enough place to stash the vehicle and
find a replacement. The Dumpsters were all nearly empty, which
meant the trash had just been picked up, probably yesterday. The
trucks wouldn't be coming around again for days, and he'd be long
out of the picture by then.

Not far down the road toward the town, he'd noticed signage
of various sizes and shapes and colors. There had to be multiple
businesses around—a strip mall, a factory, a warehouse, anything
where people would be. Surely Trout Run was no different from
every other small town in America. And where there were people,
there were cars.

It didn't take him even ten minutes of walking to arrive at the first building, a construction supply company with eleven cars in a newly coated and sealed parking lot. Nobody was around, but the lot was in direct view of the building and its front office. He didn't want to do anything that might look suspicious and draw the attention of someone inside. The police would be called and there would be a search on for the creep nosing around parked cars.

The next building sat about a hundred yards down the road, a two-story office building housing a dental supply company, a paper supplier, an accountant, and a doctor's office. No luck there either as the wall facing the parking lot was nearly all glass. Too visible. Too risky.

He moved on down the road, stopping at a trucking company near the ramp for Highway 15. The lot was mostly populated by big rigs, but a few cars and pickups sat unattended as well. Lines of trailers blocked any view of the lot from the front office. But there were cameras, lots of them, mounted on every light pole and corner of the building. Seemed the trucking company was taking no chances when it came to their trailers being broken into. One time was all it would have taken for them to go overboard on the surveillance.

Just inside the town line, Peter came upon a strip mall with a small grocery store, a pizza place, a Laundromat, a hair salon, and a beer outlet. Scanning the area, he found no security cameras but only a handful of cars sitting quietly, waiting for someone running for his life to come along and sweep them into a race against the clock. It was still early and the townies hadn't hit the stores yet.

As he crossed the parking lot, he noticed a blue pickup headed his way. It slowed in front of the grocery store and turned into the parking area. A kid drove it, a teenager, maybe eighteen or nineteen. He glanced at Peter, nodded, then steered the truck into a spot near the back of the lot.

Quickly Peter turned and headed for the truck. The kid had parked so the driver's side faced away from the grocery store, putting any confrontation that would occur there out of view of the store but in full view of the road that passed the mall. Fortunately for Peter, the town of Trout Run was in that lull between clock-in time at most of the warehouses and factories and starting time at the retail places. Peter rounded the back of the truck just as the kid stepped out.

He heard Peter's footsteps, spun, and wide-eyed and startled, said, "Hey, what...?"

Peter positioned himself between the kid and the road, slipped the handgun from his pocket, and stepping close to the kid, pointed it at his abdomen. "I need your truck."

The kid wore a pair of baggy khakis and a maroon polo shirt with the name of the grocery store—Jane's Market—emblazoned over the left chest. He was pudgy but not obese and had shaggy hair that covered his ears and hung nearly to his eyes, partially hiding a twisted and satiny scar that ran from somewhere around the hairline above his right eye, down across the bridge of his nose, over his cheek, to his jawline. His nose sat slightly askew on his face, as if someone had haphazardly positioned it there and glued it in place without bothering to center it first. The kid tried to step back, but the open door blocked his retreat. Peter had him cornered. He opened his mouth, stuttered, then finally said, "Don't kill me, man."

A twinge of guilt hit Peter, and he almost walked away. The kid had no doubt suffered years of torment and bullying because of his scar and as a result had learned the art of a quick surrender. Peter had become just another bully scratching another scar into the boy's psyche.

As if he knew the routine because he'd done it a thousand times with lunch money or candy bars or movie tickets, the kid produced the keys and tried to hand them to Peter. "No," Peter said. "Get back in. You're gonna drive."

He couldn't afford to have the kid run for the store and call the cops. They'd know what vehicle Peter was driving and would track him down by air or land in no time. Peter didn't want any more chases; he didn't want any more shooting. Though he knew that before he got to the bottom of all this, before he found Karen and Lilly, there would be more of both.

The kid shook his head, his eyes as wide as melons now. "No, really, man. Take 'em. Here." Again he tried to shove the keys at Peter.

Peter poked the barrel of the gun into the kid's stomach. "Get in and do exactly as I say, and you won't get hurt."

"You won't shoot me?"

"I won't hurt you."

"But if you shoot and kill me, it won't hurt. You know, one shot to the head. I gotta know you won't shoot me, man. It's, like, one of my fears. I have this thing about being shot."

Peter didn't have time for this. Every second they stood there, the risk grew that some passerby would spot them and grow suspicious. He dug the barrel of the gun harder into the kid's stomach. "Get in."

"Okay, okay. All right, man. I'm gettin' in." The kid climbed in behind the wheel. "You sure you want me doin' the driving?"

"Shut up and don't move or I'll shoot you and not even think twice about it. You understand?"

The kid didn't move but nodded.

Peter shut the door and rounded the front of the truck to get in the passenger side.

Once in, he turned to the kid, gun trained on his stomach. "You have a smartphone?"

"Uh…" The kid lifted his butt off the seat and fumbled with his pocket. Pulling out a phone, he said, "Here. Who you gonna call?"

Peter took the phone. "Shut up and start driving."

The kid started the truck and put it in gear. "Where we goin'?"

Flipping through the apps on the phone, Peter said, "Just start driving. East. And listen to me. I killed more men yesterday than I care to count, and I won't hesitate to shoot you if you get a mind to be a hero. Just do as I say. Exactly as I say. And you'll be okay. Do you understand me?"

Pulling out of the lot and onto the main street, the kid stole a look at Peter, then at the gun. "You killed guys with that?"

"Do you understand me?"

"Yes. Yeah. I got it."

Peter found a map app and located Centralia on it. He then located the town of Trout Run. "Okay. I'm going to give you precise instructions and I need you to follow my directions exactly. No detours. No shortcuts. You understand?"

"Dude, I said I got it. Now can you get that thing away from me? Quit pointing it at me?"

Keeping the handgun trained on the kid, Peter opened the glove box and pulled out the vehicle's registration form. "Your name is Ronald Little?"

"Ronnie."

"Ronnie, I know where you live now."

Ronnie swallowed hard, his Adam's apple bobbing in his neck.

Peter doubted that in all the years Ronnie had endured bullying, torment, and teasing, he had ever had someone pull a gun on him, had his truck carjacked, nor had his family threatened.

Peter studied the map on the phone, then set it on the seat beside him. "Okay. Ronnie, I want you to circle back around through town and get on 15 south."

"We going to Williamsport?"

"Not exactly."

They drove in silence for several miles. The interior of the truck was surprisingly clean for a teenager's vehicle. Ronnie took good care of it. From the rearview mirror hung an air freshener with an image of Iron Man on it. Along the dash were decals of other super-heroes: Hulk, Thor, Captain America, Flash, and Thing. Ronnie's key chain even included a pendant with Iron Man on it. So the kid was into superheroes, defenders of those who couldn't defend themselves.

Peter instructed Ronnie to get off the highway and onto a sec-ondary route. The major thoroughfares were too populated with state troopers who might identify him. He had to assume there was an all-points bulletin out on him with photos sent to every police barracks and station in the state. He also had to assume that who-ever was after him knew where he was headed, so they had a general idea of where he'd be.

"How'd you get that scar, Ronnie?" Peter asked.

Ronnie hesitated, checked the mirrors, the speedometer. "My dad gave it to me." He said it as if the scar were a birthday gift care-fully picked out by a loving father.

"Not exactly something a normal dad gives his son to remember him by."

"My dad was anything but normal."

"Did he do it purposefully?"

"Purposefully." Ronnie spoke the word as if it were something foreign and curious. "I don't think he did anything purposefully. He was a drunk."

"A mean drunk?"

"A mean drunk with a fascination with knives. Never a good combination."

"How old were you?"

"Nine. I was nine." Ronnie's eyes glazed as if he had transported himself back to that time and was mentally reliving the moment of violence. His hands tightened on the steering wheel and his jaw muscles clenched.

"Ronnie," Peter said.

Ronnie relaxed a little. "It took a hundred and five stitches to put my face back together and reattach my nose."

They drove in silence again, and Peter thought of instructing Ronnie to stop and get out. The kid had been through enough violence to last him a couple lifetimes. Instead he said, "You said *was*. Your dad *was* a drunk. Did he get help?"

Ronnie licked his lips. He glanced at Peter. "No. He got dead. When I was fifteen, I killed him."

"Self-defense?"

"That's the way the jury saw it."

Once more an uncomfortable silence filled the cabin. The tires hummed on the asphalt, rhythmically, quietly. Suddenly the interest in superheroes made a whole lot more sense. The wounded warrior overcoming trials and personal tribulations to conquer the villain.

A few minutes later, Ronnie again looked at the gun. "So you some kind of fugitive or something?"

Peter said, "Or something."

"Did you do it?"

"Do what?"

"Whatever they say you did or think you did?"

"Doesn't matter." And it didn't because he had no idea what he'd done or what he'd been accused of doing.

After more time in silence and three more turns onto different roads, Ronnie fidgeted in his seat and looked over at Peter. "So how many men did you kill?"

Peter kept his eyes straight ahead but could see the kid clearly in his peripheral vision. "Just drive."

"Are you CIA or somethin'? Gone rogue?"

Peter said nothing.

"You some kind of assassin? Messed with the wrong dudes?"

Peter shifted the gun to his right hand and with his left jabbed quickly at Ronnie's face with an open hand, catching the kid in the side of the head.

Ronnie's right hand went to the spot. "Man, that ain't—"

Peter reached across the space between them and grabbed a handful of Ronnie's shirt. He leaned toward the kid. "Listen, Ronnie, I have nothing against you, okay? You seem like a good kid. You got a job; you must be reasonably responsible. I admire you for how you handled the whole thing with your dad. I even like the superhero thing. I get it. But you really need to shut up and drive. I will shoot you if I need to. I will. I'll drop you right where you sit, steer the truck to the shoulder, open the door, and just kick you out." He let go of the kid's shirt and relaxed. Of course, he had no intention at all of harming the kid. Not after what Ronnie had already endured. "Don't make me do that, Ronnie, okay?"

Ronnie nodded.

TWENTY-SEVEN

. . .

An hour later, Ronnie, who had been quietly gazing out the windshield and effortlessly guiding the truck down the road, making all the turns Peter instructed him to, shifted again in his seat, scratched his head, and rubbed his face. "Hey, uh, dude?"

Peter gave the kid his attention.

"Uh, what's your name, anyway?"

"Dude works."

Ronnie shrugged. "Whatever, man. Hey, uh, we're gonna need some gas soon. We're on E."

Peter checked the fuel gauge. The kid was telling the truth. "You always drive around on an empty tank?"

"I was gonna get some after my shift. I wasn't planning on getting carjacked. This is a carjacking, right?"

Peter turned his body toward Ronnie. "Ronnie, it's whatever you want it to be. Now listen to me: here's what we're gonna do. Up ahead here about a mile, take a right. There's a small town about a mile more down the road from there. There's gotta be a station there. Pull in and up to a pump."

Ronnie threw several quick glances at him. "And then what?"

"I'll give you more instructions when we get there. I don't want to overwhelm your brain."

Ronnie made the right as instructed and a mile and a half farther steered his truck into the parking lot of Jerry's Quick Pump & Mart.

Peter said, "First turn off the engine."

Ronnie turned the key and the engine quieted to a rhythmic tick.

Presently there were no other cars at the pumps or the mini-mart. Jerry's was out of the way enough that the commuter traffic had already come and gone. It wouldn't see steady business again until afternoon quitting time.

"Now, get out and fill it up. You'll pay cash inside."

"I don't have that kind of cash, man. I always use a card."

"This one's my treat. Just do as I say. When you've filled the tank, come back to the window and I'll hand you the money. And don't even think about running or doing anything stupid. I'm a dead aim and will drop you with one shot before you can get past the tail end of the truck."

Ronnie looked at the gun pointed at him, then at Peter. "Got it. Fill it up, get money from you. Don't do anything stupid."

Peter smiled. "You're a fast learner, Ronnie."

The kid exited the truck and unscrewed the fuel cap. After pumping twenty-three gallons of gas, he replaced the nozzle on the pump and returned to the window.

Peter handed him the cash but, before allowing Ronnie to take it, said, "I want you to do exactly as I say; you got it?"

Ronnie nodded.

"Ronnie, I need to hear you say it."

"Yes."

"Good. Go in, get some drinks—water for me and you get whatever you want for yourself—then pay for everything. No small talk, no talk at all except what's necessary. Got it?"

Ronnie nodded again.

"Ronnie."

"Yes. I got it."

Peter let him have the money and watched as Ronnie crossed the pavement and entered the convenience store. He did not turn his head side to side but walked straight and rigidly, his movements mechanical, as if he were a programmable windup doll carrying out the instructions given him. Ronnie disappeared from view for a minute or so, then appeared at the counter. The clerk, a mid-twenties stocky guy with a thick goatee and wire-rim glasses, rang the items up, then turned his head and looked directly at Peter. Ronnie's head snapped up, and he said something and the clerk looked quickly away.

Ronnie glanced at Peter, and there was fear in his eyes and sorrow—apologetic sorrow.

He talked. The kid talked.

Peter pushed open the truck's door and stepped out. He crossed the parking lot with long, quick steps. Inside, Ronnie left the counter and ran toward the back of the store. When Peter opened the door, the clerk met him with a shotgun. Peter didn't flinch or hesitate. He grabbed the end of the shotgun's barrel and yanked it from the clerk's hand, then jammed the butt of the gun into the clerk's face. He stumbled back, crashed into the wall of cigarette boxes, and fell to the floor.

Still holding the shotgun, Peter rushed to the back of the store and caught Ronnie by the collar of the shirt just as he was shoving open the back door.

"Get back here, Ronnie." He dragged the kid through the store, Ronnie stumbling and sputtering something about not wanting to die.

At the counter the clerk was just climbing to his feet. Peter pointed the shotgun at him. "Get down and stay down. And keep the cops out of this or I'll be back and it won't end nicely for you."

But Peter knew he'd call as soon as they left. They'd have a description of the truck and Ronnie. There would be state troopers crawling over this area like mice in a cheese factory in no time, helicopters too. It would be an all-out manhunt.

"Grab the drinks, Ronnie."

Ronnie did as he was told and didn't resist when Peter pushed him forward and said, "Get back to the truck."

At the truck Ronnie hesitated. He shook uncontrollably. "Are you gonna shoot me?"

Peter aimed the shotgun at Ronnie's chest. "Get in the truck and start it up."

Eyes wide, Ronnie said, "Dude, you know you could just leave me here. Take the truck. You can have it. I won't call the police, I promise."

"I wish I could trust you, Ronnie; I really do. Besides, your friend in there is going to call the cops as soon as we leave anyway. And I need you in case things get hairy."

"As a hostage? Are you taking me hostage? People don't kill their hostages, right?"

Peter motioned to the driver's seat. "Get in."

This time Ronnie obeyed without further argument.

Peter got in the passenger seat. "Drive." He pointed straight ahead. "That way."

Ronnie shifted the truck into gear and stepped on the gas. The back tires screeched on the concrete and the truck lurched forward.

Peter's face was still hot with anger. His pulse raced. So many things could have gone wrong back there. If there had been other shoppers in the mini-mart or at the pumps... "That was stupid, Ronnie. So stupid."

"I'm sorry, man, okay? I panicked. It's not every day I get carjacked and kidnapped and held hostage."

"Up here," Peter said, pointing to an approaching road on the right. "Turn here."

Ronnie steered the truck onto the road and hit the gas again.

"Drive faster. We need to get out of here quickly."

"You think he's gonna call the cops?"

"Why wouldn't he?"

"'Cause you said you'd come back and kill him."

"That won't stop him."

"I don't know, man. He looked pretty scared."

"Here." Peter motioned toward the next road. "Go left."

They were putting good distance between themselves and the gas station. Ronnie went as fast as he could while still maintaining control.

After a few minutes, Ronnie said, "Are you gonna kill me?"

Peter didn't answer. Instead he continued to give Ronnie instructions. Turn here, turn there, go faster, turn again. They were doing a good job of avoiding primary roads and sticking to secondary and even tertiary roads that were concealed from above by heavy forestation. But still Peter knew he'd need yet another new vehicle, and he'd need to get rid of Ronnie.

"Pull over, Ronnie," Peter said.

"What? Why?"

"Pull over."

Ronnie slowed the truck, pulled to the side of the road, and stopped. His face flushed, and beads of sweat formed on his brow and cheeks. "What're you doing?"

"Get out."

"Why? I don't—"

Peter shoved the barrel of his handgun against the side of Ronnie's head. "Get out."

"You gonna kill me here? In the woods? Dump my body where it won't be found? Is that how you work? I thought you said you needed me. I'm your hostage, remember? Hostages need to be alive to be any good."

"You're no longer needed. Get out."

With his hands up and fear trembling his lips, Ronnie said, "Okay, okay," and exited the truck.

"Listen to me, Ronnie. You're a good kid, you hear me? A good person. The world needs more people like you. Don't ever let anyone tell you differently and don't let anyone make you feel like you're worth less than they are. You aren't. I want you to understand something. Are you listening?"

Ronnie nodded, wiped at the sweat on his forehead.

"That scar and everything it represents played a role in shaping who you are today. You're a fighter, a survivor. You remember that." Peter waved him on with the handgun, motioning toward the forest. "Now walk. Get going."

Ronnie hesitated, looked at the gun, then at Peter, then back at the gun. "You gonna shoot me in the back?"

"You're a survivor. Walk and keep walking until you can't go any farther. Don't turn back. Don't turn around. Just walk. Okay?"

Ronnie nodded and stepped off the road and into the forest. Peter watched until the kid was about a hundred yards away, then got in the truck and took off. He had Ronnie's mobile phone, so even if the kid turned around, he'd have no way of contacting any-one. The nearest town was miles away now, and they hadn't seen a single vehicle on this road or any of the roads around here.

He should have killed the kid—that's what he'd been trained to do—but he couldn't. Ronnie didn't deserve that. As he drove down the road, Peter checked the rearview mirror; he hoped Ronnie would find his way out of all this.

TWENTY-EIGHT

. . .

The road leading into Centralia was as pocked, creviced, and scaled as a crocodile's back. Tendrils of smoke, like the final breath of those occupants who were long ago driven from their small community, rose from the ground as testaments to the memories that were made there, memories of families and lovers and children playing and men working, memories of community and friendship. In the air hung the pungent odor of sulfur and the smell of decades of death.

Highway 61, which had at one time passed through Centralia and brought travelers and business, had been detoured around the town, and now the only way in was the old Route 61, a service road lined with trees stripped of bark and leaves and bleached as white as limestone by the heat radiating up from the underground fire.

Peter Ryan parked the truck along the side of the road and set out on foot. He stuck to the road's shoulder, avoiding the buckles in the pavement. Ahead he could see where the town line had once been. A sign, faded and vandalized and harkening to better times, read *Welcome to Centralia.*

Above, the sky was overcast and gray as slate, the clouds as scarred and rutted as furrowed soil.

All was quiet. Too quiet. No birds sang; no squirrels chattered. The only sound was the distant hum of traffic on the highway as it sped past the abandoned and forgotten town.

Peter stopped and reached his hand around to one of the pistols tucked into the waistline of his pants. It was within easy reach should he need it. Over each shoulder was slung an automatic rifle. He switched off the safety on each. He had come prepared, not knowing what to expect.

Walking forward as if entering the most combative of combat zones, scanning the surrounding woods and growth for anything that appeared threatening or ill-boding, Peter reached the town line and stopped. There were only a few houses left; the rest had been dozed and cleared, empty stone or concrete foundations now overgrown with witch hobble, honeysuckle, and greenbrier the only sign that a home had ever been there. To his right, the road branched but was claimed by underbrush and saplings not thirty yards beyond. To his left, a side street ran a good distance, then turned left. There were two homes on the street: one appeared to have been gutted by fire, its roofless second-story frame jutting upward like blackened fractured bones; the other was obviously abandoned. Windows had been broken out, the front door knocked off one of its hinges, and spray-painted graffiti boasting an assortment of names and a variety of vulgarities covered the exterior walls.

There was no sign of anyone else around, no other vehicles, no cameras. Nothing. The place was as much a ghost town as any forsaken whistle-stop in the old west.

Peter approached a small sinkhole along the side of the road and knelt beside it. A memory hit him then, a flash of summer lightning.

"Welcome to Centralia, Sergeant."

It's that man's voice again. Deep and thick.

He's in a room, white walls, white floor, white ceiling, white table and chair. No pictures, no color. Only one door in or out. The lights are bright—so bright he needs to squint and shield his eyes.

"Are you ready to become the soldier you were born to be? The soldier your country needs?"

He was a soldier? Why didn't he remember being in the military? Or did he remember? There were those flashbacks of combat, Baldy, the dog, the Humvee. But he had no personal ties to any of them. To him, they might as well have been scenes in a movie once watched but not entirely forgotten.

Another flash of memory struck him.

He's bound by his wrists and ankles and strapped to some kind of bed. Above him the white ceiling seems to draw closer as if to crush him.

Then the shocks come, electric jolts in waves, coursing through his body like gunshots, making every muscle tense enough to tear at its moorings, jamming his teeth together, scrambling his eyesight.

He grits his teeth, grinds his molars, and finally, when the torture stops, lets out a hideous holler.

Peter rubbed his eyes and face. What was this place? What kind of horrors had he endured here?

He needed more information. But there was nothing here. It

was an empty town, uncivilized, deserted, left to rot. Why would Karen bring Lilly here?

Peter then remembered the phone number from his dream, the one he'd found in the notepad on the desk. Nichols. He had no recollection of a Nichols, didn't know the name from any other name. But it had to have some meaning if it was in his dream. Nichols had to be someone of some importance to him or his mind wouldn't have stored the name and number. And he wouldn't have found it in the room.

Sticking to the tree line and growth along the side of the road, Peter walked as cautiously as one might traverse a minefield. He went another block, then another. It was more of the same. Gutted homes, barren foundations taken hostage by brush. The ghosts of a perished town, lost memories, forgotten futures. The road was scarred and faded, cracked and littered with witchgrass and waist-high weeds. There were no street signs, no mailboxes. Occasionally he'd see the remnants of a driveway that led to no home, just a barren lot overgrown and claimed by the wild.

Three blocks off what was once the center of town, in a large clearing, stood the shell of a one-story building. The faded and vandalized sign on the facade said it was the elementary school. Most of the windows were knocked out and the words *Do Not Enter* were spray-painted on the front door.

Peter walked the perimeter of the school. It was the only building other than a handful of homes still standing. Why was the school left intact? Why not raze it like they had nearly every other building?

In back of the school were the remains of the playground. A swing set sat undisturbed, the swings still suspended by their chains, waiting for the long-lost children of Centralia to come out for recess. To the right of the swings, a jungle gym sat quietly, the orange paint mostly chipped off. The grass around the school was long but not untidy. It looked as though it hadn't been cut in a couple weeks. Someone was keeping it mowed, keeping the weeds at bay, keeping them from encroaching on the school. The woods and undergrowth that had taken over much of the rest of the town had been warded away from this spot. But why?

Approaching the school, Peter peered through one of the broken-out windows and into what once was a classroom. Desks lay on their sides; chairs were toppled; a thick film of dust covered everything. Scrawled across the blackboard in bold letters were the words *KEEP OUT*. Posters encouraging students to do their best, to persevere, to study hard for a solid future, hung in shreds like torn wallpaper.

Peter looked around the property one more time before climbing through the window and into the school.

Standing in the midst of the decay with the smell of dust and mold in his nose, Peter had another memory, which consisted of nothing more than a series of quick images highlighted by a slow strobe.

He's a kid, no more than twelve, sitting at a desk. Alone. There's no one else in the room.

A teacher enters, female, middle-aged, slender, hair loose around her shoulders. She's wearing a dark skirt and light-blue blouse, plain.

Now the teacher is next to his desk, hovering over him, hands on her hips.

She wags a finger at him. "When will you learn to apply yourself, Mr. Patrick?"

Peter snapped back to the present and the ruin that used to be Centralia Elementary School, but the woman's voice resonated in his head. Not Patrick, but Mr. Patrick.

He moved through the classroom, stepping over and around fallen ceiling tiles and school supplies that spilled from the overturned desks. In the hallway he drew in a deep breath of the musky air and let it out. What little light filtered into this area of the building colored the walls a chalky gray.

The next room was another dilapidated classroom. More fallen ceiling tiles littered this room, like skin peeled away, exposing the electrical circuitry overhead. Peter tried the light switch, but nothing happened. He really didn't expect the electricity to still be on.

In another part of the building, several rooms down the hallway, as faint as the movements of ghosts, he heard the scuff of shoes on tile.

TWENTY-NINE

. . .

Peter's first thought was that the sound had come from a vagabond who'd found shelter from nature's mood swings in the abandoned school. After all, someone had broken the windows. Someone had trashed the rooms. Someone had colored the walls with graffiti. He was certain this old building housed more than just forgotten lectures and misplaced homework assignments, that it had become home to many a homeless traveler, especially during the colder months.

Peter withdrew the handgun from his waistband and held it in front of him with both hands. It might only be a drifter seeking shelter, but he didn't want to take any chances.

Moving slowly down the hallway, sticking close to the wall, Peter checked and cleared each room. He was no less careful than if he'd been searching for a lost child, maybe his own Lilly.

Again he heard the shuffling, the scuffing of soles. This time he was able to pinpoint the location of the sound: it came from the far east end of the building.

Peter followed the direction of the sound and entered what appeared to be the school's library. This room was carpeted and most of the space was taken up with rows of bookshelves. Many of the shelves had been cleared, but what books remained were scattered on the floor, pages splayed, bindings broken, like a mass collection of dead birds with fractured wings. Whoever had been in here, vagabond or vandal, was obviously not a lover of books.

Stepping from aisle to aisle, Peter swept the gun back and forth. And though his pulse thumped out a quick rhythm in his neck, his finger was steady.

When Peter was confident the library was clear, he moved to the next room, which turned out to be the cafeteria. The tables remained, rows of them, but the ceiling had been totally ripped out, and the mineral-fiber tiles lay broken and crumbled on the tabletops and floor. A row of windows lined the far wall, some of them broken, the ones still intact covered with cloudy grime. Light illuminated the large room and accented the decay that had taken place over the decades.

From the kitchen area came a rattle, then a clatter, like metal on tile. Peter hurried to the wall and followed it around to the kitchen entrance, listening for the now-familiar scuffing of shoes.

The kitchen consisted of four large steel islands, three industrial-size ovens with six-burner stove tops, three stainless refrigerators, and three upright freezers. Compared to the rest of the building, the kitchen had fared well against the decay and wasting that passing time encouraged. A few pots lay on the floor by one of the stoves, and a collection of cutting boards of various sizes and thicknesses had been tossed around the large room as if someone had grown bored of walking the halls and decided to play Frisbee with them. A coffeemaker had also been pushed over, the tile floor stained brown around it. But the appliances did not appear to be in disrepair, the ceiling tiles remained overhead, and surprisingly there was no half-eaten food decaying on the islands.

Peter inched into the kitchen, moving silently and slowly, sweeping his eyes over the floor and around the islands, listening, watching.

Behind him something moved, a muted scraping, then scratching. He spun, pointing the gun at one of the refrigerators, and nearly pulled the trigger when something gray and quick jumped out from between the refrigerator and its neighboring freezer.

It was a cat, more afraid of Peter than of his gun and the bullet that could have stolen one of its lives. The thing slipped on the floor, its legs going like they were attached to electric motors, then finally found its footing and tore out of the kitchen.

Peter lowered his weapon and leaned against one of the islands, letting the breath out of his lungs. He left the kitchen and the cafeteria and made his way back down the hall to the other end of the building. He wanted to check out the offices and gymnasium. There had to be something in this town that would give him a clue—some reason Lilly would send him here. So far Centralia offered nothing but a few disjointed memories that had no connection to anything tangible.

At the gymnasium Peter stopped before opening the double doors that led to the basketball court. Another memory was there, displaced and poking its way into his mind.

He's a kid again, twelve or thirteen, skinny as a rail and standing in the middle of a basketball court. Other kids are there, mulling around, talking, laughing. Some shoot hoops; some stand in a circle and hit a volleyball around. But not him. He's alone.

Something plunks him in the back, between the shoulder blades. He turns and finds a volleyball bouncing at his feet. Picking it up, he looks around.

"Over here, Sped."

He looks to his left and sees a couple guys standing there, staring at him with expectant looks on their faces.

One of them holds out his hands. "Well, you gonna give it here or what?"

He tosses the ball. It bounces twice before reaching them.

The taller of the three shakes his head. "When you gonna learn to stop throwing like a girl? And you wonder why we call you Sped."

One of the others laughs and as he turns away says, "Jed the Sped strikes again."

Peter rubbed his face. *Jed.* The name triggered no recognition. He couldn't be sure the memory was even accurate. For all he knew, it was nothing more than a collection of odd images and moments in time jumbled together, much like a dream.

He swung open the doors to the gym and stepped through the doorway. Daylight barely reached this part of the building. There was only a single row of narrow windows near the ceiling, and they were soiled with water stains and smut. The gym appeared mostly untouched. The wood floor was covered with a thin film of dust. The basketball hoops were still intact; even the nets still hung from the rims. The place looked nearly ready to host the next Friday night game. But something seemed out of place on the far end. The floor didn't look right, like an object had fallen from the ceiling and embedded itself in the hardwood.

Peter slipped the handgun back into the waistline of his pants and, sticking close to the bleachers, walked the sideline. At half court he stopped. The far end of the gym floor, near the exit, had buckled and caved as if giant hands had lifted it and folded it in on itself, cutting off one whole corner of the court and pulling some of the bleachers down as well. There must have been a sinkhole under that corner of the building, and over time, without the careful eye of a building inspector to diagnose the problem and prescribe a fix, gravity had gained the victory and pulled the foundation and flooring down toward the burning veins of coal beneath the surface.

Walking out onto the court, Peter approached the sinkhole and stood at the edge. The flooring before him sloped at a forty-five-degree angle, creating a gulf of five feet between the intact portion and the portion that had given way to the crumbling earth beneath it. The crevice stood open like a gaping mouth with an endless throat, so deep and black that it appeared to be solid matter. The hole belched a steady flow of air hot enough to singe and rank with the odor of sulfur.

Peter backed away from the crevice. Eventually the hole would grow, more ground would give way, and the entire gymnasium would be swallowed up. The earth here was hungry, and the fire beneath it was unquenchable.

Peter wondered if his very presence would shift the balance of the floor, maybe the entire building, and expedite the inevitable. In fact, if he stood completely still, he thought he could feel the floor shifting beneath his feet, moving on unstable ground.

And then he heard it. Crying. More like a soft whimper than a sob. Peter froze and listened, the hairs on the back of his neck standing on end. It was Lilly. He knew his own daughter's cry as well as he knew the sound of her laugh or voice. Suddenly his heart was in his throat, and he moved quickly across the gym, no longer concerned about upsetting the precarious balance of the floor on the edge of the earth.

He knocked through the double doors, back into the hallway, and stood still, listening. The crying was louder now, closer. *Oh, Lilly.* He rounded the corner and caught a glimpse of a figure, small, petite—Lilly—entering the office suite.

Peter followed, not caring about anything other than holding his little girl again. He reached the door to the suite and pulled it open. This area seemed untouched by the passage of time. Desks stood on their legs, chairs remained upright. On one of the desks a stack of papers remained in place, not a single sheet disturbed. Peter glanced back at the entrance, half-expecting to see a bustling school full of children on the other side of the sliding window at the receptionist area.

"Lilly?" His voice echoed in the empty place.

The crying had stopped.

Peter walked over to one of the desks and lifted a sheet of paper from the out-bin. It was dated October 17, twenty years ago.

Weaving around several desks, Peter called for his daughter, but still there was no answer. The suite consisted of the common come-and-go area and then offices: principal, vice principal, and nurse's station.

Somewhere toward the back of the suite, in one of the far offices, he heard the scuffing again, then the quiet, frightened whimper.

"Lilly," Peter called. "I'm coming, baby. Hold on. Daddy's here."

Bypassing the principal's and vice principal's offices, he went directly to the nurse's station and opened the door. The crying stopped again. There was a small desk, a couple chairs, a cot, and a metal supply cupboard in the room, all appearing as they did two decades ago, the last time the nurse occupied this office and fulfilled her duties. The faint aroma of alcohol rubs still hung in the air.

"Lilly? Baby? You in here?"

But his inquiry was met with silence.

Then: "Peter."

Karen's voice. Behind him. Peter swung around and incredibly found Karen standing in the doorway of the office. His legs nearly buckled. She smiled at him, then stepped away and disappeared into the hallway.

Peter rushed out of the room after her, dashed down the short hallway to the come-and-go area, and was met by Baldy pointing a gun at him. A white bandage covered half his face, and his left hand was wrapped heavily in gauze.

"Stay there, Patrick," he said, holding his weapon shoulder-high.

THIRTY

• • •

Instinctively Peter went for his gun, but Baldy advanced and gripped his own pistol with both hands. There was an intensity in his eyes that Peter hadn't seen before, even when he was shoving the man's face onto a hot grill. "No, you don't. Keep your hands where I can see them."

Peter looked over Baldy's shoulder but didn't see Karen. She'd disappeared as if into thin air, as if she were nothing more than an illusion, a sleight-of-hand trick played on him by a master magician. He nearly climbed out of his skin. He glanced behind him at the nurse's office door, expecting Lilly to appear or at least call to him. But there was nothing.

"You don't understand," Peter said. "My wife. My daughter."

He took a step, but Baldy blocked his advance. "Hands where I can see them, Patrick."

"No! I need to get to them."

"Hands where I can see them!"

Peter stepped forward, stopped, stepped again. He tightened the muscles in his arms, clenched his fists. He could make a run for it, charge the big guy. He wouldn't be expecting that, and it might just catch him with his guard down even for a split second.

But as if Baldy were the magician and also had the ability to read minds, he too moved in. They were less than ten feet apart now. "I said, hands where I can see them."

Baldy didn't appear to be the kind of man to give commands he didn't expect to be obeyed. Peter stopped and raised his hands to shoulder height.

"Please. My wife." He couldn't let Karen get away. Somehow she had found him. It was unbelievable, and yet he had seen her just as plain as day. And Lilly was still in the room behind him. He stepped back but stopped when Baldy inched forward.

Holding the gun in front of him at an arm's length, Baldy said, "They're not real."

Peter shook his head. "No, they are real. I saw them." Baldy was trying to play mind games with him.

"Patrick, listen to me. They're not real."

"I saw them."

"You saw a hallucination. You saw what you wanted to see."

No. It couldn't be. Baldy was lying, attempting to trick Peter, to get inside his head and scramble his ability to reason. Karen was there, as was Lilly. He'd not only seen them but heard their voices. He thought he even caught a faint whiff of Karen's perfume. "No." Peter scratched above his right ear. He refused to believe it.

"It's a hallucinogen. It's in the air coming from the crevice in the gym. It makes you see what you want to see."

Again Peter shook his head. "No." But now he wasn't even convinced by his own denial. "Who? Who's behind this?"

"I can help you," Baldy said.

"Help me what?"

"I can help you find your wife and daughter."

Peter jerked like someone had hit him. "You know where they are?"

Still holding the gun on Peter, Baldy said, "I know more than I should."

Peter mentally relaxed a bit, but his muscles remained coiled for action. He was near the principal's office and could make a dive for the doorway, test Baldy's reflexes and aim. But at this range, it would be a fatal move. Even an amateur could hit a large moving target at ten feet. And the big man in front of him did not appear to be an amateur in any way.

Baldy once more showed his propensity for telepathy, or possibly he was just great at reading and interpreting body language. He said, "Pull your weapons out slowly and toss them on the floor."

Peter did as he was instructed and tossed the handguns in front of him. They clanged on the floor and slid to about two feet in front of Baldy.

"Now the automatics," Baldy said, motioning toward the rifles slung over Peter's shoulders.

Peter obeyed and slipped the rifles off his shoulders and tossed them onto the floor. The only defense he had now was his hands, should it come to that. Again he searched the space over Baldy's shoulder, hoping the hit man was wrong and that Karen was real and was there. It was nothing but empty office space. Maybe his mind had concocted the whole thing. Maybe his captor was right about the hallucinogen.

Baldy motioned again with his pistol, this time to the right. "Over there, against the wall. And keep your hands where I can see them."

Peter sidestepped to the wall. "Where are Karen and Lilly?"

"We'll get to that later."

At the wall Peter stopped with his back against it, hands still in the air, palms forward. "We'll get to it now."

Baldy shook his head. "Patrick, you're not calling the shots. Not this time. I need your help."

"My help? For what?"

"We'll get to that later too."

"How do I know you won't just kill me? You tried to before."

Baldy smirked. "If I wanted to kill you, you'd be dead already."

"What's your name?"

"Habit. Lawrence." Habit tilted his head a little to the right and studied Peter. "You don't remember me at all, do you?"

Peter lowered his hands to his waist. Habit was familiar to him, but he couldn't recall where he'd seen the big guy before outside the splinter memories he'd had. "Should I?"

"No. You shouldn't. Not after what they did to you." He paused and stared at Peter. "But you do, don't you? You're beginning to remember."

Peter said nothing. Remember what? What had he forgotten?

"And that's why they're after you," Habit said.

"Where are my wife and daughter?"

Habit pointed at one of the desks in the come-and-go area. "Sit down, Patrick."

"I'll stand. Why do you keep calling me Patrick?"

"That's your name. Jed Patrick."

Jed Patrick. *Jed the Sped*. It meant nothing to him, though. It was just a name and might as well have been pulled out of some unknown book in some remote library. And yet it lined up with the images and snippets he'd been recalling. Amy's words came back to him: *"Things aren't what they seem. They're not what you think."*

"My name is Peter Ryan." But he wasn't convinced of that anymore.

"That's the name they gave you. Your real name is Jed Patrick."

Peter's head began to swim frantically as if caught in a whirlpool that sucked and pulled at his sanity. He sat on the corner of the desk and rubbed his temple. The name they gave him. They. Who? *"Things aren't what they seem."*

"Who gave me?"

"The agency."

"They're not what you think."

"Agency. What agency? I don't remember any agency."

A memory hit him, the same memory as before:

"Welcome to Centralia, Sergeant."

It's that man's voice again. Deep and thick.

He's in a room, white walls, white floor, white ceiling, white table and chair. No pictures, no color. Only one door in or out. The lights are bright, so bright he needs to squint and shield his eyes.

"Are you ready to become the soldier you were born to be? The soldier your country needs?"

Keeping his handgun trained on Peter, Habit said, "I only know them as the agency. They're government, though."

"Centralia."

"Yeah. The Centralia Project. You remember?"

Peter stared at the floor. "Only images, moments. Brief. So brief. Bits and pieces of something." But his memories were so disjointed, like a scattering of puzzle pieces from three different puzzles, so jarring and disconnected they made no sense.

"It's a military project. I think it falls under the DOD, but no one can be sure. It's got no direct lines to anyone or anything, so there can be no blame, no accountability, no oversight."

The images of the Humvee were there again too. The explosion, the gunfire, the blood. Peter looked at Habit. "I was a soldier."

"Sergeant."

"What?"

"*Sergeant* Jed Patrick. Army Rangers."

Again, it meant nothing to him. Not the name, not the title. There was no sense of pride. No sense of duty. Habit might as well have been speaking of a total stranger, a fictional character he had created. Peter's true memories, the ones he recognized and could identify with, the ones that defined him and who he really was, only went so far as to label him Peter Ryan, psychobiology research assistant. "I'm a researcher."

Habit shook his head. "No, you're not. Not really."

The strange man's deep, thick voice echoed through Peter's head. *"Welcome to Centralia, Sergeant."*

"Things aren't what they seem. They're not what you think."

Then who was Amy? How did she know...? A deep, familiar sense of betrayal shuddered through Peter. Anger ignited inside him and bloomed in his chest.

"Who's in charge?" he asked Habit. "Who runs Centralia?"

"The man we've got to find: Nichols."

THIRTY-ONE

· · ·

"Nichols?"

"Yeah, but he's a ghost. He doesn't exist anywhere. You'll find no record of him; he's on no payroll. I don't even know if that's his real name. I doubt it is."

Peter couldn't make sense of this. It was too much. This man, who'd nearly killed him, was asking him to believe that the very reality he knew and understood was all a lie. Where was the truth? How could he find it? Was there any such thing, or was it all just a matter of whose perspective, whose spin on the facts?

But even as the thought occurred to him, he knew it was faulty reasoning. Regardless of any lies that were fed to him, something had *actually* happened. Truth—reality—was more than just the way somebody told the story or the way he remembered it. He just had to find a way to sift the truth out of it, like panning for gold—whatever's real will settle at the bottom.

Maybe this man, his captor, had some of the answers, but could Peter trust Habit? The guy might be the one feeding him a bunch of lies, luring him in as one would a starving dog with a slab of raw meat only to capture it in a kennel and haul it away to be euthanized. He might be feigning camaraderie when his intent was catastrophe.

But there was a Mr. Nichols. That much at least was corroborated by his dream. And Peter had a phone number to go with it. But how had he ever learned the number? How did he know this Nichols? How did that information wind up in his dream? Somewhere and at some time, Peter must have had some interaction with Nichols, even if it wasn't directly.

"I have his phone number," Peter said.

"Who?"

"Nichols. And what about Abernathy? Do you know him?"

Habit paused and shifted his eyes. "Abernathy." He said it like he was surprised Peter knew the name. "If Nichols is a ghost, then Abernathy is a mere idea. He has nothing to do with this now. Not anymore. Though if he did…" Habit tensed his jaw for a moment, then winced at the pain this must have caused in his cheek. "How did you come by Nichols's number?" Habit seemed truly surprised that Peter would possess the number of such an enigmatic man, as if the number was more elusive than Nichols himself.

Peter wasn't sure he wanted to tell Habit the truth. Just yesterday Habit might have killed him if Peter hadn't grilled his face. "That's none of your business."

Habit's eyes narrowed. "You forget I'm the one holding the gun."

Peter glared at him.

"And," Habit continued, "I'm the one who can help you find your wife and daughter. Karen and Lilly, right?"

The way Habit said their names, with a kind of familiarity he didn't deserve to have, made Peter's skin burn with anger. He slapped the desk and jumped to his feet. "Where are they?"

Habit took a step closer and tensed. "Sit back down, Patrick. Not so quick. I have something I need you to do first."

• • •

Lawrence Habit was in no mood to negotiate. This was survival time. Kill or be killed. He had to get to Nichols, and Patrick was his way in. He had no idea how Patrick could have gotten Nichols's phone number, but if he was telling the truth, that number was worth a trainload of gold to Lawrence.

Patrick sat back down on the desk, his hands balled into fists, neck tense and veins bulging. Lawrence had seen him like this before, on the field of battle, in the heat of a mission.

"Here's the deal," Lawrence said. "You get me to Nichols and I'll get you the truth about your wife and kid."

"Why do you want Nichols?"

Lawrence smiled. "Now that's none of *your* business."

"What do you want me to do?" Patrick was ready to concede. Lawrence knew he would. The guy's family instinct was too strong; it was always his weakness. No matter how hard the agency tried, they couldn't scrub him of that. "I want you to call Nichols, arrange a meeting with him."

Patrick's face showed no emotion, but Lawrence knew he was surprised by the request. "How do you know he'll meet with me?"

"Oh, he'll meet with you. Trust me. You're a top priority."

Patrick seemed to think about that. He pushed his hand through his hair, rubbed his face, the back of his neck, then his temples. Finally, "Okay. Then what?"

"Then you let me handle it from there. You just get Nichols out in the open. Get him to reveal himself. He will for you." Lawrence shook the gun at Patrick. "You really don't know how special you are, do you?"

Patrick's eyes dropped to the floor. "I don't even know who I am."

"I told you. You're Sergeant Jed Patrick, Army Rangers." Lawrence could see Patrick didn't believe it, though. "It'll come back to you. Give it time."

• • •

Jed Patrick. Peter said the name over and over again in his mind, tried to imagine Karen saying it, tried to hear her voice saying *Jed.* But there was nothing there, no recognition.

"Do I have your cooperation?" Habit asked.

Peter said, "Do I have a choice?"

"You always have a choice. Life and death, it's always a choice."

"Tell me what you know about Nichols and the agency. Why can't I remember? What are they doing with Karen and Lilly?"

Habit wagged a finger at Peter. "That's not how it works, Patrick. You don't get to negotiate here. You only say whether you want a chance to recover your wife and kid. That's it. We get through this with Nichols out of the picture, and I'll tell you everything I know. Until then, I've already told you too much."

"Too much? You haven't told me anything."

"I told you your real name, and I gave you the name of the man behind your problems. And I gave you my word that I'll take care of him. Isn't that enough?"

It wasn't enough, though. Not nearly enough. Peter had so many questions that had gone unanswered. But Habit wouldn't waver. That wasn't his style. "What do you need me to do?"

"You got a phone?"

He still had Ronnie's smartphone. "Yes."

"Good. Call Nichols. Tell him you want to talk. In the open. Tell him he needs to come to you. He needs to come to the surface."

"What does that mean?"

"You'll understand in time."

"And what if he doesn't come?"

Habit smiled and shook his head. "You don't get it. For you, he'll come. You're worth so much to him. And you could do so much damage. People like him are all about self-preservation, covering their tracks, avoiding exposure."

Peter didn't like the sound of the deal. It was too risky, and there wasn't enough assurance for him that Habit would uphold his end. "And how do I know you won't just kill me too?"

Habit's smile melted and he furrowed his brow. "I'm not like that, Patrick. If you remembered me, you'd know that."

"You already tried to kill me."

"I was trying to bring you in. That's how bad they wanted you. But that was different, anyway. It was work, an assignment, nothing personal."

"So what's changed now?"

"Everything. I don't work for them anymore, and now it's personal. You do this, you get Nichols in the open, and I'll keep my word." He pointed at the bandage covering his face, protecting the burns Peter had caused. "I'll even forgive this and let it go." His eyes unfocused for a moment, looking at something beyond the confines of this room, this town. "After all, it's the least I can do."

"Why is it so important for you to get Nichols?"

The grin was there again, pushing Habit's eyes into crescents. "That's not your concern. Stay focused, Patrick. That's what you were always so good at."

"And what if I say no to this whole plan? What if I want to take my own chances at finding my family? What then?"

"Like I said, you have no choice here but life and death. That's it. Accept my help and live, or I leave you for the wolves, and your wife and kid lose all hope of ever seeing the sunshine again. Believe me: Nichols will keep sending his goons in greater numbers, and they won't stop coming until you're in custody or dead."

THIRTY-TWO

. . .

They took her daughter again. Three men—three different men—came and escorted her out of the room. The woman fought them this time; she ran at them, swinging her arms, kicking her feet, hollering like a mother bear bent on fighting to the death. It wasn't like her; she wasn't the violent type. Never had she lashed out at her husband; never had she struck her daughter. Never before had she balled her hands into fists and gone after someone with all the latent fury and ferocity within her. But all it got her this time, her first time, was a swollen lip and a bruised cheekbone. Regardless of the indignation her vigilance ignited, she found out rather quickly that she was no match for three men.

She knew they'd be torturing her daughter again, and it drove her nearly mad. They could call it whatever they wanted to, but it was torture. They were torturing an eight-year-old.

Her daughter, God bless her, never showed any fear. She willingly stepped forth, her faith intact even if her emotions were shaken, and kept telling the woman that she'd be okay, that God would protect her, that he would comfort her. He wouldn't let anything happen to her.

The woman wished she had that kind of faith. She wished she could be as steadfast. So fierce was her mettle that in spite of several blows to the head and face and one to the abdomen, she fought the men right up until they shut the door; then she fell to her knees and railed at God. Why had he allowed this to happen? How could he just stand by and let them abuse her daughter, her precious little girl? How could he reward a child's faith with such disinterest?

And she cried—oh, how she cried. The tears poured from her eyes like water from a hose. She cried until she had no more tears to cry, until her head throbbed and her throat was as raw as if she'd swallowed barbed wire. She was so helpless and the situation was so hopeless. What kind of a mother couldn't protect her daughter?

The anger intensified then to rage, against the men for taking her baby, against her husband for abandoning them, against God for doing nothing. For what seemed an hour, she pounded the bed and pulled at her hair.

And then, fully exhausted and drenched in sweat, she cried again. But this time it was tears of remorse and sorrow that leaked from her eyes. This time, as she fell to her knees, it was not to question or accuse God but rather to petition him, to beg his forgiveness, to ask for strength and courage and most of all faith. Her husband had not abandoned them. God had not deserted them. He was there; he was very present.

Her daughter knew that. The woman knew it too.

• • •

Peter Ryan clutched the phone in his hand and stared up at the late morning sky as if expecting the clouds to suddenly reconfigure and form a map showing him the way to Karen and Lilly, giving him a way out of the fix he'd found himself in. The cloud cover that had previously blanketed the area was breaking up, revealing patches of bright blue. But other than clouds, the sky was empty. No birds flew overhead; no contrails from planes striped the sky; no messages materialized; no maps appeared. And the town was still eerily quiet.

Habit had taken Peter's guns and given him precise instructions. He was to go to an abandoned house on what used to be Elm Street, call Nichols, and demand he meet Peter outside the house. Alone.

Peter didn't like the plan. It left him too exposed. Men from the agency had been after him since yesterday morning. What would keep them from coming for him now? And he still didn't trust Habit. Peter had been backed into a corner with the only way out directing him into a trap. But if he ever wanted to see Karen and Lilly again, he'd have to go along for now, comply and take his chances, and somehow stay alive.

The house was not much of a home anymore. All the windows had been busted out, the paint had peeled and disintegrated decades ago, and the wood trim was bare, worn smooth by years of exposure to rain, sleet, snow, and wind. The roof had caved in on the east end, leaving a gaping hole the size of a small car. The sidewalk leading up to the house lay splintered and cracked. Whole slabs jutted out of the ground as if the soil beneath had opened its mouth and attempted to swallow the walkway only to spit it out again after chipping its teeth. Lastly, the house had shifted atop a crumbling foundation, creating a kind of lopsided fun house where the only thrills one would experience were the near-death type. Peter half expected a machine gun–toting clown to emerge at any moment and welcome visitors to his house of confusion.

Forcing his hand to move, Peter put the battery back into the device and dialed the number from his dream.

After two rings a man answered. "Peter? Is that you?"

The voice. It was the man from his flashbacks. *"Welcome to Centralia, Sergeant. Are you ready to become the soldier you were born to be? The soldier your country needs?"*

As Peter expected, they were waiting to track Ronnie's number and triangulate his location. But it didn't matter now, since the whole purpose of the call was to arrange a little face-to-face. And it only made sense that Nichols would know, would be expecting this call. Like the creator of a fantastically creepy world where nothing was as it seemed but much more mysterious and bizarre, Nichols had been there from the beginning, whenever that was, lording his command, reveling in his control. He held the key to Peter's identity. The memory flashed back so quickly it nearly caused him to drop the phone. The water. The suffocating, drowning. *"Ryan, get up!"*

That voice.

"Peter. Are you there, son?"

Anger clawed at Peter's gut and climbed into his chest and up his throat. He clutched the phone so tight he felt he could easily crack its casing. "Who are you?"

"Who I am is irrelevant to you, Peter. We need to talk, don't we?"

"Who am I? What did you do to me?"

"You don't remember?" There was a pause, a few awkward beats of silence. Then, "But it's coming back to you, isn't it?"

Peter remained quiet while he struggled to calm himself. Anger

clouded the mind and made a person more prone to foolish decisions. And besides, he didn't want Nichols to hear the desperation
in his voice. Finally he said, "Where are my wife and daughter?"

"We need to talk, Peter. Straighten all this out. You deserve to
know. Why don't I send some of my men to get you, and we can
talk in a safe place."

And be trapped and shot like a dog? "No. We talk out here in
the open."

Another long pause—so long, in fact, that Peter thought Nichols
had disconnected. "Okay then. It'll be your way. I'll come to you.
But I hope you see this as the gesture of goodwill that it is."

"Of course."

"Where are you?"

Either he genuinely didn't know yet where Peter was or he was
bluffing, feigning ignorance so as not to raise Peter's sense of alarm
and alertness.

Peter said, "By the old house on Elm Street, the only one left
standing."

"I know it." And then the phone went dead.

Peter stood there for a few seconds with the phone still to his
ear, his heart thundering, sweat beading on his brow and chin. He'd
have one chance at this. He'd determined already that he couldn't
trust Habit to keep his word. After he killed Nichols, he'd kill Peter.
So Peter had to quickly formulate a plan to both get the information he needed from Nichols and get out alive.

Peter checked his watch. Five minutes had ticked by and no
sign of Nichols. Then ten minutes. Fifteen. He was about to leave
when he heard footsteps inside the house, floorboards creaking,
shoes scuffing.

A middle-aged man emerged from the dilapidated structure just as casually as if he lived there and was exiting to welcome visitors to his humble dwelling. No more than sixty, Nichols was slightly overweight, thick in the midsection, with rounded shoulders. His eyes were heavy and tired, and he had thick jowls, like a bulldog. A healthy crop of white hair sat atop his head, ruffled and mussed. He wore a white shirt, tan dress pants, and a tie loosened around his neck. Not appropriate attire for a man who apparently spent his time hiding out in abandoned homes.

To the surface, Peter thought. There must be an entrance in the house to an underground structure. The ramshackle house was merely a front, the tip of an iceberg or network of icebergs housing a government agency as ghostlike and shadowy as any paranormal hunter's film negatives.

Nichols stepped down off the porch and carefully navigated the ruined sidewalk.

Nothing about the man was familiar to Peter. Not his face or his dress or the way he walked. If he'd ever known Nichols, if he'd ever seen him before, he didn't remember it now.

Stepping onto the road, Nichols walked up to Peter and said, "We really need to do something about that sidewalk, huh?"

Peter said nothing. He looked past Nichols at the house. It appeared empty, but appearances could be deceiving. Nichols would be an important man, and men like him rarely, if ever, traveled alone. He had backup; they were in there, hidden in the shadows, looming in the darkened places. Habit must know it too. Peter didn't know where the big guy was, but he assumed Habit remained at a safe distance, ready to pick off Nichols with one squeeze of the trigger.

Nichols stuck out his hand. "Peter Ryan, what a pleasure it is to meet you. Again."

In another place and another time Nichols would appear to be anyone's father or grandfather, a gentle man, cordial, polite, friendly. But here, he was a menace and a phony, every movement calculated, every sentence carefully parsed. And for this reason Peter didn't shake his hand. "Don't you mean Jed Patrick?"

Nichols smiled. "Your name is Peter Ryan." He looked deep into Peter's eyes as if through them he could peer directly into a place he'd been before and had spent some time: Peter's soul. "But I think you know that."

Peter stared back at him, feeling naked and vulnerable and trying not to show the emotion that was building within him. He didn't know it. Or did he?

Nichols tilted his head to one side. "What is it you want, son?"

Peter didn't know what Habit's plan was. He presumed there would be a shot, a single shot, that would drop Nichols. But he'd also presumed it would have happened fairly quickly. What was Habit waiting for?

"Why were those men trying to kill me yesterday?"

Nichols sighed, shook his head. "I'm afraid that was a misunderstanding. A terrible misunderstanding. And unfortunately it cost a few lives." Nichols coughed, then coughed again, harder this time. The cough quickly became a hack, loud, forceful. His face turned red; he loosened his tie even more as his coughing fit continued, almost doubling him at the waist.

Peter was considering what to do when Nichols stopped coughing and stood upright and somehow had a gun in his hand. He pointed it at Peter's head. They were more than an arm's length apart, taking away any defense the quicker Peter might have had if they were closer.

Peter took another step backward.

"Hands where I can see them," Nichols said.

Peter turned his palms toward the older man.

"On your knees." Nichols motioned with the gun toward the pavement. "Now."

Peter hesitated. Where was Habit? Why hadn't he taken the shot? Maybe he was in it with Nichols. Maybe this was a ploy to take Peter alive. But Habit had had Peter at gunpoint in the school. He could have taken him then. Why hadn't he?

Peter's heart raced like the hooves of a herd of wild stallions. Something had to happen now; he had to do something.

Nichols took a step closer. "Now, Peter! On your knees."

Suddenly the concussion of gunfire sounded, and Nichols's head snapped back.

THIRTY-THREE

• • •

Nichols wobbled on his feet like a bowling pin. His eyes were empty windows; his mouth hung slack. A hole the size of a dime near his hairline oozed bright-red blood.

Two things happened simultaneously then: Peter noticed two gunmen taking aim in the windows flanking the front door of the house, and before Nichols's knees could buckle and carry his weight to the ground, Peter stepped forward, grabbed the gun with his right hand, spun the older man around, and fired two shots at the window to the left of the door. Both shots caught the shooter in the upper chest. He toppled out of the window, lifeless. The other gunman ducked back behind the wall, but without hesitation, Peter aimed and squeezed off three rounds, placing them in the exterior wall between the window and the doorframe. The walls of the old home were thin, and the asbestos siding did nothing to stop a bullet traveling more than two thousand feet per second. The gunman dropped and landed in the doorway.

Peter let go of Nichols and, still clutching the gun, hurried up to the house and entered it. Inside, the air was still, and light was sparse. The doorway opened into what would have been the living room if the house were indeed a home where a family dwelled instead of a facade for a covert government agency. To the right was another, smaller room, and behind it, to the rear of the home, was the kitchen.

Sticking close to the wall, Peter searched and cleared each room. Occasionally he'd peer from one of the broken-out windows to make sure Habit wasn't coming to gloat about his kill and then finish Peter off.

After checking the entire first floor, Peter headed up the stairs, every sense alert. He needed to make sure there weren't more gunmen in the house waiting for an opportune moment to ambush him from behind.

The second story consisted of three bedrooms and a bathroom. In each bedroom was a closet. Peter checked them all, still keeping watch out the windows for Habit. But if Habit had stuck around after the shot, he wasn't celebrating his victory over Nichols in the open. He was nowhere to be seen.

From the second story, Peter returned to the first floor and found the door to the cellar. The door opened on a wooden staircase, which descended into a dimly lit cavern. Gun out in front and held tight with both hands, Peter took the steps one at a time, pausing on each one to listen. If there was a secret passageway to some underground bunker, the cellar was where he'd find it. And if backup was coming, which no doubt it was, that was where they would emerge.

Midway down the steps, Peter got a look at the cellar. Hazy light filtered through four small windows in minimal amounts. Dust floated in the air, riding subtle currents that wafted from the open door to the first floor. The foundation walls were constructed of fieldstone; the concrete holding the stones together had long ago begun to crumble, leaving piles of dust on the dirt floor. The rafters supporting the first-story flooring held an intricate network of cobwebs tying them all together. The entire webbed labyrinth looked to be more intricate than anything a team of structural engineers could reproduce.

The area was clear of clutter. In the far corner was a utility sink and next to it, a thick wooden workbench. And in the center of the cellar sat a rotund coal furnace rising from floor to ceiling. From it reached eight round ducts like the arms of a manacled octopus imprisoned in this dungeon below the house.

Peter followed the north wall of the cellar to a door secured by two slide bolts and a hook-and-eye lock. Peter disengaged all three and opened the door. It creaked on hinges as dry as old bones. Behind it lay a root cellar under the front porch. The room was no more than eight by eight and housed a collection of old containers and boxes. It smelled of mildew and mold. Peter moved some of the boxes to the side and there found another door, but this one didn't fit the surrounding motif. It was protected by a small biometric fingerprint lock concealed inside a gray box.

Hesitantly Peter placed his thumb on the scanner. He didn't expect anything to happen, but a second later it blinked green and the door's lock disengaged. He'd been there before, several times maybe. But how? He remembered none of it.

The door opened to another passageway descending farther into the ground beneath the house. Walls, ceiling, and floor were all concrete, and the total height was just over six feet, barely tall enough for Peter to stand in. Exposed lightbulbs every fifty feet or so illuminated the corridor, which wound its way deeper and deeper into the earth. At the same intervals were one-foot-by-one-foot metal ceiling vents. Peter stayed close to the concrete walls, stepping carefully to avoid making any noise. There had to be some kind of alarm system that sounded an alert when the door was unlocked. Surely whoever was at the other end of the tunnel monitored such things.

But why hadn't they sent anyone after him? Stuck in this tunnel, he was easy prey for a team of men with automatic weapons. There were only two explanations: this was a trap and an end consisting of automatic weapons was still in his future, or Habit had been telling the truth about them wanting to take him alive.

Either way, he'd keep going, keep moving ahead. Karen and Lilly were somewhere at the other end of the tunnel. He'd stay alert, remain quiet, and be ready to strike when needed.

The corridor descended in a spiral fashion, some of it sloped concrete, some of it wide but shallow steps. Around every bend, Peter expected to find men waiting, prepared to light the place up and destroy him, but the tunnel was empty.

A humming began, quiet, almost unnoticeable, like the machinery of a distant factory. Coming from the walls. Or the ceiling, maybe. Peter put his hand on the wall; the concrete vibrated. He then put his hand to the ceiling vent. Cool air poured out. The air-conditioning had kicked on. But why? Underground it was cool; there was no need for air-conditioning.

Quickly Peter turned from the vent, covered his mouth, and drew in a deep breath. There was something in the air—had to be. Whether it was the hallucinogen he'd experienced in the school or a toxic element, he had no doubt that what came out of the vents was anything but innocent.

Picking up his pace, he continued down the tunnel, still staying close to the wall. He had no idea how long he could hold his breath but figured no more than two minutes. He had to get to the end of the tunnel before he needed to breathe.

If he encountered any resistance, he'd have to make quick work of them, which meant he'd have to take risks. Fortunately he found the end of the corridor before the oxygen in his lungs was spent. And there was another door.

This door had no lock, only a simple lever handle. Peter depressed it and slipped through the doorway, shutting the door behind him and filling his lungs with clean, filtered, recirculated air. To his right and left was an empty concrete hallway fifty feet in either direction. Solid plain doors lined each wall, four to a side. Holding the gun chest-high, Peter sidestepped to his right to the first door and tried the knob. It was locked. As were the second, the third, the fourth.

Finally he made it to the corner. There he stopped, frozen by another memory.

He's in this hallway or one similar. Long corridor, concrete, fluorescent lighting, doors lining each wall.

One of the doors opens and two men dressed in black commando gear emerge. One holds a knife and thrusts it at him. He blocks it with his left arm while jabbing the aggressor in the neck with his right fist. The man crumples to the floor clutching his throat. The other man brandishes a gun and points it at Peter's head. Peter grabs the gun with both hands and thrusts upward while delivering a paralyzing kick to the man's groin. The gun comes loose, and Peter engages the slide action and points it at the two commandos on the floor.

A man emerges from another room. Peter can't see the man's face, but he can tell who it is. He just knows. The man says, "Well done, Sergeant. You've come a long way. You're almost ready."

Peter shook his head, confused. Distracted. The man in this memory was Nichols, but it wasn't the man who met him outside. Before he could make sense of the disparity, he felt something hard and cold against the back of his head.

Then a voice: "I knew you'd come to us, Peter." It was Nichols.

Something hard hit him on the back of the head, his legs turned to paper, and he fell to the floor. The hallway spun, then went dark.

THIRTY-FOUR

· · ·

The house again. Second floor. Peter found himself in a bedroom. He wasn't sure which one it was, but it wasn't the first. Nothing in here was like that one—no bookshelf, no desk—except one thing; one thing was the same. In the corner, just like in the other room, stood the floor lamp with the *C* on the shade from Audrey Lewis's office. Besides the lamp, this room was sparsely furnished, just a worn overstuffed chair, a small wooden table, a two-drawer metal file cabinet, and an old television, the kind equipped with a dial to turn channels and a rabbit-ears antenna.

Peter went to the file cabinet and slid open the top drawer. It was stuffed with hanging folders. Each one was labeled differently. *High School. The Academy. The Force. Bills. Credit Cards.*

He pulled the one for *The Academy* and opened it. An acceptance letter to the police academy in Indianapolis and a graduation certificate. Officer Peter Ryan.

He closed the file and placed it on top of the cabinet, then took out the one labeled *The Force*. Inside was a letter announcing his employment with the Indianapolis Police Department. There was also a photocopy of his badge and a photo of him in his uniform. He had been a cop. The memory was there again: seated in the coffee shop, sipping coffee. Even as it struck Peter strange that he could recall his memories in a dream, another memory surfaced.

He busts down a door by kicking it alongside the knob. It's in an apartment building of some sort. Hallway on either side, more doors, all closed. The door swings in and Peter follows it, gun raised. He rushes in, feeling other cops close behind him. They're all hollering, shouting orders. A group of men drop to the floor, but one flees. Peter chases him, catches him in the kitchen, tackles him against the refrigerator.

The memory blurred, then faded as quickly as breath on a mirror.

Peter shut the folder and placed it with the other one on top of the cabinet. He fingered through the folders in the drawer again and found one labeled *Karen*.

Opening the file, he found only one sheet of paper, which seemed odd to him. It was facedown, but he could see the imprint of an official seal of some sort. He flipped it over, scanned it, and let it drop softly to the floor. With it, his heart dropped into the pit of his stomach.

It was an intent to divorce, signed by Karen, stamped by the state.

He had been a cop, and he was divorced. Reality twisted in on itself, a snake coiling into a tight ball. He was divorced? Was that why he'd awakened by himself yesterday morning? Was that why he couldn't find Karen or Lilly? They no longer lived with him? He wondered how many mornings he'd awakened calling Karen's name, looking for her, looking for Lilly. But then, why had other people been convinced they'd died in a car crash?

Peter shut the top drawer with his thigh and opened the bottom drawer. It contained one object, a book. The same Bible from the first room. He lifted it out and cracked it open to the same spot as before. The pages crinkled and smelled of dust and much use. John chapter 10.

As before, he read the words and was overcome with peace. Hope. A feeling of complete contentment, as if he hadn't a care in the world and whatever care happened to come his way would be dealt with properly. But as before, the feelings were fleeting and vanished, leaving him with a rock in his gut.

Disregarding the open drawer, Peter crossed the room to the closet, something the first room had lacked. Something drew him toward it, urged him to open it. An uneasy excitement built inside him, like the feeling a child has right before Christmas morning, wondering if he'll get everything he asked for, especially that one special thing. But when he placed his hand on the knob, he was suddenly in the hallway, standing before the fourth door, trying to turn the knob but once again finding it locked. He shook the door, banged on it. Took a step back, then forward and kicked at it. Nothing. It was locked tight and impenetrable.

And as always, that shadowed pacer tracked back and forth, steady, unwavering.

Then, as a mist lifts and reveals the light of day, bright light filtered in and overcame Peter's vision.

He was in a solid concrete room. Bare except for the metal chair on which he sat. His hands were cuffed behind him, his ankles shackled to the chair's legs. Above, six fluorescent tubes glared at him. His mind swam in murky water, and for a moment he forgot where he was. But as his thoughts cleared, he remembered his journey down here: the corridor, the vent; he'd held his breath and made it to the main tunnels. There were rooms, locked doors. And then... then what? He awoke here. Helpless, chained down like an animal.

He also remembered the dream and the memories within the dream. So strange. He was a cop, wasn't he? Or had been a cop. That certainly explained his ability to use a weapon, his instincts for survival, his familiarity with hand-to-hand combat. But those memories were distant as well, like the others. They seemed to not originate from within him at all but to have been fed to him by some outside source. Like seeing pictures of your childhood and not remembering a moment of the events in the photo but knowing they happened because the picture is there to prove it.

And then there were the snippets of military action. How did those fit in? The only memories that really seemed to be his were from his life as a research assistant, but he was even starting to wonder how much of that had actually happened to him, as if that too was part of a script written by someone else. And what of the divorce paper he'd found? Was that real? Had Karen left him and taken Lilly? He couldn't remember any of it, and yet it felt distantly possible. Maybe that explained why he knew she wasn't dead. She was just gone, gone from him, a stranger to him. In the swirl of memories, it felt like Karen and Lilly were the only solid ground he had. That and the strange, unshakable feeling that despite what his mind told him about God, his soul seemed to know better.

Peter shut his eyes hard and tried to sort it all out, but his mind was a blank screen, an empty box. He had memories of Karen and Lilly's accident, of the funeral . . . that was it. But if they were false memories, then Karen and Lilly were alive and they were here, in Centralia. This was why Lilly had left him the note.

The door to the room opened, and an older man in a shirt and tie entered, followed by a guard of some sort.

"Welcome to Centralia," the older man said. It was Nichols. Again. Only it wasn't the same Nichols that Habit had shot outside the house.

This Nichols was shorter, heavier, older. He had full lips and a bulbous nose, thinning gray hair combed to one side. His shirt stretched tight over his belly, and his necktie was too short.

"Nichols," Peter said.

Nichols stopped about eight feet from Peter and motioned to the guard. "Unshackle him, Corporal. He's not an animal."

The guard approached Peter and unlocked the cuffs around his wrists and ankles.

"There," Nichols said. "Now, let's have a talk, shall we?" He paused as if waiting for Peter to respond, but Peter said nothing. "You know, Peter, you used to call me Mr. Nichols. You used to respect me."

He then turned to the guard again. "Please get me a chair, will you?"

The guard left the room.

"You have questions, I know," Nichols said, pacing with his hands behind his back. "And I have all the answers you need."

The guard returned with another metal chair and set it on the floor facing Peter. "Thank you, Corporal." Nichols sat in the chair and sighed. "There. Now, let's talk. I have nothing to hide, and I think it's time you know the truth. The full truth. No more secrets, no more mysterious memories."

Peter couldn't help his eyes twitching ever so slightly.

"Yes, I know about your memories," Nichols said. "I don't know the exact images you've been recalling, but you have been having memories, haven't you? Strange ones. Memories with no source, no roots, floating out there like a ship in a dark sea with no compass."

"Who am I, really?" Peter asked.

"You're Peter Ryan. You were born in Indiana. Loogootee, Indiana. It's near the Hoosier National Forest. Beautiful area."

Peter remembered none of it. He had only fleeting memories of childhood, but none that included details and none involving a forest.

"Who is Jed Patrick?"

Nichols shifted in the chair and crossed his hands over his belly, narrowed his eyes. "Peter, it's time you hear the whole truth. That's what you want, isn't it?"

Peter nodded. But how did he know he could trust Nichols's version of the truth?

"Good," Nichols said. "I'm tired of this secrecy. I'm getting too old for it."

"I want to know where my wife and daughter are," Peter said.

Nichols smiled. "We'll get to that, but first we have to lay some groundwork. You joined the Army right out of high school, asked the recruiter what the most demanding thing to do in the Army was. He told you it was to become an Army Ranger. You signed up, and that's just what you did. In fact, you became the best Ranger. Top of your class. And in the field you showed . . . skills. Valuable skills."

"What kind of skills?"

"Well, for one, you were a dead shot. Every time. I don't mean you were a good marksman. No, they come a dime a dozen in the military. Lots of farm boys out there good with guns. You were special. You simply didn't miss. Regardless of distance or circumstances. Regardless of distractions. Hit the mark every time."

Now it was Peter's turn to shift in the chair. Nichols's tale held no familiarity, but it certainly explained Peter's comfort with a firearm.

"As you can imagine, skills like that are very valuable to the Army," Nichols said, his smile turning smug. "You were a great asset. We trained you as a sniper and sent you to Afghanistan."

Peter's memories of combat surfaced again. Habit was his spotter.

"You remember, don't you?"

Peter looked at Nichols. "Habit."

"Yes, Lawrence Habit was your spotter. You and he trained together. You were quite the team."

"What happened?"

"Oh, you were perfect. So much so that we wanted to broaden your skill set. And thus began the Centralia Project. We trained you to become the perfect soldier. The perfect weapon. You could do it all. Your natural instincts, your athleticism, your abilities—we enhanced them, perfected them, gave you everything you needed to be a pure killing machine. We poured a lot of resources into you, Peter, spent a lot of taxpayer money making you the model for our future work in Centralia. Imagine if every soldier we trained was a super soldier like you. Imagine what that would mean to our military dominance. We'd be leaner, meaner, more agile, stealthier. Fewer lives lost, more wars won."

None of this made sense. "So what happened?"

"Simply? You failed. We didn't know where the training went wrong. We pored over our techniques, the results, your performance. Everything was perfect, spot-on. But still you failed."

The memory. The man by the pool. "I didn't take the shot."

Nichols nodded slowly. "You didn't take it. Couldn't."

"His wife was there. And his daughter, the little girl."

"He was enemy number one, Peter. A ruthless killer, a mastermind terrorist. That was the only look we've ever had at him. We had one chance and you couldn't take the shot."

Peter drilled Nichols. "His wife and daughter were there."

"He'd killed hundreds of other men's daughters. Thousands."

"Why did Habit call me Patrick?"

"Jed Patrick was your code name. Jedi. You were that good. *Were* that good."

"And I disappointed you, didn't I?"

Nichols laughed, but it was anything but humorous. "You were so much more than a disappointment. You were the poster boy for the one glaring flaw in the Centralia Project."

"And what was that?"

"Training soldiers. By the time we get them, they're what? Eighteen, nineteen, sometimes older? Too old. Too much past. Too much baggage. Too much conscience."

Peter stood and stepped behind the chair, gripped it with both hands. He wanted to throw it at Nichols, attack the man, break his neck. Nichols seemed to sense that too, the anger, the hurt, the frustration, the desire to inflict harm, but he remained calm, as if what he was telling Peter were no more important than revealing who won the last game between the Steelers and Ravens. But it would do no good to kill Nichols. Peter was locked in a concrete room located in the middle of a subterranean bunker. Where would he go? Besides, he'd killed enough.

"So why am I having memories of being a cop? And how did I become a lab researcher? And how did Amy Cantori know anything about this?"

Nichols stood and walked to the door. "Peter, take some time to let this digest. Get your emotions under control. I'll be back later and we can talk some more."

The door opened and he slipped through. And Peter was once again alone.

THIRTY-FIVE

· · ·

Sometime later Nichols returned and sat in the chair again. Peter couldn't tell how much time had passed, but it must have been hours because his stomach was beginning to grumble.

"Are you ready to hear more?" Nichols said.

"Where's Karen and Lilly?"

Nichols ignored his question. "When you failed, my colleagues wanted to discontinue you."

"You mean kill me."

Nichols smiled. "We prefer *discontinue*."

"Of course."

"That was protocol. It's how we handled the other agents that didn't... work out."

"There were others?"

Nichols's eyebrows lifted. "Of course. We were building an army unlike any the world had ever seen. Others came after you, Peter. But you were the best."

"And you killed them?"

Again, the smile. "Discontinued them. But I convinced them to let you live. I had plans for you. I, unlike my colleagues, have a heart, and I hated to see such talented agents—soldiers—gone to waste. So I convinced them to let me experiment with you."

An image of being underwater flashed through Peter's mind, and the feeling of drowning, suffocating, was there too. "You tortured me."

"No, no. Nothing barbaric like that. I wanted to put you back into society. Let you live a normal life again. But the information you had, the training you had, the missions you'd carried out—it was all very classified. We couldn't trust you to sign a few forms and promise to keep your mouth shut. Time changes people. And besides, if you would have ever fallen into the hands of our enemies... well, they can be very persuasive. We couldn't take any chances."

"That's why you killed the others?"

Nichols tightened his lips and breathed in deeply and noisily through his nose. "Discontinued. We couldn't take any chances. But I had this idea, see. What if we could erase your memory? Scrub your mind clean and give you a new memory. A new identity. A new life. We could introduce you back into society as someone totally different and give you a second chance."

Like a cauldron of oil over an open fire, anger boiled inside Peter. He clenched his fists and clamped his jaw.

"Easy now, Peter," Nichols said. "You haven't heard everything yet. There's more to this story."

"You brainwashed me."

Nichols shrugged. "Call it what you like, but we prefer to call it scrubbing and imprinting. We scrub your mind of the old and imprint the new. Kind of like erasing the hard drive in a computer and reprogramming it with all brand-new information. But with you it was different. Your mind was extraordinarily strong. It's what made you so unique, so valuable. We had to imprint three different realities to block out the original."

Peter rubbed his temples in a futile attempt to ward off the ache that had settled there. Of course—that's why he had different memories that didn't coincide. They weren't his; they were false memories, junk they'd gotten from some box off a shelf and fed him. It also explained the four rooms in his dream. He was a lab jockey in one, a cop in the other. He'd never searched the third room, and the fourth, the locked door, must be his original reality, who he really was.

"You're figuring it out," Nichols said. "I can see it in your eyes." He sounded pleased. "That's good. You deserve to know. The truth is liberating, isn't it?"

"What about Amy Cantori? How does she fit into this?"

"Well, we couldn't just drop you back into the world without a support network. You were a dangerous man, and we'd tinkered with your brain an awful lot. We weren't sure how you'd get along, if it worked at all. Amy worked for the project... sort of. She was contracted by us to keep an eye on you."

"So everything that happened between us was an act? It was all scripted?"

Nichols paused and stared at his hands for a long time. "Your relationship with Amy had gotten too close. It had to be changed. We needed to remove her."

"You had her killed."

"That, unfortunately, was not part of the initial plan."

"But she never said anything." Peter wasn't going to mention Amy's words at the very end, her warning. He realized now it was a kind of confession as well.

"No. She didn't. She was quite the actress. They all were."

"They?"

"Yes. There were others who had knowledge too, but in varying degrees. Dean Chaplin, Dr. Lewis, Susan and Richard Greer. Keeping you away from the truth proved to be quite an elaborate and expensive task."

Peter sprang to his feet and rushed across the room at Nichols with every intent to strangle the life out of the old man.

Nichols put up both hands. "Wait, Peter. You haven't gotten your question answered yet, the most burning question."

Peter stopped, panting, sweating, clenching his fists. A sense of great betrayal ate at his heart like a raging cancer. They'd turned him into a monster and then erased his very existence. Populated his new world with false friends, with lies. "Where are Karen and Lilly?" He almost didn't ask it because he was afraid of the answer, afraid Nichols would tell him that the funeral was indeed real and Karen and Lilly were gone.

"Sit down," Nichols said. He lowered his hands to his lap. "If you want to know the truth, you need to sit down and take it like a soldier, like the soldier you still are."

Peter drilled Nichols with burning eyes, then turned and sat in his chair.

"Peter...Karen and Lilly don't exist. They aren't real."

Peter gripped the seat of the chair so hard he nearly bent it. "You're lying."

"I wish I was, son. In order for the imprinting to work, we had to give you some strong connection to each reality, a common factor that would travel through each one, something you'd be willing to die for in order to hold on to your life as you knew it. Some emotional tie that bound you to it. So we created Karen and Lilly. We were all very surprised by how quickly and fiercely you latched on to them, by how thoroughly you accepted them. The emotional tie was incredible. Unbreakable even. It was a perfect scenario. A little too perfect, though, and that's why we had to make you believe that they had died in a car accident. You'd still have the emotional tie, the anchor, but without the problematic issues of keeping their existence going."

Peter shook his head. "No. You're lying." The room spun around him as if his chair were the axis of a giant wheel. His head swam; bile pushed its way up his throat. He thought he'd vomit right there in front of Nichols.

"I wish I was, son. I do." Nichols stood. "I'll leave you alone to process this. I know it's hard news to accept. I wanted to tell you the truth, though, and you wanted to hear the truth. Now you have the truth. I'm sorry." He walked to the door and opened it. "Some guards will be by for you in a little while. I suggest you be on your best behavior when they arrive." He left, and the door closed.

Peter stood, picked up the chair, and threw it against one of the walls. It clattered and landed on its side on the floor. It was a lie—it had to be. Everything else felt fabricated and mass-produced, except Karen and Lilly. It wasn't possible that they were mere figments of his imagination, concoctions of some lab tech who'd fed him information while he was being *imprinted*. They were real; the memories he had of them were as real as the skin on the back of his hand. Uniquely his. He refused to believe what Nichols had told him.

But what if Nichols was right? What if he was telling the truth? Everything else he'd said made sense. It was a twisted, demented form of sense, but it all added up. Why would this be different? If Karen and Lilly really didn't exist, then Peter had no reason to live, no reason to fight and go on. His life was a sham, his relationships phony; everything about him came out of a lab, where his mind had been *scrubbed* and *imprinted*. He was a man who didn't exist, a mirage. No one would miss him if he died now because no one knew he was still alive. All his old friends, relatives, and whoever else knew him from his original life had probably accepted his death and moved on.

If he didn't have Karen and Lilly, he had nothing.

THIRTY-SIX

· · ·

Peter was about to fall asleep in a very uncomfortable position in the chair when the door opened and three guards entered. They all wore black commando garb and carried Glocks, standard issue for these types of grunts.

The lead, a broad-shouldered guy with a wide, angular face and deep-set dark eyes, stepped forward and said, "Mr. Ryan, please stand and turn around, and put your hands on the wall."

Peter didn't move. He sat in the chair and stared at the guard as if he'd suddenly gone deaf and hadn't heard a word the man said. The other two had positioned themselves on either flank of the lead. Both had their guns trained on Peter's head.

Peter noticed that each of the guards wore a utility belt that contained several magazines of ammo, pepper spray, handcuffs, and a Taser. They'd come prepared for whatever might transpire. He also noticed the lead gripped the gun with his left hand; the guard to the right of the lead was sweating terribly, soaking the collar of his shirt; and the guard to the left continuously shifted his feet.

"Sir," the big lead said. "I'm going to ask you again to stand and put your hands on the wall."

As if he were a Trappist monk and had taken a strict vow of silence, still Peter said nothing and did not move.

The lead guard circled Peter and stood behind him. The barrel of his gun nudged Peter's head. "I'm not going to ask you again." He spoke forcefully, confidently. "If you don't stand on your own, I can make you do it."

Peter knew he could. He had a Taser, and its fifty thousand volts would incapacitate Peter long enough that the three could pounce on him and cuff him in seconds.

Slowly Peter complied. He rose and walked to the wall. The lead guard followed.

Peter stood a foot from the wall.

"Hands on the wall," the guard said.

Peter hesitated, testing the man. If his stare didn't hold the power to atomize concrete, the least he could do was try to draw the man in closer. It worked. The guard stepped nearer and pressed the barrel of his gun against Peter's back, between the shoulder blades.

Quicker than the lead could react, Peter spun to his left, knocking the guard's arm out of the way. The gun discharged, sending a round into the concrete inches from where Peter stood. The gun then clattered to the floor. Peter continued his spin, using his momentum to place a tight choke hold on the guard with his left arm while grabbing the man's Taser from the utility belt with his right hand. It took him less than a second to aim and fire and hit the sweating guard in the thigh. The guy twitched and grunted like a marionette dangling from a tangled mess of string and finally collapsed to the floor.

The remaining guard shouted something unintelligible and squeezed off a round that nearly struck Peter's head but slammed into the wall behind him. Shards of concrete bit the back of Peter's neck. Still holding the lead guard, Peter groped for the man's pepper spray canister, found it, and coated the remaining guard's face. The guy stumbled back, pawing at his face; he gagged, sputtered, spit, and wheezed.

Peter released the lead guard from the choke hold and smashed his elbow into the side of the man's head, then delivered a kick to the chest of the man he'd just hit with the pepper spray. The guard backpedaled and slammed against the far concrete wall. Peter followed and easily disarmed him. He went to the guard he'd Tased, who was still lying on the floor, salivating and sweating profusely, and retrieved his gun. The lead guard's gun was in the corner. Peter picked it up too.

All three guards were suffering the effects of the pepper spray now, coughing, wheezing, clawing at their eyes. It was only then that Peter noticed his own eyes burning and nose running. Ignoring the pain, he quickly handcuffed the three men together, both at the wrists and ankles, forming an interlaced mess of arms and legs. He crossed the room to the door and cracked it open. A woman stood there as if the sudden burst of violence had telepathically drawn her to the room. She was young, blonde, and dressed in a neatly pressed navy-blue pantsuit and white blouse. "Come with me," she said.

Peter hesitated, unsure if he should trust her. He held one of the

Glocks in his hand and had tucked the other two into the waist of his pants. He raised the gun and pointed it at the woman.

She looked at the gun but didn't seem alarmed. Then, as if she'd peered inside his head and seen the question there, she said, "I'm on your side."

Whether or not he could trust her, Peter decided he'd take the risk at this point. He slipped out the door and closed and locked it behind him.

"Quickly—this way," the woman said. She hurried down the hall with the confidence of someone who had traveled these corridors many times. It was like the other halls Peter had seen in the underground bunker. Concrete, lights every fifty feet or so, electrical wiring and plumbing running along the ceiling. Vents at even intervals with the lights.

They passed a couple rooms until finally, at a solid brown door, the woman stopped. "In here." She placed her thumb over a fingerprint scanner, the door unlocked, and she pushed it open.

Once they were in the room and the door shut behind them, Peter pushed the woman against the wall and pointed the gun at her. "Who are you? Why are you helping me?"

Lips parted, muscles tight in her neck, she shifted her eyes from the gun to Peter. "You mind getting that thing out of my face first?"

"Actually, I do," Peter said. He suddenly felt he'd been led into a trap.

The woman forced a smile and glanced at the barrel of the gun again. "You have a gun and I don't. You have me by at least fifty, sixty pounds. And you're some kind of karate ninja guy. I don't see how I pose much of a threat to you. Not nearly enough to warrant a gun in the face."

Peter released his grip on her and lowered his gun. "Who are you?"

"I'm April. I'm a counselor here."

"Did you work on me? Were you part of brainwashing me?"

April shook her head. "No. Not my department. I work with other kinds of subjects."

Peter looked around. They were in some sort of control room. Television monitors with blank screens lined one wall. Against an adjoining wall were three desks, empty. The other two walls were bare. "What is this place?"

"It's a monitoring station. One of many. This one is rarely used."

Peter nodded toward the door. "Won't they be looking for me?"

"They already are. But they won't look here. This is a red room, off-limits to everyone but techs and counselors like me. The only way you could gain access to this room was if you were a counselor."

"Or have a counselor helping you," Peter said.

April smiled, genuinely this time. "Exactly."

"Why?"

"Why what?"

"Why are you helping me?"

April walked over to the wall of monitors and sat at a computer. She punched the keys on the keyboard, and one of the monitors sprang to life. On it was the image of a small boy in a room just like the one in which Peter had been held. Concrete everything except for one metal chair. The kid couldn't have been more than ten. He had thick brown hair and a face full of freckles. He sat slumped in the chair until a woman entered, carrying a box. It was April.

"This is a recording from yesterday," April said.

"What is this?"

"Just watch."

On the monitor April said, *"Good morning, Tyler. How was your night?"*

Tyler shrugged.

"Well, how's your morning going so far? Did you enjoy your breakfast?"

Again, only a shrug.

April set the box on the floor in front of Tyler and squatted next to him. *"Are you ready to get started?"*

Tyler did nothing. He stared at the floor, his mouth tight and jaw tense.

"We have something new for you today." April opened the box and pulled out a small birdcage containing one finch.

Tyler stiffened and shook his head.

"What's he doing?" Peter asked. "Why does he look so frightened?"

April said nothing.

On-screen, April placed her hand on Tyler's shoulder. *"You have to, Tyler. You know what they'll do if you don't. Do what you have to do and your mother will be fine."*

Peter's muscles tensed. Something about this was wrong.

Seated on the chair, Tyler squirmed and shook his head. He moaned and whimpered.

"Tyler," April said. *"You must. You have to."*

Tears spilled from Tyler's eyes and tracked down his cheeks. He ran a hand over his face, wiping them away. Then he fell to his knees in front of the cage. The bird flapped its wings furiously but got nowhere.

"That's it, Tyler. That's a good boy. Just do it and it'll be over."

Tyler lifted a shaking hand and placed it on the cage. The bird flapped and flitted, screeched. Tyler focused on the bird and clenched his jaw. The camera zoomed in on the cage. Suddenly the bird burst into flames and fell to the bottom of the cage.

Tyler yanked his hand away and began to sob.

April rubbed his back. *"There you go. Now it's over. You did it and it's over."*

April tapped a button and paused the image on the screen. She turned to Peter. "That's not what I signed up for here."

"What is it? How did he do that?"

"The Centralia Project is about more than training soldiers. There's another branch, experimental but gaining a lot of traction."

Peter pointed at the monitor. "That?"

April nodded. "That. They found that training children was a lot easier than training adults. Less baggage. More pliable minds. More willingness to comply. Easier to coerce."

Peter stared at the monitor. Nichols had called it the glaring flaw in the Centralia Project: *"Too old. Too much past. Too much baggage."*

"Kids are easy pickings," Peter said.

"Something like that."

"But what did that kid do? Tyler. How did he do that?"

"They look for children with extraordinary abilities and then hone those abilities, perfect them to be used for military purposes."

"Yeah, but what he just did—"

"Pyrokinesis. It's not a trick. There are documented cases. And you just saw it. Seeing is believing, right? These military types, they see this and begin to think large-scale."

He had seen it; there was no denying that. "So they kidnap kids and weaponize them?"

"Well, the weaponizing part will come later, when they're adults. But they'll be raised here, in Centralia, and that will be their purpose in life."

Peter wanted to smash the monitor's screen. "That's sick. They're treated like lab animals."

April dropped her eyes to her hands. "Like I said, it's not what I signed up for when I took this job."

"Does the name Abernathy mean anything to you?"

April's eyes widened. "Haven't heard that name for a while."

"Why? Who is he?"

She shrugged. "Not sure, really. Every now and then someone around here will mention him. He's like some kind of enigma or something. Just disappeared one day and no one knows where he went. Rumor is that the brass had him—"

"Discontinued?"

"Yeah. Something like that."

April turned to the computer and tapped more keys. "Look, there's another reason I brought you here." But before the monitor sprang to life, she looked back at Peter. There was sadness in her eyes. "Your daughter is here, in Centralia."

A tingling started in Peter's scalp and ran down the back of his neck like someone had poured cold water over him. "Lilly? She's here?"

"And your wife."

"Karen?"

"It's how they get the children to do what they want them to do."

"With threats to harm their mothers?"

"Like I said, with the right motivators, children are quick to comply."

Again the anger was there. Peter's face flushed and his breathing quickened. "Where's Lilly? Let me see her."

April turned to the keyboard and tapped one key. The monitor flickered to life. It was another concrete room like the others. In the middle of the room was a metal chair and on the chair sat a young girl. Next to the girl was a cart that contained a blue box. Wires extended from the box and connected to the girl with electrodes placed at even intervals over her arms and legs.

Peter stepped closer to the monitor and shook his head. "No. That's wrong."

April remained quiet as the scene played out. A red indicator lit on the box and the girl twitched. The camera zoomed in on the box. On the top was a meter measuring voltage; the needle steadily climbed. The camera zoomed out again. The girl twitched but did not cry out. And though her muscles tensed as tight as strained ropes, her face remained calm.

"That's not right," Peter said.

April put a hand on his arm, but Peter pulled away. "No. That's wrong." He looked at April. "That's not Lilly."

THIRTY-SEVEN

· · ·

"It is Lilly. It's your daughter."

"No." Peter grabbed his head with both hands and studied the scenario unfolding on the monitor again. The girl had blonde hair; his Lilly had dark-brown hair, like Karen. And the girl in the chair looked nothing like Karen; his Lilly was the perfect image of her mother. "That's not her."

"It *is*, Peter."

Peter felt the same anger again climbing up his chest, that wolverine with claws and teeth, scratching at his mind. "I know what my daughter looks like and that's not her."

April pushed back her chair and stood.

Peter took a step away from April and lifted the gun to aim at her. He couldn't trust her, couldn't trust any of them. This was a trick, had to be. She'd lured him into this room to trap him, to mess more with his mind—as if they hadn't muddled it enough already.

April backpedaled to the wall and lifted her hands. Fear widened her eyes. No longer did she look like the venomous villain Peter had imagined just moments ago. "Whoa, listen; I can explain."

But Peter kept the gun on her. On the screen, in the concrete room, the girl took the electrical current like no human should be able to. The meter's needle hovered around a hundred volts, but she remained calm. It was an incredible sight. "Who are you? Who is that girl?"

"My name is April LaBarrie. I'm a counselor here, like I told you. And that girl, Peter, is your daughter. It's Lilly."

April moved slowly to the computer desk and tapped a few keys; the image on the screen froze. She enlarged the girl's face so it took up most of the screen.

"Look at her," April said. "Look at her face. Look into her eyes. You have to remember. Do you see how she resembles you?"

Peter studied the girl's face. It wasn't Lilly, at least not the Lilly he remembered. But he'd already learned that what he knew, or thought he knew, wasn't necessarily reality. He found himself wanting to believe April. "Okay. I'll play along. Convince me."

April shifted her eyes from the gun to the monitor to Peter. "It's all part of the imprinting they did on you. They intended to bring you back into the project to be part of these kids' training, but there was always the possibility you'd see footage like this, so they changed the image of them. To change their names, their whole identities, would mess too much with something you had such an emotional attachment to, but they changed the way your brain remembered them to make sure you'd never recognize them."

Peter lowered the gun. "How can they do that?"

"What is your past other than a series of memories? Without

memories, nothing exists in your past. You have no history.
Change the memories, change the past. Change the past, change
the present. They scrubbed your mind of all images of Karen
and Lilly and replaced them with the images they wanted you
to remember."

Peter stared at the screen as he scrolled over this new line of
thinking. He understood what April was getting at, but she was
wrong on some crucial points. He had a past. Maybe he didn't
know which past he could trust, but one of them was empiri-
cally real, beyond the scope of his own perceptions. And more
than that, there were some truths that Peter had encountered
over the past couple days that transcended facts and evidence
and whatever mixed-up stories people had tried to feed him. His
love for Lilly and Karen. The verse in the Bible in his dream. And
now, as he stared at the still image of the girl on the monitor, he
realized another truth that had been buried deep: he'd had some
faith they tried to scrub out of him. They'd tried to take him away
from God, but God just wouldn't let go.

The girl on the screen looked into the camera as if she knew
he would be looking at her at this exact moment with the image
frozen and her eyes studying his, pleading for him to remember
her. But the girl was not his Lilly. As much as he wanted her to be
his daughter, as much as he longed for his memories to be wrong,
he simply could not bring himself to accept that they were. There
was such a strong emotional attachment to how he remembered
Karen and Lilly. How could that possibly be wrong as well?
"Images of another woman and another child. But why?"

"Their work on Lilly and the other children took higher
priority than their work with you. Once you were released into
society again, they couldn't have you clinging to Karen and Lilly,

so they made you believe they died in a car accident." She glanced at the monitor. "And they told Karen and Lilly you died in action, a hero."

"But Nichols said they never really existed, that they were fabricated to give me an anchor in each of the realities created for me."

April frowned. "Nichols is a liar, then. Another reason to not like that man."

"So how do I know if anything else he told me is true or not?"

April walked to the door. "Follow me. You can't trust your memories. Don't trust them. Whatever you think is true may or may not be. Your reality has been so tampered with that you can't know for sure that anything is real. But seeing is believing, right?"

"You know where they are?"

She cracked the door and peeked out into the hall. "All clear," she said to Peter.

He followed her, gun raised, senses alert. The corridor was empty, quiet as a tomb full of dead men who kept the best secrets. In fact, though, it was too quiet. Something wasn't right. They should have guards swarming the tunnels looking for him.

April led him to the end of the corridor and down another tunnel that branched to the left. This one had no doors but stretched no more than fifty feet to a T junction. They turned right and stopped in front of a door.

April looked at the door, then at Peter. "This is it, Peter. Karen and Lilly are in that room."

The door was protected by a fingerprint scanner like the others. With his mouth suddenly as dry as sand, Peter motioned toward the scanner. "You gonna open it?"

April hesitated. She suddenly appeared very nervous. Her eyes shifted side to side, and she wrung her hands.

"April," Peter said. His intuition screamed at him, sounded an alarm, and warned him away. "Open the door."

He should run, get out of there, but not without Karen and Lilly. His desire for the truth continued to push him forward. And his desire to find his wife and daughter overrode every tactical instinct screaming at him.

"April, please, do it. Open it."

She looked to her left, down the empty corridor, then placed her thumb on the scanner. The lock clicked and Peter pushed open the door.

The room was furnished like a cheap motel. A little table and two chairs, a double bed. On the bed sat a woman. Brown shoulder-length hair, slender figure, attractive. Next to her sat a girl, the girl from the monitor.

Peter stepped into the room, confused. The woman's mouth hung open like she'd stopped talking mid-word. Tears quickly pooled in her eyes and spilled down her cheeks. The girl next to her slid off the bed and, still holding her mother's hand, smiled widely. She too began crying.

Peter couldn't think of a single thing to say. The woman stood and approached him, her mouth still open, eyes still leaking tears. When she stood before him, she let go of the girl and lifted a trembling hand to Peter's face.

"Is it really you?" she said. Her voice was weak and tight. She appeared to be doing all she could to restrain sobs that wanted to burst out of her like water breaching a dam.

Still Peter said nothing.

The woman looked deeply into Peter's eyes, studied them as if determining for herself if he was who she thought he was.

In her eyes Peter saw love and kindness and a deep sadness

that shocked him. But they weren't the eyes of his wife. At least he didn't think they were. But standing there before the woman, she peering so deeply into his soul, he lost his handle on his memory and found it too difficult to conjure an image of the Karen he knew and loved in his mind.

They stood there like that for what seemed way too much time, the woman's hand on Peter's face, his heart thumping in his ears. He realized the girl had been clutching him, her arms around his waist. The weight of her against him was familiar but surely not unlike the hug of any child.

But still, there was something about this woman and child, something—

From the corridor outside came the sound of heavy boots moving fast. Peter's eyes darted to April. Had she led him into a trap? But she appeared just as surprised as he was.

She took a deep breath and called, "Don't come any closer. He has hostages." April looked at Peter, eyes wide, lips pressed together, and flicked her hand, motioning him toward her. She was a quick thinker.

Peter stepped behind her and pointed the gun to her head, grieving over how this might appear to the mother and daughter in the room, but one look reassured him that even the young girl had noticed April's ruse and caught on.

Peter moved April into the doorway, half in the room, half out. Down the corridor at least five guards had gathered, all brandishing handguns. None had taken a shot yet, which confirmed they didn't want to risk hitting April.

Peter moved into the corridor, staying close to the wall and keeping April between him and the guards. He glanced in the room and said to the woman, "You coming with us?"

She gathered up her daughter and they both hurried to the doorway.

"Get behind us," Peter said.

The woman, holding her daughter close, did as instructed.

"Now," Peter said to April, "how do we get out of here?"

THIRTY-EIGHT

• • •

"Back. Go back," April said.

Peter backpedaled down the tunnel, holding the gun to April's head with one hand and keeping his arm wrapped around her neck with the other. She clung to his arm to avoid losing her footing. The woman and girl from the room stuck close, staying behind Peter and out of direct line of any guns. The guards followed cautiously, crouched, guns trained on him, keeping a distance of fifty feet between them.

At the next intersection, the corridors stretched in each direction like catacombs built to house the remains of long-dead saints. Dim lights illuminated the pale concrete in sections, giving it an appearance of motion as if it billowed and rolled to some subterranean tidal force.

"Which way?"

April pointed left. "That way."

They ducked around the corner, and the scuffing of boots on concrete grew closer as the guards hurried to close the distance between them.

Peter picked up the pace, but April's feet couldn't keep up. She stumbled and nearly fell from his grip. Peter pulled her up as easily as if she were made of fabric and stuffed with cotton. "Hurry. C'mon."

A moment later two of the guards peeked around the corner, guns raised; then the others joined them. They had closed the distance to no more than thirty feet now.

They approached another intersection. "Now where?" Peter asked.

April squirmed under his grip. "Straight. Keep going straight."

At the intersection, they paused. Peter could feel April's heart beating through her back against his chest. Their pursuers were still steadily closing the gap.

Behind him, in the intersection, there was a scuffle, a whimper, and the woman screamed.

Peter spun around in time to see one of the guards dragging the girl down the tunnel, one hand over her mouth, a gun to her head.

Peter nearly dropped April. "No!" he shouted. Things were unraveling quickly.

The woman, caught in the middle of the intersection between Peter and the guard, glanced at her daughter, glanced at Peter, a look of terror and hopelessness in her eyes. Her skin went pale, and her lips trembled at the sudden chill that had descended on the subterranean maze.

"You have to remember," she said to Peter, her voice cracking on every word.

And then she turned and fled in the direction the guard had taken her daughter.

The pursuing guards were now less than thirty feet away, so close Peter could see the intensity in the lead's eyes.

Confusion fogged Peter's mind, and for a moment he thought of surrendering. The way the woman had looked at him... Those eyes...

"You have to remember."

"Let her go, Ryan." It was the lead guard. Guns aimed and ready to open fire, they continued their slow advance.

Peter began to backpedal again. Karen and Lilly. After all he'd been through to find them, losing them like this... But he'd have to leave them. He couldn't catch up to them, and he might never find them in this labyrinth. He found them once; he'd find them again. "We have to get out of here, April. How do we get out?"

"End of the hall," April said, her voice tight and strained. "There's a door. It'll take us out."

Just as April had said, at the end of the hall there was a solid door protected by a fingerprint scanner. Peter placed his thumb on the scanner. Nothing happened. He tried once more with the same result.

"You don't have access," April said.

Peter swung her around to face the door. "Unlock it."

The lead guard, a thin, muscular guy with short graying hair stepped forward, crouched at the waist, and pointed his handgun at Peter. He had a kind face, the face of a dad and granddad, and when he spoke, his voice was smooth and friendly, not forceful and commanding as one might expect. "Don't do it, April. You can't trust him."

So kindly was his voice, in fact, that Peter almost believed him and released April.

April hesitated, her thumb hovering over the scanner.

Returning to his better senses, Peter pointed his gun at the paternal guard. He spoke to April. "Do it! Open the door."

"No," the guard said. "He'll kill you once he's out. He's a killer; it's what he was trained to do. He doesn't care about you or anyone. He'll do what he needs to do to survive and in this case that means killing you." Again the guard spoke as if he were April's father giving her advice about the kind of men she chose to spend time with.

Peter loosed his grip on April. "I wouldn't do that. Now it's your turn to trust me. Trust me, April."

"You can't trust him," the guard said. "He's a robot, and he's been programmed to fulfill the mission at all cost, and you're not part of his mission. You're an obstacle."

April whimpered but didn't move her thumb.

"April, listen to me," Peter said. "You didn't want to be part of all this. I know you didn't, okay? I know it. I could see it in your eyes. Now open the door and let's both get out of here."

The guard stepped closer. He was now only twenty feet away. "April, if you unlock that door and go with him, you'll be considered a traitor—"

"You can't be a traitor," Peter said, "if I'm holding you against your will."

The guard inched forward. "You'll be a traitor in our eyes because we know you had a choice. Aiding the enemy. It's called treason. Do you want that?"

April began to cry. She dropped her thumb on the scanner. The guard yelled, "April!" but it was too late.

The door's lock disengaged.

The other guards advanced in a quick run, keeping formation.

"Go, go!" Peter said. He pushed April through and shut the door as the guards arrived on the other side.

Peter leaned against the door, his heart beating through his spine and into the thick metal, and surveyed the area. They were in another tunnel, this one more dimly lit; the bulbs were spread at farther intervals. Ahead was another door, another fingerprint scanner.

"They can't get in," April said. "Only certain job codes have access and they're not one of them."

Peter's head spun. "Was that really my Karen? My Lilly?" he asked, mostly to himself.

"Yes. That was them."

But it wasn't possible. They couldn't be his family. Surely the sight of his own wife would trigger something inside him, some kind of authentic memories. The woman had an emotional effect on him, but it was an emotional situation. But then there was the fact that, though they looked like strangers in his eyes, they both seemed to instantly recognize him. After all he'd been through in the past few days, was it really so impossible to believe that his wife and daughter might look different from how he remembered them?

They didn't have time for this. The guards would find someone who had clearance to enter this corridor and would be opening the door any minute, maybe any second. "Where are they?"

April slumped against the wall. "He took them."

"He who?"

"Nichols."

"Took them where?"

"Probably up. To the top."

"Then we need to get moving," Peter said.

THIRTY-NINE

• • •

The corridor led to a staircase that spiraled upward like a cork-
screw and emerged inside a closet in the abandoned school.

If Nichols had Karen and Lilly—*Peter's* Karen and Lilly—
then Peter was losing ground on them every precious second.
"Where to?"

April opened the closet door, which led to the gymnasium.
It was early evening and the sun was low in the sky, casting
dirty, burnt light through the clouded windows of the gym. The
fissure in the floor was still at the far end, waiting like an open
mouth ready to swallow some unsuspecting urban explorer or
at the very least douse him or her with a dose of its hallucino-
genic breath. They moved quickly across the gym floor and
into the hallway.

"There's a safe house," April said. "A farm just outside the town limits. He would have taken them there. It's where the chopper lands."

A chopper. He was going to fly them out of Centralia. "And where would he go then?"

April stopped at the double doors that led out of the gym, turned, and glanced at Peter. "No telling."

If Nichols got them on a chopper, he could whisk them away to a military installation anywhere in the world, and the chances were very strong that Peter would never see them again. Whether they were really *his* Karen and Lilly he wasn't certain. But he had to get to them, had to find out the truth. "We need to find them first, before the chopper comes."

April pushed through the doors. "Follow me."

Outside the school, April led him across the property and into the woods. Trees stretched their limbs overhead, blocking out much of what little light was left. Underbrush littered the ground as though it had been planted there for the one purpose of making their journey slow and tedious.

April pushed a low-hanging branch out of the way and, slightly out of breath, said, "There's a tunnel from the bunker that goes directly to the farmhouse, but we were at the wrong end to access it." She turned and looked at Peter. "They've had a big head start."

Peter stopped and listened. In the distance the sound of blades chopping at the air grew closer. "We need to move," he said. He pressed past April and broke into a run. Branches slapped at his chest; thorns tore at his arms. He had no idea how far he was from the farm, but the growing sound of the chopper's rotor told him he needed to make better time than he was.

The helicopter grew ever closer and louder until it passed

272

overhead. The sound produced by its whirring blades was not unlike the spinning knives of a blender. Peter saw it through the forest's canopy—a dark-gray Black Hawk, flying low, just higher than the treetops. It moved ahead of him. He pushed on, pumping his arms and willing his legs to go faster.

Peter glanced behind him but could no longer see April through the tangle of underbrush. He wondered if she was still following him or if she'd taken the opportunity to escape. Regardless, he needed to get to the safe house before Nichols boarded that chopper with Karen and Lilly.

Finally he saw the forest's banded tree line and the muted light of evening on the other side. The Black Hawk's concussive beating of air was still loud. It was landing. As he drew nearer, he saw the chopper touch down fifty or so yards from a two-story German-style brick farmhouse.

At the tree line he broke from the woods and found himself in a field of ankle-high grass, taking fire. Five gunmen poured from the house, all carrying automatic weapons and firing them in his direction. Rounds hit the ground, bit through grass, kicked up dirt. Bullets whizzed by his head like bees caught in a tornado. Peter nearly fell. Hunched over, he ducked back into the safety of the woods and behind the protection of its stately residents.

From where he stood, he had a good look at the house and watched helplessly as Nichols emerged with a woman and small girl. Peter was at least a hundred fifty yards away and couldn't get a good look at their faces, but he could tell by their gait and the way they moved that it was the mother and daughter April had led him to in the bunker. They ducked as they approached the chopper, and a gunman prodded them along.

Peter fired at the men near the house and dropped one of them.

As the remaining gunman on the house's porch returned fire, the group moved as a unit closer to the chopper. Karen and Lilly boarded, then Nichols. The other gunman left the house and joined the group in the chopper. Peter held his fire; he didn't want an errant bullet to strike either the mother or the daughter.

When all were on the chopper and the door closed, Peter burst from the woods as if pushed out by an explosion and ran in a full sprint across the field. But he was too late. The Black Hawk wobbled, teetered, and lifted off the ground, its blades cleaving the air like a scythe.

Peter pushed harder though there was now no hope of rescue. If this was Karen and Lilly, they would be carried away and he'd have no idea where to begin to look for them. Tears sprang to his eyes and blurred his vision. The ground seemed to undulate beneath him as if the moorings of the earth's crust had been loosed and its tectonic plates become like jelly.

The chopper lifted into the air, turned and tilted, and flew off.

As Peter reached the site from where the chopper had lifted, something hit him high in the back of the right shoulder and bit like a hornet's sting. The force of it spun him to the side and knocked him to the ground. His shoulder throbbed. He tried to move his arm, but it wouldn't cooperate.

He rolled to his back and suddenly grew very dizzy. The ground moved, rose and fell like the waves of an open ocean. The sky swirled and spun. Darkness crept in, first around the edges of his field of view and then closer to the center. Eventually the darkness consumed everything, and all that was left was a feeling of falling, falling.

Falling.

FORTY

. . .

Down, down he dropped; head over heels he tumbled into a bottomless, ethereal tunnel like Alice into her rabbit hole. His stomach churned; his head spun. He groped at the air, kicked at the emptiness. Twisted and writhed. But nothing would slow his descent into the abyss of darkness.

Then something appeared above him. It too was falling but quicker than he was, closing the gap between them. An object or a person, he couldn't tell. As it came into view, he realized it was another person, facedown, arms and legs extended like a skydiver, wind pushing back the facial features.

As the image grew closer, he could tell it was a man; then closer still and he saw who it was. Nichols. He was laughing. A deep, red-faced, fun-house laugh. He fell to within fifteen feet of Peter

275

and hovered there, laughing, mocking. Peter was the source of his amusement.

Peter was about to say something, to ask Nichols what had him so amused, when the older man drew a gun and without hesitating, pointed and fired at Peter.

Peter's eyes snapped open and tried to focus, but his surroundings were nothing more than a blur, a collage of straight lines and bulbous figures and varying shades of gray. His head still spun, and that feeling of weightlessness was still in his gut, but he was not falling. He was in a room, in a bed, secure on solid ground. White walls, white ceiling. But not concrete. Sheetrock walls, tile ceiling. A television perched in one corner, fastened to the wall by metal brackets, facing the bed. A large window covered with partially open vertical blinds took up most of the wall to his left. Sunlight filtered in and dusted the room in a soft glow.

It was a hospital room, and he had an IV running from a pump beside the bed to his right arm. The pump clicked rhythmically.

Peter lifted his right hand and combed his fingers through his hair, felt his face. He had at least a day's worth of stubble covering his jaw. He rubbed his temples and strained his mind to think, but it was like trying to squeeze water from a dry sponge. He couldn't remember what had happened.

Slowly the memories returned. The tunnels, the bunker. Centralia. April. Their escape. The farmhouse. Karen and Lilly. He remembered the chopper, remembered it lifting off with Karen and Lilly on board, but that was it. How had he gotten here?

Like the surge and flow of a tidal wave following an impressive ebb, a great feeling of desperation overcame him. Panic, almost. He had to find Karen and Lilly, but he had no idea where Nichols had taken them. They were as lost as two pleating pins in a world full of haystacks. They had no doubt seen him running after the chopper. What must they think? Did they believe he was dead? April had said they'd been told he was dead once before.

Peter sat up in bed and reached for the IV, but before he could yank it from his hand, the door to the room opened and in walked a man. Nichols. He had a woman with him. The two of them crossed the room without saying a word and stood at the foot of the bed.

Peter sat back, tense, hands balled into fists. "Where am—?"

Nichols held up a hand. "No questions yet. Let me explain fully, and then you can ask all the questions you want. You'll get your answers."

Peter nodded. He'd go along with Nichols for now.

"Peter, this is Dr. Ambling. She's been a part of your training from the beginning. She's a graduate of Stanford, PhD in psychology, ten years in clinical practice and as many in research. She specializes in memory manipulation and replacement."

Ambling clasped her hands in front of her and dipped her chin at Peter. She was an attractive woman, midforties, brown hair and glasses. She wore a brown dress suit and white blouse. She looked like a middle school librarian.

"I brought her here to corroborate everything I'm about to tell you. No more games. No more lies."

Peter wanted to trust Nichols. The man had that air of respectability about him that was common to politicians and other government officials. Making it that much harder to tell which ones were sharks. He couldn't help but think Nichols was a predator as well and capable of any trickery or lying to feed his ego. Besides, the man had already lied to him, tricked him, manipulated him. He hadn't earned any trust.

Nichols sighed and held his hands behind his back. "Peter, everything I told you before was true. About your true identity. About your training and failure to follow through with the mission in Afghanistan. About the scrubbing and imprinting. It all really happened. And Dr. Ambling was a large part of that. She and I fought to keep you active. We knew we could recycle you, use your skills again, but in a better way, a more productive way. We only needed time." He paused, sighed again. "And that's exactly what we did. It all worked brilliantly. Dr. Ambling and her team did a remarkable job with you. You are the future of America's fighting force. An army of perfect soldiers, bred to protect our nation at all costs. What we accomplished with you will someday be the basis for curing post-traumatic stress disorder among our combat veterans. It will be used in the training of future soldiers. It will change the way wars are fought and won. Our wars. Our victories."

Ambling cleared her throat. "You were not an easy subject, Mr. Ryan. Your mental abilities are beyond that of the average soldier, beyond that of the average man. You are remarkably resilient. But it was that resilience that ultimately worked in our favor."

"Peter," Nichols said, "all that's transpired in the past two days—" he glanced at Ambling—"was a test. The home invasion, Amy Cantori, the scenario at the motel. It was all carefully choreographed and scripted to test every facet of your training."

Heat climbed up Peter's neck and face. "But what about the men I killed?"

Nichols looked at the floor. "Yes, well, sacrifices had to be made. Those deaths were all too real. Those men knew, though, what they were getting into. They knew the risks. They also knew they were part of something much larger than themselves. Their deaths were not in vain. This project, Centralia, will change America's standing in the world forever. And like I said, it will also serve as the foundational research in many medical breakthroughs. Not just PTSD but treatments for so many psychological disorders. The possibilities are limitless. And you were at the genesis of it all. You are the father of everything."

"I'm Frankenstein's monster," Peter said.

Nichols unclasped his hands and let his arms hang at his sides. "I know this is difficult to accept and process. We're going to give you time to come to terms with it. If anything I've said is false or misrepresents our work, I would hope Dr. Ambling would have spoken up."

Ambling glanced at Nichols and smiled. "I have nothing to add."

"Now," Nichols said. "Your questions."

Peter had only one. "Where are Karen and Lilly?"

Nichols again looked at Ambling. When he brought his eyes back to Peter, there was sadness in them. Whether it was genuine or not Peter couldn't tell. If the man was a liar and a con artist, he was a remarkably accomplished one. "Peter, this has been a sticking point throughout your training. Your attachment to them was beyond what we anticipated. But eventually we were able to rectify the situation and found a suitable workaround. In the end... Well, your wife and daughter are dead. The car accident was real. We didn't fabricate that; we didn't need to."

"April led me to them. She said they were my wife and daughter. I saw them get in the chopper."

"That, too, was choreographed." Nichols tilted his head back and narrowed his eyes. "You had your doubts about them, didn't you? And rightfully so. The woman and child you saw were actors. Nora and Maddy. You must accept that Karen and Lilly are gone."

Again the heat was there, radiating up Peter's neck and setting his cheeks on fire. He was overcome with anger. "Did you kill them? Did you arrange for the accident? Fabricate the circumstance so it was timed perfectly? Was that all part of your carefully choreographed plan?"

Nichols began to speak, but Ambling put her hand on his arm to silence him. "Peter, from the beginning we determined that your family was off-limits. Everything we did to you was with your permission. You don't remember it because we had to scrub it from your memory, but it was all with your consent. Never, not once, did we tamper with your wife or daughter. Our research may be controversial, but we do have ethics. I'm not about to throw a twenty-year career away by being a party to murder."

"Thank you, Dr. Ambling," Nichols said. Then, to Peter, "Any other questions?"

"How long have I been in here?"

"Two days."

"Was I shot?"

"Tranquilized."

Peter shook his head. It was too much to process, too much to accept. He couldn't trust Nichols—he knew that—and Ambling didn't seem to be worthy of his faith either. But what was reality? How much of what they told him was real and where were the lies?

In his heart he felt Karen and Lilly were still alive, that they were out there somewhere, but gone was the certainty. The memories of their funeral, though spotty, were all too real. Conflicting visions of his past waged a contentious turf war in his head. If he couldn't even trust his own memories, then what could he trust? Peter's brain scrambled to latch on to something solid when everything seemed to be subliming before him, evaporating into thin air.

"Peter, some of Dr. Ambling's assistants will be by later to get you out of here. They'll take you to a secure location, where you'll be placed in a dark room. It's only temporary and will allow your brain to clear the fog and reset itself. This is for your good."

Nichols and Ambling excused themselves and left the room, closing the door behind them. Peter thought about trying to escape, but what was the point now?

Instead he closed his eyes and found himself battling an urge he could never remember having before. He felt he needed to pray, that he should pray, that it was the natural and right thing to do. But he couldn't; he didn't want to. He knew he had at one time, that prayer came naturally to him and was a source of power. He didn't know how he knew, but he did know it. Things were different now, though. The world was different; *he* was different. Maybe even God was different.

But still the urging nagged him, poked at him, prodded him. So he prayed. He pleaded with God to show him the truth, to not let it all end like this. He told God there needed to be more; Karen and Lilly needed to be alive. *Please let them be alive.*

Surprisingly, the words came easy, but he didn't know if they were sincere or not. And as he feared, his prayers seemed to go unheard, unable to get past the ceiling of the hospital. Whether God was intentionally ignoring him or Peter had lost all privileges with the Almighty, he didn't know. What he did know was that he was alone. And suddenly despair, like an untimely and unwanted visitor, crowded into his room, climbed into his bed.

Was there any hope of ever finding Karen and Lilly? Were they even alive? Maybe Nichols was finally telling him the truth. Maybe they really were dead. Maybe all the trouble he'd gone through, all the lives he'd taken, all the danger he'd faced and tragedy he'd avoided, was in vain. Maybe it was all for a smoke cloud of hope.... It was all for nothing.

FORTY-ONE

. . .

He'd been hooded and escorted by vehicle to an unknown building in an unknown location. He was placed in a room that couldn't have been more than ten by ten, just big enough to accommodate a cot and latrine. Darkness as black as octopus ink surrounded him, forming long tendrils of despair that wrapped around his limbs, torso, and neck and found their way into every orifice, penetrating to his soul, bringing a lightlessness that breathed and felt and thought.

But Peter didn't care anymore.

In fact, he welcomed the darkness, even embraced it. It offered him the solitude he needed, the protection from his own senses. It took him to a place where there were no more lies, no more stories, no more conflicting memories, a place where there was just darkness. And yet at the same time, it tormented him terribly, loomed everywhere and over everything, threatening to over-shadow every last memory he had, whether real or not. All Peter had now was his mind, as fractured and fragmented as it might be, and he didn't want to lose it too.

Day after day he'd sit on his cot and relive the events in his home that morning the men came, the morning he shot and killed all three of them. He'd run through every event—and every sense-less death—that followed: Amy, the Oceanview, Ronnie, Habit, Centralia.

Day after day he relived what memories he still had of Karen and Lilly. He focused on the details of their personalities, their lives, wondering what had been real and what had been fabricated as part of his imprinting. What had he really experienced, and what had he only imagined? Worst of all was that he couldn't even pic-ture them in his mind without second-guessing what he saw.

And day after day he rehashed the words as they circled through his head.

"Remember your training, Patrick? Huh? It'll come back to you. It always does."

"You don't remember yet. You will. Give it time."

"Things aren't what they seem. They're not what you think."

"What's not what I think, Amy? What do you mean?"

"This. You. Me. Everything. We need to find Abernathy. It's—"

Peter flinched at the sound of the shot echoing through his head. The memory of it still startled him. The way Amy's head had snapped back, the way her body had slouched and slumped to the pavement, still twisted his stomach.

"Things aren't what they seem. They're not what you think."

When the darkness entered and tyrannized his world, the

dreams of the house ceased, replaced by that dream of falling. Always falling but never hitting bottom. And always coming face-to-face with Nichols. Night after night he fell; he groped at the air; he fought to avoid Nichols's grinning face. And every time he'd awaken when Nichols drew his gun, aimed, and fired.

Nichols's "few days" had turned into what seemed like weeks. Hopelessness, with its featureless face and formless figure had emerged from the darkness and wrapped its smooth, chalky hands around Peter's mind, around his heart, squeezing out what little faith was left. Day and night meant nothing to him anymore. His biological clock no longer functioned properly. He'd sleep in spurts with no concept of how long he'd slept or how long he'd stayed awake. At times he'd awaken on the concrete floor and think he was on the wall, stuck there like a fly. He'd feel the air for the cot only to find it just feet from him.

His movements now felt sluggish, as if gravity's pull had increased in the darkened room, tugging at him with greater force, straining his muscles.

His thoughts had also turned dark. He tried to remember Karen and Lilly, but their image was fading in his mind like an old photograph exposed to the sunlight for too long. His memories, false or actual, were slowly being replaced by thoughts of death and a myriad of interesting ways he could quicken it. He'd be better off dead.

And still the dreams of falling continued. But the feeling encompassed so much more than just his dreams now. Even in his waking hours he'd suddenly feel as though he were falling and clutch at the floor and walls to steady himself.

His body wasted; his muscles atrophied. His legs wobbled as if they were jointless when he stood. The tasteless food they fed him was not enough to nourish a child, let alone a grown man.

He knew what they were doing, that they were breaking him all over again. This was part of the scrubbing process. Or maybe they weren't. Maybe he had it all wrong. Maybe they'd locked him away in this dungeon and forgotten about him. And this was where he'd slowly fade away and die alone. Of all the exotic ways he'd come up with to welcome death, oddly, starvation was not one of them.

But there was a moment when things changed for Peter. Whether it was day or night he did not know, did not care. He was awake, lying on the floor, arms and legs outstretched, contemplating death and how easily he might accept it, when he suddenly had the compulsion to pray. As before, he didn't know where the urge came from. He'd had no inclination to talk to God since that day in the hospital when he'd pleaded with him and received no acknowledgment. His begging had gone unanswered, his pleas unnoticed. God was silent. But now the yearning to speak with the Almighty was very real. A need. He *needed* to pray. At first he resisted it as he had last time, fought it as if it were not just a waste of time but an adversary seeking to rob him of his last sliver of sanity. God could not reach him in the pit. Peter was too far gone, too resolved to his own hopeless death, too given to the darkness that now infused every fiber and cell of his body.

But still the urging persisted.

For an undetermined yet lengthy period of time, it went on and Peter resisted, used his remaining ounces of resolve to combat it. And though the pressure to pray tormented him, he was thankful for it because it gave him something to think about, something to focus on.

But over time his willpower faded and the persistent voice inside him grew louder and louder until he could block it out no longer. He had to give in; he had to surrender. There was no fight left in him. Finally he dropped to his knees on the concrete floor, covered his face with both hands, and prayed. It was not an earth-shattering prayer of celestial proportions. It was not anything you'd hear in a church from the pulpit. It was not anything you'd read in a book, nothing that would get a host of angels excited. But it was a prayer. And this time, he knew it was sincere. It felt right, familiar, like a glove that had been stretched and molded to fit only his hand.

When he had uttered the last word, Peter lowered himself to the floor, prostrate, limbs splayed. Oddly, peace surrounded him in the darkness of the pit. The thoughts of death had not been banished, his wounds had not been instantly healed, but for the first time since lying in that hospital, he felt a spark of hope.

Eventually he fell asleep on the floor and awakened inside the house.

FORTY-TWO

· · ·

The second-floor hallway loomed like a hotel's endless corridor. What a relief it was to see light again. For a moment, Peter basked in the sunlight of this dreamworld, until the third room beckoned him, pulled him in as if it had some magnetic power. Keeping his hand on the wall to steady himself, Peter walked the hallway and stopped in front of the third room. The door stood open, waiting. Before, when he'd looked into this room, it had been furnished with one bed—the bed he'd had in his childhood room—a dresser, a desk, and a collection of objects one would acquire in the military. A footlocker, helmets, a flak jacket, uniforms folded neatly on the bed. There were no weapons. This was the room where Peter would usually find Karen, sitting on the edge of the bed looking like she wanted to tell him something, like she *needed* to tell him something.

Now, though, the room's decor had changed. It was set up to appear identical to Lilly's bedroom. The same bed and pink bedspread. Same light-green shag area rug. Same dresser and lamp. The shades were pulled to cover the windows and not allow in any light. Only one thing remained out of place. In the far corner, between the bed and wall, stood the floor lamp with the *C* on the shade.

Peter entered the room and reached for the lamp on the dresser. He clicked it on and noticed the Mickey Mouse watch next to it. He picked it up and rubbed its face with his thumb.

Replacing the watch, he crossed the room to the floor lamp and ran his hand over the glass shade and traced the *C* with his finger. Why had this lamp affected him so much that it now appeared in every room of this dream house?

He heard a shuffling in the hallway behind him. Peter turned and faced the doorway. More movement in the hallway drew him out of the room.

Lilly was there—his Lilly, as he remembered her, wearing the last outfit he'd seen her in: pink capris and a white T-shirt with a red-and-pink floral design on it. Her hair hung loosely around her shoulders. She was no more than ten feet away, facing the door of the fourth room. The locked door.

Peter wanted to run to her and scoop her into his arms. He wanted to hug her and bury his face in her hair, breathe in the fresh scent and never let go, never leave her again. But she was a mirage, a sleep-induced figment, as much a counterfeit as any three-dollar bill, and he wasn't sure he could trust this version of his daughter.

So instead he stayed where he was and said, "Lilly, what are you doing?"

Still turned away so he couldn't see her face, she put her hands in her pockets and shrugged. The image was so much like her. The way her shoulders lifted and dropped, her posture. It was all Lilly to a tee. His mind had remembered so many details that made his sweet girl unique.

Peter knelt. He didn't know why but he felt compelled to, like it was just the right thing to do when you saw your daughter after so long and so much.

"Lilly, baby, please turn around and look at Daddy."

Slowly, as if to move too fast would cause her to lose her balance and fall, Lilly turned. She was the girl from the bunker, the girl that had hugged him so tight and stirred him so deeply.

Was this still Lilly? She was only an actress—Maddy.

The girl smiled at him, a genuine smile that went all the way to her eyes. Peter wanted to push away, though, to move back down the hall. He wanted to wake up. But he couldn't. He couldn't move and couldn't stir himself to awaken.

The girl took a step toward him.

"Stop," Peter said. "You're not—"

"I am Lilly, Daddy," the girl said. "You have to remember."

That was what the woman had said right before she left Peter in the tunnel to go to her daughter, who had been taken by the agency. *"You have to remember."*

"Remember what?"

The girl's smile disappeared and was replaced by a pouty frown. "Me. Mommy. You have to remember."

"You're the girl from the—"

"I'm Lilly. You saw what they did to me." Her eyes teared and reddened.

The monitor, the electric shocks. The poor girl had been

through so much and now Peter was rejecting her. He couldn't. Even if she wasn't who she thought she was. Maybe they'd brainwashed her too. Scrubbed and imprinted her mind.

She advanced again and stopped not two feet away and tilted her head to one side, studying him like Lilly did, the same way Karen did. The corners of her mouth turned down and she said, "You're scared. Why are you scared?"

It didn't matter what she looked like, Peter realized. In his mind's confusion of a dream, this girl was his daughter, and it had been so long. No matter what Peter thought of her, he couldn't hurt her any longer. She believed she was Lilly, and there was no harm in playing along.

Peter said, "I miss you."

"But I'm right here."

"In a dream, yes. But when I wake up, you'll be gone."

Her smile returned again. "I'm not gone, silly. You have to find me."

Inexplicably, tears pushed on the backs of Peter's eyes, and he suddenly found it impossible to swallow. "Where? Where do I look?"

She reached for his hands and held them. Her touch was the touch of his daughter. "I'll pray for Jesus to help you."

"I need it," Peter said. "I need his help."

"Mommy and I will be okay."

"How do you know? How can you be so sure?"

She let go and cupped his face in her hands. As much as Peter didn't want to cry in front of her, he couldn't help but let a stray tear slip from his eye.

"Jesus will take care of us, Daddy. Don't worry, okay?"

But Jesus hadn't taken care of them yet. Jesus seemed nowhere to be found.

She studied his eyes, looking past them and into his soul. "Don't think that, Daddy. It's not true."

She'd read his mind. She'd seen past his exterior armor and looked right into the hurricane that engulfed his heart. As if someone had run an ice cube down Peter's spine, he shivered.

"But he hasn't helped you." Peter couldn't believe he was verbalizing his deepest struggle to this eight-year-old.

She frowned again. "But he *has* taken care of us. He hasn't left me alone, not for one second."

More tears pushed from behind Peter's eyes and found their way out, cascading down his cheeks.

"Trust him, Daddy. Do you trust him?"

Peter hadn't. He'd given up on trusting God, trusting Jesus. But now it seemed different. This child, this imposter of his daughter, had strangely given him hope. She'd begun the process of renewing the faith he once had, the faith that had survived multiple brainwashings or scrubbings or whatever Nichols wanted to call them. They could take away his old mind, his old memories, his old life, but they couldn't take away the underlying core of who he was. That much survived.

It wasn't a knock-'em-over, tingle-and-break-into-laughter experience. It was as subtle and natural as a trickle of springwater from a rock, and as deep and real as the water vein from which it flowed.

He was ready to trust again. He was ready to embrace the faith he'd once had and the faith that remained. He was convinced it was the only way he'd find the real Lilly and Karen. Peter nodded. "Yes. I trust him. I'm ready."

The girl broke into a wide smile, her eyes bending into crescents. She even giggled a little. "Good. You need to start with the Bible in my room."

"I didn't see a Bible in there."

"It's on my dresser, my Precious Moments Bible."

"There wasn't anything there but your watch."

"Go look again with your new eyes."

Peter stood and entered the room again. And there on the dresser was Lilly's little pink leather-bound Bible. He lifted it and balanced the weight of it in his hands. As he shifted it to the other hand, the book fell open, and the pages parted to the same passage he'd read the last two times in the Bible he'd found in the other rooms.

He traced the words while he read in the gospel of John. *"I am the door. If anyone enters by Me, he will be saved, and will go in and out and find pasture."*

Peter closed the book and placed it back on the dresser. It was the passage he'd read before but couldn't remember.

That last conversation he'd had with Audrey Lewis walked through his mind.

"I think it means your subconscious mind is keeping something from you."

"So what do I have to do?"

"Find the key."

She'd made it sound so easy when Peter thought it would be impossible to find the key. The door would remain locked for the rest of his life and he'd spend the rest of his sleeping nights wrestling with it and the rest of his waking days wondering what secrets it protected.

But now he knew it. The Bible. The verse. *"I am the door."* It was the key. Or more specifically, Jesus was the key.

And it had happened just like Amy said it would at the Ocean-view. A trigger. This girl and her faith. Faith was the trigger.

Peter left the bedroom and stood in the hallway. The girl was now gone, the hallway left empty. All that stood before him and the door was ten feet of flooring and a mountain of faith. He needed to stop trusting in himself; that's what Karen would tell him. Stop trusting his skills and ability to fight out of every situation. Ultimately it had gotten him nowhere. He needed to let go of the reins he held so tightly and give them to God. He needed to admit he couldn't do this on his own, to stop striving and just surrender.

Then, from the first floor of the house came a terrible banging noise, like someone taking a sledgehammer to the very foundation of the home with an intent to destroy it and bring the entire structure down.

Peter fought the ache in his bones and rolled to his back, opened his eyes. The dream was over; he was awake. The door to his room was open about six inches, and light, beautiful light, poured in and colored the concrete floor a pale gray. He squinted as it opened the rest of the way. Before him stood the backlit silhouette of a woman.

FORTY-THREE

· · ·

The woman stood in the open doorway, hands hanging at her sides.

Peter righted himself and pushed back so he was seated against the wall. He could tell by the woman's figure that it wasn't Karen. Too small and thin. She wore a pantsuit and lab coat, and her hair was pulled back off her face in a bun.

"How are you, Peter?"

He recognized the voice. Ambling. She was going to take him away and experiment on him now. Poke him, prod him, maybe torture him. He knew how it worked. They'd break him down to nothing, then rebuild him into the man they wanted him to be. Again. Into the soldier they wanted him to be. Again. After all that had transpired, they still weren't done with him. How much could one mind handle before it suffered too much tampering and shattered like a crystal vase?

She opened the door wider, and Peter shielded his eyes from the light.

"How do I look?" he asked.

"Like you need a shower, a shave, some clean clothes. How do you feel?"

"Like I need a shower and a shave. Definitely some clean clothes."

"Would you like a hot meal too?"

"What are you serving?"

"Whatever you want."

"Fast food? I could really go for a greasy burger and fries."

Ambling turned to leave. When she spoke, he could hear the smile in her voice. "We can arrange that."

She exited the room, and three men dressed in gray scrubs entered. Orderlies of some sort. They lifted Peter from the floor and escorted him into a hallway. It appeared they were back in the bunker under Centralia. Same concrete, same doors lining the walls.

The men took Peter to a bathroom, handed him a towel and change of clothes, and shut the door without saying a word. The bathroom was small but not cramped. It consisted of a toilet, sink, and shower stall with a frosted-glass door. Tile lined the floor and walls; the ceiling was concrete. Everything was white and clinical.

Peter undressed and stood before the mirror. He hadn't lost as much weight as he thought he had, nor had he lost much muscle mass. After getting a few meals in him, he should regain his strength quickly.

The hot water energized him as it washed away the grime that coated his skin. The shower was already supplied with a bar of soap and a small travel-size bottle of shampoo. Peter lathered his hair and stuck his head under the nozzle, letting the water wash the bubbles over his shoulders and chest and down his back.

From outside the shower, a woman's voice said his name.

Peter rinsed the soap from his face and wiped the water from his eyes. Through the steamy, frosted glass he could see the figure of a woman. He assumed it was Ambling again.

"What do you want with me?" Peter said.

The woman said nothing but stepped closer to the shower stall, and Peter instinctively stepped back and covered himself.

"What are you doing?" he said.

The woman did not respond but neither did she move.

Finally she said, "Why did you come here, Peter?"

Despite the hot water hitting him in the chest and abdomen, despite the clouds of steam billowing within the stall, Peter broke out in chills. It wasn't Ambling at all. It was Karen. His wife. But how?

Karen put one hand, fingers splayed, on the frosted-glass door and said, "You did this. Don't you remember?"

Frozen with his back against the wall, Peter opened his mouth, but nothing came out. He tried to form words, but his throat produced no sound. He tried to lift his hand, but he couldn't.

Karen didn't move, didn't open the door. She remained motionless with her hand resting on the glass. "Only you can make this all right again," she said. "You need to let them change you, this time for good. Then we can be together. You. Me. Lilly."

It sounded like Karen, but it wasn't her. It couldn't be. Karen would never want him to change. She'd never go along with Nichols's scrubbing and imprinting.

"No."

"You must, Peter. For us."

Anger took over him, flooded his blood and made it boil. They had no right to do this to him.

"I won't. I can't." If he gave in to the process, he might forget Karen and Lilly for good. As far as he would be concerned, they would never have existed. He couldn't allow that to happen. He couldn't live without them, didn't want to.

Peter forced himself to move. He lifted his arm and practically threw it at the door, slid it open.

But there was no Karen. She'd been a mirage. Or a hallucination.

They were gassing him again, like in the school gymnasium, causing him to see things that weren't there, to hear voices that didn't exist. They were toying with his mind, disassembling it memory by memory.

Peter shut off the shower and stood in the stall, his skin crawling, dripping water, his heart pounding. The chill had intensified, and now he shivered as if he were standing naked in the middle of Antarctica. He slid the shower door open the rest of the way and suddenly felt very dizzy. The shower's tiled floor moved beneath him; the walls waved. His legs grew weak, wobbled; he was standing on stilts of rubber.

Peter reached for the towel and dropped to his hands and knees, half in the shower, half out. The floor spun faster and faster until he thought he'd faint.

The bathroom door opened. Peter's mind was muddled, could barely make sense of what was happening. Men entered, grabbed his wrists and ankles. They loomed over him like demons, their eyes hollow sockets, their mouths gaping chasms. A strange hissing sound emanated from their mouths.

Peter was dragged along the floor, the room still turning circles around him. As he passed the sink, he saw Lilly there—her old self, the way he remembered her—standing in a white shirt and pink jeans, her hair in pigtails. She held a teddy bear, the one Karen's parents had given her for her sixth birthday.

"Daddy," she said, her voice soft and urgent, "listen to them. Do what they tell you to do. For me and Mommy."

Peter tried to speak, tried to tell her he loved her and that he'd rescue her, but his throat seized as if concrete had been poured down it.

The men continued to drag him as Lilly faded from his view and the room around him grew darker. He tried to fight it, to keep his wits about him, but resistance was futile, and soon everything went dark.

FORTY-FOUR

. . .

Peter felt as though he were floating on a cushion of air, and he would have believed it too if not for the annoying squeak of wheels in need of oil. The ceiling passed by slowly, concrete, lights, and air vents. His head still in a fog, his brain seemed stuck in one gear, and any attempt to comprehend the situation caused an awful grinding in his ears.

He attempted to lift his arms, to sit up, but his wrists were secured. His ankles too. He watched the bland wall slide by. How long was this corridor?

Peter tried to lift his head, but it weighed too much; he could only roll it from side to side.

He rolled his head to the left and this time saw Lilly standing there. She seemed to float alongside the gurney. Peter's eyes

303

had difficulty focusing on her, but he could vaguely make out the downward turn of her mouth, the sadness in her eyes. Once more he tried to speak to her, to tell her he'd make it all right. He wanted to tell her that he trusted Jesus, that he'd listened to her and Mommy and surrendered and had faith that all would be okay, regardless of the outcome. But his tongue felt like it was three sizes too large for his mouth and he'd lost all control of it; he could only produce garbled words, incoherent jumbles of sounds and syllables.

Lilly put her finger to her mouth, silencing him, and said, "Do what they tell you to do, Daddy. You must go along with them."

Peter shook his head. He wouldn't. She didn't understand, poor kid. They'd brainwashed her, and probably Karen too. He couldn't let them steal everything from him. He shut his eyes to refocus, but when he opened them, Lilly was gone. Peter turned his head to the right, but she wasn't there either.

He tried to say her name, to call to her, but all that came out was a mess of slurred letters. Peter strained against the straps, but it was futile.

The gurney turned right. A man's voice spoke, but Peter couldn't make out what he said. A few more feet and the gurney slowed. Above him a fluorescent bulb hummed. A door opened and the gurney was pushed through the open doorway and into a dimly lit room.

Peter shut his heavy eyes as the gurney was pushed across the room. When he opened them again, he noticed a large circular LED operating room light suspended above him. Somebody across the room spoke and the light flipped on, blinding him. He shut his eyes and again fought the restraints at his ankles and wrists. A warm hand rested on his forehead. Peter opened his eyes and found

Karen standing over him, smiling. But when she spoke, it was not with Karen's voice but rather Dr. Ambling's.

"Don't struggle, Peter," she said. "It's okay. We're going to give you something to relax you."

Peter shook his head, tried to tell them he didn't want anything, didn't need anything, but his tongue didn't work and his lips felt swollen and clumsy.

Ambling disappeared, replaced by a man wearing a surgical mask and scrubs. His eyes smiled at Peter. "You'll just feel a pinch."

Again Peter shook his head.

The prick came, and suddenly Lilly was there in the room with him, by his side. Only it was the new Lilly, the girl from the bunker. She lifted her little hand and rested it on his arm. Her touch was so soft and warm. "Trust him, Daddy. Do you trust him?"

Her eyes were urgent, and the tightness around her lips and jaw changed the shape of her face.

"Daddy, do you trust him?"

Peter knew whom the girl spoke of, and it wasn't Nichols or the man in scrubs. He nodded.

She smiled. "Good. Then trust him. You'll need to…"

But before she could finish, the light above him faded and the room grew dark. A severe weight pushed down on Peter until he thought he'd suffocate. Finally light was overcome with darkness and everything faded away.

• • •

Peter awoke with his eyes still closed. At first he didn't know where he was and imagined himself back in his home in his bed, the light of the sun filtering through the blinds to awaken him. But the bed on which he lay was hard and cold, not at all like his bed at home.

He tried to focus and remember where he was, but his mind swam in a murky soup, images coming and going, ebbing and flowing. Lilly was there, smiling at him, her hands extended as if she were begging him to come to her, to rescue her. Karen was there too, her eyes pleading with him. She mouthed words, but there was no sound. Then Amy appeared, urging him to come to her. Her face showed panic, fright. Gunshots rang out, sharp and distinct, a staccato of them, accompanied by flashes of light and explosions. Outside of this convoluted collage of images, he heard the soft, indistinct warble of two men's voices in conversation and behind them a gentle clinking, like the sound of small screws being dropped into a metal pan.

It came to him then. He was in some kind of operating room buried deep in the bunker beneath Centralia. As his mind cleared, Peter remembered more of what had taken place. The dark room, the shower, the hallucinogen. They had strapped him to the gurney and wheeled him beneath a bright light. He'd seen Karen and Lilly, but they were false images, like a Pepper's ghost on a flimsy glass pane.

He brought his mind back around to the room, the gurney, the light overhead, and the clinking of metal. Were they planning surgery?

One of the men in the room said something and the other laughed. Peter knew he had only one chance at this. Apparently they thought he was still unconscious, still under the effects of whatever sedative they had given him.

Seconds passed and with each tick of the clock, Peter's mind cleared more. He rolled his right arm palm up, then palm down, and did not feel the restraints around his wrist. They'd unsecured him, perhaps to transfer him to an operating table, then not bothered to reapply the restraints, thinking he was no threat while he was safely unconscious.

Soft footsteps approached and Peter held still. He could hear breathing so close it seemed to be only inches away.

Peter had to act now. He opened his eyes while simultaneously sitting up. The man, a twentysomething dressed in a lab coat, stepped back and dropped the instrument he had in his hand. He couldn't have appeared more surprised if Peter had been dead and suddenly sprang to life.

Peter swung his right foot around and caught the guy in the side of the head, shoving him sideways. He grunted and stumbled into a metal cart, dumping tools and instruments, then fell to the floor. There was one other technician in the room, heavyset, middle-aged. He made a move for the door, but Peter was off the table and across the room before he could reach it. Peter's movements were clumsy, his limbs heavy. The anesthesia was still in his blood. Grabbing the guy by the lab coat, Peter yanked him back and pushed him hard into the adjacent wall, nearly falling on top of him. The guy reached for a pair of forceps, but Peter awkwardly slapped his hand away.

Behind Peter, the other technician was on his feet. He exhaled loudly and made a charge at Peter, some sort of stainless-steel instrument in his right hand.

Still gripping the taller technician's coat with both hands, Peter swung him around and drove him into his colleague. The men's heads collided, sending them both to the floor in a conglomeration of arms and legs.

While they were dazed and struggling to reacclimate themselves, Peter found a roll of surgical tape and quickly bound both men by their wrists and ankles. He also shoved a roll of gauze in each man's mouth and taped it in place.

With both technicians bound and gagged, Peter collapsed to the floor, fatigue overwhelming him. He needed to rest, to replenish his energy. He felt he needed to sleep for days but knew he had mere minutes, maybe seconds, before his escape was discovered. He had to keep moving. Willing his limbs to function, he pushed himself to stand and leaned on a counter. His stomach roiled and churned with boiling bile, and he felt like he might vomit.

A can of soda sat on the counter. Peter glanced at the two technicians bound on the floor and grabbed the can. Taking huge gulps, he downed more than half of it in two swigs. The sugar would do him good, give him a burst of energy. He drained the rest of the can.

Glancing around the room, checking all four corners, he saw no cameras. Odd, given the seeming omniscience they'd shown in other situations. Maybe the agency didn't want any recorded evidence of what happened in this lab—something so unethical, so egregious, the agency took precautions against whistle-blowers.

At the door, Peter paused and turned toward the technicians. They blinked and glanced at each other. He hesitated, then reached for a pair of surgical scissors on the counter and walked toward the men. Their eyes widened. If there was even a slight chance that Karen and Lilly had been returned to the bunker for more experiments, Peter had to know, and these two were the only sources he had.

Peter squatted in front of the men and held up the scissors. "Guys, there's a couple ways we can do this and one of them will be awfully painful for you. I want to know where my wife and daughter are. Karen and Lilly Ryan."

The men glanced at each other again but made no show of wanting to talk.

Peter shrugged. He had to work quickly. He grabbed the younger technician by the belt and yanked him forward. He then grabbed the man's bound hands and pried open his fist. Extending the man's little finger, Peter opened the scissors and placed them around the quivering digit. "I wonder how well these scissors cut through bone. I'm guessing not so well."

The man's eyes widened and he moaned, tried to pull his hand away. The other technician hollered as well and squirmed, trying to get himself into position to resist Peter. Peter punched the man in the face with the side of his fist, then replaced the scissors around the shorter man's finger.

Finally the man opened both hands and his eyes pleaded for Peter to stop.

Peter cut the tape holding the gauze and removed the roll from the tech's mouth. "Tell me," he said, "or I won't hesitate to remove your fingers one by one."

The man swallowed, then said, "I need some water."

"I don't have time for this," Peter said, grabbing the man's hand again and lifting the scissors.

"No, no, no. Wait. I'll tell you." Tears spilled from the young man's eyes now. "They don't pay me enough for this."

"Where are they?"

"I don't know, man."

Peter slapped the man in the mouth.

"It's not our job to know."

Peter hit him again. "Where are they?"

As if he'd just been told that not only had his position with the agency been terminated but he'd been selected to be discontinued, the man tilted his head back and moaned. He glanced at his partner, who widened his eyes and shook his head. "I don't care anymore, man. It's not worth losing my fingers. I don't know where they are—"

Peter put some pressure on the scissors, starting to dig into the man's little finger.

"But I know the room where you can find what you're looking for. It's in B corridor."

"Where is that?"

"Two corridors away. This is D."

"Which way?"

The man said nothing. He licked at a trickle of blood that had seeped from a cut on his lip and tried to wipe at it.

Peter hit him, even more fiercely. "Which way?"

The other technician grunted and shook his head.

"Please, man, stop. I'm just a tech. I'm nobody around here. Make a right out of here and go to the end of the corridor, then go left. Two more intersections, then the first room after you turn right. That's what you're looking for."

Peter replaced the gauze in the man's mouth, stood, and crossed the room to the door. He paused before opening it and said a quick prayer.

"Do you trust him?"

Yes, I trust.

FORTY-FIVE

· · ·

Cracking the door, Peter listened for footsteps or the scuffing of boots on concrete, but the corridor was silent and still. His little revolt and escape had yet to be detected. He poked his head out of the doorway; the corridor was empty. Slowly he closed the door behind him, then proceeded to the right down the hall, sticking close to the wall. At the end of the hallway he rounded the corner and headed in the direction the technician had indicated.

He didn't know whether the man had told him the truth or directed him into a trap, but he had had nothing else to go on. His only protection now was diligence. At the junction of the next corridor, Peter paused and checked the hallway. It was lined with doors like the other tunnels and also was clear. Quickly he crossed the junction and headed to the next passageway.

Again he paused, waited, listened, then peered around the corner. A woman in a white lab coat was headed the opposite direction, her back to him, her heels clicking on the concrete like a clock wound too tight. Peter waited until she rounded the far corner, then shuffled down the hallway to the first door on the right. His heart pounded in his chest, filling the space between his ribs and spine, and he could feel his pulse in his fingertips. He rested his hand on the door's handle.

Peter depressed the handle all the way and pushed open the door. Without hesitating, he stepped inside and shut the door. A light automatically flickered on, illuminating a room whose four walls were lined with gray file cabinets. In the center of the room sat a metal desk with a computer, printer, and scanner.

"The room where you can find what you're looking for." Wasn't that what the technician had said?

Peter locked the door, then sat at the desk. The computer was equipped with a fingerprint scanner. He placed his thumb on the small pad and waited. A box popped up on the monitor with a bar that traced back and forth across the screen. The word *VERIFYING* blinked in time with the bar's movement. After a few seconds the screen went black, then blinked on again. Against a light-blue background, black text read:

Confirmed
Jedidiah Patrick
Welcome!

Peter sat back in the chair and clasped his hands to steady the tremor that had overtaken them. The computer knew him as Jedidiah Patrick, not Peter Ryan.

Moments later the screen blanked again, then sprang back to life, displaying some kind of home page with various icons. Peter clicked on the Files icon. From there he clicked on a link labeled Personal.

A list of pages appeared. Peter clicked on one labeled Family.

When the page popped up, an involuntary gasp escaped Peter's mouth. On the screen were two photos of Karen and Lilly, the wife and daughter Peter remembered. The first was posed, Karen seated with Lilly standing by her side, her delicate hand on Karen's shoulder. Both wore pretty dresses with small floral prints. Their smiles were forced for the camera.

The second photo was not posed; in fact, it appeared to have been taken without Karen or Lilly's knowledge. They were by a pond, Karen squatting and holding something out to Lilly. Karen wore jeans rolled to her calves and a red-and-white gingham blouse. Lilly wore shorts and a white T-shirt with flip-flops.

Instinctively Peter reached out and touched Karen's face on the screen.

He scanned the text on the page. It stated that Karen Aubrey Wells was born on March 6 and that Lillian Marie Patrick was born on July 12. Both correct. Except for the last name. There it was again: Patrick, not Ryan.

Peter read on as a chill like the thready legs of a thousand spiders climbed down his neck and back and caused him to shiver. The document claimed both Karen and Lilly had died in a car accident.

Peter let his hand slide off the mouse and fall onto his lap. That word—*DECEASED*—burned a hole in his eyes, his mind, his heart. It couldn't be true. He refused to believe it, but there it was. The images were of Karen and Lilly, *his* Karen and Lilly—there was no mistaking it. They had the right people. Was Nichols right all along? Had he been telling Peter the truth? Or was this just another trick, another step in his mind-altering torture?

"That's what you're looking for." The technician had known Peter would find the truth here.

With a numb, trembling hand, Peter forced himself to exit the file and clicked on one labeled Military.

Another photo appeared, this one of himself, a bit younger and leaner and sporting a full beard. He wore an Army uniform and looked scared or angry or maybe both.

Peter stared at the photo for what seemed a long time, studying the younger man on the screen, probing his eyes, trying to decipher what was peering back at him.

Finally he scrolled down to the text below the photo. Scanning it, he felt his heart rate become even more pronounced. Words and phrases jumped out at him and seemed to sock him in the gut.

...Sergeant Jedidiah Patrick, First Battalion, 75th Army Ranger Regiment...
...Medal of Honor... Purple Heart... Distinguished Service Cross... Silver Star...

Once again Peter's hand slipped off the mouse and rested in his lap. He sat there, dumbfounded, confused, an odd mixture of fear and anger growing in his chest. He had absolutely no recollection of ever earning those medals.

Back on the Files page, Peter moved the cursor to a file named Centralia and clicked. A page popped up that briefly described Sergeant Patrick's accomplishments, the medals he'd earned, the battles he'd fought. Another paragraph described him as stable, reliable. It included testimony from a military psychologist, stating that Jedidiah was competent and in excellent psychological health despite the combat action he'd seen in Iraq and Afghanistan.

Scrolling down the page, Peter found the mission Patrick had volunteered for. It was called the Centralia Project. The page offered only a brief description, stating the project's aim to develop the "perfect soldier, focused, disciplined, courageous, skilled, possessing the ability to make decisions quickly."

It stated that "Sergeant Patrick possesses all of these qualities and would make an ideal candidate."

At the bottom of the page was a scanned copy of a legal release form, signed by Patrick. Below the release form was an agreement to confidentiality forbidding Patrick to ever speak of the Centralia Project, the work, the members, or anything else he might know of it, with the consequence of imprisonment or death for treason if he did. Both forms were signed by Sergeant Jedidiah Patrick.

At the bottom of the page was a link that simply read MK-ULTRA (ABERNATHY). Peter clicked on it, and the screen went black with a single sentence in white letters blinking in the center of it:

Files no longer exist.

Outside the room, in the corridor, he heard a commotion, voices speaking hurriedly, someone shouting. They were looking for him.

FORTY-SIX

. . .

Quickly Peter shut down the computer, crossed the room, and stood by the door, his ear to the metal. The corridor was quiet now; his pursuers had moved on to another section of the bunker.

Slowly, quietly, Peter depressed the handle and opened the door. The hallway was empty. Part of him wanted to find the nearest occupant of this subterranean tomb and just surrender, but his survival instincts wouldn't let that happen. If there was a sliver of a possibility that Karen and Lilly were still alive, then he had to get to the top and begin the search for them. Nichols said they were dead. The computer said they were deceased. But he'd heard enough lies from Nichols that he wasn't ready to take that at face value. For all he knew, Nichols wanted him to find that computer and read those files.

Sticking close to the wall, Peter made his way down the corridor. At the end he paused. He thought about going back to the room where the technicians were bound and conscripting one of them to lead him to the surface, but he decided against it. By the time he got there, they might be free, and he'd find himself surrounded without a weapon. No, the best decision was to keep moving through the bunker. Eventually he'd find an exit.

This end of the bunker was apparently rarely used. Peter turned down the next passageway and stopped at the first door. Behind it something hummed steadily, and beyond the hum was a rhythmic thrum, like that of a huge clothes dryer.

After looking both ways, Peter opened the door and peeked inside. The lights in this room were already on, and Peter saw rows of big machines but no sign of human presence. He ducked in and eased the door shut behind him, then turned and found himself looking down the barrel of a handgun. A sloppy move, and he couldn't afford to get sloppy.

A man stood on the other end of the pistol, middle-aged, short gray hair, handlebar mustache, wide eyes and lips parted. His hands trembled ever so slightly. The man took two steps back, out of Peter's reach.

Peter raised both hands and showed the man his palms. "Easy now. I don't want any trouble."

"You're him, aren't you?" the man said.

"Who?"

"The guy who escaped. You're him." He stood with his feet wide and the gun shoulder-high. His respiration was quick and shallow. With the gun he motioned for Peter to move to the left. "Slowly now. I don't want any trouble either."

As Peter sidestepped, he said, "Who are you?"

"Bob. Maintenance."

Behind Peter was a chair. Bob motioned for Peter to sit in it.

Sitting, Peter said, "I just need to get out of here, Bob."

Keeping the gun trained on Peter's chest, Bob stepped backward several paces toward a small metal desk with a phone on it.

"Bob, don't pick up that phone, okay? Let's talk about this."

But Bob reached for the phone.

Peter stood and stepped forward, causing Bob to temporarily abandon his idea of calling for help. "You stay there, you hear me?" Bob waved the gun back and forth. His eyes were so wide Peter thought they might pop from their sockets. "Don't you come any closer."

Peter took another step toward the maintenance man. "Bob, you don't want to shoot me. If you wanted to, you would have already. Put the gun down. I don't want any trouble. I just want to get out of here. This doesn't have to be complicated."

"You're makin' it complicated. Now you just sit back down there."

"I'm not going to sit. And you're not going to shoot. Right?"

Another step forward. He was now no more than ten feet from Bob.

The gun teetered in Bob's hand. "No closer. Stop!"

Ignoring Bob's warnings, Peter inched nearer, keeping his hands where they could be seen to assure Bob he had no intention of harming him. When he was five feet away, Peter stopped.

One of Bob's hands now rested on the phone; the other held the gun pointed at Peter's chest.

"All I have to do is pick up the receiver," Bob said. His voice quivered. "It automatically places a call to HQ. If I don't respond, they'll think something's wrong and send someone to check on me."

"Then don't pick it up."

Bob's face twisted into a terrible grimace. "Get on your knees then."

"I can't do that, Bob."

Peter kept his eyes locked on Bob's, but in his peripheral vision he saw the man's hand tighten around the receiver. He was going to do it.

As quickly as a snake strikes from the cover of high grass, Peter lunged at Bob, taking hold of his wrist with one hand and the handgun with the other. Before Bob could even reflexively squeeze off a shot, Peter had the gun pointed at the man's face. Startled, Bob made to step back but stopped. He still had his hand on the phone.

"Take your hand off it, Bob."

Bob shook his head.

Before Bob could lift the receiver, Peter slapped him across the face and shoved him back. Bob stumbled, lost his balance, and fell to the floor. But in doing so, he knocked the receiver from its cradle.

Both men stared at the phone for a second. On the other end a steady beeping began.

Peter stepped between Bob and the desk. "I'm sorry. I am. I didn't want to hit you. But I need your help."

Bob looked at the phone. "It'll keep beeping until I give my password. And if I don't within twenty seconds, they'll send someone."

Peter approached him and grabbed his shirt with one hand, lifted the man to his feet. He pointed the gun at Bob's face. "Say it."

Bob hesitated, his lips trembling, right eye twitching uncontrollably.

"Do it," Peter said.

Bob gasped and contorted his face again.

Peter lifted the receiver and put it against Bob's mouth. "Say it." But Bob refused. Finally the beeping stopped.

Peter shoved the maintenance man back. "Bob!"

"I'm sorry," Bob said. He began to cry.

"Is there a way to the top from in here?"

Bob retreated against the wall and pointed to a door at the far end of the room. "Ventilation chimney. There's a ladder to the top."

"How far below are we?"

"Seventy feet."

That wasn't too bad. Peter had to make quick work of it, though. If security arrived while he was still on the ladder, he couldn't trust Bob to keep his mouth shut. If they found him midway up the chimney, he'd be a dead Santa.

With the handgun tucked into the waist of his pants, Peter ran for the door, threw it open, and launched himself onto the ladder. Hand over hand he climbed, as fast as his legs could push him upward. Above him there was a grate, and on the other side of the grate was daylight. As he climbed closer to the top, he noticed trees, leaves, clouds. Freedom. He only hoped the grate was not bolted shut from the outside.

When he was ten feet from the top, his shoulders and legs now burning, his lungs working hard to deliver oxygen to his racing heart, he heard the door from the corridor to the room below slam open and men shouting.

He pressed on, ignoring the pain, ignoring the fatigue. Five rungs to go.

His single focus was on the grate above him, growing ever closer. He imagined himself pushing on it and it flying up and off the hatch.

Two rungs to go. His legs felt as though they were made of wood; his arms felt dead, limp. But still he willed himself to continue.

Finally Peter reached the top. He pushed against the grate, but it didn't move, didn't budge. His heart sank. His shoulders were on fire, and his legs threatened to give out and send him plummeting the seventy feet to the concrete floor below. He pushed harder but still nothing.

Peter climbed one more rung so his upper back was against the grate. Lifting with his legs, he pressed against the grate. It moaned and moved ever so little. It wasn't bolted in place, only rusted shut. Again he pressed upward with his legs, gritting his teeth, straining every muscle. And again the grate moaned and creaked.

On the ground level the door to the ventilation duct opened. Peter looked between his feet and saw a man poke his head through the doorway and look up. He stayed like that for a full three seconds. From the ground level, anything at the top would be merely a silhouette against the daylight on the other side of the grate.

Peter remained motionless, his back against the wall of the duct, his shoulders and head against the grate.

The man stepped into the shaft and continued looking up.

Beads of sweat that had formed on Peter's brow now gathered at the bridge of his nose. He held his breath. To move and wipe at them would certainly give away his position. The sweat moved down his nose and stopped at the tip.

Below, the man continued looking up, not sure of what he was seeing.

A droplet of sweat dislodged from the tip of Peter's nose. Before it could hit the man below, Peter launched himself upward one more time, shoving with all his force against the grate. It creaked, snapped, gave way, and flew open, swinging up and out on hinges that moaned terribly. Sunlight rushed in like water over a breached levee.

The man at the bottom shouted something to his colleagues,

and with his torso out of the shaft, Peter heard a gunshot. A round ricocheted off the shaft. Peter twisted and writhed. Another shot sounded. Peter's legs cleared the top of the ventilation shaft, and he tumbled to the ground, breathing heavily, sweating profusely. His legs and arms felt as lifeless as lead.

He lay there, panting like he'd just run a mile at top speed, but he knew they might start climbing at any moment. Peter sat up and slipped the gun over the edge of the chimney, firing off two rounds. He heard a low grunt and a soft expletive from below. Not a fatal wound, but certainly no fun to climb with. And now that they knew Peter was armed and shooting, they might not risk being such easy targets inside the shaft. Even so, Peter didn't want them sneaking up behind him. He fired two more shots down the shaft and flipped the protesting grate closed again. There was a slot where the grate could be padlocked, but he didn't see anything sturdy enough to do the job. As a last resort, he jammed the barrel of the handgun into the opening, sealing his captors below. He hated to lose the weapon, but it was better than having an armed posse right on his tail.

After a minute of rest, Peter climbed to his feet and surveyed the area. The shaft had opened into the woods surrounding Centralia. All around were trees and underbrush, leaves and dirt. He had no idea which direction to go. He wanted to get back to town and find his truck. From there he could go somewhere safe where he could think about his next move, contemplate how he would lure Nichols out, and formulate a plan.

The shaft was on an elevated area of land, and a gentle slope downward lay directly in front of Peter. He knew Centralia was in a bit of a valley with hills all around, so he figured he'd try going downhill and see where it led. It was his best guess.

After five minutes of hiking, he noticed a home set back in the trees. It was dilapidated and in ruins, the roof caved in, the windows shattered, but a sure sign that he was headed in the right direction. Another five minutes and he came across what remained of a road. The asphalt was now broken and eroded, mostly covered with dirt and overgrown with serviceberries and saplings.

Peter followed the road to the edge of Centralia. From there he stayed in the woods along the perimeter of town until he came across the service road that led to where he'd hidden his truck.

Moving carefully but quickly and staying concealed by the growth around him, Peter located his truck, found the keys he'd hidden. At the driver's side door he reached for the handle and heard the crunch of leaves behind him. Before he could swing around, the cold, hard metal of a gun's barrel pressed against his skull.

"Don't make a move, Patrick."

Habit. It was Habit.

Without saying a word, Peter lifted his hands.

"Now slowly," Habit said, "on your knees."

Peter did as he was told.

"I'm sorry to do this to you, Patrick. Really, I am. But don't think you didn't have it coming."

The barrel pulled away, and a second later a terrible explosion went off in Peter's head. He felt his body go limp and then sank into oblivion.

FORTY-SEVEN

. . .

Peter awoke feeling confused and disoriented, as though he'd just been through the spin cycle of a washing machine and the whirling had yet to stop. Only he wasn't awake; he was in the house again, sitting at the top of the stairs, staring down at the first floor and its nearly empty rooms.

On the second floor everything was the same as usual, only this time the three doors nearest him were closed as well. It was as if his subconscious mind, the ringmaster of his dreams, were telling him that he'd looked there, done that, and now it was time to move on to the fourth room or give up altogether.

Peter wasn't about to give up.

He stood, holding on to the banister until his head stopped swimming, then proceeded down the hallway. At the fourth door he tried the knob, but as usual it was locked.

Then the girl's voice. Peter couldn't tell whether it was Lilly or Maddy. Or maybe both of them together. If there truly was a Lilly. Or a Maddy. *"Do you trust him, Daddy?"*

And that verse in the Bible: *"I am the door. If anyone enters by Me, he will be saved, and will go in and out and find pasture."*

The words echoed through Peter's head again and again. *"Find the key"* . . . *"Do you trust him?"* . . . *"I am the door."*

He reached for the knob again but stopped. No, he couldn't do this on his own. It wasn't about him, not really. It wasn't about finding the secret behind the door. It wasn't even about finding Karen and Lilly.

It was about giving up his hold on everything he'd been trying to control. It was about giving it all to him regardless of what he found, regardless of the outcome. Give it all to *him*. In fact, it wasn't about the room at all. It was about the door; it always had been.

Peter put his hand on the knob but did not try to turn it. He closed his eyes and felt a warmth pour over him. It started at the top of his head and traveled down his face, neck, shoulders, and chest, to his waist and over his legs, all the way to the soles of his feet. And then it reversed direction and moved up, like water defying gravity, to his waist, to his chest, and back to the top of his head.

"I trust." He said it aloud and meant it. He had no power to find Karen or Lilly, no power to find the truth, let alone face it head-on. He had no ability on his own.

"I surrender." He whispered the words. Sweet words. Words he'd never said, or at least didn't remember ever saying, but fully felt.

Beneath his hand, the knob moved on its own as if someone from the other side of the door was turning it. Peter lifted his hand from the knob and exhaled. The door swung open and the room with all its precious secrets was finally revealed.

And it was empty. Stark empty. Nothing there but four white walls, a white ceiling, and a wood floor. No furniture, no memorabilia, no person. The shadow pacing back and forth, always back and forth, had disappeared and proven to be bodiless.

Peter entered the room and stood in the middle of it, half-expecting Lilly or Karen to round the corner and join him. But they didn't. The emptiness was almost overwhelming, almost enough to spring tears from his eyes and release sobs from his throat. Where were his answers? Who was he? Where were Karen and Lilly? He had put so much hope in this room. His subconscious had done so much to protect him from its contents. And now that he'd discovered it was empty, the disappointment was nearly too much for him.

He ran from the room and tried the other doors. Maybe there were more clues in each of them, pieces of a puzzle he could assemble and get the full picture of who he was. But they were now locked.

No, God, no. Please. I trust you. I do. Please.

He fell to his knees outside the first door, and the hallway once more began to spin as fog moved up the stairs and swallowed the hall as slowly as it rolls in off an early morning ocean.

Yet again Peter awoke disoriented after being hit on the head. Slowly the world around him cleared and it all came back. He was outside. He'd escaped the bunker and found his truck. Then he'd been approached from behind. No, more than approached... assaulted. Habit. It was Lawrence Habit. He'd come back. Or maybe he'd never left.

Peter realized he was sitting in the passenger seat of a car, a sedan. Leather seats. Black interior. He was seat-belted but that was the only restraint. His head rested against the window, his cheek and ear pressing against the cold glass.

Slowly Peter lifted his head and looked to his left. Habit was driving, the burns on his face still bandaged from the grill. That seemed like such a long time ago—months, maybe years. How long he had been shut away in the dark was still a mystery.

Habit glanced at Peter but said nothing. He had both hands on the steering wheel, and there were no weapons in sight. Peter did not feel immediately threatened.

"Where are we going?" Peter said.

Habit checked the rearview mirror, looked out the side window. "There's someone you need to meet."

"Who?"

"Someone."

"That doesn't tell me much."

"He'll tell you everything."

"How do I know you're not going to kill me?"

Habit motioned toward a duffel bag on the floor at Peter's feet. "Thought you'd like a change of clothes."

Peter ignored the bag. "How do I know you're not going to kill me?"

Habit lowered his brow. "We've already had this conversation. If I'd wanted to kill you, I would have done it already. Besides, why would I bring you clothes only to kill you before you had a chance to put them on?"

"Then how do I know you won't turn me over to Nichols?"

"I could have done it while you were out."

"How'd you even know I'd escape?"

"You'd be surprised. There's more than just me who're less than pleased with the way Nichols runs the show. And it pays to still have some friends inside. When they told me you were out of the hole, I had a feeling you'd make it back to your truck sooner or later."

Habit bit his lip. He checked the mirrors again, then leaned forward and, peering out the windshield, scanned the sky.

"What are you looking for?"

"Making sure we're not being followed."

"By Nichols?"

"And whoever he sends after us."

Peter rubbed his face, then the back of his head. There was a lump there, tender to touch.

"Sorry about that," Habit said. "But I knew you wouldn't come voluntarily."

"No, I probably wouldn't have."

"No probably about it."

Peter was quiet for a moment, thinking, watching the trees blur by outside the car. "You know, I was once one of Nichols's soldiers. So were you."

Habit nodded. "Once. I'm not anymore." He glanced at Peter. "And neither are you."

"Sounds like we didn't have much of a choice."

A slight smile curved Habit's lips upward. "I had a choice. At first. But things get complicated when you deal with Nichols."

"*Complicated* doesn't seem like the appropriate word."

"Dangerous."

"There it is."

They were both quiet for a while. Peter watched the outside world slide by in a silent blur as the hum of the car's tires tugged at his eyelids. He fought sleep, though. He still didn't fully trust Habit; he couldn't. He couldn't trust anyone. Finally, still looking out the window, he said, "Why are you doing this?"

"Doing what?"

"Helping me. I thought guys like you worked alone. Acts of kindness usually aren't part of your repertoire."

"Is that what you call this? An act of kindness?"

Peter said nothing. He really wasn't sure what it was, but he knew Habit was telling the truth when he said he could have killed Peter on multiple occasions and had chosen not to. And that—sparing his life—was certainly an act of kindness of sorts.

Habit shifted in his seat, glanced at the rearview mirror, adjusted the collar of his shirt. "I owe you."

"You owe me?"

"You don't remember. You saved my life."

"In combat?"

"Not the kind you're thinking of." Habit once again checked the mirror.

For the first time, Peter noticed a hint of vulnerability in the set of the big man's jaw, the arch of his eyebrows.

"We'd come home after a tour in Afghanistan," Habit said. "I hated coming home because I had nothing to come home to. Only an empty apartment and a head full of nightmares. See, we were different. You did what you were ordered to do. I did that and so much more. Evil stuff. Violent stuff. And when I came home, I had time to dwell on it. This particular time I returned in a dark place. All I could think of was death. The killing I'd done and my own. I wanted to end it, you know? Just put a stop to it all. I was ready to—I was literally seconds away from pulling the trigger—when you called."

Peter remembered none of it, but he wished he did. He could see reliving those dark days was painful for Habit, and he wished he could assure the man he didn't have to retell the story. But Peter felt he needed to hear it.

Habit glanced at Peter. "You talked to me, walked me out of the valley. You told me there was hope for me and I believed you. I don't even know why I believed you. I think it was because I wanted to believe there was hope. Then you told me about your wife and daughter. You'd talked about them before but never like that. It made me want what you had. And I wanted it bad enough, I began to believe maybe it was possible."

"Wasn't it?"

"No. Not for me. After you disappeared, I thought you were dead. They wouldn't tell me what happened to you. I lost whatever hope I'd had, and that's when I started working for Centralia, doing their dirty work."

"But I wasn't dead."

"Nope. When I saw you at Cantori's house, it was like all that hope came rushing back. I'm not sure I could have killed you then even if they'd ordered me to. I'd all but forgotten what you did for me. They messed with my head too. But I remember it now. I owe you my life."

"You can repay me by helping me find Karen and Lilly."

"You'll get answers where I'm taking you."

Habit slowed the car at an intersection and turned right. The landscape changed from forest to farmland. On the left side of the road, an open field stretched to the horizon, undulating in rolling hills.

Peter said, "So will this mystery man be able to tell me where Karen and Lilly are?"

Habit's eyes moved from the road to the mirror to Peter, then back to the road. "Yes, he will."

FORTY-EIGHT

· · ·

They drove in silence for a couple of hours. Peter watched the world go by outside. Mostly, Habit stuck to rural roads that passed through forests of maples and oaks and sycamores and eventually turned to pines. Occasionally they'd pass through a field, newly harvested and brown with the death of autumn. Deer were there, foraging the grains left by the heavy equipment that had recently scoured the land. The roads took them over mountains and through valleys, across streams of glistening water and under remote railroad overpasses.

They were headed north. Ever north.

After two hours of travel, they passed a *Welcome to New York* sign, and Peter said he had to use the restroom.

Habit pulled the car into the next gas station and shut off the engine. They both sat there, watching an older man fill his Ford with gas.

"We need to keep moving," Habit said, "so make this quick."

Peter unlatched his seat belt. "How do you know I won't run?"

"Because you want to know the truth."

"I could find it on my own," Peter bluffed. He needed Habit now but didn't want the bald man to know that.

Habit frowned and shook his head. "Not this truth."

Opening the door, Peter said, "I'll be just a few minutes."

The bathroom in the convenience store was clean and empty. After changing into the clothes Habit had brought him, Peter was out in less than five minutes. He thought about running. Even after all Habit had told him, he still didn't fully trust the man. Like Peter, he'd been trained to kill, educated to be heartless and singularly focused. Could Peter believe that he'd had a change of heart, that seeing Peter again had really caused him to alter his course that much? Then again, he had come to find him.

Returning to the car, Peter closed the door and hooked his seat belt. He'd decided he had no other option than to play along with Habit and see where this trip took him.

Twenty minutes into the second leg of their journey, Peter said, "You know Nichols is still alive? That guy you shot wasn't him."

"I know. I knew then."

"Then why'd you take the shot?"

"To send a message."

"Do you think he got it?"

Habit slowed the car and turned left onto a road that appeared to be freshly paved. The yellow center lines hadn't even been painted yet. "Nope. That's another reason I came back. They'll come after us. They're not going to give up on you."

"And you're using me as bait again."

Habit shook his head. "That's not exactly what I have in mind."

The big man was being intentionally enigmatic, giving Peter just enough information to keep him interested. Peter had had enough for now. He turned his head and watched out the window as they passed through a small town. There was one intersection and one light. A police car was parked just beyond the light, the officer keeping watch on the traffic, waiting to catch someone violating the law—speeding, running a red light, making an illegal turn. The officer met Peter's eyes as they passed, but there was no sense of recognition in them. Peter realized then he had been holding his breath and exhaled.

"Where are we going?" Peter said.

"I told you—there's a man you need to meet."

"The mystery man. I know. I mean where, a location, like on a map."

Habit glanced at him. "Ever hear of Utica?"

"Sure."

"Just north of Utica is the Black River Wild Forest. That's where the truth is."

Two hours later Habit turned the car onto a dirt road that wound its way up a mountain dotted with pines as tall as five-story buildings. The road was narrow and rutted, and at times the sedan bottomed out and scraped on the stony ground. Habit did his best to avoid the potholes and ridges. He cursed under his breath each time the ground rose or dipped sharply.

At the top of the mountain, concealed by trees that stood as tall and straight as telephone poles, sat a cabin. It wasn't much to look at—just four walls and a slanted metal roof—but it was solidly built to withstand the harsh winters of upstate New York. Smoke puffed from the chimney and threw the aroma of burning wood into the air.

Habit parked the car alongside the cabin and shut off the engine.

"Someone wants to be left alone," Peter said.

Habit studied the cabin with intent eyes. "More like someone else wants him to be left alone."

"What did he do?"

Habit turned toward Peter. "What makes you think he did something?"

"This has the feel of exile rather than escape."

Habit didn't answer. He opened his door and exited the car.

Outside, the air was cool and crisp, and the combination of smoke and pine scents intensified. Above them, the tall canopy of trees blocked most of the sunlight. The ground was barren and rocky, blanketed with dry needles.

"Though it would be a nice place to escape from the world," Peter said.

The cabin had a sprawling front porch that stretched the length of the front wall. On it were four wooden rocking chairs and a small table. Before Habit could knock, the front door opened and an elderly man appeared. Without saying a word, he hugged Habit and clapped him on the back. He appeared to be in his eighties. He was slightly shorter than Peter with a shock of thick white hair. His chest and arms were thick, remnants of a physique hardened by manual labor or strenuous exercise. Even in his advanced years, he moved with an athletic manner.

When he pulled away from Habit, the old man looked at Peter and studied him with serious gray eyes. "So this is him?"

Habit nodded. "It's him."

The man approached Peter and stuck out his hand. Peter took it.

"Son," the man said, shaking Peter's hand. "I'm Roger Abernathy. We got a lot to talk about."

FORTY-NINE

· · ·

Abernathy turned and entered the house; Habit and Peter followed. The interior was furnished with antiques and rustic pieces. The door opened to a great room with a cathedral ceiling. To the right was a small kitchen and two closed doors, no doubt a bedroom and a bathroom. Deer antlers and rifles of every size and caliber decorated the walls of the great room, and from the peak of the ceiling hung a chandelier made of moose antlers.

Abernathy headed for the kitchen. "Sit down. Sit down. Would you like some coffee? I just put some on."

Habit declined but Peter, both intrigued and intensely curious, agreed. "Please. Sugar, no cream."

Minutes later Abernathy returned with two steaming cups of coffee, handed one to Peter, and sat on a chair opposite the sofa where Peter sat.

Abernathy sipped at his coffee, not taking his eyes off Peter the whole time. "So I hear you're looking for answers. Is that right?"

Peter held the mug with both hands and nodded. "The truth would be nice for once."

"Yes. You've been fed a buffet's worth of lies, haven't you?"

"It seems that way." Peter took a sip of his coffee but didn't take his eyes off the older man. "I just want to know the truth about my wife and daughter."

Abernathy shifted a glance at Habit, then looked back to Peter. "Ah, yes, and we'll get to that. But first, Lawrence brought you here to me because I'm the only one who can give you the whole truth and nothing but. Do you know who I am?"

Peter shrugged. "Someone important enough to exile. You need to be kept quiet but also kept alive."

Abernathy smiled and sipped from his mug. "Very good."

"Whose side are you on?"

Abernathy turned his head slightly and fixed Peter with narrow eyes. He'd taken offense at Peter's question. "Does my side matter if I have the truth?"

"Trust matters, don't you think?"

"Certainly. Then what are the sides? The lines can be rather ambiguous sometimes, you know."

Peter paused. What was happening in that hole under Centralia was wrong. "With Nichols, or against him."

Abernathy studied Peter as if he wasn't satisfied with that answer. Finally he said, "I'm on your side, Jedidiah."

Peter straightened and placed his mug on the coffee table. "Why do you call me that?"

"It's your name. Your real name. The name your mother gave you at birth. Jedidiah Patrick. It has such a nice sound to it."

Peter was growing anxious. This Abernathy was as nebulous as Nichols, and no answers had yet to come out of his mouth.

As if he'd read Peter's body language, Abernathy crossed his legs and said, "In the 1950s the CIA began a project it called MK-ULTRA. Ever hear of it?"

"'Files no longer exist,'" Peter said, remembering the empty folder on the computer back in the bunker.

"You're a resourceful man, Jedidiah. MK-ULTRA was a program developed to determine how far the human mind could be altered and controlled. Experiments were done on human subjects, some aware of what was happening, others not so aware. All sorts of methods were used. Drugs, hallucination, deprivation, torture. The early results were astounding but unpredictable." He paused and looked at his hands, twisted them as if he were massaging an invisible lump of dough. "I was a researcher. We studied ways to program multiple personalities. But then in the early seventies, we were exposed, and ULTRA was shut down. The files were destroyed. There was much outrage over the experiments."

"What does this have to do with me and my family?" Abernathy's story was intriguing, but Peter failed to see the connection between some secret CIA project so many decades ago and him.

"The outrage, Jedidiah, was a front. We made such great strides, there was no way the government was going to just give up on our work, cast it aside as if it had never taken place. ULTRA was discontinued, but Centralia was born. And I was asked to head it up. It took us a while to get our bearings again after all the congressional hearings in the eighties and after the dust settled."

"I'm still not seeing the connection."

Abernathy leaned forward and rested his elbows on his knees. "You were born in Pennsylvania Dutch country. Your parents were young, unmarried, and scared. Your mother was Brethren, your father Catholic. A most unlikely union that never had a chance. Your mother ran away from her family, gave birth to her son, and promptly gave you up for adoption. Her family eventually took her back but not before intense shaming. Your father disappeared."

Peter found his heart racing in his chest, and blood surged through his neck and ears.

"As a child," Abernathy continued, "you spent time in a handful of foster homes. The system became your family, but it made a poor one. At eighteen you joined the Army, full of fight and attitude. You served your four years, got out, got married, and had a child."

"Lilly."

"Yes. Lillian. Sweet girl. But you missed the service. You missed the security, the structure, the predictability, so you rejoined. You were the best, Jedidiah. Absolutely the best in every way." Abernathy hesitated and looked as if he might begin to cry. "Until tragedy struck. It was outside Kandahar. Your unit was ambushed and driven into a warehouse. There were no survivors except one."

"Me."

"You. And barely at that. Amazingly, you had few physical injuries. But you suffered severe head trauma. We essentially brought you back from the dead, gave you new life, a new purpose."

"Centralia."

"I saw the potential in you; of course I did. You were our hope for resurrecting the work begun in MK-ULTRA. Nichols was heading it up then, and he, too, saw the opportunity you presented us with."

Still Peter remembered nothing. His flashbacks were there, but they were so spotty, so irregular and unreliable. Abernathy's story was totally unbelievable, and yet Peter found himself wanting to believe every word of it. "How do I know you're telling me the truth?"

"I know you've been lied to so much, haven't you? But the lies stop here. I have proof that will convince you." He motioned to Habit, and the big man got up, crossed the room, and retrieved a laptop. Abernathy ran a hand across his forehead and rubbed his eyes. "Nichols was a liar even back then. He told you your wife and daughter were dead, told them you had died in the mission. He said it was the only way to get you to volunteer. And for the programming to be effective, he needed a willing subject. I disagreed with his tactics. I've done a lot of things in my life I'm not proud of—not now, at least—but what he suggested crossed the line for me. I got out. Told them I was leaving. And that's when they banished me to this mountain. They knew the secrets I keep would bring down kingdoms, crumble the White House, the CIA, Congress, everything Americans trust."

Habit set the laptop on a coffee table and swiveled it so the screen faced Peter. He hit a key, and a video began to play. The picture was grainy and the filming amateurish, but the person front and center was definitely Peter. He wore Army fatigues with sergeant's stripes on the sleeve. He sat at a desk, back straight, hands resting on his thighs. Across from him at the desk sat Nichols. What was visible of the room was bare save for an American flag next to the desk.

"Name and rank," Nichols said.

Peter lifted his chin. "Jedidiah Kurt Patrick. Sergeant. US Army Rangers. Sir."

Jedidiah. Peter's face flushed and heat burned in his cheeks. That was him in that video. It wasn't some digital trickery or any such thing. He knew it was him. The real deal. And his name was Jed, just like Habit and Abernathy had said.

On the video, Nichols said, "Do you understand the mission of the Centralia Project?"

"Yes, sir."

"And do you, Jedidiah Patrick, willingly volunteer for the Centralia Project?"

"Yes, sir."

"Why? What is your motive?"

"To serve my country, sir. To do my duty. Sir."

Nichols slid a piece of paper and pen across the desk. "Sign at the bottom, Sergeant Patrick."

Without hesitation, Jed picked up the pen and scribbled his name on the paper.

The video stopped with a freeze-frame of Jed looking at Nichols. The look on his face was one of determination, of resolve and purpose. He knew full well what he was getting into. Or at least he thought he did at the time.

Peter pinched the bridge of his nose, then looked toward Abernathy.

"I know it must come as a shock, son, but you're not the man they made you think you are."

Habit crossed his arms and nodded.

"So why have they kept you around?" Peter asked Abernathy.

"I'm valuable to them. I'm not proud of this, but over the years, I've been able to help them. Give them information they need."

"Why? Why would you help them?"

"To stay alive. Without my cooperation they'd have no reason to keep me around. I was biding my time, waiting, hoping for an opportunity like this."

Peter was quiet for a long moment. "So why bring me here and tell me this?"

Abernathy smiled again. He had a nice smile, warm and welcoming, a smile one could come to trust easily. "You're our last hope for shutting it all down. The project has gone awry, experimenting on children and holding them and their mothers prisoner. It's grown dark under Nichols and needs to be exposed for what it is. Nichols needs to be stopped."

"Why can't you expose them? You were part of it. You have all the inside information."

Abernathy sipped his coffee and let out a long sigh. "My past is very dark and checkered. I've done some wicked things." He paused and a shadow moved across his eyes. "Things I'm ashamed of. Things that have tarnished my reputation. Outside of the project my word means little. Most in Washington think I'm dead, and I can tell you no one mourned. If I suddenly showed up and wanted to pull the cover off a project few even know exists, I would not be taken seriously."

"Can't Habit do it then?"

Abernathy leaned over and patted Habit's knee. "Lawrence is part of the plan. Voluntarily, I might add. He found me a week ago and asked me for my help. When I met him, I knew the opportunity had come. But you, Jedidiah, you're the missing piece of the puzzle." He stopped to sip his coffee again. "You see, this is my last chance to make things right. To do some good for a change. A lot can happen on a mountaintop, you know. One can even find God and forgiveness. Consider this my final act of restitution."

Abernathy dug in his pocket and pulled out a small thumb drive and handed it over. "This is everything you need. All the names of everyone who knows about Centralia. Locations. Documents. Videos. It's all there."

"And what do I do with this? Just walk into the president's office and hand it to him?"

Abernathy laughed. "Goodness no. You might get slightly farther than I'd get but that would do no good. No one wants this information exposed. Be careful with it."

"Then what do I do with this?"

"You'll know when the time comes."

"I don't like that answer."

A smile pushed the corners of Abernathy's mouth toward his eyes. "Neither do I, but I knew what to do with it when the time came."

"Give it to me."

Abernathy nodded.

"So I can pass it on to someone else?"

"When the time comes, if you feel that's the answer."

Peter—Jed—didn't like this. He didn't want to be this involved. He only wanted to find Karen and Lilly, disappear somewhere for a long time, and regroup his life. But from somewhere inside him, a voice whispered and told him this was the right thing to do. He didn't know how he'd accomplish it. He hadn't any idea even where to begin. But he knew he had to at least try. He glanced from Abernathy to Habit. "Where are Karen and Lilly? Does this lead back to them?"

"It does," Abernathy said. "They tampered with your mind. Programmed multiple personalities."

"I know that. What does it have to do with where my wife and daughter are now?"

"They fed you what they wanted you to remember, to see, to

know, to experience. But what they fed you is merely images and ideas; remember that."

Throughout the entire conversation Habit had sat quietly and listened. Now he spoke. "Your real memories, the real you, is still in there. They call it scrubbing, but they can't delete what's already been recorded in your brain. The truth is in your mind; it's just buried under layer after layer after layer of false images."

Peter's heart began to thump again, and suddenly his fingers started to tingle. "Why are you telling me this?" He feared the worst, that they'd tell him Karen and Lilly were really dead, that they were saving the most devastating news for last.

But instead, Abernathy motioned to Habit and said, "There's a couple you need to meet."

Habit rose from his chair and crossed the room. He stopped in front of a wooden door, placed his hand on the knob, and looked back. Then he opened the door.

FIFTY

• • •

The woman and girl from the bunker emerged. Nichols had called them Nora and Maddy. But then, Nichols had said a lot of things. Peter's heart beat harder, faster; he could feel his pulse in his throat, temples, ears. Sweat wet his palms. He rose slowly from the sofa and faced the woman and child, who stood just outside the room, holding hands. The looks on their faces said they recognized him, knew him. There was sorrow there yet a glint of hopefulness.

Behind Peter, Abernathy stood as well and walked past him. He stood beside the woman and girl and rested his hand on the girl's shoulder.

She was the girl from the dream, the girl who claimed to be his Lilly. Now that he faced her again in daylight in a much less stressful situation, he found himself wanting to believe that it was true.

"Jedidiah," Abernathy said, "I gave you all that information so you'd be ready for this moment, so you'd understand it better, be able to place it in context and accept the truth. The images in your mind of what your wife and daughter look like are false, placed there by Nichols's staff of psychologists. You must look past them now; you need to have faith—believe without seeing." He paused, squeezed the girl's shoulder, and smiled at the woman. "Jedidiah, this is your wife and daughter. Karen and Lillian."

Peter began to tremble, as faintly as a shiver runs over the surface of skin. He had an inclination to shake his head, to demand the lies to stop, to run from the cabin. But he couldn't. Something held him there. A desire to know, a need to explore the possibility and probe for the truth—the truth that transcended whatever false realities were piled up in his fractured brain.

He took a step closer to the couple. The woman who claimed to be Karen stared at him with wide, hopeful eyes and mouthed his name. *Jed.* Tears formed in her eyes, and her lower lip and chin began to quiver.

"Don't rely on what your brain is telling you, Jedidiah," Abernathy said. "Listen to what your heart says. And your soul. They can tamper with your mind but they can't touch those."

"They told you we died, didn't they?" the woman said.

Peter did not respond. He needed to hear more, but how much more would convince him?

"They told *us* that *you* died," she said. "In Afghanistan. They wanted Lilly to go to their school. Do you remember? The Centralia School?"

He did remember. The dream, the room, the brochure. The Andrews Academy. The school for gifted children.

"After they told us you died, that man visited us again. Several times. He wouldn't give up." She pulled the girl close and hugged her. "Lilly didn't trust him. She kept saying that you wouldn't want her to go there. She warned me." Tears formed in the woman's eyes and one spilled down her cheek. "I didn't listen, though, and eventually gave in. That's how we ended up in that prison."

Her words sounded like truth, and why wouldn't they? He remembered the man, the school, the decision they had made not to send Lilly there. But his memories were populated by a different wife and daughter.

"Daddy," the girl said. Her voice was sweet and innocent. "You found my note, didn't you? That's why you came looking for us."

A chill raced down Peter's spine. She knew about the note. But how? The only other person he'd shown it to was Amy. Could it be…?

The woman released her grip on her daughter and drew closer. "My Jed."

The sound of her voice was beautiful, but it wasn't Karen—at least not Karen as he remembered her. They were asking him to look past that, though. Believe without seeing or hearing.

She was before him then, barely a foot away. He looked deep into her eyes, searching for the truth, for some unquestionable evidence that she was indeed his Karen.

The woman moved even closer and rose onto her toes to place her mouth against his. The touch of her lips sent electric impulses through his body, not enough to move him but enough to stir images from some depth he didn't even know existed. There was no flood of memories, no onslaught of revelations. But he was suddenly certain: there was no question now who this woman was. And with their lips still touching and him leaning into the kiss,

Jedidiah Patrick began to cry. He wrapped his arms around Karen, his wife, his sweetheart, and pulled her close.

He eased away from Karen as his daughter, his precious Lilly, ran to him and wrapped her arms around his waist. It was really them. It would take some getting used to, but as unbelievable, as unlikely as it was, he was ready to believe it was them and—

In the distance, the faint sound of a chopper's blades beating the air grew closer.

Abernathy moved across the room to the front of the house. His swiftness defied his age. "They're coming."

Habit joined him. The sound of the chopper grew louder.

"Jedidiah, you'll have to take them and go," Abernathy said.

"What about you?"

"I'll hold them off. You need to get out of here."

"We can't leave you."

Abernathy grasped his arm and squeezed. The intensity in his eyes could ignite a fire. "Listen to me. I'm an old man. I've done things of which I'm too ashamed to ever mention again. This is my time to make it right. To do some good. Now you and Lawrence take Karen and Lilly and get out of here."

Habit stepped close to Abernathy. "I'm staying with you. Patrick, you take your family and go."

The chopper grew closer and louder. "No, I can't leave both of you. I won't."

"I owe you," Habit said. "Remember? Hope. You gave me hope. Now it's my turn."

Abernathy crossed the room, opened a gun safe, and began pulling out a stockpile of weapons. He tossed one rifle to Habit as he spoke. "There's an emergency exit through the floor, a tunnel that will drop you out farther down the mountain."

"Won't they be expecting that?" Karen said.

Abernathy lifted an area rug to reveal a trapdoor in the wood flooring. "They don't know about it. I thought this day would come, sooner or later, when they'd need to get rid of the evidence. I had years to prepare myself."

Outside, the chopper's thumping grew still closer.

"Quickly now," Abernathy said. "Down you go." He passed off a rifle and a handgun. "Just in case."

Habit handed over an envelope. "Hang on to this too. It's your ticket out of this world. Good luck, Patrick."

It would take a while to get used to, he knew, but even now the name Jed Patrick was starting to sound more and more like himself.

Habit lifted the trapdoor. Beneath it was a dirt tunnel lined with corrugated piping that dropped about twenty feet, then turned south. A wooden ladder fastened to the wall provided a way to descend. It must have taken Abernathy years to complete.

The chopper was now overhead, the concussion of its blades almost deafening. The windows of the house rattled; the floor vibrated.

"Go," Habit shouted. "We'll hold them off."

Crouched by one of the front windows, Abernathy looked their way, gave a thumbs-up, then waved them on.

Jed squeezed Karen's shoulder. "I'll go first, then Lilly, then you."

She nodded, worry and fear etching deep lines in her brow.

"Let's go," Jed said.

He descended the ladder and waited for Karen and Lilly to do the same. When Karen's head had cleared the floor, Habit lowered the trapdoor back into place and darkness closed in on them.

Jed helped Lilly off the ladder, then Karen. He hugged them both.

"It's really you, isn't it, Daddy?" Lilly said.

Jed held her close and stroked her hair. Sporadic memories were falling into place, pieces to a complex puzzle slowly fitting together. "Yes, darling. And it's really you."

Karen pressed herself against her husband's side. "I'm afraid, Jed." Even in this terrifying moment, the sound of his name—his actual name—on her lips was like a balm washing over him.

"It's okay," he said. "Stay put and let me get a feel for where we are."

The darkness was oppressive, almost palpable, and seemed to have a weight all its own. But unlike the darkness of the underground cell, this was a pregnant darkness, one that promised a new start on the other end.

Above, they could hear hurried footsteps on the floor, then the *pop-pop-pop* of gunfire.

Jed frantically felt the walls of the tunnel, searching for any source of light. He had no idea how long this tunnel was or what kind of turns or drops it took. He didn't like the idea of groping around in the dark, buried two stories underground, in a metal tube barely wider than his shoulders. Finally his hands found a small plastic box. He unlatched it and lifted the lid. It was filled with objects of various sizes and textures, but there was one that was unmistakable. A flashlight. Jed switched it on and a swath of light illuminated the tunnel.

The firefight continued above. Gunfire, muffled by earth and floor, sounded like raindrops on a tin roof.

"C'mon, let's go," Jed said. "We need to move fast." He knew Habit and Abernathy wouldn't be able to hold them off for long. If the chopper had found them, it was a sure bet that ground forces wouldn't be far behind. Soon the two men would be overwhelmed by sheer numbers and would be forced to either surrender or fight to the end.

On all fours, the threesome crawled, Jed in the lead, keeping the light pointed southward. Behind them darkness loomed and in front the light reached twenty, thirty feet, then was swallowed by what appeared to be an abyss of emptiness.

They crawled in silence for what seemed to be at least a quarter of a mile. Finally the tunnel took a slight turn upward and the light found an exit hatch.

Karen blew out a breath. "Oh, thank God."

The exit hatch was round and had a hand wheel in the center to seal it from outside exposure. Jed grasped the wheel and tugged it counterclockwise. The wheel moaned as it broke loose from its locked position and began to turn.

Muted sunlight flooded the tunnel when the hatch swung open. Jed half expected there to be armed men waiting for them, but the surrounding forest was void of any gun-toting hit men. In the distance they could still hear the beating of the chopper blades and an occasional concussion of gunfire. Whether Abernathy and Habit would survive the ordeal, Jed couldn't know, but they had succeeded in delaying their pursuers.

Jed helped Karen and Lilly from the tunnel, then surveyed their surroundings. The tunnel had opened on the side of a hill, the opening protected and hidden by a stand of serviceberries. Around them stood giant pines, oaks, and maples, their branches offering a shield from any hovering aircraft looking for three fugitives.

"Will Mr. Abernathy and Mr. Habit be okay?" Lilly asked.

Jed pulled her to him again and hugged her. The feel of her body against his was somehow so familiar, so ordinary. "They can take care of themselves."

Karen looked around and rubbed her forehead. "Which way do we go?"

Jed reached into his pocket to retrieve the envelope Habit had handed him. He slipped the contents from the envelope and unfolded a bundle of papers. They were birth certificates, three of them. One for Eric Bingsley, born in Baltimore, Maryland; one for Angela Tiegel, born in Hartford, Connecticut; and a newer one for Abigail Bingsley, also born in Hartford. Included in the bundle was a map of the Coeur d'Alene National Forest in northern Idaho. A star marked a location along a service road deep in the heart of the forest.

Also in the bundle was a smaller sealed manila envelope. Jed broke the seal and slipped out a pair of keys, two driver's licenses for Eric Bingsley and Angela Bingsley, and a fold of hundred-dollar bills totaling ten thousand dollars.

"What's it for, Daddy?" Lilly said.

Jed tucked all the contents back into the envelope and stuffed it in the front pocket of his pants. "A new life, sweetie. For all of us."

Trekking down the mountain, Jed led the way. The terrain was rough but not impassable. The soil was soft, but the carpet of pine needles, as well as the stones that jutted from the ground like worn molars, provided some traction.

They'd traveled not even twenty minutes, picking their way along at a pace slower than Jed liked, when he felt something slam into the back of his left shoulder and heard the distinct crack of a gun. The impact threw him forward and spun him around. Immediately he hollered for Karen and Lilly to get down even as another gunshot ripped through the still forest air.

FIFTY-ONE

• • •

Karen lay on the ground, facedown, Lilly pressed up against her.
Jed had hit the ground too. His shoulder burned like a hot poker
had worked into the muscle surrounding it and now wrenched this
way and that. He tried to move it, but it was useless; any activation
of the muscles surrounding the shoulder sent that poker deeper
into the tissue.

Below them, about forty feet, sat an outcropping of boulders.
They needed some cover.

Dirt kicked up to Jed's left as another shot sounded.

Jed slid Karen the rifle. "Take it and head for the rocks. I'll cover
you. Stay low and use the trees for protection."

Eyes wide with fear, Karen grabbed the rifle and nodded.

Jed rolled onto his left side, ignoring the pain that ate at his nerves, and lifted the handgun with his right hand. "Go," he said to Karen and Lilly. He squeezed off three rounds as they scrambled to their feet and took off for the rocks.

More shots came from the higher ground. Jed returned fire and prayed Karen and Lilly had made it to the outcrop safely. He stole a glance behind him and didn't see them.

Rolling to a tree five feet to his right, Jed got to his feet and used the thick pine for cover. He had seven rounds left, and the best he could tell, there were at least five gunman. He needed better cover than this tree; he too needed to head for the rocks.

Holding his left arm close to his body to minimize the jarring, Jed took off running, one tree to the next, zigzagging his way down the hill. Bullets zinged around him, took chunks out of the trees, and sprayed dirt. One nicked the flesh on the back of his right arm. It bit like a snake.

When he reached the rocks, he ducked behind them and found mother and daughter crouched, holding each other tightly.

The gunfire had stopped. Their pursuers were advancing.

Jed said to Karen, "Take the rifle and go with Lilly. You need to get out of here." He handed her the envelope. "Here. I'll hold them off."

"We're not leaving you," Karen said.

"You have to. I'll find you." Though he knew he wouldn't. He'd hold off the gunmen long enough for Karen and Lilly to escape, but the odds of his survival were not in his favor. "Now go. Quickly. They're coming."

Mother and daughter stood, Karen holding Lilly's hand with her left and the rifle in her right.

"Ready?" Jed said.

They both nodded.

"It'll be okay. You'll see."

"God's with us, Daddy. I know that."

Jed wished he had the faith that Lilly possessed. Truth was, he honestly didn't know if this would be the last time he'd see them. How tragic, he thought, to be brought together after so much only be torn apart again. A lump lodged in his throat. He had so much he wanted to say to them; they had so much missing time to relive. But there was no time now; there might never be time. He reached out and touched Lilly's hand, then Karen's. "Go!"

Hand in hand, they took off down the hill. The moment they cleared the rocks, Jed popped up and scanned the area above them. Two gunmen slid out from behind trees and raised their weapons, but before they could fire, Jed dropped them both with two quick shots.

Another round came from his left and ricocheted off the rock. Jed spun, found the shooter, and squeezed off a shot. Bark exploded off the tree next to the man.

Four rounds left.

Movement higher up the mountain caught Jed's eye. Two more men dashed out from behind a tree. Jed fired twice, hitting one in the chest but missing the other.

Two men remained, one about thirty yards to his left, ten o'clock, the other higher up the mountain, fifty yards, at one o'clock.

He had only two shots left. He needed to draw them out into the open. He knew he was a quicker aim than they were. If they exposed themselves, he could get off a round before they could. But he didn't want to initiate a confrontation too soon. Karen and Lilly needed time to descend the mountain and get a safe distance away.

Jed moved around to the right of the boulder, putting the bulk of it between himself and the gunman to his left. From this vantage point he would be able to focus on the gunman farther up the mountain without worrying about the other man getting off a clean shot. Every movement sent jarring pain through his arm, shoulder, and neck. The left side of his shirt was now soaked and clung to his body like plastic wrap.

Leaning against the cool rock, Jed again breathed a quick prayer, for Karen, for Lilly, for himself. It occurred to him then that he was falling back into old patterns, thinking it was up to him to save Lilly and Karen. Maybe he wasn't the protection they needed. If he was to get out of this alive, it would not be by his own doing.

Before he could talk himself out of it, Jed lunged away from the rock. Pine needles crackled; leaves crunched. But instead of committing himself forward, he stopped his progress and quickly pushed back.

The distraction worked. Hearing the commotion, the gunman peeked out from behind his tree, rifle raised. Jed had only the smallest target. He aimed, pulled the trigger. Bark flew and the gunman cursed. Jed had only succeeded in knocking the rifle from the man's hands.

Without a moment's hesitation, Jed stepped out again, this time far enough that the man to his left could see him. The gunman on the higher ground hadn't retrieved his gun yet. He was crouched by the tree, holding his hand. Pressing his left arm to his body, Jed ran forward, up the hill, keeping an eye on the position of the gunman to his left.

As planned, the man showed himself. He swung out from behind the tree, rifle raised, and as he dove to the ground, Jed saw the muzzle flash. As he fell, Jed raised his handgun and fired at the gunman, hitting him square in the chest. The man's arms flew up, the rifle sailed, and he fell back, motionless.

Frantically Jed continued scrambling up the hill. If he could reach the other gunman before he retrieved his gun, he would have a fighting chance. But when he was still thirty feet away, the man launched himself forward, scooped up the rifle with his left hand while holding his right hand against his chest. He spun around and pointed it at Jed.

"Hold it! Stop right there!"

Jed pulled up, panting, sweating. His arm was going numb, his hand and forearm swelling. Blood dripped from his fingertips. He was growing weaker by the second.

"Hands up," the man hollered.

Jed raised his right hand. His heart hammered in his chest. This was it. This was how it would all end. In the woods, alone, with no one but this killer to even witness his death. He was glad for that, though. He wouldn't want Karen or Lilly to see this. He prayed again that they were far enough away and that they'd make it to the cabin in Idaho, someway, somehow, that they'd be safe and able to start a new life.

A familiar voice spoke then from an unseen location. "You're a difficult man to hold on to, Peter."

Nichols. His voice was unmistakable. He emerged from behind the trunk of an ancient oak, hands behind his back, head held high, like a big-game hunter who had just brought down his prize trophy and now wanted to gloat in his victory.

The gunman approached Jed cautiously, making sure to keep enough distance between them to avoid any hand-to-hand engagement. As he drew closer, though, Jed noticed two fingers missing from his right hand. He held the rifle tight against his shoulder, but still it wavered. He'd gone pale and his skin glistened from a cold sweat.

"They want me to discontinue you, you know," Nichols said. He too made his way closer to Jed, carefully navigating the rocky, sloped terrain.

Jed said nothing because there was nothing to say, no argument to make, no sentence to deliver. He didn't want to give Nichols the joy of hearing him beg, either.

Nichols and the gunman stepped closer to Jed until they were fifteen feet away. Nichols put a hand on the gunman's shoulder. "I don't want to kill you, though. There's still more to do. But you know those military types—they do want their orders followed. They're so obsessive about it." He drew in a deep, melodramatic breath. "So I guess I have to reluctantly comply."

Jed's mind whirled, searching for any way out of the situation, but there was none. He was trapped, had no plan and no options. End of the road.

"But I don't have to watch," Nichols said. He tapped the gunman on the shoulder. "Whenever you're ready." Then he turned his back to Jed and began making his way up the hill.

The gunman repositioned his feet and tucked the stock of the gun even tighter against his shoulder. He tilted his head to the left to bring Jed into the gun's sights.

Jed tensed. He had to do something; he wasn't about to go down without a fight. But if he lunged at the gunman, he'd be dropped before he could take one complete step.

Nichols continued making his way up the hill. Every now and then his shoes would slip on the pine needles.

Before Jed could do anything, the crack of a gun sounded, and he flinched, thinking it was the gunman. Nichols spun around. The gunman wavered, lowered the rifle slowly, then went to his knees. A hole the size of a quarter oozed bright-red blood from side of his head.

Nichols reached inside his coat, but before he could draw his own weapon, Jed snatched the rifle from the falling gunman and aimed it at Nichols. "Don't do it," he said.

Nichols froze, his hand still buried in his coat, feet wide, eyes intent and serious.

Jed quickly closed the gap between himself and Nichols, keeping the rifle trained on Nichols's head. "Pull it out and drop it."

Nichols slowly removed his hand, which grasped not a handgun but rather an envelope. He held it high.

From Jed's right, Karen and Lilly emerged from behind a stand of three close pines. They walked quickly to Jed, Karen still grasping the rifle she'd just used to put down the gunman. When she reached Jed, she said, "I told you we weren't leaving you."

Jed gave them both a subtle smile, then said to Nichols, "What's that?"

"My insurance."

"Throw it on the ground in front of you."

He did. The envelope landed midway between Jed and Nichols. Jed asked Karen, "Can you open that, please? Tell us what's in it."

Karen moved forward carefully to retrieve the envelope, then opened it and slid out a packet of papers. She unfolded them and scanned the top sheet.

"What is it?" Jed asked.

Nichols stood relaxed, arms at his sides, his eyes bouncing back and forth between Karen and Jed.

Karen held out the papers. "You'll want to see this for yourself." She handed over the papers, then trained her own rifle on Nichols.

Jed stared at the documents, not sure he wanted to know what was printed there. He'd been told so many lies already; how could he ever sort it all out? He was still getting spotty, sporadic memories stuttering through his mind, images and voices and feelings, as valuable to him now as pure platinum and yet so foreign.

Jed took a deep breath and read the top page. It was a birth certificate for Peter Ryan, born in Baltimore, Maryland, on August 15. His own birthday. The parents were Richard and Serena Ryan.

"It's yours, son," Nichols said. "Your true identity. Abernathy told you your name was Jedidiah, didn't he? That you were an orphan and the military became the only real family you ever knew."

Jed flipped to the next page, a military medical report for a Sergeant Peter Ryan. Ryan had apparently spent time in Walter Reed Medical Center after suffering severe head trauma, six contusions across the cerebral cortex. Words like *blunt force trauma, comatose, unresponsive, vegetative state*, and *death* jumped out at him.

"It's just a name. Peter Ryan could be anybody," Jed challenged, even while an eel squirmed in his stomach.

"Keep reading," Nichols said.

Jed flipped to the next page and nearly dropped the papers. There was a picture of him in his dress blues, an official Army photo. Peter Ryan, Ranger.

The forest floor seemed to shift beneath his feet. The trees overhead and all around loomed menacingly, their branches reaching for him. It couldn't be him.

"You were the best," Nichols said.

Jed didn't look up from the paper. He stared at it but read none of the words. They were just black letters floating in a white sea.

Nichols took a step closer. "It was an ambush. You were part of a team sent to rescue our ambassador to Kenya. His convoy had been attacked, everyone killed except him. A group of rebels held him hostage and we needed to get him out. But someone must have tipped off the rebels. They knew you were coming. Casualties were high." He paused to shove his hands in his pockets. "You were beaten to within an inch of your life. It was a miracle we got you out and even more of a miracle that you survived. The doctors at Walter Reed wanted to pull the plug on you, but I wouldn't let them. I believed in you, Peter. You were the best I'd ever seen. I knew if anyone could pull out of that coma, it would be you. And you did, but..."

Jed looked up. "But what?"

"You had complete amnesia. Couldn't remember a thing. Doctors said, considering how extensive your brain damage was, you would probably never regain your memory."

"So you decided to give me a new memory."

"That's simplifying it, but yes. Physically you made a complete recovery, maybe even in better shape than you were before, if that was possible. Emotionally you were stable. You just had no memory. Your mind was a complete blank."

"And what about my family? Did you contact them?"

Nichols sighed, ran the toe of his shoe in a line in the dirt. "You had no family, Peter. Your father walked out when you were ten and was never seen again. Your mother and little sister were both killed in a car accident." Nichols hesitated, stared at Jed as if giving him a moment to process this new information. "You were raised by your aunt in Wisconsin. She died of cancer when you were nineteen. She was the only family you had until the Army became your family. And after your injury and recovery, we retrained you. That's what the Centralia Project was all about. You were the first and the best until bits and pieces of your past started resurfacing. We tried to weave them seamlessly with the imprinting we were doing, but there's no substitute for the real deal. Finally we had to retire you."

"Jed." It was Karen. For a moment, he'd been so absorbed in trying to process this new rendition of his past that he'd almost forgotten the two of them were standing there. "What about us? This man says you're some stranger named Peter Ryan, but look at us."

Nichols's eyes twitched between mother and daughter. He shifted his feet in the leaves and adjusted his collar.

But as Jed turned his gaze, though his eyes saw two strangers, his soul recognized two people who truly loved him.

"You're Jedidiah Patrick," Karen said. "Papers can say anything. We've got a stack here with yet another name on them. I don't care what you remember or what you've been told. We're standing here, in the flesh, and telling you who you are. And whose you are. And I know one thing: you don't belong to him."

Nichols caught his attention. "Peter, there's no conflict here. They're only telling you what they think is true. But they don't have all the answers. I told you they're actors. They've been scrubbed too. Don't you see? They're only regurgitating the reality we put in their heads. How else could we guarantee their performance would be convincing? They're not trying to deceive you. They're just—"

"Enough! I've listened to too much already." Holding the papers in one hand and the rifle in the other, Jed kept his eyes on Nichols as he said, "Karen, take Lilly and head down the mountain."

Karen started to protest, but Jed silenced her. "Please, Karen. I'll catch up with you."

She and Lilly left, and Jed stood statue still until he no longer heard their footsteps. He then balanced the rifle against his leg while he grasped the papers in his hand and crumpled them into a small ball.

"Lies," he said. "More lies." He tossed the ball of paper onto the ground.

There was no mistaking the truth of what he'd seen in Karen's eyes, of what he'd felt in her kiss, in the touch of her hand on his face, the feel of her body against his. Abernathy had told him the truth, the complete truth, and it had opened a floodgate of memories. His past was coming back to him in streams of revelation.

Jed reached into his pocket and lifted out the flash drive Abernathy had handed him. "I have some insurance of my own."

Nichols eyed the drive. "What do you think that is, son?"

"The truth. About you, Centralia, everything. It's all right here and I'm going to blow it wide-open."

Nichols shifted his weight and forced a smile. "Is that what Abernathy told you? Maybe Habit? They're both liars, you know. Abernathy is a traitor, convicted of treason. It's only because of me that he's still alive. Did he tell you that? They were gonna give him the death penalty and I saved him, convinced them that exile would be just, fair."

"Just like I should be grateful for the way you saved me? Well, I didn't see you jumping to anybody's aid a few minutes ago." Jed nodded toward the soldier near his feet, then held the drive higher. "We'll find out who was lying, won't we?"

Nichols started to advance, slowly and carefully on the rugged terrain.

Jed pointed the rifle at Nichols, who stopped and raised his hands, stepped backward, and almost fell.

"Peter, wait. Please. You have to listen to me. Listen to the truth."

"Take out your wallet," Jed said.

Nichols hesitated.

"Now! Do it."

Nichols reached inside his jacket and pulled out a black wallet. "Throw it to me."

Nichols tossed the wallet to Jed.

"Now your phone."

Nichols retrieved his phone.

"Throw it to me."

He complied.

Jed picked up the phone and wallet, wincing from the stabbing pain in his left arm. "Now, turn around and get on your knees."

"You can't do this, son," Nichols said.

"On your knees. Now."

Nichols's face twisted into an awful scowl. "If you're going to kill me, do it while you look me in the eyes. This isn't how you were trained."

Jed walked to Nichols and stopped no more than six feet away. "Fine. Get on your knees facing me."

Nichols straightened his back and glared at Jed.

Jed swung the butt of the rifle around and caught Nichols along the side of the head. He listed to the side, stumbled, and struggled to regain his balance. While he was fumbling, Jed shoved Nichols with his foot. Nichols fell and landed on the ground, facedown.

Quickly Jed put a foot on Nichols's back and the barrel of the rifle to his head. "You know what I've been trained for. Kill without mercy, without remorse. You put that in my head, didn't you?"

"So do it!" Nichols hollered. His voice had a defiant edge, but Jed could feel the man's shoulders quaking.

Jed pulled the rifle away and lifted his foot. "I guess I've been reprogrammed. Roll over."

Nichols turned over on the ground. His face was red and wet from tears and sweat. Fear widened his bloodshot eyes.

"Don't try to follow us," Jed said. "Let us disappear. Leave us alone."

"You know I can't do that."

"If we meet again, I'll look at it as self-defense and I won't hesitate to kill you." Jed turned and left, not looking back once to see if Nichols had climbed to his feet.

FIFTY-TWO

. . .

The map Habit had given Jed led to a large stretch of forest in the Coeur d'Alene National Forest near the Montana state line. A small cabin sat miles off any regularly traveled path, tucked into a clearing and surrounded by towering spruce and fir trees.

Jed, Karen, and Lilly gathered around an outdoor fire, something they'd been doing every clear evening since arriving at the site two months ago. The fire writhed and gyrated, sending sparks crackling into the chilly night air. Above, a cloudless sky shimmered with millions, maybe billions of stars. Jed was no longer wearing the sling to support his left arm. The shot was a flesh wound, a lot of blood loss and torn tissue, but nothing more. Stitches, the sling, and a robust course of antibiotics had made it just about good as new.

Once a week they all trekked into the town of Coeur d'Alene for groceries and other supplies they needed and to pick up reading material at the library. Other than that, the remote homesite was where they spent all their time, away from people, away from cameras, and miles off the grid.

Karen leaned forward and poked at the fire with a stick. Firelight reflected off her face, softening the corners of her jaw and smoothing the roundness of her cheeks. She was a beautiful woman, caring and patient. They'd spent every day talking, reviving memories, reliving moments, laughing, crying, holding each other. So much had returned to Jed, but there were still whole blocks of missing time, absent memories. And occasionally the imprinted memories would interfere in disjointed segments and disorient him. But he was learning to decipher the difference between the reality past and the manufactured one, developing ways to cope with the false memories. And always there was the truth, the deeper truth that no amount of brain manipulation had managed to entirely scrub out of him.

Karen poked at the fire again and said, "I keep thinking, how do we know they won't find us here?"

She'd mentioned similar concerns several times before. The captivity she'd endured and her inability to protect Lilly from harm had left scars that would take a long time to heal, if ever.

Jed broke a stick and tossed half into the fire. "If we're careful and limit our exposure, we'll be okay. This place is a speck on a map, one in any number of hunting and camping sites just like it. The forest is dense and desolate. It'd be like finding one particular pine needle in a forest of pines." He looked at Lilly, who smiled at him. Her smile always gave him strength, for it radiated confidence and certainty, faith and trust. "We'll be fine," he said. "We just need to stick together."

"The money will run out eventually," Karen said. "And then what will we do?"

Jed dropped the other half of the stick into the fire and watched as the flames received it. "We won't run out. I think I should look for a job next week."

Karen looked up, her eyes wide. "What? How? Where?"

"The people here don't know me as Peter Ryan or Jed Patrick. They only know me as Eric. They don't know where we're from or anything else about us. I'll get a job lumberjacking. I think I'd like that."

Karen was quiet for a long moment. Finally she said, "I don't like it, but if you think it's safe…"

"It'll be all right," Jed said. "Besides, the townsfolk will begin to wonder where we got all our money from if I don't soon go to work. They'll start talking, getting curious. Better to avoid giving them reason to take a second glance at us."

Lilly rested her head on Jed's arm. "It will be okay, Mommy. Daddy will be careful and God will be with us. Just like he always has been."

Karen had told Jed how he'd encountered Jesus, how he had come back after his first tour in Afghanistan a changed man, solemn, introverted. Dark thoughts had tormented him, pushed him inward and haunted him with nightmares. She told him how she'd urged him to read the Bible and how under compulsion he'd complied. It was there he'd found the light and the hope it brought. He remembered most of it now. The scrubbing Nichols had done had tucked it into a dark and remote corner of his mind. But it was still there, and nothing Nichols did could erase it.

They all sat quietly while time passed slowly and the fire danced before them, crackling and popping to its own disjointed beat.

Karen eventually lifted her face and said, "Jed, I've been thinking a lot about the dream you said you used to have and about the last room, the empty one."

"Yeah?"

"You know how you said you thought it meant your past was gone, that there was just nothing there?"

"That's what I thought at the time, but I'm not sure what it means now. Why? What are you getting at?"

She jabbed at a glowing log, and sparks floated into the night air ten feet or so before cooling and disappearing. "Well, maybe it didn't mean your past." She paused but Jed could tell she wasn't finished, that her mind was churning with some thought that had been bouncing around in there for days, ever since he told them about the recurrent dream he'd had. "I mean, the house kinda reminds me of a book, and each room is a chapter or a bunch of chapters. And what if the last room is the last chapter and it's blank because God isn't finished writing it yet? For any of us."

Jed had to pause and reframe the entire dream. She was right, of course. Jed had been spending too much time looking back, trying to relive the past, when it was now time to look forward. God wasn't finished with him yet; his story was still being written.

Karen pulled her eyes away from the fire and fixed them on Jed. She stared at him for a long time, seeming to read his thoughts. Finally she just smiled at him and went back to studying the movement of the flames.

Lilly half giggled and sighed loudly. "Do you know what would be really cool?"

Jed smiled. "What would be really cool, kiddo?"

She giggled again. "If you two got remarried."

Karen looked at Jed, firelight dancing on her face, and at that moment he almost lost himself in her eyes. "I think that's a great idea."

"But we're already married," Karen said.

"And I even remember most of it." Jed laughed and pulled Lilly close. "Would we get married as Eric and Angie Bingsley?"

"No. As Mom and Dad."

"Mr. and Mrs. Mom and Dad? That would look awfully silly on a marriage certificate."

Lilly was quiet for a time, staring at the flames and thinking. "You could just renew your promises. It would be like a new beginning."

Jed and Karen looked at each other, grinning softly.

That new chapter, unwritten, blank, waiting for words to be penned.

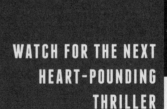

Acknowledgments

This is the part of the book where I get to thank all those who played a role in the creation of this story. Contrary to a popular misconception, writers do not just speak a story into existence. We all wish it would be that easy, but that power is reserved for God alone. The reality is that it takes multiple individuals months and months to bring you the story you now hold in your hands. Furthermore, I would be a complete jerk if I tried to take all the credit for the finished product. And I'm not a jerk. Well, we all have our moments, don't we? I'm at least not a complete jerk.

So, with everyone else in mind and in the spirit of giving credit where it is really due, I'd like to acknowledge and thank the following people:

First of all, Jesus. Yes, this might seem clichéd, but I can assure you, to me there is nothing clichéd about Jesus. He is my Savior, my Lord, my Friend, my Guide, my Rock. All of this, ultimately, is for him, and without him none of it would be possible. I am nothing. He is everything.

I also want to thank my wife, Jen. She supports me, encourages me, pushes me, admonishes me when I need it, and spends a lot of time and patience just putting up with me. She is truly a gift from God.

My daughters need to be thanked as well. I'm not the dad they deserve and they love me anyway. They inspire me to be more and do more than I think I can be and do. I love being a dad, and they are the reason for that.

Thanks to my agent, Les Stobbe, for his guidance and wisdom. It's nice to have someone like him in my corner. I am privileged and blessed.

Big thanks go to my readers who stick with me book after book. Without them this wouldn't be possible. What's a book without readers? Just words. Readers give it a soul and a life. Readers inspire. Readers fan the flame. Readers pay the bills. Special thanks to my Darlington Society for the continuous prayers and support. They are a special group, indeed.

Another big thank-you goes to my editors at Tyndale House, Jan Stob and Caleb Sjogren. These are the folks who make sure this book has its shirt tucked in and hair combed neatly before it shows its face in public. If there are any mistakes, any inconsistencies, the fault is mine. These two are pure professionals.

Thanks to the marketing team, the sales team, the design team, and anyone else at Tyndale who has a played a role in the production of this story. We are all members of the same body!

Lastly, thanks to my parents and family for never giving up on me, for seeing what could and would be, for praying, and for encouraging. Their support does not go unappreciated.

Discussion Questions

1. Though Peter's faith was buried deep in his mind, it is still
    present. The Bible says nothing can ever separate us from God's
    love (Romans 8:38-39) and "I give them eternal life, and they
    shall never perish; neither shall anyone snatch them out of My
    hand." (John 10:28). So we can never be taken from God, but can
    our faith ever be taken from us?

2. Throughout the book, Peter uses lethal force to defend himself
    and others. He feels remorse for this, but he sees no alternative.
    Are his choices justified? When, if ever, is a person justified in
    taking another life?

3. Where does faith in Christ reside? In our minds or someplace
    deeper? Our soul?

4. Peter is led to believe many things that turn out to be lies.
    Think of a time when you've heard conflicting stories and
    were uncertain which was true. How did this uncertainty
    make you feel? How did you discern truth from fiction?

5. How would you describe Peter's faith at different stages of
    the story? Are there turning points, or is his spiritual growth

gradual? What exactly does it mean for a person to believe in Jesus?

6. Peter finds it difficult to surrender to Jesus. What is the natural, human response when asked to surrender? What makes it harder for some and easier for others?

7. Have you ever questioned your faith? What were the circumstances, and what was the outcome? Where is the line between honest questions and faithless doubting?

8. Do you know anyone who lost their mental capabilities but retained their faith in Christ? How would you explain that? What role does the Holy Spirit play?

9. Have you ever been in a situation where your brain was telling you one thing and your heart was telling you another? Which did you listen to? Was that the right decision? When is it appropriate to be guided by facts, and when should we trust our instincts and intuition?

About the Author

MIKE DELLOSSO is the author of eight novels of suspense, an adjunct professor of creative writing and popular conference teacher, a husband, and a father. When he's not lost in a story or working or spending time with his family, he enjoys reading and dabbling in pencil sketching. Mike has a master's degree in theology and serves with his wife in their local church. He is also a colon cancer survivor and health care worker. Born in Baltimore, Mike now resides in southern Pennsylvania with his wife and four daughters. Besides *Centralia*, his other books are *The Hunted*, *Scream*, *Darlington Woods*, *Darkness Follows*, *Frantic*, *Fearless*, and the novella *Rearview*.

Have you visited TYNDALE FICTION.COM lately?

YOU'LL FIND:

- ways to connect with your favorite authors
- first chapters
- discussion guides
- author videos and book trailers
- and much more!

PLUS, SCAN THE QR CODE OR VISIT **BOOKCLUBHUB.NET** TO

- download free discussion guides
- get great book club recommendations
- sign up for our book club and other e-newsletters